# CHAR DILEMMA

by

George Donald

*Also by George Donald*

Billy's Run

Charlie's Promise

A Question of Balance

Natural Justice

Logan

A Ripple of Murder

A Forgotten Murder

The Seed of Fear

The Knicker-knocker

The Cornishman

A Presumption Of Murder

A Straight Forward Theft

The Medal

A Decent Wee Man

**CHAPTER ONE**

He had arrived only moments before at the station and was standing just inside his office door, hanging his dripping wet overcoat on a peg driven into the wall when the door burst open.
Tall and heavy set, Eric Kyle stood with one hand on the doorknob and stared at him.
Charlie Miller, his complexion still florid from the icy wind and rain turned pale and instinctively knew.
He felt his stomach lurch and turning to lift the coat from the peg, he sighed.
There had been another one.
"So Eric, what's the story," he slowly turned towards the tall, stocky Detective Sergeant as he slipped his coat on. "Where is she?"

The drizzling rain had ceased when with Kyle driving, they arrived ten minutes later at the locus. A uniformed constable, a slim dark haired lassie Miller had seen about the office, raised her hand and indicated that they park in Hope Street behind a police van.
Kyle skilfully manoeuvred the unmarked Ford Focus into the tight space and got out.
Already a number of passersby, mainly local office workers were forming up two deep at the entrance to the lane that Miller could see had been cordoned off with blue and white tape. A second constable, a young man who held his notebook in his hand, stood behind the tape staring vacantly into space.
Kyle popped open the boot and fetching out two sealed plastic bags, handed one to Miller.

"Detective Chief Inspector Miller and DS Kyle on scene," he heard Kyle inform the constable who bent his head to write their names and arrival time in his book. It didn't escape Miller's notice the young mans hand was shaking and asked him, "Has the Casualty Surgeon arrived yet?"

The constable used his free hand and raised the tape to permit them to duck under it.

"She got here a couple of minutes ago, sir. She asked if you would join her. The woman," he hesitated and swallowed hard, cocking his head as he nodded behind him. "The body, it's about thirty yards along the lane. That's where the doctor is."

"Is there another officer manning the other end of the lane, son?" asked Miller, unconsciously shivering as the cold of the November morning bit at him.

"Aye, sir," the constable nodded. "There's a car crew standing by the lane entrance on Wellington Street. It's been secured so there's no access into West Regent Lane to the public from there."

"What about offices or commercial premises that lead into the lane? Back doors or garages I mean?"

The constable stared at him and he softly shook his head. He realised he was overwhelming the lad and correctly guessed this was his first murder. "Forget it," he sighed and turning to Kyle, said, "Eric, I'll meet with Sherlock if you get onto the blower and fetch a couple of the lads down here pronto. Have them canvas the front of the properties that back into the lane and issue instructions to anyone working in these buildings," he nodded at the tenements, "that for the meantime, access to the lane via rear doors or garages is restricted unless we say otherwise. I'm guessing that there might be private cars parked there, but tell the guys they've not to take any shit from anybody. The lane's out of bounds and that's it, okay?"

"Right boss," Kyle nodded and turned to duck back under the tape.

"While you're at it," Miller called after him, "find out what's keeping the Scenes of Crime boys. I need them here now."

"Got it, boss," Kyle waved a hand and made his way through the crowd of rubbernecking morning commuters and made his way back toward the parked Focus.

Miller turned to the constable. "What's your name, son?"

The younger man straightened up almost to attention and replied, "Constable Burton, sir."

Miller stifled a grin and clapped the younger man on the shoulder.
"What's your first name?"
"Eh, it's Paul, sir.
"Right, Paul. On the way here, DS Kyle informed me that it was you and your neighbour that discovered the body."
"Yes, sir," he nodded toward the young policewoman who was encouraging the pedestrians to move along, hearing her loudly calling out, that there was "…nothing to see. Come along now, move away."
"Siobhan and I…sorry, I mean Constable McKay and me, we were taking a shortcut through the lane to get our…" he stopped and his eyes widened.
Miller stifled a grin.
"Let me guess, your morning tea and toast at a howff, would that be right?"
Burton blushed and nodded.
"Well, we'll keep that between us so your section sergeant needn't know, eh?"
Burton grinned self-consciously and continued. "Along there," he pointed towards the lane, "I saw a woman's foot…well, her shoe, really, sticking out from beneath an old soiled carpet."
"So, the body was covered over?"
"Aye, sir, I pulled the carpet aside and that's when…" he gulped.
"Okay, Paul," he nodded. "That's all I need for now. I'll get your full statement in due course, but I need you to do something for me. When backup arrives, the SOCO and my guys…"
He stopped when he saw the young cops eyes narrow and tightly smiled.
"SOCO means Scene Of Crime Officers, Paul"
"Oh, right, sir."
"So, like I said, when the SOCO and my guys arrive, keep them all here until I've viewed the body. I don't want anyone trampling across my crime scene until I get a good look at our victim. Which begs my next question; where's your shift Inspector and section sergeant?"
"I'm not sure where the sergeant is, sir, but I heard Inspector Brogan tell him on the radio that because of the lack of resources the Inspector was away back to Stewart Street to have a word with the sub-divisional commander about getting more men out here," then

lowered his voice as though imparting a great secret. "He said something about expecting an argument because of overtime."
Miller grimaced. He'd had enough arguments with Superintendent Neil Murray when trying to procure overtime money for his own department. He knew Pat Brogan was a former CID officer who had decided to pursue promotion through the uniform ranks, but a good man nevertheless.
"Right son, hold onto that for me," he told Burton as standing to one side, he pulled off his over coat that he then handed to Burton.
Tearing open the plastic bag, he fetched from it an oversized white coloured Forensic suit that easily encompassed his tall, sturdy frame. With his back to a grimy wall, he slipped on the Forensic overshoes, a facemask and lastly blue coloured, thin nylon gloves.
Now satisfied he would not contaminate the crime scene, he left his coat with Burton and carefully made his way along the lane, ensuring he stuck as near to the wall as was possible.
Just as the young cop had said, after a distance of about thirty yards and tucked into a two-metre recess in the wall, he saw where a stained and sodden carpet that was dragged to one side.
"Morning Sherlock," he quietly called out, careful not to startle the similarly attired hunched figure bent over the body of a young woman who like some broken and discarded mannequin, lay on her back, her skin pasty white and her eyes open. The woman's black coat was unbuttoned and her short, scarlet coloured skirt had ridden up to expose her thighs and undergarment. One black high heel shoe was still on her left foot while the other lay some three feet from the body. Miller gave an involuntarily shiver for it seemed to him the woman had died with a look of surprise fixed on her face.
An old, stressed brown leather medical bag lay open, sat upon a two foot square of plastic sheeting on the ground by the body.
The duty Casualty Surgeon for the Greater Glasgow area police divisions, Doctor Elizabeth Watson, known throughout the CID as Sherlock and inwardly proud of her nickname, didn't turn from her examination of the body, but softly called back, "Morning, Charlie. How's your day been so far?"
"Same old, same old," he quipped in reply, but stood well back from her to permit her room to stand upright.
"Youngish, no more than late twenties or early thirties," she began as she rose to her feet. "Obviously I haven't turned her over until

you have viewed the body and she's been photographed, but my tentative examination of her would seem to indicate a massive trauma to the back of her head."

"The same type of blow to the head as the others?"

She turned and though the mask hid her mouth, he saw her eyes smile at him.

"Come on, Charlie, you know as well as I do I can't confirm that until I perform a more thorough examination and besides…"

"Just give me the short version, please," he interrupted, his voice sounding a little harsher than he intended.

She stared at him and he immediately guessed he had annoyed her.

"What the *hell* do you want me to tell you, Charlie? The poor bugger's been bashed on the back of the head, yes! She's still wearing her knickers and seems to be fully clothed so there's no *apparent* indication of sexual molestation! She fits the age group of the other victims, yes! Her handbag is here beside her," her voice rising, she angrily pointed towards a red coloured, faux leather clasp purse that lay nearby, "so even though I'm *not* a detective, it doesn't look like she's been robbed! So yes, on the face of it she fits the profile of the other two victims, but without a formal medical examination I can't be certain. Is *that* information enough for you at this time, Detective Chief Inspector?"

"Sorry," he mumbled.

"What was that? I didn't quite…"

"I'm bloody sorry, Sherlock, so let's get past it, okay?" he sighed heavily, then more contritely, asked, "What about her hair, is there any indication…"

"For heavens sake, Charlie, look at her," Watson snapped at him. "She's being left here in the rain and is soaked through, the poor soul. How can I tell under these conditions if her hair has been cut? Like I said, when I get her to the mortuary …"

Her shoulders slumped and shaking her head, she audibly exhaled then said, "No Charlie, it's me that should apologise. I shouldn't have snapped at you like that. It's just that, well…"

"I know, Liz," he nodded down to the dead woman. "It just seems somehow so bloody unfair."

He bent down and visually examined the red clasp bag. Kneeling beside it and careful not to disturb its location on the ground, he prised the clasp bag open and extracted a black leather wallet purse from inside.

"You're right," he nodded as he saw the purse contained several currency notes, "it doesn't seem like she was robbed." From a slot in the purse he pulled a Bank of Scotland VISA debit card and holding it up to the morning sunlight, squinted as he read aloud, "Miss J Maxwell." He held the card out towards Watson and standing, said, "Here, hold that for me," as he pulled down the zip of the Forensic suit and fished in a jacket pocket for his mobile phone.

Watson returned the bankcard to Miller and listened as he called his incident room. "Mark? It's Charlie Miller. I've a possible identification for the deceased female down here in West Regent Lane," and proceeded to provide the woman's name, bank sort code and account number. "Get onto that right away and have one of the guys follow up with an address from the bank. You know what we need to ID her and Mark," Miller paused and licked at his lips, "delegate the inquiry to somebody with a wee bit of compassion just in case I don't get back to the office in time, but if possible, I'd like to be the one to…yeah," he unconsciously nodded, "I knew you'd understand. Thanks."

She watched as he grimly smiled before he ended the conversation with, "Aye, I'll not be much longer here."

He re-zipped his suit, but kept the phone in his hand. Turning to Watson he said by way of explanation, "Mark Barclay. He's the DI in charge of the incident room. Good man."

"Yes, I know DI Barclay. Widowed a couple of years back, wasn't he?"

"That's him," confirmed Miller.

They stood for a few seconds in respectful silence, then he asked, "If you've pronounced…"

"Yes, yes, of course." She peeled back the glove on her left wrist and glanced at her watch. "Give or take the five minutes I've been here, I'm officially pronouncing life extinct at eight-forty-five. The post mortem will likely provide you with a more definitive time of death. You can call your crime scene people in now, Charlie."

"Right, I'll get them along and Liz…" he hesitated, unsure whether this was the right place to refer to such a delicate issue. "I heard about you and Steven. Sorry that you're going through…"

She raised a hand to silence him and gave a short, mirthless laugh. "I knew it wouldn't be long before the grapevine found out. I'm almost fifty, Charlie. How the hell can I compete with a twenty-eight year old primary teacher?" She shook her head as she bent to close and then lift the leather bag. "At least the kids are on my side and even though I haven't said a word against him, he's complained to me that they're not returning his calls."

"So, he's moved out then?"

"Last week. Said he has to," she wiggled the forefinger of her free hand in the air, "…find himself. Not that it surprises me because for a guy who's supposed to be finding himself, I know for a fact he's holed up with her in her flat over in Carntyne." She smiled at his raised eyebrows and without explanation, added, "Oh, I have my sources."

Miller thought it better not to press her how Watson had come by that particular piece of information, but instead said, "It's his loss, Liz."

She pulled her facemask down and grinned at him. "You always know just the right thing to say, Charlie."

Beneath his mask he smiled in sympathy while his eyes narrowed as he appraised the slim and good looking woman before him. Turning, he began to walk with her to the entrance of the lane.

"How're the girls taking Steven's…departure? You said they're not returning his calls?"

"You'll recall that Elspeth's in her third year up at Uni in St Andrews. She's worrying herself sick about me, so I'm getting at least half a dozen phone calls and texts each day," she sighed, but Miller suspected she was pleased with her daughter's concern. "Janice on the other hand is still local, sharing a flat in Partick with two pals, but twenty's too young to take anyone else's life seriously. She's so wrapped up with her latest boyfriend that other than a passing comment about Steven's departure, she doesn't seem too fazed though to be honest I think there's more going on in her head than she's letting on."

"Well, just remember Liz that if you need a wee night out or a home cooked meal then don't forget Sadie and me are home most evenings," he quietly reminded her.

"Thanks Charlie, I know that and I really do appreciate it," nodded Watson.

They stopped at the blue and white tape and conscious of the presence of the young cop Burton, Miller formally acknowledged Watson and said, "Well, thank you Doctor, we'll speak later," and nodded towards her. He watched her duck under the tape held aloft by the young cop and walk off to her car parked on the street nearby.
"Right you lot," he waved the Scenes of Crime personnel and a young detective forward who all similarly attired and laden with their equipment, ducked under the tape and waited in a small group for their instruction.
"Okay, guys," began Miller, "we'll walk while I talk and here's what little I know so far."
While her team prepared their equipment, Miller instructed the matronly SOCO supervisor about the photographs he wanted snapped and items of interest to be seized and quietly admitted he had rifled the woman's clasp bag to obtain the purse.
"But you didn't move anything else?" she frowned with disapproval in her voice.
"Jean," he raised his hands in surrender, "you know I've been doing this for a long time now, hen. I didn't touch anything else. Honest."
"Aye, well Charlie, I'm sure you know what you're doing."
Suppressing a grin, Miller accepted the unspoken rebuke and standing to one side, watched as the SOCO team quietly and efficiently carried out their tasks.
After a few minutes Miller was satisfied there was little else he could do there and instructed the detective that when the SOCO team had competed their work, he was to summon the waiting mortician team to enter the lane and for continuity purpose, accompany the body to the mortuary.
"I'll have somebody from the office meet you at the mortuary to bring you back to the office," and hid a grin at the younger man's pale face.
"Is this your first murder?"
"Aye, sir, it is."
"Well," he deliberately kept his face expressionless and nodded towards the SOCO supervisor, "if you've any questions, Jean will keep you right, but a wee word of warning; don't even *think* about puking on her crime scene."

He was still shaking.

Sat on the edge of his bed he listened as downstairs his wife worked in the kitchen, his eyes tightly shut and his teeth grating against the sound of pots and pans being lifted from the dishwasher and banged into the cupboard and he wished that she had been the bitch he'd dragged into the lane.

Slowly, he exhaled and felt a little better while he concentrated on forcing himself to be calm.

He opened his eyes and cast a nervous glance at the closed bedroom door. Standing, he walked to the built in cupboard located on the opposite wall and sliding the mirrored door open, he pushed aside the overcoat and the suit and licked at his lips as his hand reached into the pocket of his anorak, surprised that the material was still slightly damp from the previous nights rain.

He groped in the pocket and withdrew the small, clear plastic food bag. Almost reverently holding it up against the light shining through the window, he gazed with awe at the thick, but slightly damp twist of hair inside the bag and fought the urge to open the bag and hold the hair against his cheek.

His eyes narrowed and wondering if the damp hair might rot in the plastic bag, he glanced down at the radiator under the window. Opening a drawer in the cupboard, he fetched out a clean handkerchief and carefully wrapped the plastic bag in it before bending down and slipping the folded handkerchief behind the radiator.

There, he smiled. That should ensure the hair would dry before he tied it with the ribbon and placed it with the others.

He stared at the radiator and almost changed his mind, but knew that since her loss, she never came into his room these days anyway so he had no fear of it being discovered. The hammer was safely hidden, wrapped in an old towel in the spare wheel compartment in the boot of his car.

Rising to his feet he glanced at his appearance in the full-length wardrobe mirror and taking a deep breath, prepared himself to go downstairs to face the bitch.

He ignored the angry sound of the car horn and the single digit aimed at him as the driver behind swerved to avoid his sudden stop at the kerb outside Craven and Son's (Wholesalers) large warehouse in Cook Street.

Pulling his large bulk from the driver's seat of the gleaming black coloured Mercedes S Class saloon, Martin Craven took a few seconds to again stand and stare at the freshly painted frontage of the building that bore his name in large, black letters. He sighed and involuntarily grinned with unmitigated pleasure. It had taken almost three decades of hard graft for him to achieve this, his name on the front of the building of his own company. From his overcoat, he fetched a cigar case and extracting one of his favourite Havana's, lit it with his personalised gold lighter before striding towards the door. Since moving his operations base from Maryhill to the Tradeston area in the south side of the city, he had enjoyed not just a better address for his business, but easier access to the motorway where most of his stock either arrived at or was dispatched from. That short distance in time and fuel made a difference at the end of the financial year and besides, he reasoned, it made his journey from his Newton Mearns home to the office that little bit less stressful. It was also a matter of pride to him that he brought all of his staff with him and though he could not know it, endeared many of them to him for his thoughtfulness.

He pushed his way through the newly installed double-glazed doors and smiled at Shelley McPhail, the tall, slim and busty blonde haired teenager who sat behind the reception desk. The desk had no modesty board and he could see she wasn't wearing any tights on her long legs.

Employing Shelley had been another of his better decisions and as she coyly returned his smile, he briefly considered calling her into his office for a short, ten minute liaison, but Monday mornings were always busy and instead winked at her and said, "Fetch the post through in a couple of minutes with a mug of coffee, hen. I want to get myself settled in before I start tackling the mail."

"Right, Mister Craven, will do," smiled Shelley, conscious that Alex Mason, the warehouse manager who sat in the reception area and had awaited Craven's arrival was all ears and the biggest gossip in the place. She knew that any hint of familiarity with her boss would be open to discussion on the shop floor within minutes.

Turning to Mason, Craven told him, "Give me ten minutes, Alex and I'll see you then. In the meantime, grab yourself a cuppa to bring in with you."

With that he pushed through the door into his office and slipped out of his overcoat.

Seated behind his large desk, he sighed with pleasure. It never ceased to amaze him that though he had left school at fifteen with no qualifications, through hard work and diligence he now found himself to be the sole owner and Managing Director of a large distributing company. Not that he was naïve enough to believe that the business would ever grow large enough to challenge the blue chip companies but still, he was doing okay for a wee Glasgow lad and smiled with satisfaction. Aye, he drew deeply on the cigar, I've come quite a way since running a stall in the Glasgow Barra's.

His thoughts were disturbed by the ringing of his desk phone.

"Shelley, I thought I told you…"

"Sorry, Mister Craven," she soothingly replied in her soft Northern accent and he guessed Mason was still in reception, "but I've got your Davie on the line. He says he needs to speak with you and it's urgent."

"Right," Craven sighed and rubbed with the heel of his hand at his forehead, "put him through, hen."

He heard her phone being replaced then his son's voice asked, "Dad? Are you there?"

"What is it this time, Davie?"

"Dad, listen, I'm sorry to bother you, but I'm going to be late in. The car's not working. I don't know what's wrong. I just tried to turn the key…"

"Where are you?" he impatiently asked, immediately regretting the sharpness in his voice.

"I'm at the house. I've been trying for, I don't know, maybe half an hour…"

"Did you not think to call the RAC, Davie? I mean, you *are* a member. I distinctly recall getting you signed up for recovery and home assistance; the whole package."

"Oh, I thought maybe I should phone you first, Dad. Should I do that then? Phone the RAC?"

"Aye, son," he forced himself to remain calm. "Phone the RAC and make sure you've got your membership card handy. They'll want the details. Okay? Can you do that Davie?"

"Aye, Dad, of course I can do that," his son huffily replied before adding, "Thanks. I'll be in to the office as soon as I can. Bye, Dad, bye."

Craven slowly replaced the handset in its cradle and sitting back in his chair, rubbed at his face with both hands.

It still maddened him that it wasn't till Davie was in his early teens that he had finally been diagnosed as Dyslexic, though not profoundly so. However, the teasing and bullying at school where his son had been dismissed as just another slow learner had seriously impacted on Davie's development and almost destroyed his self-confidence. To Craven's shame, he had been so wrapped up in creating his business that he allowed his wife to deal with their son's formative years and been unaware of the difficulties Davie was experiencing at school. The lad wasn't stupid, far from it, but such was his insecurity that he needed his hand held for every little decision. He loved his son, but no matter what advantages he bestowed upon him, he knew that Davie would never be the man that Craven hoped for unlike his father, the thirty-year-old Davie was a follower, not a leader. Yes, he could and did adequately perform the role in the company as a supervisor, but he guessed even that job Davie found difficult. He slowly shook his head for no matter what else he was, Davie Craven was a good father and pleasant young man and at least for that his father was grateful.

Even his sons short-lived and disastarous marriage to that money-grabbing wee cow Jean Anderson, for which Craven was still paying her a monthly allowance, hadn't taught the trusting Davie anything about life.

Despite himself Craven smiled, for the monthly allowance paid to Anderson ensured that she didn't squabble about custody of the only good thing resulting from Davie's marriage; his granddaughter, wee Elsa. He suspected that even if he were to quit paying the allowance, Anderson would quite happily continue to foist Elsa onto her ex-husband rather than have the wee girl interfere in her social life, but it wasn't an issue he was prepared to risk.

In the deep recess of his mind, it often occurred to Craven that his former daughter-in-law's fondness for drink and men might cast doubt on Davie's paternity of the little girl, that her pregnancy was merely a means to trap Davie into the marriage, but he forced himself to ignore this doubt and instead loved the little girl without question.

He swallowed hard and again ignored the ache in his chest. Perhaps the doctor was right, that maybe he should get himself signed into Ross Hall Hospital for a check-up.

He forced his body to relax and wished Davie had been more like his sister Moira.

He slowly exhaled and smiled when he thought of his daughter. If anything, though he would never dare admit it, Moira was the son he wished he'd had. The image of her mother, his daughter was a sharp and shrewd, good-looking young woman, but just as her brother did, had made a bad marriage. Unlike Davie though, Moira was still tied to her spouse and shaking his head Craven wondered what she had seen in James Bain that caused her to be tied to such a waster. Of all the men she could have married, she settled for a bloody telephone clerk! But Martin Craven was no fool, for the house in Blantyre and the cars he had purchased as their wedding gift were in Moira's name and if she ever came to her senses and got rid of the idiot, he'd walk away without a penny of Craven's money.

The door rattled once and was pushed open by Shelley who carried the morning mail in one hand and a mug of coffee in the other.

His eyes opened wide. Seated behind her desk when he'd arrived at the office, he hadn't realised how short her denim skirt was and marvelled that the long legged, tall young blonde managed to walk without exposing her underwear. He watched as she used her backside to push the door closed behind her.

"There you are, *Mister* Craven," she pouted and brushing her thigh against his arm, laid the mail and mug down onto the desk.

He watched as slowly taking a step back, she seductively undid the top button of her blouse to reveal milky white breasts bulging from the top of her bra as she bent over to arrange the mail in front of him.

"My rents due this week," she whispered, dropping her voice to deliberately sound husky.

He felt his chest tighten as smiling up at her, he placed a hand on her backside and squeezed as he replied, "Then after work this evening, maybe I should pop down to your flat and we'll discuss how we can deal with that."

**CHAPTER TWO**

He was as satisfied as he could be that he had seen enough and now that the necessary Scene of Crime work was being conducted in the lane, Charlie Miller realised there was nothing else that could be done by him at the location having instructed the body be removed to the mortuary located in the newly constructed Queen Elizabeth University Hospital in Govan.

"What about the lane, boss?" asked DS Kyle, standing against the tenement wall and sheltering against the drizzle of falling rain with his back against the door of a closed property. "Do you want it to remain closed or will I have the uniform guys re-open it?"

"We'll give it twenty-four hours for now, so keep it closed meantime, Eric. There might be something comes to mind during the day, so no point in having the ghouls picking over the locus. If there's any problems from the shift Inspectors about having cops manning the lane, refer them to me, okay?"

"Right, boss," nodded Kyle, who hearing Miller's mobile phone activate, walked off to the nearby CID car.

"Sadie," Miller smiled into the phone and unsteadily leaning against a nearby wall, used his free hand to tear at the white overshoes on his feet.

"I didn't hear you leave this morning," his wife said.

"No," he shook his head, "I didn't want to wake you after the night you had with the baby, so Jellybean and me had our early breakfast then I dropped her to your mother's before I headed into the office. Your mum will walk her to school and before you ask, yes; I made her a lunch up and she's got it with her."

"You, you're just a big softie, aren't you?" She paused then said, "I can hear traffic. Are you outside?"

"Aye," he glanced about him and awkwardly trying to step out of the white Forensic suit, gave up and tore it from his body. "I'm standing in Hope Street. You're hearing the commuter traffic. It's a bit noisy…"

"You're at a locus?"

"I am."

"Oh God, Charlie, don't tell me there's been another one."

He heaved a sigh and nodding into the phone, replied, "Listen, hen. I don't want to go into it on the phone, but yes, you're right. It *seems* to be what you think. Let me give you a call later from the office. For now, you and wee Ella try to get some rest. Give her a cuddle from me and..." he glanced about him to ensure he wasn't overheard and whispered, "I love you."

He didn't wait for her reply, but ended the call and strode towards the CID car where Kyle sat in the driver's seat with the engine running.

"I had a message from the control room, boss. The team's already assembling at Stewart Street for the morning briefing and there are an additional half a dozen guys from the Murder Investigation Unit on their way there too."

Miller sensed there was something else. "And?" he turned to stare as Kyle gunned the engine and quickly shot out into the busy traffic, incurring the wrath of a bus driver.

"The word is that Miss Mulgrew is on her way through from Gartcosh. The controller says she'll be there in half an hour."

Miller sighed.

As the area Detective Superintendent responsible for overseeing major inquiries in the three divisions that covered the Greater Glasgow area, Miller and the DCI's of the adjoining divisions had found Cathy Mulgrew to be a hard taskmaster.

It didn't matter that he and Mulgrew were close friends and several years previously, when both were Detective Sergeants, worked together on a case that resulted in the three inch scar that run across his right cheek when he got too close to a car that exploded. Though the official story at the time was that the vehicle experienced some sort of fuel leak, the truth of the incident was furtively whispered among the CID that a bomb had been set off and killed the driver, a well known and high profile Irish republican supporter from Glasgow's east end. Miller had suffered a life-threatening injury and in the weeks that followed the incident, his now wife Sadie, Mulgrew and her partner Jo saw him through the difficult months of recuperation that was to lie ahead of him.

The experience had created a bond between him and Mulgrew that encompassed their private lives.

While Kyle steered the car through the heavy morning traffic, Miller thought about Mulgrew and knew that close friend or not, she would be on top of him if he didn't get his finger out and catch who was responsible for the murder of three young women in the city centre. That said, he also knew that while Mulgrew was an ambitious and career conscious police officer, she would give him every bit of support she could muster and provided he didn't make a complete cock-up of the inquiry, back him to the hilt. His thoughts were interrupted when his stomach growled.

"Right, Eric," he waved a hand at the front windscreen, "we've half an hour before the briefing, so let's stop at the roll shop on West George Street first. I'm starving."

Eric Kyle weaved the car round a stationary taxi and came to a halt right outside the local CID's favourite morning takeaway on West George Street.

"I'm on the bell so is it the usual?" asked Miller as he paused at the open door.

"Aye, but brown sauce this time, not that shitty red stuff they use."

Miller grinned and closed the car door before making his way through the pedestrians and into the shop.

Remaining in the car, Kyle glanced across the busy road towards Albion Street and morosely reflected on how the city had changed since he'd walked the beat. With a little over five months left to serve before his thirty years was in, Miller had a few weeks earlier offered him a desk job that effectively meant he'd be away from inquiries and therefore would not be involved in cases that would mean receiving court citations in his retirement. He had appreciated the offer, but sitting behind a desk wasn't for him and though he hated to admit it, he really needed the income the overtime provided. Besides, the routine of a nine to five, five-day week had never appealed to him so God alone knew how he'd cope in retirement. Maybe, he unconsciously nodded he'd get himself a wee part time job.

He shifted his weight in the seat and with some relief, expelled trapped wind. Quickly, he opened the driver's window and used a cardboard file to wave the nauseous air from the car.

Retirement had been on his mind now for some months and again he thought of his wife, Paula. His eyes narrowed and his brow furrowed as he wracked his brains trying to work out what exactly was going on there. He was no fool and the new clothes and the expensive make-up could only mean one thing; but not again, he angrily shook his head as he sighed.

"Penny for them," Miller startled him as he snatched open the rear door and dumped a bag of hot food on the back seat.

"Bloody hell, boss, don't be scaring a man of my age like that!"
"You did say red sauce?"
"Brown," snarled Kyle, but almost immediately realised Miller was winding him up.
Miller was grinning now and getting into the passenger seat, turned and glanced at Kyle and said, "Eric, you've been working harder than anyone on this inquiry and you've put some long hours in. You've stayed enough nights and…" he held up a hand to stifle a protest, "I want you to quit early this afternoon. Get yourself home and have dinner with your missus. It'll make a change from all those chip suppers and Chinese carryout's at the office. I'm sure she must wonder what the hell you look like. I mean, she'll be thinking she hardly sees you these days."
"Aye, maybe you're right, boss," Kyle nodded and forced himself to return Miller's grin. "Thanks, I'll do that."
"Right, Stewart Street and quick as you like," Miller said, belting himself into the front passenger seat, "and if you're sharp enough, Eric, we'll get to eat those rolls before Ma'am arrives and grabs one for herself."

Cathy Mulgrew impatiently drummed her fingers on the steering wheel of her gold coloured Lexus and glanced at the dashboard clock. Bugger it, she thought and with one eye on the slow moving traffic ahead of her, pressed the button that activated her hands free mobile. Tapping her finger on the screen she selected the mobile number for Charlie Miller who answered almost immediately.
"Charlie? It's me," she said. "Traffic from the M73 has been diverted onto the M8 because of an accident and now I'm stuck in a jam on the motorway next to Ruchazie, so I'll likely be delayed by another twenty minutes or so, but if you could be good enough to hang fire with your briefing till I get there, I'll be grateful. So, I know that without the PM Sherlock won't have given you a definitive decision, but what's your opinion?"
She listened as he took a deep breath and guessing from the background noise he was in a car, he replied, "I'm only ten minutes away from the locus, Ma'am…"
She smiled at the formal use of Ma'am and assumed he wasn't alone in the vehicle.

"…but my humble opinion is that we're looking at number three. As you say, Sherlock will be able to confirm our suspicions at the PM and on that point, my office have informed DS Kyle who's with me that there's a slot open this afternoon at 1pm, so we should have an answer about that time. However, I intend briefing the team with what I've got so far and of course will include our victim as part of the ongoing inquiry. That is, unless the PM indicates otherwise. I see no reason at this stage to open a second murder room, but we'll maybe discuss that when you arrive at Stewart Street."

"Agreed, Charlie," she angrily glanced in her rear-view mirror at the young, blonde haired moron in the Mini who was applying her lipstick while she was tailgated Mulgrew. "There's little point in any further discussion meantime, so…did I hear you say you're with Eric Kyle?"

There was a definite pause and she grinned because she guessed where they had been.

"Aye, you did," he cautiously replied like a man who knew what was coming.

"Well, tell DS Kyle that a man of his age should watch his cholesterol and doesn't need two rolls and sausage, so he's to keep one aside for me."

She ended the call to the sound of laughter.

A hubbub arose from the incident room at Stewart Street police office when it was learned that a female's body had been discovered within a lane in the city centre. In the room, a large white board on one wall already bore the photographs of two murdered women. The general feeling and whispered supposition among those detectives and support staff that had already arrived that morning was that the killer had struck again.

Seated behind his desk, Detective Inspector Mark Barclay sighed. So much for a bloody paperless society, he thought and miserably stared at the mound of paperwork stacked in the in-tray.

"Coffee, Mark?" asked Elaine Hamilton, his senior Home Office Large Major Enquiry System (HOLMES) operator as she carefully placed the steaming hot mug on the desk in front of him.

"That's it," he nodded his head, "you're on a pay rise Miss Hamilton. Anyone who can put up with my moods and tolerate a miserable old sod like me *and* bring me morning coffee deserves a pay rise."

Hamilton blushed and slightly confused, backed off towards her own desk.

However, while the rest of the inquiry team quietly sniggered and joked about Hamilton's open affection for the crusty, widowed Barclay, he was himself totally oblivious to the feelings the middle-aged and attractive woman harboured for him.

His desk phone rang and snatching it up informed by the control room that DCI Miller was a few minutes away and requesting all officers involved in the current inquiries be in the incident room for the briefing.

Replacing the phone in its cradle, Barclay shot to his feet and clapping his hands together loudly called out, "Right you lot, the boss is due in a couple of minutes, so get yourselves together and if you need a pee, now's the time to go because nobody and I mean *nobody* is to be absent for the briefing!"

The bawled instruction was met with a shuffling of chairs as the team got themselves together and the hubbub died to a whisper.

Eric Kyle popped his head into the incident room and catching the eye of Barclay nodded that he follow him from the room.

Together the two men stepped across the corridor to the DCI's room where Miller was hanging up his coat. Turning, he nodded to the chairs on the other side of his desk and sat down. Opening the paper bag on his desk, he retrieved three rolls and handed one each to Kyle and Barclay.

"Sherlock will likely confirm it, but I'm as certain as I can be we're looking at number three. No sexual motive or robbery as far as she could tell, but it was too soon to tell if the hair was cut."

He took a bite of his roll and chewing, asked Barclay, "Who have you sent to deal with the identification, Mark?"

Barclay swallowed and replied, "Myra and her boy, Kevin Feeney. They're away down to the Sauchiehall Street branch of the bank. They should be able to get a full name and address there. If the bank tries any of that Data Protection shite, Myra will handle that, trust me on that issue."

Miller and Kyle both grinned. Detective Sergeant Myra 'Whiplash' McColl was no shrinking violet when it came to dealing with uncooperative neds or members of the public and it was generally agreed that nobody in their right mind got on her bad side. Miller chuckled at Barclay's description of 'her boy, Kevin Feeney', a young constable who had just recently been appointed to the CID as a trainee detective and was in awe of his mentor and followed her about like a puppy dog.

"Once she has an address…" began Miller, but was interrupted by Barclay who forestalled him by raising his hand and said, "She won't attend the address until you give the say so, boss. I thought that you'd want to be there yourself when the news is broke."

Miller stopped chewing and exhaling, slowly nodded. He never relished breaking the news of a loved one's death. It was a difficult enough task and even more so when that loved one had been murdered.

The door knocked and was pushed open by Cathy Mulgrew. Wearing a bottle green coloured trouser suit, the copper haired Mulgrew's piercing green eyes narrowed as she said, "Morning gentlemen and Eric, you're in big trouble if you've eaten both those rolls."

Miller grinned and leaning across the desk, handed her the paper bag containing the last roll and sausage.

Mulgrew thanked Kyle, but declined the offer of his chair and leaning back against the wall, said, "Any update on our victim yet, Charlie?"

"No, Ma'am," replied Miller, who nodded towards Barclay and continued, "Mark's sent Myra McColl and her lad to the bank for details of a full name and home address and we await her getting back to us."

Mulgrew, chewing at the roll, nodded thoughtfully. "What's your gut instinct?"

Miller sat back in his chair and replied, "I think…no," he slowly exhaled, "I *believe* we're looking at victim number three; the third in six weeks."

Mulgrew didn't immediately respond, but then half smiled at Barclay and Kyle in turn before asking, "Gentlemen, can you give us a minute, please?"

When they had left the room and closed the door behind them, she sat in the chair vacated by Kyle and staring curiously at Miller, said,

"Number three, Charlie? My God, we're talking about a serial killer here!"

"Not a term I'm comfortable with, Cathy, but yes, you're correct. Some bastard is out there targeting young women." Shrugging, he added, "There's no apparent robbery or sexual motive so far, so the question is, why?"

They sat for a few seconds in uncomfortable silence before Miller continued, "How do you want to play it here? Do I continue as the Senior Investigating Officer or as my boss, do you want to run the show?"

She thoughtfully shook her lowered head, her lips tight and her eyes narrowed then turned to stare at him, before replying, "I'm not certain, Charlie. My instinct is to let you continue as the SIO. Hell, you know as much if not more than me about running a major inquiry," she snorted. "Look, I don't need to tell you that if the powers that be decide otherwise it will be out of my hands."

He looked blankly at her and said, "Look at this way, Cathy. If you do take charge of the inquiry and you get a result, it won't do your career any harm. On the other hand..."

"Fuck off, Charlie!" she exploded and standing, placed both hands on his desk as she stared down at him. "Do you *really* think I give a shit about my career prospects when some bampot is out there murdering women?"

He opened his hands in surrender and shaking his head he grimaced and replied, "Sorry, Cathy, that didn't come out right. I didn't mean to imply..."

But as quickly as her temper arose, she raised her own hand and now calmed, said, "No, I know you didn't mean it like that. Sorry, I was out of order..."

"No, it was me who was out of order," he smiled at her and was relieved when she returned his smile with a grin.

"Charlie Miller, you can *really* get up my nose at times. It's just as well we're such good friends because otherwise I think I'd want to punch your head now and again."

"No need, I've a wife for that," he quipped.

She sat back down and asked, "I'm digressing, but how is Sadie and the kids anyway," but before he could reply, she raised her hand as she added, "Sorry. Jo and I should have been over more often, but since she got that promotion at work, she's been back and forward to London each week so anytime together has been precious."

"That's what you get for having a highflying partner," he continued to grin, "but no need to be worrying about Sadie because the baby is keeping her far busier than she ever expected. In fact, though she hasn't said anything, I don't think she's that keen to get back to work anytime soon."

"Why would she want to when she's got two gorgeous wee girls to look after? How is Ella coming along?"

"Great," he smiled, "and wee Geraldine is a wonderful help to her mum."

"You're a very lucky man, Charlie Miller," she returned his smile and he thought he detected a wistfulness in that short reply.

"Right," she rubbed her hands together, "we'd better get in there and let the team know what we've got so far. How do you want to do this?"

"Well," he slowly drawled as he got to his feet, "I'm thinking that I'll let the team know what details we have so far and that it's a likelihood the deceased is victim number three, but *that* is still to be confirmed. With your permission and in the meantime I'll work on the premise that it's the same killer for all the women. That way I can conduct the inquiry from one incident room and there's no need to diverse and split my resources."

"Agreed," Mulgrew again nodded and then asked, "I presume knowledge about the cut hair is still a tightly held evidential issue?" Miller nodded and replied, "Aye, just you, me, Eric Kyle, Mark Barclay, Sherlock who conducted the previous PM's and Jean Galbraith, the SOCO supervisor that did the PM photographs. By the way, it's Jean's team that's currently at the locus the now, so she'll put an Urgent on the snaps and we should have the book of photographs by lunchtime. As for the cut hair, to my knowledge none of the team has learned of it and I've Mark Barclay keeping his ears open should any of the team mention it."

"Good, that should sort the wheat from the chaff if any of the nutters in the city try to claim responsibility," she nodded as he held the door open to permit her to pass through and then adopted a serious expression before saying, "Right then, DCI Miller, let's get this done."

Arms wrapped about her, she watched from behind the curtain as her husband drove off to work and again wondered what had possessed her to marry such a weak, dull man like James. God, she shook her head and snarled at her own stupidity. Seducing the extremely handsome, but nervous James had been easy and showing him off to her friends had soon become boring when she realised what a dullard he really was. The pregnancy after just a few weeks courtship had come as a complete shock and she hated the fact she had so easily given in to her father's persuasion, his outdated values that for the sake of the unborn child, she be married. On hindsight, she realised that among the business community, the scandal of his daughter's unwanted pregnancy might have cost her father more than just a few contracts, for it would have been whispered that if he couldn't keep his own house in order how could he hope to run a successful business.

Moira was shrewd enough to realise that in business, reputation was everything and nobody took prisoners.

The arrangements for the wedding were conducted by her father at a speed that had taken her breath away and who had called in a number of favours, but ironically the relationship between her husband and Moira lasted only as long as the pregnancy which terminated after four months.

Following her miscarriage and her short spell in hospital, her husband's apparent indifference to what she had suffered ended any illusion she had about continuing her relationship with James and upon her return home, he had since occupied the guest bedroom.

She watched as the silver coloured Ford Fiesta disappeared out of sight on Dalcraig Crescent and turning from the window, sighed and cast an eye about the expensively furnished lounge.

She could fool others, but not herself and knew exactly what the appeal was that had attracted him to her. Strikingly good-looking and physically desirable though undoubtedly James was, it had not taken her long to tire of his boyish, witless charm. The marriage was just weeks old when she became bored with him and it wasn't long after that she came to learn that her husband was not just lazy in the house, but beyond his initial charm, had no motivation or work ethic. Nor had she realised until too late that James was a loner, for he had no one he could truthfully call a friend and she attributed this to the suffocating upbringing by his unmarried mother. She quickly realised that James had always relied upon his good looks to open doors, but when prospective employers realised that intellectually he was a complete sham, he never lasted in any job or was quickly encouraged to leave. The best he could manage these days was working in an insurance company's call centre and even her part-time job at her father's warehouse paid almost double what her husband earned.

The main advantage she had was learning early in their relationship that her husband was not just easy to manipulate, but that morally he was weak and spineless and would go to any lengths to avoid verbal confrontation with her; in fact though he had a muscular physique, she also suspected him to be a weak and cowardly man.

At the outset of their relationship it suited Moira to be the dominant partner and it pleased her that at the few business events they attended as a couple, his physical appearance turned many eyes and made him the ideal and compliant partner to support her with her future ambitions. Unlike her older brother Davie, Moira had her father's fire in her belly and an ambition for the company that was far beyond what Martin Craven had so far achieved.

However, since her miscarriage the situation had now changed and her husband was proving to be a burden she could well do without. In the kitchen, she switched on the kettle and while it boiled, spooned coffee into a china cup and her thoughts turned to Davie. A cold feeling enveloped her and inwardly raging, wondered why it was when her father was so aware of her accomplishments and her brother's incompetence it was her fathers wish that Davie inherit the business.

She despised her brother and considered him a feckless fool who had not nor ever would amount to much more than a menial supervisory position in the company. It was common knowledge and even her father suspected that the staff treated Davie like the idiot he was and jokingly whispered behind his back.

Her own position as a manager without portfolio overseeing the human resource department was a bloody joke; a part-time job created by her father simply to provide her with employment and to give her a stake in the company. Yes, it provided her with a salary, but without a staff to manage she was unable to prove to her father what she was capable of and gritting her teeth, acutely aware that a sixteen year old school leaver could probably do the administration of the ninety-seven staff personnel files just as well as Moira.

Her hands turned to fists and teeth clenched she arched her back and angrily shook her head at the unfairness of it. Davie, for even whom a private education could do little, while she achieved top marks in all her subjects and graduated from Strathclyde Business School with a First in Economics.

Davie, whose failed marriage to that slut Jean Anderson was the talk of the city's business community.

Failed marriage? Her shoulders heaved as she gave a mirthless laugh and poured the boiling water into the mug as she quietly laughed at the irony. After all, who was she to criticise Davie's failed marriage when she was tied to that feckless idiot James.

Stirring the coffee granules she thought of her own wedding just eight months previously. The cost to her father of the reception alone must have exceeded forty grand and already other than in name only, the marriage was finished.

She glanced around her at the newly fitted replacement kitchen and eyes narrowing, wondered just how much her father had paid for the detached house in Blantyre, as well as gifting the newly wed couple both her fire red coloured Audi A3 and James's Fiesta. Generous to a fault, she knew that her father doted on her and though he quite blatantly disapproved of her choice of husband, Martin Craven would never create any situation that might result in a rift between him and his daughter.

Following the death of her mother five years previously, she had for that first year of his drunken grief been her father's mainstay, tending to his needs while ensuring that the company stayed on track as well as attending to her own studies and achieving her Degree. During that awful period, her brother Davie had been of no use whatsoever, constantly whining about his wife's infidelities and while temporarily occupying their father's chair, losing so many contracts that but for Moira the company might have went under.

It had taken most of that year for Martin Craven to get back on his feet and what thanks did she get.

Upon his retirement, he promised that Davie would succeed him as the MD.

Bastard!

Not that Moira would be cast aside her father assured her, for after all the company would still require a Deputy MD and told her that, Davie would remain "…at the helm" he called it while she was off making babies. She knew that the position of Deputy MD had been suggested to appease her, for her father was wise enough to know Davie's limitations and she had little doubt he would continue to maintain control of the company through Davie. That was his way and always had been. Even during her parent's marriage, Moira's mother had little to do other than look pretty, arrange the meals and keep the house tidy.

As a female, Moira knew exactly where she stood in her father's pecking order; no more than a breeder for his future grandchildren and one night during his year of agony when he was the worse for wear through drink, vividly recalled him telling her of his anticipation that she bore him grandchildren.

She turned to stare through the kitchen door at the framed wedding photograph that still hung on the lounge wall and scowled; like that's going to fucking happen!

Sipping at the coffee, she made her way upstairs and in her bedroom, glanced in the wardrobe mirror. Her reflection showed a medium height, slim brunette with collar length hair and a face that would easily attract attention from any man.

However, at twenty-six years of age, Moira Bain's primary ambition was not to attract the attention of men.

She already had her father's affection, but what she really needed was to overcome his old-fashioned chauvinistic attitude and misguided belief that Davie was the natural choice to succeed him. And that she vowed, would most definitely occur by any means at her disposal.

## CHAPTER THREE

Charlie Miller took a deep breath and stared round the room at the thirty-odd detectives and support staff that were seated or stood silently watching him. During the preceding weeks it had been difficult motivating his team. The lack of progress in the investigation had weighed heavily not only on Miller, but on each individual who served under him. It was his custom to brief the team on what little was learned daily then go round the room, seeking comments or suggestions, but the discovery this morning of the woman's body had changed today's format.

"Ladies and gentlemen," he formally began, "firstly, I apologise for keeping you all waiting. As you can see, we're honoured by the presence of Detective Superintendent Mulgrew stood at the back of the room there," who he nodded to with a twinkle in his eye, "who has promised to kick my arse if we don't get a result by the end of this week."

The comment drew a few chuckles and he continued, "Right then, you'll all have heard the news of the discovery of another body; a young woman as yet unidentified who we believe to be in her late twenties or early thirties. She was discovered by two uniformed cops covered over by an old carpet in West Regent Lane. For those of you not familiar with the topography of the city centre, the lane runs east to west between West Campbell Street and West Nile Street and also crosses over Hope Street and Wellington Street too. The body was discovered between the Hope Street entrance to the lane and the West Regent Street entrance. As you'll appreciate because it's still early days, we're attempting to formally identify the deceased and that's currently being done by Myra McColl and…" he hesitated, forgetting the young lad's name and turned towards Barclay who called out, "Kevin Feeney, the acting DC, boss."

"Right," Miller nodded. "Anyway, Myra and her lad are away to the bank for an address and once that's obtained I'll be knocking on some poor sods door. For now though, with the permission of Ma'am," he nodded again to Mulgrew, "this latest development, the discovery of the deceased, will be investigated as part of the ongoing inquiry. A tentative examination by Doctor Watson," continued Miller, "indicates the deceased was bludgeoned on the back of the head and the wound is similar to that of our other two victims." He turned to the white board behind him and in turn pointed to the two photographs as he called out, "Linda Docherty, discovered almost six weeks ago in Dalhousie Lane in Garnethill and Allison McVeigh, found two weeks ago in Douglas Lane round the corner from our old HQ at Pitt Street. There is no immediate indication of sexual activity or any suggestion the motive was robbery. However, as the SIO I can confirm to you that there *is* a direct link between both these murders. For those of you experienced in murder investigations, you will appreciate this link is currently confidential. For those of you not previously involved in this type of investigation, let me explain. This type of inquiry attracts nutters and bampots who will come forward to claim responsibility. The card up our sleeve is that *when* we make an arrest…" he pointedly glanced about the room, "as we surely will, only the killer will be aware of this link between the victims. Does everyone understand that?"

There was a general nod of heads and a murmur ran through the assembled team causing Miller to raise his hands to quieten them. "Okay, settle down, I know what you're thinking and yes, while it *is* already confirmed there is a linkage between the first two victims, we have no *conclusive* information that the deceased *is* number three. In the meantime, Ma'am has agreed that we include this mornings deceased as part of the inquiry. I realise maybe we're adding two and two together and coming up with five, but that's how I intend working the latest murder for the minute and I have my reasons for that," he held up his hand to forestall any questions.

"Moving on, once the deceased is positively identified, DI Barclay will issue Actions to you and that will let us get on with our profiling and tracing of witnesses. In the meantime I want you all to continue with the Actions you already have been issued with relative to the murders of McVeigh and Docherty."

He glanced around the room and could almost read the thoughts of every man and woman there and his shoulders slumped as he slowly exhaled.

"Right, I know what's going through your head, folks, that we might have a serial killer to find. There's no easy way to say it. Three murders in just under six weeks and we all know what this will mean if the media latches onto it. In particular, that wee bugger Ally McGregor who does the crime beat for the 'Glasgow News' is already suggesting a connection between the first two murders so we can almost guarantee when the news of this latest murder breaks, the headlines will scream out serial killer."

His eyes met with Mulgrew's who gave him an almost imperceptible nod as he continued, "What we as the investigating team need to remind ourselves is that absolutely *nothing* about the investigation is to be leaked. I'm sure that you are all aware of the damage that has been done in previous murder inquiries when a casual reference or misplaced word has reached the ears of the media and caused all sorts of damage to an investigation. Well, I'm confident that this won't occur in our inquiry, but that doesn't mean to say we become complacent. Be on your guard against discussing the inquiry with anyone, police or otherwise who is not a member of this team. Don't forget, the worlds worst gossips are the polis. In particular, be careful when answering the phone. Some reporters are not beyond pretending to be cops or CID when they're looking for information. Now, any questions?"

At the back of the crowd a hand was raised by a young female detective who introduced herself, "I'm DC Mhari McGhee from the MIU, boss," she said. "Me and the other guys that have just been sent over to assist were wondering if there will be a catch-up briefing re the first two murders."

Before Miller could respond a desk phone rung and almost immediately answered by a civilian intelligence analyst who he saw began to scribble something on a notepad.

Ignoring the interruption, Miller addressed McGhee and her colleagues and replied, "DI Barclay, the incident room manager will organise that and thanks for coming guys, we certainly could do with your help," but his attention was then distracted by the analyst who was waving the notepad at him.

"Yes, Melanie?" he smiled at her.

"That was DS McColl, sir," gasped the young woman. "She's passed us the address of the deceased and will be here in about ten minutes."

"Good, thanks Mel," he nodded towards her and again asked, "Anymore questions?"

A hand was raised by a male detective, also from the MIU.

"Is there anything that connects the first two women together or to the third victim, sir?"

"Good question, but nothing we have so far discovered and at the minute, the attacks seem to be random. However, that doesn't mean to say we should rule it out."

Turning to Mark Barclay, he said, "Maybe add that to your list of Actions, Mark, Have someone profile the three women's early lives just in case there is a connection there."

"Sir," replied Barclay as he scribbled a note on his pad.

Miller cleared his throat and continued. "As you will learn when DI Barclay briefs you later, there does not at this time seem to be any motive to the murders. By that I mean there is no obvious sign of sexual assault or robbery for nothing seems to have been stolen from the deceased," but quietly thought, apart from a lock of their hair. "What *is* evident is that both women were struck on the back of the head with what Forensics have assessed as a hammer type implement, with the wounds inflicted being roundish in shape and roughly about one inch in diameter," he smiled and added, "For you younger folks, in metric that would be two and a half centimetres. Its Forensics opinion that the weapon used and I might add used with such force to shatter the skull, is probably a carpenter's hammer. However, do *not* discount anything that you might come across during the course of your inquiries that could make this type of wound and of course it does *not* mean that the suspect *is* a carpenter. Enquiries so far have discovered that carpenters hammers are on open sale from hardware and DIY stores, the Internet and even some supermarket chains."

He stared round at the room, conscious of all the eyes that stared back and said, "Any further questions, then? No? Right then, thanks folks and let's get this bugger arrested, eh?"

As the team dispersed to their duties, Miller was handed a torn sheet upon which Mel the analyst had written the deceased's address. He was joined by Mulgrew who quietly said, "That was a timely warning regarding the press, Charlie. I'll contact our Media Department and give them the heads up to expect a flood of calls. Right now though," she glanced at her watch and in a voice dripping with cynicism, added, "I'd better head back to Gartcosh and meet with Mister Freeman because likely he'll want an update as to why you've not yet solved the first two murders."

Miller grinned for he knew that beneath Mulgrew's sarcastic comment was an underlying deep dislike for the Assistant Chief Constable (Crime). Not that she was the only detective who disliked Freeman for the portly East Anglian was unpopular with most if not all his senior CID staff. It was widely rumoured that Freeman's appointment was political, that he was being groomed for the top job in a large English constabulary and under budget pressure from the UK Government's Home Secretary, there was little the Scottish Government's Cabinet Secretary for Justice could do to remove him. However, this information was of little help to his beleaguered CID officers from whom Freeman demanded drastic cuts in their

Divisional budgets and of whom he continually made unreasonable demands.

"Well, good luck there then," he smirked and then added, "if you can squirm some overtime out of him for my budget, it would really help."

Mulgrew pulled a face and replied, "No promises, but I'll see what I can do."

With a final, "Keep me apprised of any developments," she winked as she turned to leave. It didn't escape Miller's attention that more than a few of the male detectives cast a furtive glance at the good-looking, copper-haired Mulgrew as she walked from the room.

"Boss," Miller turned to find the florid faced DS Myra McColl at his side.

"Whiplash," he smiled in greeting. "Right, my office and you can fill me in with your visit to the bank."

Davie Craven parked in the large car park at the rear of the warehouse and switching off the engine, slumped down into the seat. He breathed a sigh of relief and hoped the tenner he had bunged the RAC guy to keep his mouth shut was enough. He'd decided to just tell his Dad it was something in the engine. No way was he going to admit he had forgotten to get diesel. Bugger it. He hadn't even considered that the tank needed topped up. Weren't these bloody Merc's supposed to run forever?

He sat for a few minutes in the bottle green coloured car, watching as the two articulated lorry trailers were loaded with goods. He could see Alex Mason, the warehouse manager standing there with a clipboard in his hands, supervising the dozen staff that carried the goods from the warehouse rear door. He disliked Mason who always made him feel like he was a useless bastard, but exhaled and shook his head. He *was* a useless bastard. Never in a thousand years would he understand the logistics of the warehouse. Too many figures and details for a dyslexic like him to comprehend and it didn't help that he'd no real interest in the running of the place, anyway. He wasn't like his sister Moira, who could easily manage the day to day managing of the company. She was wasted sitting in her pokey office, dealing with that stupid admin stuff. Why his father couldn't see that, he never understood though he suspected that maybe his old man *did* know of her capabilities, but just wouldn't accept that his daughter was a whole lot brighter than his son was. It terrified him that he was expected to take the reins when his father retired. Besides, he was hopeless when dealing with people and particularly the warehouse staff. He knew they laughed at him behind his back; the boss's son. Well, most of them anyway and smiled. Not Mary, though. No, Mary wouldn't talk about him behind his back. He liked Mary who a bit like him, was shy and reserved. She'd been hired just a month ago and they'd hit it off and when he could he'd take his break with her. All he had to do now was pluck up the courage to ask her out. One afternoon, when his sister was out at lunch, he'd visited Moira's office and sneaked a look at Mary's personnel file and with some difficulty, managed to read that she lived with her parents in Bridgeton and that at thirty-two, was two years older than him. More importantly, she wasn't married but did have a wee boy who was aged six. That didn't bother Davie who had his own child, three year old Elsa.

He glanced up and saw that Mason had realised he'd arrived and was peering at him.

Bugger it, he'd better get out there and taking a deep breath, opened the driver's door.

Myra McColl drew up outside the mid-terraced house in Fairway Avenue in the Glenburn area of Paisley and switched off the dashboard SatNav. In the passenger seat beside her, Charlie Miller took a deep breath and simply said, "Okay Myra, here we go then." The name on the door was the same and their knock was answered a few seconds later by a slightly built, middle-aged man who stared curiously at the officers. He was about to smile, but his face turned pale and his shoulders slumped.

"I...I listen to the radio. Is it her then?" he asked.

Miller realised there was no need to produce the warrant card he held in his hand, but instead took a deep breath and replied, "Mister Maxwell, my names Charlie Miller and this is Myra McColl. We're from the CID and we're here about your daughter, Janice. Can we come in, sir?"

John Maxwell shivered before leading them through to a neatly furnished lounge where a woman wearing a wrap-around apron, his wife Miller correctly guessed, sat nervously in an armchair by the fireplace twisting a white handkerchief in her hands. Her eyes opened wide with hope when she saw them, but turned to dismay when her husband said, "its Janice. They're from the CID and they're here about our Janice, hen."

"Oh God, oh my God," she said and then head down, began to softly weep.

With compassion, McColl quickly moved towards her and bending down onto one knee, took the woman's shaking hands in her own while Miller's attention was briefly taken by a framed photograph of a smiling young woman wearing a university gown and mortarboard cap and hung upon the wall.

There was no mistake.

He recognised the face as that of the young woman who had been discovered lying dead in West Regent Lane.

"We heard it on the radio, that a body had been found," said Maxwell, his voice faltering and shaking his head as he fought to contain his tears. "She never stayed out without letting us know when she'd be home or where she was. She's a good girl, always…" but his shoulders heaved as a tide of tears enveloped him and reaching behind him, he sank back into the other armchair.

"I'll put the kettle on," McColl quietly said and rising, made her way into the kitchen.

Miller was at a loss. The distraught parents each occupied an armchair while he stood helplessly staring at them in turn before deciding that he could do nothing other than sit down on the couch and let them weep.

A few minutes later, McColl returned from the kitchen with a tray upon which rested a pot of tea, four mugs, milk and sugar. At her nod, Miller arose from the couch and placed a side table in the middle of the carpeted floor.

Maxwell exhaled loudly, blew his nose and said, "I'm sorry, I didn't mean to…"

"Please, Mister Maxwell," interrupted Miller, his hands held up before him. "You have every right to be upset and absolutely no need to apologise. I'm just so very sorry to be the one to bring this awful news to your door."

"There's no doubt? I mean…"

Miller nodded to the framed photograph and asked, "Is that Janice?"

"Aye, that's here. It was taken when she graduated from the Caledonian Uni."

"Then I'm sorry," Miller shook his head, "there's no doubt."
They spent almost an hour with Janice Maxwell's parents. Her father Alex Maxwell fought his sorrow to tearfully provide Miller and McColl with the information they needed while throughout their visit, her mother Esther wept uncontrollably.
They had been through this before, breaking the news of the violent death of a loved one with other parents, with spouses and even on occasion to children and it never, ever got easier.
When at last they returned to the CID vehicle, they both sat to catch their breath and if they were brutally honest, to silently give thanks that it was someone else's child, someone else's loss and not their own.
"Sometimes boss, I hate this job," McColl said as she stared through the windscreen.
"Aye," he blew through pursed lips. "I can't think of a worse thing than what we just had to do there." His eyes narrowed and as she started the engine, he said, "When we get back to the office, Myra, give Paisley CID a courtesy call and on the QT, inform them of the address of our victim. Once the media release her details there will be press knocking on that poor couple's door, so tell them I will be grateful if they'd be kind enough to get the uniform to put a car outside the Maxwell's house for at least twenty-four hours to chase the buggers off. I know they can't be there all the time, but…well, use your charm, eh?"
She grinned as she gunned the engine and drove off before replying, "Well, boss, if Paisley can't manage it, I'll fucking sit outside the house myself and I'll have Mister Hickory with me."
Miller grinned because it was a standing joke that the steel grey haired and stoutly built McColl had never returned her old wooden baton, preferring it to the recently issued modern friction locking baton and if the stories that Miller had heard about McColl were even half correct, she wasn't adverse to using it either.

Unusually, James Bain found an empty bay in the underground car park and hurrying round the corner to the main entrance on Bothwell Street, rushed through the door to catch the lift to the third floor where the insurance company's call centre was located. He glanced at his watch and seeing he was already ten minutes late, silently thought 'Shit!' He'd already received two verbal warnings from his cow of a team leader about his time keeping and a third verbal automatically led to a written warning and a written warning was merely the prelude to dismissal. With his employment record he couldn't afford to be sacked and urged the lift to hurry. To his dismay, it creaked to a halt on both the first and second floors and when it did reach the third floor he exited with his head down, hoping not to be seen.

Fortune seemed to favour him for Annette Bell was on the other side of the large room with her back turned towards him. Partially hidden by the tall cubicle dividing walls, he made his way to his workstation and with a sigh, slid into his seat.

That's when he saw the handwritten note on his desk that instructed upon his arrival, he attend at the managers office.

With a groan, he crumpled the note and angrily flung it into his wastebasket. He clasped his hands behind his head and sat back in his chair to ease the throb in his head. The bitch Bell had got him at last. If ever a woman deserved to be…he took a deep breath and slowly let it out. Shaking his head he got to his feet and pushed the chair back so sharply it tipped and fell over.

"Breaking the furniture won't help, Mister Bain," said the high-pitched voice behind him.

He turned to find the small and overweight redheaded Bell staring at him, her glasses perched on the tip of her nose.

"It was an accident," he stammered, "I didn't mean for…"

"I believe you and I are due at the manager's office, Mister Bain," she retorted and without waiting for a response, turned and waddled off in the certain knowledge he would follow.

His hands clenched into fists and for a few, heart-stopping seconds he thought about leaping upon her, grabbing her by her fucking hair and smashing her head off the nearest brick wall then stomping her bleeding skull into pieces.

But he didn't.

Head down in defeat, he followed the portly woman through the narrow corridors that separated the cubicles, conscious of the curious stares of his co-workers who shook their heads or grinned with relief he passed them by that it was James and not them being censured. The manager, tie undone, shirtsleeves rolled back onto his forearms and jacket slung over the back of his swivel chair, was sat encased in his own glass cubicle and invited both he and Bell to sit. Clearly though, he had other things on his mind for they'd hardly been in his office for a few minutes when he raised a hand to stop Bell's whining complaint and curtly told Bain, "That's your third verbal now James. I will have a written warning issued to you and remember your contract agreement. No more verbal warnings," he shook his head as he glanced at his watch. "The next time you fuck up, it's a straight written notice that will of course result in your dismissal. Now, if you don't mind…" he tightly smiled and with a wave of his hand, summarily dismissed them.

Outside the office Bain turned to speak with Bell who simply raised a hand to stop him and wordlessly, walked away.

He was infuriated that she could treat him like that, but knew exactly why she did.

It had happened several weeks before at the office party to celebrate the company's takeover by the American conglomerate, when the tipsy Bell had trapped him in a storeroom and tried to proposition him. Drunkenly he sneered at her and told her to fuck off, that he wouldn't dream of shagging a wee fat, redheaded dwarf like her.

The morning after the party, it had begun; her relentless campaign to get him sacked.

It had commenced with her monitoring his calls to clients and complaints about his handling of the calls, then graduated to this; clock watching his every shift.

The worse thing was he was stupid enough to continue being caught out by her.

He had never disclosed the storeroom incident to anyone, least of all Moira.

He slowly made his way back to his workstation and sighed. These days he and Moira didn't communicate anyway, so why would he tell her about Annette Bell?

Women!

Fuck them all, he inwardly seethed and glancing about him, stared intently at the females who worked in the nearby cubicles. If he could, he'd do for the lot of them. What a collection he'd have then, he mused.

The telephone on his desk rung and he lifted it then with a resigned sigh and practised smile, repeated the company greeting and added, "James here. How can I be of assistance?"

Elaine Hamilton worked steadfastly at her desk, accounting and filing the inquiry team's returned Actions, disseminating those that she considered worthy of further investigation to her civilian staff, the intelligence analysts that occupied the three desks behind her. She was good at her job as a senior intelligence analyst and since the formation of Police Scotland her team's services were in high demand from SIO's across the country.

As she worked she sneaked a glance across the room to where Mark Barclay occupied the incident room manager's desk and stared at him for a brief few seconds. She had known the bespectacled Barclay for most of her seventeen years service as a HOLMES operator and had worked with him on numerous major inquiries. Such close proximity had permitted her an insight into his private life and she suffered with him when two years previously, his wife had finally succumbed to the cancer that had plagued her for several years prior to her demise. It was during these years, at functions and shift nights out that Elaine had got to know Barclay and his wife and through the couple, lived the lives of their two sons, now both grown and with wives of their own.

While his colleagues often thought of Barclay as an impersonal and sometime abrupt man, Elaine was aware of his true character for beneath his gruff veneer was the caring, selfless man who through a decade of nursing his ailing wife almost single-handedly raised both sons. It was during these years that her respect turned from fondness to unrequited love.

Of course she would have been horrified had Barclay learned of her affection and hated herself for the feelings she experienced. Many nights she would weep with shame as her thoughts turned to what life would be like if Barclay's sick wife died and left him free for Elaine to pursue.

It was this shame that decided her.

No matter what, she would never disclose to him how she felt; she would accept and be content with her lot.

Staring down at the Action in her hand, she startled; so wrapped up was she in her own thoughts that she had not properly read the document in front of her and with a shiver, glanced guiltily at the Actions she had already dismissed to the filing basket. With a sigh, she retrieved the Actions and prepared herself to again read through them.

Cathy Mulgrew swiped her security card at the barrier and nosed her Lexus through the narrow lane and into the large, secure car park. Though the newly formed Police Scotland headquarters was temporarily situated at the Scottish Police Training Centre in Tulliallan prior to being moved to Randolphfield in Stirling, Mulgrew's appointment as the Detective Superintendent in charge of the three divisions in the Greater Glasgow area gave her some leeway and so she had chosen to locate her office at Gartcosh.
As she walked through the security gates and towards the main building, she never failed to marvel at the tall, concrete structure that now housed the five main agencies of the Scottish Justice system. Her decision to locate her office at Gartcosh was she believed sound, for she argued she was better situated for liaison purposes close to the where the Crown Office and Scottish Police Authority (Forensics) was also located as well as being relatively handy to attend incidents within her area of responsibility.
Passing the security desk she nodded politely at the duty officers and opting for the stairs rather than the lift, made her way to her office on the second floor. It was as she was opening her door that her mobile phone rung.
She frowned and sighed when she saw who was calling as she answered, "Good morning, Mister Freeman. I've just arrived back at my office. Are you still able to attend our meeting, sir?"
"I'm here already," Freeman irritably growled, "so if you would be so kind as to meet me in the conference room on the third level and soon as you can, Miss Mulgrew. I do have *other* responsibilities, you know."
Before she could respond, Freeman abruptly ended the call. Angrily, she banged her handbag down onto her desk, while thinking, but not before I have a bloody pee!

It took Mulgrew a few minutes to negotiate her way through the three security doors that permitted her access to the third floor conference room where opening the door, she found Freeman seated at the top of the long table. His staff officer, a uniformed Inspector who was little more than a flunky, stood in the corner with his back against the window that overlooked the atrium on the ground floor below.

"Good morning, sir," she politely greeted him and waited respectfully to be asked to sit.

To her annoyance, Freeman chose to ignore her and instead pretended to read the report that lay in the cardboard folder in front of him.

However, diplomacy was never Mulgrew's strong point and after a moment's hesitation at his rudeness, pulled out a chair to Freeman's left and seating herself, deliberately banged her handbag onto the floor beside her.

In response, Freeman half turned towards her and with a mocking smile, said, "Time of the month, Miss Mulgrew?"

She felt the blood drain from her face and teeth gritted chose not to respond, but instead said, "You called this meeting, sir. How can I help you?"

Freeman flipped the folder closed and turning towards her, belched loudly and exhaled the smell of onions into the room. "Pardon me," he said with a mirthless smile and sat back in his seat, his fingers making an arch in front of his nose as he stared at her.

Again Mulgrew chose not to comment and folding her arms, pressed her back against the unforgiving plastic of the chair.

"I understand our killer has struck again in Glasgow city centre, Miss Mulgrew. What exactly is your DCI…ah, Miller, doing about catching this man?"

"Well, sir, two things," she calmly replied. "One, it is still to be confirmed that the recent murder is related to the murders of the two young women Linda Docherty and Alison McVeigh. Secondly, we have no evidence at this time that the killer *is* a man."

A small point scored, but one with which Mulgrew took deep satisfaction.

Freeman, his face turning red at the obvious rebuke, tightly smiled and replied, "Yes, very good Miss Mulgrew, but my question remains. *What* is DCI Miller doing about catching the killer of the two women and this new victim?"

"DCI Miller is doing all he can with the limited resources at his disposal, sir."

"Limited resources? My God woman, he's got a full divisional CID, a HOLMES staff and about a dozen MIU officers seconded to him. Isn't that enough to catch one bloody killer?"

"With respect, sir," she seethed because it grated on her to call him 'sir', "DCI Miller is not only trying to catch the killer of the three women and yes," she forestalled him by raising a hand, "I accept it is likely the third victim is related to the first two murders, but you have to realise that he's doing so on a budget that does not permit him to offer his team overtime. A budget, if I might remind you, *sir*, imposed by you. You might not know it, but some of his own divisional personnel are working overtime without pay just because they respect their boss and want to catch the person responsible for these murders."

Freeman leaned his bulky figure across the desk and stared with beady eyes as he pointed a finger at her, then sneeringly said, "Well, that's very commendable of those officers, but if your man Miller is unable to run the inquiry within the hours I permit him, then maybe you should think about getting someone else to run the bloody inquiry!"

She stared at his finger, revolted as she saw for the first time how his hand and fingers were covered with warts, some of which had clearly been picked at.

"DCI Miller is a good detective, sir. I have complete confidence in his ability, but as I said you have to permit him some leeway, some overtime to conduct inquiries outwith the working day and don't forget; the inquiry team is depleted by a number of his officers who are tasked to attend to the divisional crime that still occurs daily. As a former operational officer…"

"What do you mean former?" he thundered at her. "I still know how to be a copper, lass!"

She stifled a retort and instead replied, "What I mean, sir, is that if you have experienced working a major inquiry, then you must know that it's a twenty-four hour, seven day working week. Miller *needs* the extra allocation of overtime to clear the large number of Actions that are constantly being generated by the inquiry…"

"Nonsense," he swept a hand in front of him as though dismissing her complaint. "When I were a detective down in Great Yarmouth…"

"Again with respect sir," she interrupted, "you can't *possibly* compare a seaside town in East Anglia with a major city centre like Glasgow! My God, there *is* no comparison. I'm guessing that more people socialise in Glasgow city centre on a Friday night than *reside* in Great Yarmouth!"

His face flushed and she knew she had erred, that she was mocking his brief experience as a Detective Constable in the CID.

"Well, that may be," he conceded with reluctance and banged a fist heavily down onto the polished wooden table, "but when *I* were a detective, lass, we didn't have fancy computers to work with and we *didn't* need extra hours to catch our criminals!"

No, she thought, because both of them were probably fucking known to you anyway, but kept her mouth tightly shut.

She knew she had lost the argument.

Charlie Miller wasn't getting his overtime.

Pale faced, she stared at him and asked, "Will there be anything else, sir?"

He turned away from her and waved a hand in dismissal. "Keep me abreast of how your DCI is getting on and lass," he turned to her with a look of malevolence on his face, "if he doesn't get a result soon, he'd better think about dusting off his uniform."

The subject of Mulgrew and Freeman's conversation was at that time in his office, studying the daily synopsis of Actions compiled by his office manager Mark Barclay when the door knocked.

"Come in," he called and looked up to see Barclay shoulder the door open, two steaming mugs grasped by their handles in one hand and a report in the other. Using his backside, Barclay pushed the door closed,

"I thought you might need a coffee, boss."

Miller sighed and grinned. "What I need is a large whisky, but I've been sober for a number of years now, Mark, so no sense in going back now, eh?"

Barclay sat the mugs down onto the desk and nodding, he grimaced. "I remember when it happened. That must have been a hard time for you, losing your wife and son together like that."

"Aye, it was, but no harder for me than you losing your wife and don't forget, I was lucky. I met and married Sadie." He took a sip of his coffee and stared at Barclay. "What's that now; a year and a half?"

Barclay sensed a moment of intimacy had arisen and replied, "Just over two, actually, but I'm moving on, Charlie. The lads have been a great help. Good boys, both of them."

Miller lifted his mug and with a smile, toasted Barclay and said, "Here's to family."

"Aye, to family," agreed Barclay.

"Right then, what have you got for me?"

"Not much I'm sorry to say, but Elaine Hamilton picked up on one of the MIU team's Action's with a statement attached. Apparently DC Mhari McGhee, who took the statement, spoke to a prostitute who works in the Drag area round Blythswood Square and was working the night that Linda Docherty was murdered. The woman remembers it was the same night because the Rangers were playing at home against the Aberdeen and there was quite a few Aberdonians knocking about, looking to get serviced."

Miller laughed and repeated, "Serviced?"

Barclay grinned and nodded. "That's how she McGhee describes it in the witness's statement and the woman also says it was memorable because the Don supporters are the most miserly buggers she's ever had to deal with and she was pissed because one of them gave her a forged twenty pound note!"

"I hope she didn't make a complaint of fraud," chortled Miller.

Barclay returned his grin and continued. "Anyway, she's worked the Drag area for a number of years and says that she's become familiar with most of the cars that do the circuit, looking for the prostitutes and the way they're driven." He held up his hands and smiled, "I know, but that's what the witness claims. Anyway, on the night the first victim was murdered, the witness remembers it was dry that night and says that a light coloured Ford, she's positive it was a Fiesta, did the rounds several times, but the male driver never stopped to speak with any of the women. She thinks the car was white or silver in colour and in the Drag for about an hour and there was something odd about the car, but she couldn't for the life of her recall what it was. Anyway, she was so suspicious of the driver that she passed the word on to the other women. Apparently they've got some sort of a warning relay set up. You know, passing the word from corner to corner or something like that if there's a punter who seems to be suspicious."

Miller's brow furrowed with interest. "Did the witness get a clear look at this guy? I mean, would she know him again if she saw him?"

"She says she didn't get a good look and can't describe him other than to say she thought he was a youngish guy, certainly not middle aged or older, maybe with dark hair. One thing that came across and was commented on by DC McGhee in the statement is that cars are this woman's passion. She's one of these people who regularly attends classic and vintage car shows and she told the detective that part of the reason she solicits is to fund her travelling and for the upkeep for her own 1970 Ford Capri that she takes to events up and down the country." He grinned when he added, "She also told McGhee that the events are good for business too and she has a regular clientele she meets at these occasions."

"She sounds to be a switched on businesswoman," Miller dryly commented, then continued, "Talking about the driver again. Surely the driver not speaking to the women is not that unusual. I mean maybe he was rubbernecking or just couldn't make his mind up."

"It's a possibility," agreed Barclay, "and McGhee noted that in the statement, that she did put that to the witness, but the witness was apparently adamant that the driver just seemed suspicious, like he was looking for someone in particular."

Miller's eyes narrowed. Linda Docherty, a young and vibrant single mother of twenty-eight, had been on a shift night out with some friends from the restaurant where she had been employed as a waitress when she left the pub in Charing Cross to catch a taxi. She was heading home to let the babysitter away, but her body had been discovered the following morning in Douglas Lane, a short dead-end lane located not far from the former Strathclyde Police headquarters and a stone's throw from Glasgow's red light area, more commonly known as the Drag.

"Okay, Mark. Might be something, might be nothing. Let's have the witness in for a formal interview, see if she can remember anything else or recall the thing about the car she mentioned. If she's not happy about attending here at Stewart Street, maybe we can arrange to have her interviewed somewhere she feels more comfortable; her home perhaps or a hotel foyer or a café or somewhere like that."

"Right, boss," replied Barclay, finishing his coffee.

"One thing before you go, Mark," said Miller, his eyes betraying his concern, "how's the morale out there?"

"Could be better if our illustrious leader ACC Freeman was to release some funds for overtime, but apart from that, it's pretty positive so far."

Miller nodded. "Okay, thanks, Mark. Here's hoping that Cathy Mulgrew gets something squeezed out of him."

"Aye and I'd be first in the queue to squeeze the miserable bastard, preferably by the throat," Barclay said and shook his head with some feeling as he closed the door behind him, leaving Miller to grin at the closed door.

## CHAPTER FOUR

Martin Craven decided to take his sandwiches down to the staff canteen and sit with some of the warehousemen and women. It was something he tried to do at least once each week and gave him the opportunity to share some craic and hear their gripes and complaints. His own working experience was that if the coalface workers had access to their boss it helped with any difficulties when they were asked to work late or extra hours at the weekend. Besides, he paid a better hourly rate than most local employers and always rewarded their graft with staff nights out where he would provide a generous kitty. His care for his staff also included ensuring they paid into a company pension he had set up and turning a blind eye to the very occasional theft. His philosophy, based on a business research paper he had read some years previously, was after reading about a major retail company with a large number of UK outlets who permitted a university team of psychologists to conduct research and monitor theft in two of its outlets. During a given period, the company relaxed security and ignored minor thefts from one store, but cracked down sharply on security in the other store. The results over the fixed period surprised the psychologists who learned that the store where minor theft was tolerated demonstrated a sharp rise in profit whereas profit in the store where security was tightened had rapidly declined.

The results fascinated Craven, yet didn't surprise him for he remembered his own formative working life and the occasional pilfering he himself conducted and decided he would permit the infrequent theft as long as it did not interfere with the company profits.

So far, his gamble had paid off and he had not been disappointed. He pushed open the door of the canteen and cast a smile to the turned heads. He saw that his son Davie was seated at the far end of the canteen, apparently deep in conversation with a dark haired young lassie that Moira had recently hired, though for the life of him he couldn't recall the girls name. He hesitated, but then Davie turned and saw him, so with a fixed smile he walked down the aisle and joined them at their table.

"Not intruding I hope," he smiled at the girl.

She was clearly embarrassed, sitting not just with the boss's son, but now with the boss himself.

"About this morning, Dad…" Davie began, but Craven raised a hand to stop him and said, "Don't worry about it, son. Did you get the car fixed?"

"Eh, aye, the mechanic turned up and got it going, Said it was something in the engine, but I'm not sure what it was," replied Davie, glancing away.

Craven wondered why his son was blushing and mistakenly thought it was because he had been caught sitting with the young woman. Plain looking but with nice eyes, he thought she seemed a wee bit shy and correctly guessed his presence had thrown her. "Sorry, hen, what's your name again?"

"It's Mary, sir. Mary McLaughlin."

He hoped his smile would put her at ease and nodding, said, "Well, Mary, I hope my lad here isn't keeping you back from your work?"

Mary might not have attended university, but she was sharp enough to recognise a dismissal and continuing to blush, hastily packed her Tupperware container and spoon into her plastic carrier bag. "Eh, I'll see you later then, Davie," she smiled shyly and nodded to Craven as she left the table.

When she had gone from earshot, Craven asked, "Friend or work colleague?"

"She's a friend, Dad and probably the only real one I've got in this place."

"Maybe you should think about putting yourself about a bit more, mixing with the other staff I mean, Davie, because after all," he waved a hand about the room, "one day this will all be yours."

"I wish you'd listen to me, Dad," hissed Davie, "I *don't* want to be the top man here. For heaven's sake, we both know that Moira would do a far better job than I ever could. My God, how many times…"

"Perhaps we should discuss this at another time son," interrupted Craven, conscious of the heads turning as Davie's voice rose.

"What's the use, Dad, you *never* bloody listen," Davie angrily shot to his feet and crumpling the paper sandwich bag, grabbed at his mug of tea, spilling some across the table top and causing Craven to jerk back to avoid being splashed. "You just don't want to hear the truth that *Moira* is the smart one, not me!"

Stunned, Craven watched him walk off past the bemused staff, their eyes following Davie to the door that he slammed behind him.

He took a deep breath and stirred at the mug of tea in front of him, his appetite for the sandwiches gone. He wondered what the relationship was between his Davie and the girl…Mary, she had said her name was and decided it might be prudent if he were to have a word with Moira. He'd already paid off one gold-digging wee bitch and wasn't prepared to go through that hassle again.

His thoughts turned to the receptionist, Shelley.

Yes, maybe he was an old fool, keeping a young girl like that in a flat down in Govan, but even at his age, he still had physical needs. Besides, though he would never openly admit it, he cared deeply for the teenager and then couldn't help but grin.

If he was going to have an affair, then it might as well be with a smart and sexy young teenager like her and smiled in anticipation of another exciting evening.

Myra McColl knocked on Charlie Miller's door and popped her head round to tell him, "Anytime you're ready to leave for the PM boss, just give me a shout. I'll be in the incident room."

"Have you made arrangements for the lassie's father, Mister Maxwell, to be brought to the mortuary for the official identification?"

"Mark Barclay did that, boss. The mother wants to attend too, so one of the MIU team is collecting them as we speak and they will meet us there."

"Right, Myra," he nodded and then added, "Your aide, the young lad Feeney. Have you told him he's coming too?"

She grinned. "Aye, he's never been to a PM and I don't think he's looking forward to this one."

"Well, if he's intent on a career in the CID he has to start somewhere," sighed Miller. "Give me a couple of minutes to make a phone call and I'll be with you."

Nodding, she closed the door.

He lifted the desk phone and dialled his home number. It rang for almost a minute and he was about to replace the handset and try her mobile when a breathless Sadie answered, "Hello?"

"I thought you might have gone out to the shops or something, love."

"No, the wee bugger has just gone for a sleep so I thought I'd take the opportunity and have a relaxing bath."

"Oh, sorry, did I get you out…"

"Aye, Miller, you did," she interrupted.

He grinned at the handset and said, "Well, that's made my day, imagining you standing there naked and dripping wet."

"Is there a point to this call," she testily asked.

"Oh, ah, I just kind of wanted to hear your voice."

He listened as she sighed deeply and then replied, "Well, if you weren't so busy, Miller, I'd ask you to come home and dry my back for me and then rub me down with baby oil, but…"

"Okay, that's too much information when I'm supposed to be concentrating on the job. I might be a bit late tonight, but I'll let you know."

"Right," she laughed in his ear, "I'll keep you some dinner just in case. Bye."

He was still smiling when he was standing and pulling on his coat.

Myra McColl drove with Miller in the front passenger seat and the young aide Kevin Feeney sat quietly in the back. Beside Feeney was a cardboard box filled with paper and plastic bags, evidence labels, a roll of blue adhesive tape, small sample jars and a stapler. He glanced briefly at the items contained in the box and tried to remember what McColl had instructed him regarding the seizure of the deceased's clothing and personal possessions and the manner in which these items were to be sealed in the paper bags. It was when she explained the purpose of the sample jars that his blood run cold and he hoped he would be able to hold it together, that he wouldn't puke like he guessed she expected him to.

Miller half turned in his seat and said, "You all right back there, Kevin?"

"Yes, sir, I'm fine."

"Good. DS McColl informs me that this will be your first post mortem?"

"Yes sir."

"Don't be getting yourself stressed about it, son. What you will be witnessing is something that nobody should have to see, but what we intend doing today is acting for the young woman who was murdered. She's no longer able to speak for herself, so that's our job now. We are the people who will do our very best to ensure that she obtains justice for the terrible thing that happened to her and to ensure that the person who killed her pays for it. Her parents will be there and the first thing that will happen is they will be asked to formally identify their daughter. It's not an easy or a pleasant task, standing with a parent or family member when they're going through that, but it's a necessary part of the job so you'll be with me when we do that, okay?"

"Ah, yes sir."

"When the identification part is concluded, the deceased will be removed to the examination room where Doctor Watson will perform the post mortem examination. Prior to this though, you and DS McColl will seize the deceased's clothing and personal items that might adorn the body. The clothing and items will be bagged and labelled. DS McColl will keep you right regarding that and thereafter you will both convey the seized items to the Forensic laboratory for examination. You know why that's done, I assume"

"Yes, sir, DS McColl explained it all to me and says it's for continuity of the evidence, sir."

"Good. When the deceased is stripped of clothing the SOCO, Jean Galbraith it will be, will photograph the body and the doc and I will examine the deceased. While that's being done I'll have to ask you and DS McColl to wait for a few minutes outside the room while the doc and I examine the deceased. I'll then call you and DS McColl back into the room and with me you will witness the PM."

"So, I'll be present throughout the PM, sir?"

"That's right," nodded Miller, who then paused and turned to stare at the younger man. "Remember this though, Kevin. At all times we do our level best to treat the deceased with the utmost dignity so if at any time during the autopsy or at any time during any part of the procedure you need to leave the room, then don't wait for permission; just go, because its better you get fresh air than puke all over the place." He shook his head as he added, "Nobody will think the less of you, son. Do I make myself clear?"

"Yes, sir," Feeney gulped and then added, "thank you sir."

Miller turned away while beside him, McColl concentrated on her driving. Inwardly she thought that no boss she had ever before worked for would take the time to explain to a trainee detective what was expected of him.

Her respect for Charlie Miller just did not end.

Moira Bain parked her Audi in her designated bay and saw that both her father and brother Davie's cars were already in the car park. She didn't immediately leave the vehicle, but sat for a few minutes, thinking again about her failed relationship with her husband James. She knew it irked him that she insisted on calling him James while most people knew him as Jim, but she didn't care. It simply presented her with another opportunity to needle him.

She glanced across at the rear loading bays and saw the fair headed Davie standing close in deep conversation with a woman, her dark hair tied tightly back in a ponytail. Peering at them, she recognised the woman as Mary McLaughlin, a recently employed member of staff who worked at labouring and stacking shelves in the warehouse. As she watched she saw Davie reach out and with an apparent quick glance about him to ensure there was nobody about, pulled the woman to him and hugged her.

The hug lasted but seconds and then the woman patted Davie on the cheek and made her way back through the roller shutter bay doors into the warehouse. A few seconds later, Davie again glanced about him then followed her through the door.

Moira's eyes narrowed as she considered what she had witnessed, what it had meant. Was her brother again falling into another hopeless relationship?

She ground her even white teeth and guessed this would be another problem her father would need to fix and likely more mean money being spent to get rid of McLaughlin.

During a recent audit of the company's finances, she had inadvertently discovered that monthly, her father paid off Davie's former wife Jean Anderson from his private account. Moira knew that the allowance was like a festering wound, a constant drip that hurt the company profits for her father had increased his annual company salary to compensate for the payments; money that Moira believed was being wasted just so her father could enjoy Davie's grandchild; that shitting, puking little toddler they both doted on. And now this, another floozy who had apparently turned her stupid brother's head.

She angrily shook her head when she recalled that McLaughlin's probationary month had expired and it wouldn't be so easy now to sack her.

No, she would have to find some plausible reason.

Getting out of the car, she made her way across the rutted concrete car park and entered the warehouse through the staff door. The elderly pensioner who acted as the security for the door and the nearby loading bay, a former employee that her soft hearted father had kept on when he should have been got rid of, greeted her with a smile and was about to speak, but Moira tacitly ignored him and walked on.

On the way to her office on the upper floor, she passed a number of employees, most who smiled or greeted her with "Hello", but Moira was not known for her manners and as she had done with the elderly doorman, ignored them.

Pushing open the door to her cramped office, she slipped off her coat and hung it on the hook behind the door. Patting at her collar length hair, she stood and looked about her, again annoyed that her father had chosen this squalid little cupboard to accommodate his daughter while he sat behind a huge desk in his large office downstairs with that little tart Shelley at the front door reception attending to his needs. Her eyes narrowed for she had a vague suspicion Shelley's attendance of her father went beyond the office.

She slowly sat down behind her desk and thought about Shelley. Moira had no part in hiring the young teenager and would not have even considered giving her a job. It was her father who one day completely out of the blue brought her into the warehouse, though God knew where he had found her and against her forthright advice, hired her. Her attire at work was totally inappropriate, though she guessed that her father enjoyed having the short-skirted little madam running back and forth for him.

It revolted her, but while she suspected her father was having an affair with Shelley, was uncertain how to could broach the subject with him. Moira had little doubt Shelley was yet another money-grabbing parasite who was after her father's cash.

Since the death of her mother, when she alone had held the company together, her father had for the first few years been the shell of the man who had built the company from nothing.

It had been her belief that when finally he came round to his former self, he would recognise her achievements. But no, her fists tightened.

Once more Davie had been the apple of his eye, the chosen one even though he was completely useless in business affairs. The cock-up's he made during the brief period he was acting MD were forgiven by their father and all but completely forgotten, but not by Moira.

It was then as she sat at her desk, her rage knowing no bound that a cold fury overcame her and she came to her decision.

Just like his latest infatuation Mary McLaughlin, her brother Davie would also need to be removed from the company, but how she would accomplish this would need some thought. All she had to do was come up with some sort of plan that did not involve her.

She startled when her door was knocked and to her surprise, pushed open by her father. Martin Craven smiled at his daughter and said, "Morning, love. I wonder if I might have a wee word."

Taken aback and feeling a little guilty, Moira could only dumbly nod and point to the seat opposite her desk.

"You should have called me on the internal phone, Dad. I'd have come down to your office."

"No," he raised a hand, "I thought I'd come up here because I want you to check your files anyway. Eh, it's about your brother, hen. I sat with him at lunch…" he paused, "Well, actually, I *tried* to, but he got a wee bit annoyed with me," he added without explanation. "Anyway, the thing is he was sitting with a young dark-haired woman, a new lassie that you hired and I was wondering…"

"You mean Mary McLaughlin?"

Craven's eyes opened in surprise. "My God, Moira, it seems you're better informed than I am, hen. Did you know that our Davie is seeing this woman?"

Moira maintained the pretence that she knew more than she did and nodded. "It's no great secret, Dad. After all, I *am* the personnel

manager so it's my job to know what the employees are up to." She frowned and saw his eyes narrow and decided to seize the initiative. "My only concern is, as we both know of course that Davie's track record with women isn't great so I'm worried that he's about to make a fool of himself again with this woman McLaughlin."
"Why, what do you mean?"
Moira pursed her lips and with her elbows on the desk leaned forward to support her clenched hands, shrugged. "Of course, I'll need to have another look through her previous employment record, but if I recall correctly McLaughlin was fired from her last job; waitressing I think it was, somewhere in the city centre. I can't recall what she told me, but I remember that's she got a wee boy and lives with her parents or perhaps its just her mother; I'd need to check the file. The point is I felt a bit sorry for her and decided to give her a chance here with us. I'm only sorry that she's abusing my trust and using the opportunity I've given her to latch onto Davie, particularly after the ordeal of his divorce from Jean Anderson. After all, he's making good money now and she'll likely be aware that he's being groomed for the MD position in the company; he is, isn't he Dad?"
She forced herself not to sound as spiteful as she felt. The lie about Mary McLaughlin being fired rather than the truth that the restaurant business failed and her previous employer was unable to keep the staff on, tripped easily from her lips. Added to that, the reference to Davie's former wife and Moira's insinuation that McLaughlin was an opportunist fell on fertile ground for she saw the seed of doubt take root in her father's face.
Martin Craven slowly shook his head and asked, "To be honest, hen, I thought it might do him some good, seeing a woman. He's been kind of lost these past couple of years, what with losing your Mum and then that ex-wife of his taking him to the cleaners. I don't know the lassie…what's her name again?"
"Her name's Mary McLaughlin, Dad."
"Aye, Mary McLaughlin," he repeated with a nod of his head. "What do you suggest, hen?"
Moira worked hard at keeping her face straight and stared levelly at her father. "I think it might be prudent to find a reason to dismiss McLaughlin and get her out of here for as they say, out of sight, out of mind."

He thought about it for a moment, then remembering the heartache that Davie went through with his former wife, Jean Anderson, decided that it just wasn't worth taking the risk of Davie again becoming obsessed and falling head over heels in love with the wrong woman. With a heavy heart, he asked, "How will you go about that?"

"Leave it to me, Dad," she smiled encouragingly at him.

Mark Barclay took the call on his desk phone. "Hello, Mark, it's Cathy Mulgrew. Has DCI Miller left for the PM? I know he was meeting the parents and didn't want to call him on his mobile and interrupt in case he was already with them."

"Aye, Ma'am, he and DS McColl and the aide left over an hour ago. I think the PM will be underway as we speak."

He heard her sigh and then she asked, "Are you free to speak?"

He glanced about him and nodding to the handset, replied, "Go ahead."

"Mark, inform Charlie that ACC Freeman has refused any further money for overtime. That and he wants an immediate result to determine if the third victim is the work of the same killer. Can you get Charlie to phone me when he's got some news? I'm in my office at Gartcosh, but if there's no reply there, I'll have my mobile with me."

"Will do, and Ma'am…" he paused and bit at his lower lip, "thanks for trying anyway. It's no great secret what you're up against."

He thought he'd maybe overstepped the mark, but she carefully replied, "I appreciate your understanding Mark. Here's hoping that the team do, to."

In her office, Mulgrew thought it wise that though she knew Barclay of old and he was a trusted man, she had decided not to mention the threat issued by Freeman that if Miller didn't soon get a result, he would be returned to uniform duties.

Her good friend Charlie had enough on his plate and just didn't need that extra pressure.

With his arm wrapped around his distraught wife's shoulder, Janice Maxwell's weeping father followed DS McColl to the side room where the MIU detective sat waiting to convey them home.

Returning to the viewing room, she smiled softly at the pale faced Kevin Feeney.

"It's not easy, is it son?"

"No, Sarge," he swallowed hard. "I mean, there's nothing we can say, nothing we can do…"

"Oh there is, I mean, something we *can* do. We can arrest the bastard that brought this grief down upon them. That's what we can do, Kevin."

"Aye, I suppose you're right," he glanced at her then added, "Mister Miller says we've to go into the examination room and to bring the cardboard box."

"Okay," she nodded and then stared quizzically at him. "You sure you're going to be fine, Kevin?"

"Aye, I will be as long as you keep me right regarding the productions, Sarge."

"Don't worry, we'll get through this together," she patted him on the shoulder then led the way into the brightly lit examination room.

He saw that the deceased, the once vibrant young woman called Janice Maxwell, still fully dressed, lay in repose on her back atop a steel table that was punctured by holes located uniformly along the sides and bottom of the table. He realised with a start the holes were designed to permit the deceased's blood to flow away to a bucket located beneath the table. He then quietly gulped at the array of stainless steel dissection instruments that lay in neat rows on a nearby wheeled trolley.

DCI Miller, Doctor Watson, the SOCO woman Jean Galbraith, with a camera strapped round her neck and a male mortuary attendant stood quietly beside the body.

At Watson's nod, the attendant began to carefully undress Janice Maxwell and handed each item of clothing to McColl who placed the item in a paper bag held by Feeney.

"We'll label and seal the bags out in the anteroom," McColl whispered to Feeney.

A thin gold chain from her neck, a wristwatch and a pair of gold ear studs were also placed in separate paper bags.

When at last the deceased lay naked Miller cast a glance at the young trainee detective, curiously pleased that the lad looked shocked for he believed that nobody in their right mind should take any pleasure in seeing the naked body of a dead young woman.

But there's always one, he mused, remembering a Detective Inspector in particular who Miller always thought of as a bit of a ghoul.

Turning to McColl, Feeney and the attendant, he said, "If you could give us just a minute, please guys," and watched as they left the room, the officers carrying the evidence bags.

When the door had closed behind them, Watson moved to examine the deceased's head and slowly turned it towards Miller.

"It's as we expected. The bad news is that she's the same as the other two, Charlie. There's a sizeable chunk of her hair been cut to the scalp from the back of her head near where the mortal blow was struck."

"What's the good news," he sighed as Jean Galbraith, the SOCO supervisor prepared to photograph the area of the head missing the hair.

"It seems then that you're looking for the one killer. Right," she sharply added as she reached for the instrument trolley, "if you want to call Myra and the young guy in, we'll get started."

When details of the discovery in a city centre lane of a young woman's body was released to the press, within minutes the Police Scotland Media Department was inundated with calls from both reporters and TV and radio stations, all desperately keen to obtain the information for their outlets.

As previously requested by DCI Charlie Miller, the SIO running the inquiry, Chief Inspector Harriet 'Harry' Downes of the Media Dept kept the information to a minimum, refusing to release more than the briefest of details and denying any connection with the discovery of the two murdered females that was currently being investigated. However, such was the pressure of calls from the media that she believed it was time to review the official press release and phoned Stewart Street to speak with Miller, but her call was answered by Melanie the analyst who handing the phone to the DI, said, "It's a Chief Inspector at the Media Department, sir."

"Hello, DI Barclay here. Sorry, but DCI Miller has still to return from the PM. Can I get him to call you back or do you want his mobile number?"

"Barclay? Mark Barclay?"

"Aye, it is, Ma'am."

"Mark it's me, Harry Downes, so don't give me any of that Ma'am crap," she chided him. "How are you doing these days? Oh, I heard about your bad news, Mark, I was sorry that…"

"No, it's okay Harry, really," he interrupted her. "It's coming up for two years now, so like I was saying earlier today, I've moved on. How are you getting on these days?"

"Just the usual. Different day, same old shit," she sighed then continued, "Listen Mark, my lot are under a wee bit of pressure here the now. We're getting toasted about the body discovered in West Regent Lane and the buggers are putting two and two together and coming up with five. I need Charlie Miller to phone me…"

"Hang on, he's just walked through the door on his way to his office," said Barclay, who continued, "Look, I'll give him a minute to get himself together and have him phone you right away. Is that okay with you?"

"Don't let me down, you grumpy old sod," she laughed and hung up.

Barclay followed Miller through to his office and note pad in hand, knocked on the door as Miller was hanging up his overcoat.

"How did it go, boss?"

Miller shook his head, his eyes betraying his distaste at witnessing the dissection of a lovely young woman whose life was so abruptly and brutally ended. "No matter how many of these PM's I attend, it never gets easier," he shook his head and stared at Barclay. "To quote Sherlock, the bad news, Mark is that Janice Maxwell *is* victim number three. We've got a serial killer on our hands."

He slumped heavily down into his seat as Barclay leaned out of the door and called to a young HOLMES operator passing by, "Couldn't rustle up two coffees could you, son?"

"Right away sir," the young man nodded and hustled off to fetch them.

"Okay, what do you have for me?"

In order of calls, Barclay related Cathy Mulgrew's bad news about being turned down for extra finance and the request from Harry Downes that Miller contact her regarding a fresh bulletin for the press.

"Okay, I'll update Ma'am and then phone Harry. Nothing else came in today. No new witnesses or information?"

"Sorry, no, nothing," Barclay shook his head and as the door was knocked, stood to receive two coffees that were handed in.

"Okay, maybe I was expecting too much," sighed Miller, reaching for the mug. "Right then, regarding the lassie Janice Maxwell. As you will have guessed her folks are in a hell of a state, but they were able to tell Myra and I that their daughter had been on a night out in the city centre with some pals from the place where she worked at the passport office in Milton Street. Apparently the lassie never stayed out all night without phoning home to let her folks know she was okay. There's a boyfriend who's away at the minute working somewhere down in England, but you can have someone confirm that too. As for the pals, they gave us a couple of names, but I guess it would be better if you allocate a couple of Actions and instruct our guys to go team handed to the lassie's work to obtain statements. Myra has the details of the pals. It might be prudent to give the manager a call first to let him know we'll be speaking to his staff and ask that he set up an interview room. It *is* the passport office, so they must have more than a few rooms available."

Barclay made a few notations on his pad and replied, "Got all that." He raised his head and watched as Miller, who looked tired and drained, rubbed at his face with both hands.

"Look, I'll let you get on with your calls. I expect it might be a long night. Let me know if you'll be staying late and I'll get someone to organise a chip shop run."

Miller slowly smiled and nodded as he reached for the desk phone.

## CHAPTER FIVE

James Bain was still seething with anger when his shift finished. All that day he had avoided eye contact with the redheaded bitch Annette Bell and now it was time to return home to his own bitch; his wife.

Making his way to the underground car park, he unlocked his car and getting in, sat still, breathing slowly and forcing himself to be calm. The memory of last night, the woman, the *bitch* he had dragged by the hair into the lane and hit with the hammer was still fresh in his mind. Her attempt to escape from him was laughable as she stumbled backwards on her high heels, her hands clutching at his fingers that were wound into her hair. He felt himself become erect as he forced his neck back into the car headrest and slowly closed his eyes, hearing again and savouring the bitch's whimpering plea not to hurt her. He slowly reached down to touch himself, but stopped and quickly glanced about him. This was stupid. Anyone coming to collect their car from the car park might wonder at him sitting there and the last thing he needed was to draw attention to himself. No, he would go home and retrieve the bag from behind the radiator in his room, the bag he had wrapped in the handkerchief to dry and then place the hair with the other trophies. Then tonight in the single bed in the privacy of the guest room, he would remember what he did and rub the three bags over himself. He had no fear of Moira discovering him or the bags for she never came into his room. Not any more.

His thoughts turned to her and his blood run cold. He had never hated anyone as he hated his wife. Well, maybe his domineering and bullying mother, the woman who beat him and every other month would painfully snip his hair almost to the scalp in her obsessive hunt for head lice, but he no longer had any contact with her so she wasn't worth even a thought.

Moira, though, was a different matter. He had to see and suffer her sneering face every day.

Regardless of the pregnancy, he knew now that marrying her had been the biggest mistake of his life and no amount of money, no fancy house or lifestyle would compensate for her coldness and her overbearing ways. If he thought he would get away with it…

He felt himself again become erect and smiled to himself as he switched on the engine.

Maybe one day, just maybe, on a day not too far away, Moira's hair will be in a bag too.

With Cathy Mulgrew briefed, Miller phoned Harry Downes and greeted her with, "How's it hanging you old warhorse. Still hankering after me?"

"Aye, that'll be the day, Charlie Miller," she replied with a smile at the handset and continued, "Long time no speak, you old scarred bugger. How's that wife of yours? Still putting up with your nonsense no doubt and I heard you've another wee girl to add to the family. Belated congratulations on that, though I'm guessing somebody must have had it in for you."

"I heard that joke when the Pope was an altar boy, Harry. But thanks anyway. The baby's name is Ella and Sadie's doing great. So, what about your hubby? Still reversing into garage doors?" he laughed.
"You'll be referring to my *current* husband," she answered with a grin. "I call him that to remind him how lucky he is to be married to me. Aye, the silly bugger drives like an old woman. Just as well he's got me, Charlie. Nobody else would love him. Right then, back to business; your latest victim. Janice Marshall is the name Mark provided and gave me some of the details about where she was discovered. She was aged 29, is that right?"
"That's correct, Harry," he unconsciously nodded to the handset. "Single and she lived with her parents in Fairway Avenue in Paisley."
"Poor soul. How are her folks holding up?"
"Devastated doesn't even begin to describe it."
He heard her sigh, then she said, "I'm getting a lot of calls from the press and in particular, that wee toe-rag Ally McGregor from the 'Glasgow News'. He's told one of my staff that he intends running an article linking the three murders to the same killer. Is there any substance to his claim?"
He paused before replying, "Janice Maxwell is victim number three, Harry."
Acutely aware of the pressure that Miller must now be under, she exhaled softly and said, "Oh, oh, I'm sorry to hear that, pal. I know you'll be in the thick of it over in Stewart Street, but is there *anything* that you can give me for a press release, something that I can get out for tonight's editions and news bulletins?"
He shook his head at the handset and replied, "Nothing that won't cause a widespread panic, Harry. Suffice to say that we're looking into three murders and there are similarities between all three. You'll know better than me about phrasing the appeal for witnesses, etcetera."
"Do you want me to go ahead and arrange for a press conference tomorrow? Say, mid-morning?"
He paused and was about to tell her that he'd better clear it first with Cathy Mulgrew, but instinctively knew that Cathy would undoubtedly agree, so replied, "That might be a good call, Harry. If you can set it up, I'll have Ma'am informed regarding the time and venue."

"What about having one of her parents present or a family member? That usually attracts a sympathetic audience and can often persuade someone who's uncertain about contacting us, to give us a call."
"I'll consider that. I don't think the mother would be fit, but I'll have Myra McColl give the father a phone and see what he says. Where would be the best place to hold such a conference?"
"I think here in the Dalmarnock office is probably the best venue, Charlie. The conference room here is a good size. Leave the time to me and I'll get back to you or Mark Barclay."
"Okay, Harry and thanks. It was nice hearing from you again."
He replaced the handset then thought about it and lifting it, dialled and internal number.
"Mark, it's me. I'm going to be here for a while so put me down for a fish supper and a can of diet coke."

Sat behind her desk, Shelley McPhail sorted out the mail and sighed when she saw the letter addressed to Alex Mason, the warehouse manager. She didn't like Mason and was acutely aware that he took every opportunity to visit the reception desk where he would leer at her and try to look down the front of her blouse. She had considered telling Martin, but didn't want him to get involved for really, Mason had never said anything that could be construed as offensive or inferred anything sexual, but that didn't stop her feeling uncomfortable every time Mason passed by or called in to see Martin.
She exhaled through pursed lips and lifting the letter from the pile, went to seek out Mason in the large warehouse, not for the first time thinking it would be useful to have a tannoy system installed in the building.
She had been walking among the narrow aisles for several minutes, greeting the staff she met with a smile and inwardly smiling at the interest she provoked from the male employees.
It was as she was about to turn into an aisle at the rear of the store she saw Martin's daughter, Moira Bain walking in front of her and turning the corner. She had realised almost from the first day working in the office that Moira disapproved of Martin hiring Shelley and other than business issues, kept her association with the personnel manager to the minimal contact. She was about to turn away into another aisle when from round the corner in the adjacent

aisle a few feet away, she heard Mason's voice clearly say, "You're looking for me, Moira?"

Shelley hesitated, torn between delivering the letter to Mason yet reluctant to bump into Moira. Standing there, she was about to turn away when she heard Moira in a low voice, say, "Yes, it's about the new girl, Mary McLaughlin. How is she shaping up? Is there any issues, Alex?"

Shelley froze. The were talking about the new lassie, the dark-haired, quiet girl who had just recently been hired and who she had seen several times speaking with Martin's son, Davie.

"Issues? I'm sorry, what do you mean?"

"Time-keeping, poor work ethos, anything that might provide us with an opportunity to, shall we say, let her go?"

"You mean Moira, you want her fired?"

"Crudely put, but yes. I have my reasons, so the first opportunity that arises, I look forward to your report on my desk and Alex; one day I'll be running this company and I have a long memory. Just be sure that I won't forget those who are useful to me. Do we understand each other?"

"Oh, aye, Moira. I understand," Shelley heard him reply and fearing discovery, she quietly slipped away

Eric Kyle took advantage of Charlie's Miller's earlier instruction and didn't feel guilty about leaving the office early that afternoon for he had stayed late for most of the last six weeks, claiming overtime when it was available and hours in lieu when it wasn't. Besides, he told himself he had bridges to mend after his argument with Paula last night.

He thought of the money he was earning with the overtime and how useful it would to bring down his overdraft, but it brought little comfort. With a little over five months before he retired he had already received a projection of his lump sum and pension from the finance people, but still it irked him that his ex-wife would get almost half of the lump sum and a sizeable chunk of his monthly pension, as would the bloody taxman.

Well, he grinned to himself; that would happen only if what he was planning didn't work out.

As he drove he thought of his wife Paula and wondered if she'd be at home or again out socialising with her so-called mate.

Younger than him by thirteen years and the most alluring woman he had ever known, he'd thought that after a short romance and following the final *decree nisi* of his acrimonious divorce the blonde and vivacious Paula would continue to work at the hairdressing salon when they'd married almost a year ago. A couple of months into the marriage and only to keep her happy he'd reluctantly agreed when she suggested giving up fulltime work and instead be self-employed working from home or attending at her client's houses. It wasn't too long after that her client contact list fizzled out even after she dropped her prices and the business finally became unprofitable. Of course, she had persuaded him that something would come along, though it didn't and since then her hairdressing work had dwindled to a few regular appointments every other week that barely covered the petrol for her two years old Range Rover.

What continued to puzzle him though was after his ex-wife took her share of his weekly salary, leaving barely enough money to pay for the rent of the former local authority flat in Bankhead Road in the south side of Glasgow, Paula still always seemed to have cash in her pocket. Since she no longer contributed to the household budget, it worried him where she got the money for her new clothes and her days and nights out with her mates. Of course he had confronted her, but she simply smiled in that beguiling manner that she knew disarmed him and persuaded him that she was a more astute housewife than he credited her for.

As always, he accepted her explanation because quite simply he chose to believe her. He just couldn't face the fact that she might be lying and the prospect of another failed marriage worried him, for his retired standard of living would depend on what he currently earned. To pay alimony to another ex-wife was frankly, unthinkable and if he admitted it, the thought scared him shitless.

Besides, he didn't want to lose her and couldn't think of facing the rest of his life without her. As he drove he recalled the excitement of marrying the svelte and sexy Paula. It had been an almost physical rush he hadn't experienced with his ex-wife or any other woman and the first months had been the best of his life. It did niggle at him when he could no longer afford to take her to the pubs and clubs she enjoyed that their relationship had cooled a little, but he still loved her as she loved him; or again, as he chose to believe.

He slowly exhaled, pleased for once to be almost home so early. He knew that Paula had two tickets for that nights comedy play at the Pavilion Theatre at the top of Renfield Street in the city centre and arranged to meet her friend Jill early that evening to attend the show. He didn't particularly care for Jill Hardie who he thought was a right tart and already had two husbands behind her. If Paula was to be believed, Jill apparently had a prospective third husband in her sights, some bouncer in a nightclub in the city. However, any reservations he had about his wife associating with the promiscuous Jill were quickly dismissed when she reminded him that she and Jill had been pals since primary school. Tempted as he was he never disclosed to Paula that early in their marriage Jill had even propositioned him. He glanced at the dashboard clock and saw that even if she left early to meet Jill for a drink before the performance, he would still have a few hours with his wife and grinned. A lot could happen in a few hours.

He slowed as he approached the junction, turning from Kings Park Avenue into Bankhead Road. Almost immediately clearing the junction, he slammed on the brakes of his old Ford Mondeo and brought it to a screeching halt when he saw the football fly out over a nearby hedge and land in the middle of the road. Sure enough, a boy aged no more than six or seven came running through the garden gate after the ball. Breathing a sigh of relief, he growled at the lad who with complete indifference scooped the ball up into his arms, ignoring the angry driver and his lucky escape and run back through the gate.

Kyle shook his head and wheezed through pursed lips before restarting the stalled vehicle and continuing along Bankhead Road at a more sedate speed.

As he approached the mini-roundabout that was close to where his flat was located, his eyes narrowed.

Further along the road, he saw her.

His wife, her long blonde hair flowing down her back in the wind and wearing a light coloured, hippy style chiffon robe, was leaning on the driver's door of a bright red coloured Volvo V60 that was parked in the lay-by outside the flats. Paula seemed to be speaking with the driver, but Kyle couldn't see if the driver was male or female because the afternoon sun reflected on the windscreen. He couldn't explain why, but he had a sudden misgiving and slowed the

Mondeo and pulling into the side of the narrow road, switched off the engine. He watched for a few minutes then his heart sank as he saw her lean into the window and he knew, just knew, she was kissing the driver.

Paula backed out of the window and as the vehicle drove off towards him, she waved before turning to hurry towards the flats entrance door.

As the new and shiny Volvo negotiated the roundabout and passed him by he turned his head away, but not before he saw a dark haired man in his forties at the wheel; a man he didn't recognise.

He felt a cold sweat envelop him and he sat there, his hands gripping the steering wheel so tightly his knuckles were white.

He knew the right thing to do was to go to the flat and confront her, for having worked late for all those weeks he realised that Paula obviously didn't expect him to return home in the late afternoon.

He found it difficult to swallow and hands now trembling, he made his decision.

Eric Kyle, the man who early in his police service was commended for facing down a razor wielding psychopath, the man who just four years earlier had tackled and brought down a robber armed with a baseball bat, the man who was respected throughout the city by both CID colleagues and the criminal fraternity, was humbled and indecisive because he saw his wife kiss another man.

His instinct was that he should drive to the flat, tell her what he had witnessed and have it out with her, but afraid of what he might learn his courage failed him and so he took the decision that rather than face the truth he would return to Stewart Street and sign on for a few more hours of work.

Across the city in the small, former mining town of Blantyre, James Bain turned into Dalcraig Crescent and reversed his Ford Fiesta into the single driveway, slowly coming to a halt in front of the garage. It had been made clear by Moira that when she arrived home, she expected to be able to bring her car into the driveway and he'd learned early in their marriage that it wasn't Moira's custom to have to remind him twice.

He inwardly smiled for the plus side to being first home would provide him with the opportunity to ensure that his latest trophy had dried properly and he could add it to the other two he had hidden at the back of his underwear drawer. With that plan in mind he got out of the car, but then heard someone shout, "Hi, there."

Surprised, he looked across the narrow road and saw Lara Quinn, the woman who lived directly opposite, in her garden waving at him with a smile plastered to her face. His stomach tightened and he forced himself to return her smile, but as he turned away from the car didn't expect her to suddenly cross the road to intercept him before he got to his front door.

"Hello, Jim," she coyly greeted him. Dressed in a halter-top that left little to the imagination, her heavy thighs bulging in cut-off denim shorts and sandals on her feet, her breasts heaved and her eyes shone brightly. Almost immediately he realised she had been drinking.

In her late-forties, the dyed blonde widowed woman had taken a shine to Bain and sought every opportunity to corner him. In the honeymoon period when he and Moira had first moved into their home, they had laughed together at Lara Quinn's attempts to engage Bain in conversation. Later, her tactile advances towards him when she thought that Moira wouldn't be watching and her veiled suggestion that he might wish her to visit him some evening when his wife was detained in hospital for the aborted pregnancy, caused him to take extraordinary measures to avoid her. However, as recently as the previous week when returning his lawn mower to the garage, she surprised him from behind and ushering him into a corner, attempted to kiss him before taking his hand and clasping it tightly to her breast.

He had been shocked and stuttered an excuse to get away, but now watching her cross the road towards him, he realised that the woman was relentless.

Had she known of his background, Lara Quinn might not have been so keen to pursue the handsome Bain.

Born the only child of a unmarried, domineering and alcoholic mother, James Bain had never known his father or had the opportunity of a male role figure in his life and endured a childhood of both physical and mental abuse. The slaps and punches inflicted by his mother as chastisement for the pettiest of mistakes reduced what should have been a normal and happy youngster to a frightened and terrified child; an experience that resulted in a childhood stammer that he carried forward into adult life and projected itself during times of stress. His school years had been a nightmare and though the education department could have helped with speech and language therapy, Bain was one of those unfortunate, friendless individuals who fell through the cracks in the system. His free time during his adolescence was spent caring for his abusive mother, at her every beck and call until one day when in his early teens, he discovered her unconscious and was unable to awaken her. Her subsequent hospitalisation and diagnosis of a stroke resulted in Bain being taken into care. There followed a number of failed foster homes until eventually in his mid teens he was accommodated in a young persons hostel. Like many young people, Bain fell foul of an overworked and underfunded system and ultimately found himself freed from local care and thrust into the world at large. His attempts at finding work were hindered by his lack of educational qualifications and thus invariably led to low paid, menial jobs. However, Bain's one and only real advantage in life was his extraordinary good looks. His jet black collar length hair, piercing blue eyes and physique attracted more than a few of the opposite gender, most of whom initially believed Bain to be shy, but soon discovered him to be without question a very handsome individual, though not overly bright.

No one could ever have known that his extremely unhappy childhood and the unwarranted punishment meted out to him shaped a man who harboured a deep and malevolent hatred not just for his mother, but for all women.

Now here he found himself, his back to his front door and a cold sweat running down his spine as yet another woman attempted to take advantage of him.

Lara Quinn reaching forward to stroke lightly at his arm, suggested he might wish to invite her inside for a glass of wine.

"After all," she slurred, "Moira doesn't get home for another hour and well, a lot can happen in an hour, don't you think?"

He realised that she must have been watching them, noting the times they arrived home from work and gulped. While his mind wanted to push her off and tell her to get away from him, his mouth dried up and he could only croak, "We don't…don't have any wine."

She grinned and moved closer to him, her face mere inches from his. He saw she had plastered her lipstick on so thickly it smeared her teeth and he gagged, for her breath was stale from drinking wine and smoking heavy tar cigarettes and nauseated him. She cocked her head to one side and staring into his eyes, said, "Don't you want to shag me, Jim? Wouldn't you like to…" but got no further for he snapped and surprised her by pushing her away and hissed, "Fuck off, you old tart! Get away from me!"

Stunned, she took a step backwards, but lost her footing and fell heavily onto her backside. Helplessly, she stared up at him and her lips began to tremble and he saw tears in her eyes, but then rage took over and red-faced, she snarled, "What...what did you call me? You…you…you're nothing but a *bastard*!"

Panic stricken, he turned and with shaking hands forced the key into the lock and opening the door, quickly stepped through and slammed it closed behind him. He couldn't understand why he was shaking. Outside, he could hear her screaming and then the door was kicked and he could hear her beating hear fists against it.

His back pressed against the locked door, he closed his eyes and willed her to go away. After a few minutes of cursing and swearing, the sound of her voice faded and he risked a glance through the curtained window to see her stagger across the road towards her own house. He watched as she went through the front door and slammed it behind her and then breathed a sigh of relief.

The whole incident had taken no more than five or six minutes, but his body continued to shake. He glanced up and knew that the only thing that would calm him was wrapped in a handkerchief and hidden behind the radiator in his bedroom. Quickly, he made his way upstairs.

It was as he had left it, the handkerchief now crisply dry and unfolding it saw the plastic bag was also now dry. He opened the bag and withdrew the twist of hair it contained and almost with reverence, smoothed it against the skin of his cheek. It felt a little brittle and he stared at it, realising to his disgust that some of the woman's dried blood from her head wound had adhered to the hair. Grunting, he took the hair to the bathroom and run it under a lukewarm tap until he was certain that it was clean of blood. He decided not to return the hair to the plastic bag, but wrapped it again in the handkerchief to dry. He was disappointed that he couldn't add it to the other two straight away, but did not dare risk it spoiling.

He heard the crunch of tyres on gravel and sneaking a glance out of the hallway window, saw that his wife had returned home earlier than expected.

Hastily he shoved the plastic bag into the small, bathroom bin then returning to his bedroom slipped the handkerchief back down behind the radiator.

The front door was banged closed and slowly closing his eyes, took a deep breath for a few seconds before opening them and preparing himself, made his way downstairs.

Seated comfortably behind her desk in the CID general office, DS Myra McColl sipped at her scalding coffee and peered sympathetically at the young acting detective. "Are you sure you're okay, Kevin? I mean, I know that the PM wasn't what you might have expected. It's not a pretty sight, seeing somebody being examined like that."

Sat opposite her, Feeney slowly exhaled and laid his mug down onto McColl's desk. "To be honest, Sarge I just didn't know what to expect. I mean, you get the lecture at the Police College during training and there's photographs and things like that, but my God, what the doctor did," he shook his head and shivered as if the very movement would expel the memory.

McColl continued to stare at him with concern. "Look," she said at last, "I'd understand if you wanted to head home. Maybe take some time…"

"No, nothing like that," he sat bolt upright. "It's just that, well, you must have felt like this at your first PM Sarge. Nauseated, I mean."

"Oh, aye," she smiled and slowly nodded, "but what makes you think I still don't get nauseated?"

"You mean…"

"Listen, Kevin, the day you get used to seeing what you saw is the day you chuck it. Think about Sherlock, for example. You probably don't know it, but she's a regular churchgoer, a Baptist who attends services every Sunday morning not far from where I live in East Kilbride village. I sometimes see her if I'm out walking the dog and if there's time, she'll stop for a chat. Now, that woman has probably performed more PM's than anyone else I know, but is she used to it? Not likely," McColl shook her head. "She once told me that before she wields her scalpel, she says a wee prayer to herself that God forgives her for what she is about to do. That's what keeps her strong and the day that she doesn't see the body on the examination table as a human being is the day she quits. Her motivation is that she performs the PM to determine why that individual died and that helps her through the procedure. So the moral of my story is that you must *never* forget why the PM is performed and one other thing, Kevin. What you witness in the examination room, other than in evidence, must remain there. We always maintain the deceased's dignity, so no gossiping, okay?"

"Sarge," he was shocked, "I would never…"

She held up a hand to silence him and added, "I know, son, but sometimes we can forget and you'll hear other detectives, particularly with a drink in them, laugh and joke about PM's and particularly if the deceased has been a bad bastard, but just bear in mind what I've told you."

"Yes, Sarge," he dully replied and wondered why anyone would find anything funny about what he had seen earlier that day.

"Can I ask, Sarge, one thing that did puzzle me."

"What's that then?" she asked, glancing across to him.

"The DCI asked us two and the attendant to wait outside while he and the doctor examined the body alone. I'm not daft and I know they could easily have done that when we were in the room, so what was that all about?"

"Ah," she smiled knowingly at him. "You picked up on that, did you? Right, the easy way to explain it is that the SIO of any inquiry and particularly murders always keeps an ace up his sleeve. Something that he will hold back about the MO or the murder that only he and maybe a very few selected other officers will know. What you might call a unique feature of the murder and so unique that when a suspect is questioned he will be the only other person outside the selected officers who also knows. That way when we get the nutters and the false confessions come trooping through the door as we invariably do, the SIO can phrase his questions in such a way that he will be able to determine if the person claiming responsibility is aware of this unique feature and if that person *does* know, then that person in all likelihood is the real murderer."

Feeney's eyes widened and he replied, "So, when the DCI and the doctor were in alone with the body…"

"They were probably looking for that unique feature," she finished for him.

The door opened and to McColl's surprise, Eric Kyle walked into the room.

"I thought you'd gone home?"
Kyle walked to his own desk and tiredly took off his jacket. "When I got home Paula had already gone out for the night with one of her pals," he glibly lied, "so because I've been tied up with the murder inquiry, I've fallen behind with some reports for the Fiscal. Thought I'd take the night to catch up," and grinning, added, "what, with me but a few months left to do." Slumping down into his seat, he asked, "What's the word from the PM?"
McColl glanced at Feeney and replied, "The boss is satisfied it's the same killer, so Janice Maxwell is number three."
"The bastard!" Kyle spat out and shook his head. "Has the press tied it up with the other two murders yet?"
"I haven't seen the papers yet, but hang on," she reached for the television remote control and pressed the button for the BBC twenty-four hour news channel.
As they watched, the anchor was discussing with another reporter that day's debate in the UK Parliament, however, the breaking news ribbon scrolling at the bottom of the screen announced that the police in Glasgow were hunting a serial killer thought to be responsible for the murders of three women.
"Well," McColl said in a flat voice, "it seems they have."

## CHAPTER SIX

Martin Craven closed the cardboard file and glancing at the clock, decided to call it a day. Pressing the intercom button, he summoned Shelley through to his office and nodded that she closed the door behind her.
"I'm heading off now, hen. I want to get home, take a bath and change for tonight. Do you want me to bring some food and a bottle of plonk in with me?"
"I'd rather you *took* me out to dinner," she pouted, leaning across from him, her palms flat on the desk to permit him an eyeful of her cleavage. His nostrils twitched at the faint, but sensual scent of her perfume.
"How do you think that would look, me at my age dining out in public with a lassie young enough to be my granddaughter? What if someone I know saw me?"

"I *could* pretend to be your granddaughter," she replied and then coyly added, "in fact, I *could* pretend to be whatever you wanted me to be."

As he stared at her breasts, her offer prompted several thoughts to cross his mind, but he unconsciously shook his head and replied, "No, it could be someone that sees us who knows you work for me. After all, Shelley," he smiled at her, "you're not a young woman that a man would easily forget."

Keen to move her away from the subject of dining out, he asked, "Did you get those costumes I asked you to order online?"

"Yes, I did, so I'm guessing we're eating in after all then?" she huffily replied.

He smiled and said, "For tonight, anyway, so wear one of the costumes for me."

"Which one do you want me to wear?"

"Surprise me. I'll be down about seven."

He stared after her as she walked towards the door and sighed. He knew he was being a fool, that at fifty-one years of age he should really know better, but she was a young woman who was difficult to resist.

He thought back to almost six months previously and their first meeting; he arriving in Glasgow on the train back from a business trip to London, tired and worn-out and she with her backpack looking lost and vulnerable in the concrete edifice that was the Central Station. He didn't know what urged him to speak with her, still couldn't understand what prompted him to ask if she was okay and did she have somewhere to stay, but he did remember that the physical attraction of the young, tall blonde had overwhelmed him. He had quickly persuaded her he was no threat to her and bought her a coffee in the small cafe round the corner and learned she had just arrived from Nairn, wide-eyed and penniless with the intention of meeting and staying with a former school friend. When Shelley phoned to announce her arrival in Glasgow, the friend regretted that the room was no longer available and that her boyfriend had instead moved in with her.

Suddenly stranded, she found herself with six pounds and forty-five pence in her purse, no job and nowhere to live.

He didn't know why, but sitting there stirring his coffee, he shared with her that he was a widower, had a large house in Newton Mearns and insisting there were no strings attached, offered her a bed for the night. Recognising the doubt in her face, he had tactfully suggested she phone a relative or friend to inform them where she was going and with whom, but was surprised when she shook her head; there was no one, she had told him.

He held his breath while she considered his offer then his heart skipped a beat when she shyly accepted.

It was when they were walking together to collect his car from the council car park he realised how young she really was and he had his first misgivings. Almost panicking, he considered instead that he give her some money to find a hostel or hotel.

But he didn't utter a word.

The journey home in heavy traffic took almost an hour by which time he learned that since her parents died, she had lived in Cawdor outside Nairn with an elderly aunt and uncle who had neither the time nor the inclination to continue to share their home with a nineteen-year-old woman. Almost in a whisper she confided that her part-time job in a small local grocery store ended when the predatory owner cornered her in the storeroom and that rather than return to her home town, she was willing to do anything to get a job, but then made him smile when she hastily added, "…within reason, I mean." She had wondered round his large, detached six-bedroom home with a childlike curiosity, touching the furniture, the ornaments and the paintings and for the first time he had seen his home as others did; it was a mausoleum inhabited by a lonely man who was wasting away. He made supper for them both that included wine for him and juice for her. Try as he might, he couldn't recall who had made the first tentative approach for within days of Shelley arriving in Glasgow they were in bed together and for the first time in years, he had again felt alive.

Two days after their first union and a week after meeting she commenced working at his company and to his surprise, proven to be a capable and extremely competent receptionist. A month later he had rented a renovated and furnished, two bedroom Victorian flat in Whitefield Road in the Ibrox area of the city and installed her there. His daughter Moira had at first been suspicious and questioned his hiring of Shelley, but now seemed to have accepted her employment. It was his belief that so far neither Davie nor Moira had realised his relationship with the teenager spilled over from work to her bed.

To Martin, his budding relationship with Shelley had been an exhausting but exhilarating few months, yet not once had the young woman demanded anything of him other than his time. Visiting Shelley had been the happiest of times for him and at his request his sympathetic GP, though unaware of her identity had been wise enough to provide Craven with the stimulant he needed to continue his liaison.

Though delighted with the nights and weekends he spent with her, he worried that she seemed content to spend most if not all of that time with him.

Often, when spending the night at the flat he would awaken and in the dim light of the bedroom stare at her as she slept for during those times when his mind was at its most vulnerable he would wonder why she stayed with him, a man of his age. His uncertainty and concern at their age gap would prompt him to consider that perhaps she had a long-term plan, that she really did want something from him, but daylight would bring the stark truth she had never asked anything of him other than his affection.

He frequently encouraged her to make friends though he knew and accepted he risked losing her if a younger man took her attention. At his insistence, she did sometimes join some of the younger warehouse staff at their nights out or attend the occasional house party, but on each of these functions he would invariably receive a discreet phone call towards the end of the evening requesting that he pick her up and take her home where inevitably he would remain the night.

He could not understand the tender passion she had for him and though there was the insurmountable gap in their ages, Shelley never broached the subject other than to chide him when he would refer to himself as an old man.

The word love was never mentioned for he feared that to admit to this affection for the teenager might somehow facture the delicate balance of their relationship. And yet being a practical man he realised it could not last, that at some time in the very near future Shelley would awaken with him beside her and recognise that he was indeed an old man.

He dreaded that day, but knew it must come.

How he would handle it was something he had yet to decide.

Moira Bain was undecided. Most nights she ate alone and left her husband James to fend for himself, but tonight the steak pie she had defrosted was far too big for her alone and she considered calling him down from his room to eat with her. What the hell, she decided and opening the oven, placed the whole pie inside.

As she scrubbed at the potatoes, she thought again of her brother Davie and the woman McLaughlin. If anything came of their relationship, her father would again have to bail Davie out and once more the company profits would suffer.

The pie now in the oven with the potatoes and vegetables simmering on the stove, she set two places at the kitchen table and walked into the hallway before curtly calling up stairs, "James, dinner will be in ten minutes."

In his bedroom, Bain's eyes narrowed in surprise. She was calling him to dinner. He frowned for he couldn't recall the last time that they had sat down as a couple and eaten together. Moira usually ate in the kitchen while he would eat later in front of the television in his room.

His mind raced as he wondered what this meant. Was it some sort of appeasement? Was Moira considering renewing their relationship? He didn't know how he would react. Should he go downstairs and eat with her when dinner was ready?

What should he do?

He paced the room, trying to decide how he would react to this strange and unexpected turn of events.

Sitting alone at the table among the pre-theatre crowd in the famous Lauders pub in Sauchiehall Street, Paula Kyle was looking forward to her night out at the show with her friend Jill. With her long blonde hair tied in a ponytail and wearing a short black leather skirt and white blouse, Paula knew she was attracting a lot of visual attention and quiet comment from the men seated nearby. Used to admiring glances, she didn't feel too uncomfortable, but hoped that Jill, who wasn't known for her timekeeping, would arrive soon.

Older by just a year, Jill was good fun and completely outrageous when she had a drink in her, especially where men were concerned. She knew that her husband Eric disapproved of Jill and thought her a tart, but Paula didn't care and if she was honest with herself, really couldn't give a shit anymore what Eric thought. She hadn't realised when they first got together that his promises of good times were a load of crap and yes, it had been exciting when they first got together. Being married to the tall, former rugby prop she had envisaged a life as a carefree housewife and the thought of him being a detective had thrilled her; something she could boast about to her pals.

Foolishly, her plans to give up work completely came to nothing for Eric had insisted she continue with her hairdressing job, though in time she had been able to persuade him first to let her work freelance and then lied that her client list had all but dried up. Now she only took the odd job when it suited her or her Range Rover needed fuel or serviced or she needed some cash for a good night out with Jill. She blushed, remembering where the bulk of that extra cash came from.

It had been Jill's idea and as long as Eric didn't find out, Paula saw no real harm in it. Besides, it wasn't as if Eric was as active as he once had been and after all she told herself, a woman had certain needs.

She had been willing to overlook their age gap, but in recent months she saw through the façade that was Eric Kyle to the man beneath; the man who would rather curl up with a can of lager in front of the television than whisk her out to a pub or club.

She was slowly dying in that bloody boxlike flat and it wasn't even theirs, but rented.

What had really upset her when they had married was that he had lied about his income, that it was a lot less than he had told her and had also conveniently forgot to mention that his fucking ex-wife took a sizeable chunk of what money he did earn.

As far as Paula was concerned, she had heard enough of his bullshit and now all she had to do was work up the nerve to tell him that as far as their relationship was concerned, that boat had sailed and other than in name only the marriage was over. She wondered what kind of cash settlement she could expect after she divorced him; what was a year and a bit of putting up with him worth?

Not that she had any worries about moving out and thought that about what occurred the previous evening. Unconsciously she rubbed her left forearm at the bruise that was now mercifully fading. Of course, he had apologised like he always did, that he didn't know his own strength. Bastard! At least her friendship with Jill ensured she definitely had somewhere to live.

Her thoughts turned to today's visit from Chris. She felt a slight flutter in her bosom at the memory of him, his touch and him running his hands across her body and shivered at the thrill of him visiting her in her own bed; vividly recalling her excitement of knowing that Eric might have suddenly arrived home and caught them together, naked.

Maybe that might not have been such a bad thing, she mused.

"Sorry I'm a wee bit late, hen," said the voice behind her. She turned to see Jill, her face red and glistening with sweat, stumbling on six-inch heels towards the table where Paula sat. A couple of young guys in their early twenties turned from a table full of their mates to stare at the short-skirted, heavyset dyed blonde who passed them by, causing Jill to stop and bellow at them, "What the fuck you pair of wankers looking at? Never seen a good looking blonde with fabulous legs before?"

"The last time I seen legs like that, missus, was on a piano," cracked one in reply, prompting the table to erupt in laughter.

Paula jumped from her table to grab Jill by the arm and pulled her to the table before she could swing at the comedian, who turned back to his table to join in the laughter with his mates.

"Bastard," hissed Jill as she sank heavily into the chair. "Right then, this my vodka and coke, hen?"

Paula slid the drink towards Jill who downed the double in one fast gulp and then smacking her lips, said, "Finish yours and let's head to the Pavilion, hen. I've a half bottle of vodka and a can of coke in my handbag and we can use the ladies in there to have another drink. This place is full of shite," she turned slightly to direct her comment to the nearby table of young men and in one smooth movement, slid the two empty glasses to land with a quiet clink into her handbag. Standing, she took a deep breath and making her way towards the side door passed by the table of young men and made to swing her handbag onto her shoulder, but instead deliberately swung it at the table, scattering their drinks across the table and forcing them to jump back or fall from their chairs.

"Oooops, sorry," she pretended to be surprised by her action and followed by the giggling Paula, ignoring the mayhem and abuse shouted at her as she led the way outside.

"Right, hen," her eyes bright, she linked arms with Paula and leaning in close to her, she whispered, "tell me all about this guy Chris that you fucked today."

Seated behind his desk upon which rested the remains of a well picked over fish supper, Charlie Miller folded the polystyrene container into the paper wrapping and threw it into the waste bin beside his desk. Rubbing his fingers with a hand wipe, it also went into the bin before he clasped his hands behind his head and stared at his senior investigators, Mark Barclay and Myra McColl and the civilian senior analyst, Elaine Hamilton.
"I would have had Eric Kyle here too," he said, "but I gave him an early start to take the rest of the day off."
"Well, he *didn't* take it," shrugged McColl. "He's through in the general office catching up with some paperwork. Says his missus is out socialising tonight," and then under her breath muttered, "…again."
The others pretended not to hear McColl's sarcasm, but were aware that the cause of her dislike for Paula Kyle stemmed from an incident that occurred shortly after the Kyle's marriage. Eric Kyle, keen to introduce and show off his younger, good-looking new wife, brought her to the Divisional Christmas Dance held in the Thistle Hotel in the city centre. Almost as soon as Paula had taken her first drink, Kyle knew it was a mistake to bring her. During the evening, when McColl politely suggested Paula might wish to ease up on her alcohol intake, the extremely inebriated and surprisingly promiscuous Missus Kyle had challenged McColl to a fight and had to be physically restrained which was fortunate for Paula, for in McColl's opinion her behaviour was, "…worthy of doing her for a breach".
Extremely embarrassed by his wife's drunken behaviour and particularly towards some of his male colleagues, her husband had avoided bringing his wife to any further divisional functions and since that time there was within the CID an underlying sympathy for Eric Kyle.
"Okay, well, we'll let Eric get on with his paperwork. Right, folks, here's the latest," began Miller. "We're now looking at three victims, no witnesses and nothing of Forensic value. Statements from the witnesses who were with the first two victims prior to the

victims being discovered murdered have produced nothing of evidential value." He turned to stare at Barclay. "I assume that statements from the last people to see Janice Maxwell alive are being collected, Mark?"

"As we speak, boss," confirmed Barclay. "I dispatched a team to the passport office earlier and with the cooperation of the manager there, those individuals who were out last night with the deceased are being interviewed at their office. Anyone not at work will be contacted at his or her home address and will be visited there. So far," he sighed, "I've had nothing from the team other than Janice left the pub in Hope Street to make her way home. It was her intention to catch a train to Gilmour Street and then a taxi from there."

"So, like our first two victims, Janice had left the company of others and been alone when presumably she was attacked."

"Boss," began McColl with a thoughtful expression, "these three young women do have one thing in common. They were all pretty. Have you considered that there is a motive and that the killer just didn't like pretty women or even that the killer just doesn't like women in general?"

The door knocked and a harassed looking Doctor Watson popped her head then said, "Sorry I'm late, Charlie. I had a bit of a rush on at the mortuary."

Mark Barclay stood and smiled at her as he said, "I'll get another chair, Sherlock. Likely you could do with a coffee as well?"

"Please," she gave him a grateful smile, "milk and one sugar."

Watson sat in the chair vacated by Barclay who returned a moment later with an additional chair and crowding into the room between McColl and Hamilton, said to the doctor, "One of the girls is fetching your coffee."

"Right, glad you're here now, Sherlock," and nodding towards McColl, he continued, "we're stumped because we are unable to find a common link between the victims or a motive for their murder, though Myra has just offered the suggestion that our killer might have some grievance against pretty women or women in general. I know you have a degree of some sort in criminology, so how does that sound to you?"

"A degree of some sort?" she favoured him with a wry smile.

"Mmm, first let me explain," and slipping off her suit jacket, hung it on the chair behind her. "Aside from my medical qualifications, a number of years ago I undertook an Open University criminal psychology course that earned me a degree. To be frank, my dual role acting for the police as a casualty surgeon and pathologist keeps me very busy, so I have not had a lot of opportunity to practise what I learned on the course. However, while the subject of psychology is of course a complex issue I'll do my best to explain what I did learn. To keep it simple, in general terms there are four roles that a criminal psychologist will practise and if I may, I will summarise these roles for you. The first role is Clinical whereby an individual will be assessed regarding his or her ability to stand trial and their understanding of the trial process. The second is Experimental, which to be honest is unlikely to be of any use to your inquiry and the third is Actuarial. This role usually is more likely to come into play when either the police or the court seeks the opinion of a psychologist asked to determine the probability as to whether or not an offender might re-offend. The fourth role is Advisory and is probably the closest of the four that will permit me to respond to your question. Off the top of my head an example *might* be if a psychologist is requested to advise police about how to proceed with an investigation or the best way to interview or cross-examine an individual or more particularly, how an offender will act after committing the offence."

The door knocked and Melanie the analyst handed a steaming mug into the room that was passed to Watson.

"Ah, brilliant," she sipped at the scalding liquid. "Now, as I was saying, in response to your question and Myra's suggestion, my humble opinion," she raised both hands to indicate her opinion was not set in stone, "is that the individual who is murdering these women does have some sort of grievance against women. As it's three *women* that have been murdered I do realise that does seem self evident, however, that does *not* mean to say it is a man who is the killer." She pursed her lips and said, "Without any Forensic evidence and please remember, I'm providing an opinion here, there *is* also the likelihood you could be looking for a female killer. I just can't say. However, what you don't want to hear is that I believe the individual responsible for these murders will continue to kill. As for motive, I would suggest the killing is in revenge against women for a perceived or actual wrong that was done to the killer; perhaps something from the killer's past or maybe even something that is ongoing, but whatever it is it relentlessly drives him or her onwards to continue to commit the murders. In short, it is the killers revenge that is possibly against an individual or perhaps against women in general. I'm just not certain. Sorry."

She paused while the others digested her information and then continued. "It might not be of any help in solving your murders, but I would also like to make you aware that a number of years ago I attended a Forensic profiling seminar at Glasgow University. The guest lecturer was an American FBI profiler," she frowned. "I'm sorry, I can't recall his name, but his presentation was quite excellent. Now, as far as I recall what he told us was that most if not all serial killers will begin their killing with what he termed a trial murder; in short, the killer will pick a victim at random, commit the crime and wait for the police and public reaction. If the killer is not arrested after the first murder, then he or she will become more selective, choosing their victim and, forgive my phraseology, honing their style. What I did find interesting was the agent told us that during their killing spree, most serial killers will adapt and change their tactics, whether that be the gender or age or some characteristic of the victims or perhaps the style of murdering the victims. So, my suggestion to you guys is if God forbid there are further murders that do not immediately fit the profile of your three victims, do *not* dismiss them as separate issues. It might in fact be the same killer." She glanced around the room at the others and sighed. "So, does that help?"

Miller was the first to speak when he responded, "If nothing else, Sherlock, you've come the nearest to providing us with some sort of motive though to be frank, it chills me to the bone to know that we might be finding more murdered women."

He could not know how prophetic those words were.

Martin Craven parked the Mercedes at the closed end of Whitefield Street and switched off the engine. The aromatic smell from the paper bag on the rear seat wafted through the car and he made a mental note the next time he filled up to purchase a new air freshener for the car.

Still seated, he cocked his head and glanced up at the flat and saw the light on behind the drawn curtains. He couldn't explain it, but even after all these months he still got a flutter in his stomach when he visited Shelley.

He didn't visit her every night and it wasn't just about the sex anymore for he enjoyed her company and more often than not, after they had eaten they'd sit curled up on the couch watching some soppy movie she'd recorded. He didn't mind what they watched; being with her was enough for him. Even at the end of an evening when he was tired, she never demanded of him and was content to lie in bed with him till they both slept.

He hadn't realised in all the years of his marriage what it was like to sit and talk with a woman. Young as Shelley was, she had proven to be a smart lassie with an inquiring mind. During their evenings together he had taught her to play chess or occasionally he read the newspapers to her; they would discuss shows they watched, argue local politics or simply talked about everything under the sun.

He knew that one day it would end, that she would leave and find herself someone nearer her own age; someone who would make her happy.

For now, he treasured every moment with her and had already made the decision though it pained him to think about it, when Shelley decided it was time for her to move on he would do everything he could to support and encourage her.

With a sigh, he heaved himself from the driver's seat and collected the paper bag and bottle of white wine before locking the car and making his way to the front close entrance.

He used a Yale key on his car fob to open the close door and made his way upstairs to the first floor flat. At the door, he rung the bell and waited, grinning because he knew that she always chastised him for not using his front door key, but he liked the thought that it was Shelley's flat and it was his own insistence that he respect her privacy. Craven knew she would scowl, but suspected that she was also secretly pleased that while he paid the rent, he didn't take it for granted that he could waltz in when it pleased him.

He was not prepared for what he saw when she opened the door. Shelley stood there wearing a French maid outfit, her lips glossed, her shoulder length blonde hair now piled up on top of her head and upon which she wore a small black and white cap. Around her throat a narrow, black ribbon was tied in a bow and the top of her outfit was so low cut her firm breasts bulged from it with the material

barely covering the areola around her nipples. The frilly skirt about her narrow waist was short enough to stop at her thighs and expose the white coloured suspenders that held up the black coloured fishnet stockings. In her left hand she held a feather duster that rested lightly on her shoulder.
She smiled delightedly at his surprise and with her other hand on her hip, stepped back from the door and in a hushed voice, asked, "So, what do you want to eat first; the takeaway or me?"

Following the meeting in Charlie Miller's office, Myra McColl returned to the general office to find Kevin Feeney poring over a report and Eric Kyle, his jacket slung across the desk behind, banging noisily with both forefingers at a keyboard as he stared intently at a monitor.
"Kevin," McColl called out, "go and fetch a bucket of water, son. I think DS Kyle's keyboard is about to burst into flames."
The young aide grinned and even Kyle smiled at McColl's dry humour.
She sat in the chair next to Kyle's desk and said, "Kevin and I are on a late shift till about two am, so we're off out to have a look round the city centre and attend a couple of calls. I'm guessing you won't have had your dinner, so do you want something brought in?"
"No, you're all right, thanks," he shook his head and patting his stomach, added, "Look at me. The last thing I need is another pie supper. Paula keeps on to me about losing weight and besides, I need to watch my cholesterol too."
"Right then," she slapped the desk and said, "We'll be on the radio if you do decide you want something brought in." Her eyes narrowed and she asked, "How long do you expect to be here anyway?"
"I've a mass of paperwork to get through," he sighed, "so I could be anytime."
Kyle was well aware of what McColl thought of his wife, but smiled anyway and as if in explanation, said, "Paula won't be home till the early hours if she's out with her pal Jill, so there's no point in me going home the now and getting wakened up when she comes in."
"Okay then, Eric," McColl patted him on the shoulder and with Feeney by her side, made her way out through the office to the rear yard and their CID car.

When they were in the car, Feeney in the driver's seat asked, "DS Kyle, Sarge. He seems to be a good guy, but he puts some hours in so he does. Is there a wee problem at home?"

McColl turned towards him and coldly replied, "Why do you ask? Do you really need to know that?"

Feeney's face reddened and his stomach tightened for he knew he had made a mistake.

"Listen to me, son and take this on board as good advice," her face pale, McColl stared at him. "One thing we don't do is discuss our colleague's private lives. Eric Kyle is a good hardworking detective and his home life is none of *my* business and certainly none of *yours*!" she snapped at him.

Crestfallen, he swallowed hard and replied, "Sorry, Sarge."

A little calmer, she turned to face the windscreen and said, "Right, how about we take a turn round Argyle Street, Kevin and concentrate on our own business, eh?"

Eric Kyle stared thoughtfully at the monitor, but though he was reading the report, he was taking nothing in for his mind was elsewhere. Who was that guy, he thought. McColl and Feeney had been gone just fifteen minutes from the general office when Charlie Miller, his overcoat slung across his shoulder, stuck his head round the door and saw Kyle at his desk.

"What the hell do I have to do to keep you away from this bloody place?"

Kyle turned and grinned. "I'm just keeping abreast of my paperwork, sir."

"Aye, very commendable Detective Sergeant, but if you think I'm going to believe *that* old chestnut, then that'll day," Miller returned his grin and then entering room, Slung his coat across the back of a chair and drew another chair up to sit alongside Kyle's desk.

Miller glanced about the room as though to ensure they were alone and quietly said, "We've know each other for a very long time, Eric. Is there anything that you want to chat about, anything that is bothering you? You know it will be in the strictest confidence."

Kyle turned from his keyboard to face Miller and sighed as his shoulders slumped. He couldn't look Miller in the face when he replied, "Between me and you, Charlie, I've a bit of a problem at home. It's Paula. I think she's seeing someone else. That and I'm a bit suspicious of where she's getting her spending money because frankly, with the alimony I'm paying and her not working, well, at least not *regularly*," he grunted, "it's got my head spinning. I just don't know what the hell to make of it."

What Kyle didn't admit to was the awful thought racing through his mind; the thought that confirmed he really *did* know how his wife was earning her extra cash.

"Silly question," Miller broke into his thoughts, "but have you asked her about it? Challenged her about where the money is coming from? I mean," Miller spread his hands wide, "is it possible she's got a job on the side, one that she hasn't told you about? Maybe she's not wanting to declare it to anybody and particularly you because she's trying to keep her earnings below the radar and avoiding the Inland Revenue. Could that be it? After all, Eric," he shrugged, "you're working long hours and it might be that knowing when you'll be home she's taking advantage of your absence to work some kind of shift. If I recall correctly, she's a hairdresser, isn't she? Doesn't that mean she's maybe working freelance in customer's houses and let's face it; if women are getting a bargain price hairdo, who's going to fire Paula into the taxman?"

Wearily, Kyle shook his head and more to conclude the conversation that satisfy Miller's suggestion, replied, "That might be it. I hadn't thought about that." Then, as if seizing upon the explanation, he brightened and said, "Aye, maybe you're right. Maybe that's the reason."

Exhaling with a 'phew', Kyle suddenly grinned and nodding his head, continued, "That must be it, Charlie. Thanks, that makes me a feel a bit better. I think I'll have a word with her when she gets home tonight."

"Myra McColl mentioned you said Paula's out for the night?"

"Out with her mate Jill" Kyle scowled, his dislike for Paula's pal clearly written all over his face. "A right scrubber if ever there was one and man daft. I've tried to warn Paula about her, but they've been pals for a long time, so I just put up with Jill."

"Well," Miller pointed to the monitor, "why don't you finish up what you're doing Eric and get yourself away home." He stood and lifted his overcoat from the chair and added, "Seen as how you didn't take that time off this evening, there's no need for you for you to be in early because the briefing won't be till midday."

"Why's that?"
"Harry Downes at the Media Department has arranged a press conference for ten o'clock tomorrow morning at Dalmarnock police office. Myra McColl and the lad Feeney are late shift tonight, but they've both agreed to come out early and fetch Janice Maxwell's father from his home and bring him to the press conference. I'll be there too with Cathy Mulgrew and once that's finished, I'll be back here with Cathy to bring everybody up to speed with any developments."
"*Are* there any developments?"
Miller shook his head and his eyes narrowed. "We're still trailing way behind this bastard, whoever he or she might be."
"You know the press will go crazy when you confirm tomorrow that we've a serial killer on our hands."
"That, Eric," he shook his head and breathed uneasily as he walked towards the door, "is an understatement."

While Charlie Miller was making his way to his car in the rear yard, the 'Glasgow News' chief crime reporter Ally McGregor was at his desk in the newspapers Albion Street offices reading not just his own articles, but also the articles from rival newspapers about the murders of three young women that had occurred in the Glasgow city centre within the last six weeks. Reading the reports on his PC monitor, he made notations on an A4 pad in front of him. The notations would form the basis of the article he intended writing after the police press conference for tomorrow evenings edition of the 'Glasgow News', the article that would report the murder of the three women by a serial killer. Though it had not been officially announced, McGregor's long experience and nose for a good story had already convinced him that the same killer was responsible for all three murders and he was confident that the press conference would confirm this.
Already he had toyed with a few names for the killer that he had scribbled on his pad, but had still to firm up on the name. McGregor knew that when the story of the murders went UK wide and was picked up by the nationals if not the international press, the killer's nickname would be forever synonymous with his own and whenever the killer's deeds were discussed, he would for evermore be known as…McGregor shook his head. The name had to be something

snappy, something that would instil fear in women wherever they walked in darkness in the city.
He needed a 'Bible John' type name; something *really* memorable. He sighed and scratched at his belly. The name would come to him, of that he was certain and continued to pore over the reports about the three dead women.

Moira Bain stood up from the kitchen table and reached across to pick up her husband's plate. Conversation through the meal had been stilted and the atmosphere tense.
She had just turned to the sink to rinse the dishes when the doorbell rung. She glanced at her husband, but he shrugged his shoulders and as he made to stand her curiosity got the better of her and she curtly told him, "Sit where you are, I'll get it."
Pulling open the door, she saw it was their neighbour from across the road, Lara Quinn, now wearing a baggy sweat top and jogging pants. From the look on Quinn's face, Moira realised it wasn't a social call. She was about to force a smile and greet Quinn, but did not get the opportunity for Quinn immediately snapped at her, "I'm here about your husband and to tell you to keep that bastard away from me! I said hello to him today and he tried to sexually assault me!"
Moira, open-mouthed could only stare as Quinn pointed a forefinger at her face and continued, "If you've any sense, you'll get shot of him and if he comes anywhere near me again, I'll have the polis onto him!"
In the kitchen, James Bain heard Quinn shouting at his wife and rushed to the front door, but before he could deny Quinn's accusation's, Moira held her arm out to prevent him from passing her and in a quiet, but firm voice, said, "Now listen here to me, you drunken, pasty faced bitch! Do not ever, *ever* come to my door and make those kind of accusations against my husband! You have done nothing but chase him since we moved here, dressing up like a prostitute and throwing yourself at him. You are an absolute *joke* among the neighbours around here, with your antics," she sneered, "thinking that you're a young thing when in reality you're just an old fucking has-been!"
She took a step forward and curling her hand into a fist, waved it at Quinn as she screamed, "Get off my doorstep before I knock you down onto your fat arse!"

Quinn, her face chalk white and lips trembling, hastily stepped back and turning, tried as best she could to muster some dignity as she quickly made her way towards her own house.
Behind her, Moira, still shaking from the confrontation, slammed her front door and her face red, turned angrily to face her husband.
"I think perhaps you have something to tell me," she quietly hissed as she brushed past him.

It didn't matter that he was the victim!
It didn't matter that he told her the truth about what happened!
It didn't matter that he had no interest *whatsoever* in that fucking old cow!
It didn't matter that since they had moved into the estate, Lara Quinn had made a fool of herself over him!
It didn't matter that there had been nothing between him and Moira since she lost that *bloody* kid!
He beat at the steering wheel with the heel of his left hand and screamed "Shit!"
His attention was briefly distracted as he glanced down and reached across to adjust the radio, annoyed at the crackling sound it emitted and vowing to get a replacement for the bloody…his eyes opened wide in shock as he took the roundabout at the entrance to Drumsagard Village far too quickly and nearly lost the Fiesta on the bend. Righting the vehicle, he exhaled slowly with relief and glanced in his rear view mirror. If a passing patrol car had seen his erratic driving, he would have been pulled over for sure.
That's when he remembered the hammer in the boot under the wheel arch.
The bloodstained hammer.
He snorted. He should have got it out of the boot and used on that bitch Moira then crossed the road and battered that old cow too! How he hated his wife!
The things she had said, the names she had called him. If ever a woman needed killed…
He was now passing through the suburb of Halfway towards Cambuslang and stopped at the pedestrian crossing. A young woman, barely in her twenties he thought, crossed the road in front of him. He watched her, his hands tightening on the steering wheel, the way the stuck-up bitch paraded herself. Teeth gritted, he thought

he might…but no. There were too many people about and besides, a small place like this, somebody might remember seeing the white Fiesta.
The lights turned to green and accelerating too quickly, he forced himself to slow down. The last thing he needed was to attract the attention of the police.
It was getting dark now so he made his decision.
The city; he'd head into the city centre.

The audience stood to again applaud the raunchy Geordie comedian who before exiting the stage, took her third bow and waved goodbye as the curtain fell.
In the third row from the front, Paula Kyle and her friend Jill Hardie, who was now more than the worse for wear with drink, shuffled between the narrow row of seats towards the aisle on their right. While the balcony and rear stalls were being directed to the exits at the front of the theatre, an usher waved the audience from the front stalls towards a door that led into a passageway that in turn led out into a short lane and exited into Renfield Street.
"Another drink, hen?" slurred Jill.
"No," Paula shook her head, conscious that she was now short of cash and mainly because having finished the bottle of vodka, her friend had persuaded Paula to visit the theatre bar and drunk most of Paula's money there. "I'm for home. What about you?" she told Jill.
"Oh, I know the doorman at the casino down at Charing Cross and we've a wee arrangement," Jill winked. "I give him a wank and he lets me in for free and bungs me a voucher for two drinks. Are you not wanting to come too?" she giggled, drawing disapproving glances from two women walking beside her. "What the fuck you looking at?" she growled as the two women frowned and embarrassed, turned away from the loudmouthed Jill.
Paula stifled an embarrassed giggle and replied, "No, I'll pass on that."
"I know you've got your big motor with you, so can you not drop me down there to the casino, hen?" she pleaded in a whining voice.
"Sorry, Jill, but I've just enough petrol to get home. Right," Paula stepped out in Renfield Street from the lane, eager to be away from the persuasive Jill before she was talked into giving her a lift. She hesitated and then added, "Eh, give me a phone of there's any

more…" Paula paused and raising her eyebrows, grinned. "You know, somebody needing a trim."
For a few seconds the inebriated Jill was confused, but then the penny dropped.
"Oh, aye," she returned Paula's grin and pushing her way through the milling crowd as Paula walked off, held up her hand and rubbed her forefinger and thumb together and shouted, "I know a guy, bags of cash. I'll phone you, hen," she waved after Paula.
Paula returned the wave and turning into Renfrew Street walked with the crowd heading for Hope Street. Passing the Theatre Royal she stopped at the traffic lights and waited for the green man. Bloody heels, she grimaced and vowed that when she got home, fashionable though the shoes might be they were going into the dustbin. The beep alerted her to cross and she quickly made her way across Cowcaddens Road and headed for the underground car park beneath the flats.

Hidden in the shadows cast by the nearby building that housed the Piping Centre, he watched as the striking looking Paula hastened across and entered the dimly lit car park. Quickly he hurried after her, walking on his toes as he listened to the tap-tap of her high heels on the concreted ground.
He glanced about him, but neither saw nor heard anyone else and watched her approach the large Range Rover.
At the driver's door her head bent as she fumbled in her handbag for the keys and then he was almost upon her.
She sensed rather than saw him and was half turning towards him, a look of surprise registering on her face.
He grabbed her by the ponytail and tugged hard, jerking her head backwards and causing her to cry out in pain. Dropping her handbag, she reached behind her, grabbing at his hands in a panicked attempt to stop him dragging her backwards. Being pulled along by her hair as though it was a dog lead, she was aware that her shoes had both come off and her heels were dragging painfully on the ground as she fought to keep her balance and continued in vain to turn to grab at him, but his grip on her hair was too tight and too strong and she was unable to resist the momentum of him hauling at her as he dragged her backwards.

She had parked the Range Rover a few bays from a tenants waste bin area and it was into this area that he forced her backwards, through the unlocked wooden gate and that's where he raised the hammer high above his head and brought it down to savagely strike a crushing blow to the back of her head.

## CHAPTER SEVEN

Moira Bain put a hand on the banister at the foot of the stairs and stopped. She had forgotten to pull the wet washing from the machine. With a sigh, she turned and made her way back into the kitchen and switched on the light. The wall clock indicated it was too late to shove the washing into the dryer in the utility located beneath her bedroom for the noise of the tumble dryer would only keep her awake. With a sigh, she fetched the plastic washing basket from the small utility room and down on her knees, began to pull the sodden wash from the machine. As she knelt there, she thought again of her confrontation with that bitch Lara Quinn. She scowled when she thought of James's response to the accusation. He wasn't even man enough to fight his own battles she silently fumed, preferring to run out the door and drive off to God knew where rather than explain that he was innocent of that mad woman's accusations. Her brow creased and she wondered; where did he go most nights and then almost immediately shook her head, for the truth was she didn't really care where he went as long as he wasn't sitting in the same house with her.
She stood and heaved the full basket from the floor and started in the lounge, draping the damp clothes across the radiators, then into the hall and dining room with more damp clothes. Carrying the remaining clothes upstairs, she spread them about the radiators in the hallway, master bedroom, third bedroom and with some reluctance, carried the few that remained into the guest room used by James. She yawned and lifted a small hand towel from the basket and dropped one end behind the radiator then startled and jumped back in fright when something fell from behind the radiator to bounce off her foot. Her hand instinctively clutching at her throat as she stared down at a folded handkerchief, the wet towel in her hand for the moment forgotten. Bending, she lifted the handkerchief and opened

it. Her eyes narrowed at the sight of the thick lock of hair. What the hell is this, she thought and then, why was it hidden?
She glanced about the room as though fearing being disturbed, but then a cold fury came over her. Was this some floozy's hair that he'd kept as a souvenir? Was her husband cheating on her and a cold chill swept through her. Could it be that Lara Quinn was telling the truth, that James had tried it on with her? Shaking her head as though to clear it, she could not believe that he had been bedding some other woman when he was so incapable of fucking his own wife!
A thousand questions run through her mind and with a quiet determination, she cocked her head to try to look down the rear of the radiator, but there was nothing there that she could see. Her eyes swept over the room and she opened the doors of the built in wardrobe, pulling clothing from them that she flung onto the bed, searching trouser and jacket pockets, but finding nothing else.
That done, and now in a rage, she pulled out the three drawers from the small cabinet by his bed and emptying the first one, scattered his underwear on the already full bed and that's when she found the clear, plastic bag.

Tired and worn out, Charlie Miller arrived home and parked the car in the driveway in front of Sadie's Honda Jazz, knowing he'd be away early the next morning and probably before she and the girls were awake. He sighed heavily as he pushed the Yale key into the door and stifled a yawn. He opened the door as quietly as he could and once inside, bent to undo his shoelaces and slipped them off onto the coarse doormat for the last thing he wanted was to waken his wife or the baby.
"Want me to do that for you," came the whispered voice from the darkness.
He stood upright and saw the silhouette of Sadie framed in the doorway at the far end of the hallway, her arms folded.
"Sorry, love, did I waken you when I drove into the driveway?"
"No, I was waiting for you to come home," she replied and moved towards him to be enveloped into his arms. As he crushed her to him her body smelt of perfumed deodorant and he guessed she had just recently bathed.
"Can I make you something to eat," she asked.

"No," he wearily shook his head. "I had a fish supper at work, but I couldn't half murder a cuppa."
Taking his hand she led him through to the kitchen and switching on the light, moved to fill the kettle while he took off his overcoat and suit jacket that he laid across a chair, then sat down at the kitchen table and watched her.
Sadie reached up to the wall cupboard for two mugs and over her shoulder said, "I can feel your eyes on me."
"Actually, I'm looking at your bum, Missus Miller and wondering what you're wearing under that dressing gown."
She turned and standing with her back against the worktop, replied with a saucy smile, "Maybe something, maybe nothing. Why don't you come over here Mister Miller and find out?"
He grinned and rising from the seat moved towards her then pulled gently at the cord that held the gown closed. The cord fell open as did the dressing gown and he frowned. "You've got a nightie on," he said with a pretend petted lip.
She giggled like a schoolgirl and reaching her arms up to encircle his neck, pulled him close and whispered, "Aye, but nothing on beneath it."
A few minutes later, the kettle boiled behind them, but by that time neither Charlie nor Sadie were interested in drinking tea.

Dispatched earlier by the control room to interview an injured party within the casualty ward of the Royal Infirmary in the High Street, DS Myra McColl and her aide Kevin Feeney now sat on the uncomfortable plastic chairs in the foyer of the reception area and dispassionately watched as a drunken woman, kicking and punching her equally intoxicated husband, were hustled out the door by a number of uniformed colleagues.
"Aye," she smiled, "there's nothing like a right heavy bevy to bring out the love of a good woman for her man."
Feeney sat with his notebook opened on his knee and pretended to study it while casting a wary eye towards the nearby reception cubicle where sat the formidable and feared Constance Meikle, known by officers throughout the Central Division as the Dragon Lady on account of her fearsome breath; a mixture of strong halitosis and cigarette smoke from her preferred heavy tar fags. Meikle, who was thought to be in her mid to late fifties, applied her make-up so

heavily she resembled a Picasso reject and despite her outsize girth, insisted on dressing like a skinny teenager. It was every male cops nightmare to be dispatched to a call at the casualty department when she was on duty, for Meikle was infamous in her attempts to sexually compromise the young uniformed men of the Division.

And so it was with dread that Feeney was instructed by McColl to request from Meikle the details of the injured party, a young man who when drunk attempted to gatecrash a private party at a city centre nightclub, but instead found himself at the receiving end of a severe kicking.

"She's not that bad," McColl told him, working hard to keep her face straight.

"Are you *kidding*, Sarge? I've already had my arse groped by her when I was up here last month with a prisoner who was receiving treatment. The woman's a nutter!" he whined. "Do you know that new probationer that's on three group? The one with the red hair?"

Tight-lipped, McColl slowly shook her head, but knew exactly who Feeney referred to.

"The rumour is that he met her when he was out on the town at a stag night with some of his shift and he was pasted. Anyway, did he not come to the next morning, naked and in a strange bed and turned to find her lying next to him. She'd apparently met him in a club and kidnapped him!"

"You don't really believe that, do you?"

"What, that she kidnapped him? Bloody right I do!" he nodded.

"What does the lad say to it?"

Feeney shrugged. "Denies it, of course. I mean, look at her," he hissed. "She's like something you'd use to frighten weans with that face of hers like a Halloween mask."

"Yoo-hoo," called Meikle, waving at McColl and Feeney from her cubicle. "I've that information you need," she cooed and held up a sheet of paper.

"Go get her, Romeo," said McColl and gently pushed at the reluctant Feeney, who trudged towards the cubicle.

While watching the nervous Feeney, her mobile phone activated and fumbling it from her handbag, almost dropped it in her haste to answer it.

"Yes?"

"Myra, its Alex at the control room. I didn't want to use the divisional radio."

McColl went cold. Alex Norman was a much-experienced copper and if he wasn't using the divisional network but calling her on the mobile, there had to be a very good reason.

"There's been a murder, another young woman," Norman continued. "In the underground car park behind the office under the flats. I've got the nightshift there the now and they're telling me…Myra," he paused, "it's Eric Kyle's wife."

Standing at the public bar in the pub on George Street round the corner from his office, Ally McGregor was boastfully regaling a pretty young, female copy typist with an exaggerated version of how he had assisted the police in tracking down a rapist.

"Not that the bastards acknowledged my help," he scoffed.

His mobile phone activated and opening it, screwed his eyes to focus on the name that appeared on the screen. Colin Napier. Who the fuck is Colin Napier he wondered, but nevertheless pressed the green 'accept call' button.

"Hello, Ally McGregor."

"Ally," the hushed voice said, "It's Colin. Colin Napier. Do you remember me? I work at the mortuary."

A vague recollection of a skinny wee bearded man flashed through McGregor's head, but never one to turn away any potential source of information, he greeted Napier with, "Colin, how's it hanging. Long time no speak, pal. What can *you* do for me, my son?"

"It's about the murders, Ally. The lassies that got themselves killed. You know, in the city centre?"

The drunken haze that had been present just minutes before vanished as did the next chat-up line to the typist and pushing his way through the crowd to a quiet spot in the bar, McGregor slapped his free hand over his ear and glanced about him. It wouldn't do to have some bastard ear wigging him when his instinct told him he might just be onto something.

"Go on," was all he replied.

"You might remember we've had a wee arrangement before, Ally?"

"Oh, aye Colin. Forty quid, wasn't it."

"Your memory's not that good then, Ally. It was eighty quid, but I think that this wee tit-bit is maybe worth a lot more."

McGregor licked at his lips. "That might depend on what you've got to offer me, Colin, my son."
McGregor waited, not daring to speak. He knew that Napier was measuring his worth as McGregor's source against what the information was worth, but also knew that having contacted the reporter, Napier had committed himself. The only argument now was how much McGregor was prepared to pay.
"Look, Colin, if this information is as good as you say then stand on me; I won't let you down. I'll pay top whack for it, okay?"
"Nobody can know where the information…"
McGregor sharply interrupted him with, "Colin! You're not the only source I've got and I have never disclosed any of them, not one! I mean, for fuck's sake, who would trust me if I gave names away to the polis?"
He listened intently and heard a resigned sigh, then Napier replied, "Okay then, Ally, but the money. You'll send me cash like you've done before?"
"Here, wait a minute," McGregor scrambled in his pocket for a pencil and piece of paper. "Remind me about your address and it will be the same arrangement as before, Colin. A brown paper envelope and I'll mark it on the top corner with an AMG so you'll know it's from me, okay? Will that do you?"
"Aye, that's sound, Ally," and slowly dictated his home address that was scribbled down by McGregor. "Right, here's what I've got and please, Ally, don't shaft me with this, eh?"
Impatiently, McGregor gritted his teeth and taking a deep breath, replied, "Of course not and like I said, I'll not let you down."
"You remember I work in the mortuary down here at the new hospital in Govan. The attendant's room is in the same wee corridor as the examination room that is through the wall. Anyway, there's a ventilation pipe that runs in the wall between the examination room and the attendants room. Both rooms are aired through a vent screwed to the wall directly opposite each other. That means when I'm in the attendant's room and the vent is switched off I can hear what's going on in the examination room; do you understand, Ally?"
"Aye, Colin, I understand that you must have heard something you weren't supposed to hear, is that what you're telling me?"
"Dead on, Ally. I was present when the last lassie was brought in today and helped get her ready for the post mortem by Doctor

Watson. She's the one that did the three post mortems and I heard her and the detective, Mister Miller…"
"You mean Charlie Miller?"
"Eh, I don't know his first name. It might be Charlie. I think he's the guy in charge of the murders. A big bastard with a scar on his cheek."
"Aye, that's him," confirmed McGregor.
"Anyway, at today's PM after they took the lassie's clothes off and examined her, they cleared the examination room before the PM so there was just the doctor and Miller and the woman that takes photographs in there and then I heard them talking about it; the doctor and Miller, I mean."
With bated breath, McGregor softly asked, "Talking about what exactly, Colin?"
"The hair, Ally. I heard them talking about the bit of the hair that was cut off all of the three women. I think that nobody is supposed to know about it, just the doctor and some of the CID. Is that good information or what, Ally?"
"It sounds to be interesting, Colin," he cautiously replied. "Have you told anybody else about this?"
"No way, Ally. I would get my books if I spoke about what goes on in the mortuary. Fuck's sake, what do you think I am?"
"Now, now, Colin, I didn't mean to imply you were talking out of turn or anything."
McGregor smiled at the contradiction that Napier was willing to sell the information, but wouldn't gossip about it.
"I believe that I can use your info, Colin, so in grateful thanks, you can expect a hundred notes through your door my son, but remember this, our conversation *never* took place."

Moira lay awake in bed, listening for the sound of his car.
He had got into the habit of either staying in his room watching the nineteen-inch television or going out on a night drive to get out of her way. After she had confronted him about Lara Quinn, he had stalked off in a huffy mood, but before he left he moved her Audi into the roadway outside the house to permit him to drive off in the Fiesta.
Her eyes opened wide for she heard the sound of his car arriving home on the chipped driveway.

Conscious that he didn't want to awaken her, Bain quietly locked the car and made his
way to the front door. He took of his shoes before entering the house and in the darkness, made his way up the stairs.
She bit at her lip, hardly breathing as she listened.
He would find the room exactly as he had left it, the hidden bag of hair in the underwear drawer and the folded handkerchief with the hair inside still tucked behind the radiator.
Much as her curiosity was killing her about the locks of hair she had discovered, she had made her decision that tonight was not the time to challenge him. No, time was on her side and she would wait and pick her moment, catch him off guard and then make him tell her about these other women he was meeting with.

Myra McColl parked her car beside the vehicle entrance to the car park and glanced up at the flats above. Not a light showed and she sighed. The uniformed police officer lifted the blue and white tape to permit McColl and Feeney to pass underneath and noted their time of arrival in her notebook. As McColl thanked the young constable she thought the girl looked ill.
The car park was poorly lit and in the distance, a fluorescent light flickered on and off, giving an eerie and cold feeling to the area. McColl's attention was taken by two men who stood near the entrance to a waste bin area and approaching, saw them to be the nightshift Divisional CID, Detective Constable's Willie McGuigan and Kenny Ross.
"Hello guys," she greeted them and shivering in the cold of the concrete car park, glanced about her and asked, "Nobody else here yet?"
"No, not yet. We've summoned Sherlock. She's the duty casualty surgeon again this month and her ETA was fifteen to twenty minutes, so she should be here anytime now," replied McGuigan.
"We figured as you're the duty DS you'd want to see the body first, Myra, before we call out the boss. He's not going to be happy about this," he shook his grey haired head.
"Well, I'm not going in there in case I contaminate the locus," McColl nodded to the waste bin, "but I suppose there's no doubt?"
"No, there's no doubt," it was Ross who replied this time. "The cops that discovered her body were walking through here on their way

back to the office to sign off from the late shift when they came across the handbag and shoes lying beside the bin area and that's what made them curious. That's the two that we've kept on to secure the locus; the lassie at the entrance and her neighbour is out there stopping anyone using the pedestrian entrance to the car park," he pointed towards the gap in the wall that led through to the piping centre building. "The cops are supposed to be getting relieved by the nightshift when the buggers *eventually* get their fucking act together," his voice dripped with sarcasm. "Anyway, back to what I was saying. On their way to sign off, the cops found the handbag lying on the ground over there," he pointed towards a bag that McColl could see was lying beside a piece of blue and white tape that marked its position. "They thought it might have been slung away after a mugging and were surprised to find the purse with cash inside, a mobile phone and a driver's licence. Then they had a quick scout about here and found her shoes lying over there," and again pointed to two shoes which were also marked with blue and white tape. "The cops followed the line between the handbag and the shoes to here and saw her lying inside," this time he pointed to the waste bin area. "One of the cops, that young lassie at the entrance, went in to check if she was still alive, but she's told us that it seemed quite obvious to her the woman was dead because the back of her head's been caved in." Almost apologetically, he added, "The lassie checked for a pulse, but there wasn't one. I'm sorry, but she didn't think about transference of DNA or anything, Myra. All she wanted to know…"

McColl raised a hand to stop him and said, "The lassie did the right thing, Kenny, checking if she was alive. We can worry about the DNA thing later and when I get the chance I'll have a wee word with her to let her know that."

"Yeah, thanks and you're right," he nodded and continued. "Anyway, the cops called us from the office and we hotfooted it here. When they told us whose licence they had found I had a quick peek inside," then held his hands up and added, "but I didn't touch anything, Myra." He took a quick breath and shook his head. "I remember her from the dance when Eric introduced her. She's a looker and," he grimaced with a wry smile, "not a woman that's easy to forget. It's definitely her, Eric's wife," he concluded.

Davie Craven's imagination was once again working overtime. Lying on top of the quilt cover in the narrow bed with his daughter Elsa beneath the cover and sleeping against her father's arm, he thought of Mary McLaughlin and wondered what she was doing at this time of night. His imagination took him to a time and place when they would be together, he being a father to her son and she being the mother that Elsa really needed.

That dream finally prompted him and glancing down to ensure Elsa was fast asleep, he slid slowly from the bed to avoid disturbing her and tiptoed towards the door, picking up his mobile phone from the top of the chest of drawers as he left the room. With a final glance at the sleeping child he closed the door over, leaving a gap to permit the hallway lamp to shine through into the room and cast a wide beam of light onto the carpeted floor.

As he made his way downstairs, he dialled Mary's mobile and when she answered, smiled as he greeted her.

"Just thought I'd give you a call, see what you're up to," he said.

"Nothing much, just watching the tele with my mum. You?"

"Just put the wee one down to bed. She's always on a high when I collect her from the childminder. Even though I've told her not too I think that the childminder gives her too many sugary sweets and she's fairly buzzing by the time I get her home."

"My Mickey's a bit like that," sighed Mary. "My mother's forever giving him sweeties behind my back and I'm supposed to pretend I didn't notice."

Their conversation continued for another ten minutes about work, films and TV shows, but nothing in particular. Her female intuition was that Davie was dancing around why he had really called. At last, he said, "Does your mum look after the wee guy when you're on nights out and, eh, things like that?"

"Nights out, what's that?" she half-laughed in his ear.

"Oh, I was thinking that maybe you went out sometime, maybe with a boyfriend or your pals or something," his voice quietly died away as his inherent shyness took over.

"No, Davie," she sighed. "I'm not out that often. Maybe to the pictures now and then with Mickey, but a woman can only watch so many cartoons."

"Oh, so," he swallowed with difficulty, "if I was to ask you out..."

"Then I'd say yes," she interrupted before he changed his mind.

"Oh, right," her quick reply had taken him by surprise for he had half expected to get a knock back. "Well, how about tomorrow night, then? Oh wait, is that too soon?"
"No, no," she hurriedly replied, "that will be fine. My mum won't mind," her voice quietened as turning her mouth away from the phone, he heard her asking, "Will you mum. No, tomorrow's fine," she confirmed.
"Right then, I'll see if my Dad will keep the wee one overnight. He's not bad like that. Does me favours now and then, especially with Elsa."
The line went quiet and for a heart stopping few seconds he thought the connection was broken, but then in a hushed voice Mary said, "I don't think your Dad likes me."
"No, that's not true," Davie unconsciously shook his head at the phone and then sighed. "Listen, Mary, my Dad can be…" he struggled for the word, then said, "a bit overprotective about me. To be honest, I've let him down a few times and I think that sometimes he's really disappointed in me. I'm not…" he was embarrassed admitting it to her, but went on, "I'm not as smart as my sister Moira. Dad thinks that when he retires or dies I should be the one to run the company, but I just don't have the bottle for that kind of responsibility." He was angry with himself now and continued, "Bloody hell, Mary, it takes me all my time to run my own home let alone a factory with about a hundred people working there. That and, well, I'm not good with women."
"What does that mean, you're not good with women?" she teased.
"You know, what I mean is I'm divorced. My ex-wife, she was a real bad bitch and took me to the cleaners. She was unfaithful and you know what, I knew and I didn't even care. In the end I was just so glad to get shot of her and though he's never admitted it, I think my Dad is still paying her off because of Elsa."
There was silence again and he said, "Mary?"
"I'm still here, Davie. Look, you might not have had much luck with women, but I'm no great shakes when it comes to men either. Mickey's father, well, he was an American sailor. His boat was docked in Glasgow and I met him in a club in the city. I was a lot younger then and I believed his patter about him sending for me to go to America and getting married. How stupid is that?"
"I don't suppose you heard from him again then?"

"No, when his boat sailed away I wrote to the address he gave me, but the letters came back, then two months later I find out I'm pregnant. What an idiot I was, eh?"

"What, for believing somebody you thought you loved?"

"Well," he heard her take a deep breath, then she said, "there's something else, Davie. You see, Mickey's father Marcus, the American sailor; he was a black man."

He blinked several times and she heard his sharp intake of breath. She knew she had blown it with her admission and was about to end the call, just say goodnight, when Davie replied, "Does the wee guy's colour really matter? I mean, maybe I'm being a bit naive here, but he's your son, Mary. Do you love him any less because of his skin colour?"

She bit back tears and didn't trust herself to reply when Davie added, "I mean, Elsa's mother was cheating on me, stealing money from my wallet and seeing other men behind my back, but I don't love my wee girl any less because her mother was a right tart."

He heard her inhale, but could not know that his unquestionable acceptance of her son's parentage was exactly the correct thing to say. She fought back tears at his kind words and taking a deep breath, said, "Look, I have to go, but I'll see you at work tomorrow and we can talk about our night out, eh?"

"Aye," he grinned, "I'm looking forward to it."

"Me too," she quietly replied and finished the call.

He smiled at the phone and shoving it into his pocket, climbed the stairs to make one final check on the sleeping Elsa. It was curious that after meeting Mary just the once, she thought his father didn't like her.

Well, he would have to do something about that, he vowed.

He went down into the kitchen to make a cuppa and thought about Martin Craven. His Dad had always been there for Davie, particularly when Davie's mother died and even though yes, they sometimes argued and fell out, they soon made up. Besides, there was no doubting his father's love for little Elsa.

His sister Moira, however; that was another story. Though younger and certainly brighter than Davie she was without doubt the apple of their father's eye, but that didn't sway Martin Craven when it came to the company. His legacy, he constantly told Davie, was his son taking over the business. Yes, he agreed Moira would be included in the management team, but the boss would be Davie; even though it was a position Davie never wanted.

As the kettle boiled, his thoughts turned to Mary and his eyes narrowed. Maybe if things went well with her on their date, he might be able to introduce her to his father as his girlfriend.

Sadie Miller groaned and turning, reached across her sleeping husband to answer the phone on the bedside cabinet. "Hello," she tiredly greeted the caller.

"Sadie? It's Myra McColl. Is your hubby there, hen?"

Sadie was immediately awake with the realisation that the call from Myra must be urgent. She switched on the bedside light and turned to shake the snoring Charlie awake, hating herself for she understood the pressure he had been under since the discovery of the first woman's body and the long hours and sleepless nights he had endured since.

With a deep sigh, Miller awoke, his hair sticking out from his head like a yard brush and yawning, stared at Sadie, not quite sure where he was or what was happening.

"Charlie," she whispered to him and handed him the phone, "its Myra McColl. I think it's urgent."

As he took the phone from her she slid from the bed and draping her dressing gown about her shoulders, sleepily stumbled from the room to go downstairs and switch on the kettle for no matter what time it was, she wasn't letting her man leave the house without a hot drink.

"Myra," he said and saw the time on the digital alarm clock read was after one in the morning. "What's up?"

"Sorry to wake you, boss, but it couldn't wait. We've another dead woman, but there's a complication." She didn't wait for him to ask, but continued, "It's somebody we know. It's Paula Kyle, Eric's wife."

He took a sharp intake of breath, now instantly awake and swung his legs from the bed. "No way!"

"Aye, she's got ID on her and Kenny Ross has seen the body and recognises her, says without doubt it's Paula. She was found in a bin area in the car park under the flats just round from our office. It's not a robbery, well, it doesn't seem to be and her head's been battered from the back, the same as the other women. Sherlock's just arrived so she's in there now. What's your ETA?"

He glanced again at the clock and tucked the phone under his chin as reaching to a chair for his trousers, he replied, "Let me get dressed and I'll be with you in, say, twenty minutes. Has Eric…"

McColl interrupted and said, "No, you're the first call I've made. We've established a cordon and the control room have been instructed not to disclose any details of the discovery over the radio."

"Good, right, I want you to inform Cathy Mulgrew and when you speak to her, tell her it was me that requested her presence at the locus. I know it's going to be difficult, Myra, but do your best to keep this under wraps meantime. If there's any updates I need to know about, you'll get me on my mobile, okay?"

"Okay, boss, but just watch yourself driving. I know you'll be tired, so better a few minutes late than me having to explain to Sadie why you have crashed. Now, do you hear me?"

He grinned at McColl's strict instruction and couldn't help himself before replying, "Okay, mum. I'll watch what I'm doing," and ended the call.

It took him but a few minutes to get dressed and descending the stairs to the hallway below, he found Sadie standing there with a travel mug filled with sweetened coffee.

"Thanks love," he stooped to kiss her and took the mug from her.

"Another woman?"

"Aye," he nodded, "but there's really bad news. Myra tells me it's Eric Kyle's wife."

Sadie involuntarily raised her hand to her mouth as she muttered, "Oh, no, poor Eric."

He stared at her and it struck him how lucky he was to have found her, then kissed her again before he left.

She watched him turn from the driveway into Westbourne Drive and as the Volvo disappeared from her view, slowly closed the door in the sure knowledge that she wouldn't sleep soundly for the remainder of that night.

Wrapped in a warm quilted jacket with her hands stuffed into the deep pockets and wearing a green coloured knitted bobble hat, Cathy Mulgrew stood with Charlie Miller a little apart from the rest of the attending CID and Scenes of Crime personnel and staring at him, said, "So, we're in agreement. You and I will attend and inform Eric."

Miller nodded in response and replied, "Give me a minute to speak with Myra. I want her to bring Mark Barclay out early. We'll need to get something prepared before we inform the team about this as well as some kind of statement for the conference later this morning."

"Do you think it's a good idea to go ahead with the conference, Charlie?"

He shrugged and replied, "I can't see a valid reason for not going ahead with it. We can't cancel because the victim on this occasion is the wife of one of our own. The media would probably have a field day and accuse us of having a different set of rules because it's a detectives wife and besides, we need them to cooperate with our own Media Department to put the word out so it's better we keep them onside. Yes," he nodded, "I think we need to go ahead with the conference, Cathy. As the polis we have to be seen to treat all the victims as of equal importance. We just need to be ready for the questions that will be thrown at us."

"Okay, for that reason, I agree." She inhaled and then slowly exhaled through pursed lips, her breath leaving a small cloud of vapour in the air. Glancing about her, she shook her head and said, "What a *miserable* place to die," then staring again at Miller, said with some feeling, "We need to get this bastard, Charlie. And soon."

"Aye, but for the minute the initiative lies with the killer. We've no witnesses, no Forensic evidence that ties the killer to the victims and…" his voice, bitter and angry, trailed away as he continued, "Hang on till I speak with Myra and then we'll be off."

She watched him walk towards McColl and then made her way to Doctor Watson who a few yards away was tearing off her Forensic suit.

"Bad business, Sherlock."

"It is, Cathy. How are you these days?"

"I'm good, thanks for asking," then reached a hand to Watson's shoulder and said, "but I hear that you're having some problems."

Watson grimaced. "Like I told Charlie, the polis grapevine. There's nothing like it."

"Well, if you're needing a wee chat anytime…"

"I appreciate that Cathy and I'll bear it in mind. Right," she nodded to the bin area, "regarding my written report. Is it you or Charlie's who's dealing with this?"

"Oh, it's still Charlie who's in charge," replied Mulgrew, but in the back of her mind, she recalled ACC Freeman's threat and wondered for just how long that might be.

The three of them sat in the small lounge cradling the mugs of coffee that she had quickly brewed; Miller and Mulgrew sat together on the two-seater couch while Eric Kyle, barefooted and dressed in pyjama shorts and a worn and holed tee shirt, was seated in the single armchair.
"You think it's the same one, the bastard that murdered the three other women?" he asked.
Mulgrew licked at her lower lip and nodded. "Obviously we can't be certain until the PM, Eric, but it's got all the hallmarks of the same killer. There's no obvious sign of robbery. It seems that Paula was dragged into the…" she hesitated and glanced at Miller who agreed with the subtlest shake of his head not to distress him further about where his wife was discovered, "where she was found and she was also struck on the back of the head."
"Her hair, was her hair cut?" he glanced at her.
Mulgrew nodded and replied, "Sherlock said it had been cut, but again the PM will confirm it."
Kyle's head drooped and laying his mug on the floor beside him, he placed both hands over his face.
"It's not the time or place to do the formal statement, but we've got some questions, Eric, if you're up for them," said Miller.
Kyle stood and taking a deep breath, replied, "Give me a minute."
They watched him walk from the room and then sitting quietly, heard the sound of running water from the bathroom. His face splashed with water, he returned a few moments later and returned to the armchair.
"Sorry, it's been…well, I thought she was just having a late night out with her pal."
He exhaled and nodded to Miller. "What is it you want to know, Charlie?"
"First, I need to know where you went from the office when you left tonight."
Kyle's eyes opened wide and mouth agape, he spluttered before replying, "Jesus Christ, Charlie! You can't possibly think…!"

Miller held up his hand and interrupting Kyle, said, "It doesn't matter what I think, Eric! You've been doing this job longer than me and you know the question has to be asked!"

Kyle stared at him for a few seconds and then eyes lowered, slowly nodded. "Aye, you're right." He rubbed with the heel of his hand at his forehead and said, "I clocked off, I don't know, say just after eleven. I left the office and walked round to get my car from the bay in Glenmavis Street."

"From one of the police allocated bays, Eric?" asked Mulgrew.

"Aye," he sighed. "Once I was in the car, I drove straight home. I didn't expect Paula to be home anytime soon so I had a cuppa and went straight to bed."

"I think you told me she was at a show in the Pavilion, is that right?" asked Miller.

"Yes, with her pal, Jill Hardie. I don't have an address for her, but Paula…" he paused and bit at his lip. "Paula will have her phone number, if not the address."

"Did Paula usually park in the underground car park, the car park under the flats?"

"Eh, yeah, sometimes if she was in the town. If she's parking after six there's no charge there and because it's under cover and near to the station, she felt the big Rover would be safe, that there was less chance of it getting screwed," then as if realising what he had just said, he almost choked and loudly spat out the word, "Safe!"

Miller didn't immediately respond, but then asked, "What about family, Eric. Is there anyone we can contact for you?"

"No, Paula's mother died before I had met her and she didn't have much contact with her father or her sisters. Some argument years ago before I met her, but I can't really recall what it was about," then shaking his head, he added, "but likely I'll have them coming out of the woodwork now."

Miller glanced at Mulgrew who nodded and turning to Kyle, he said, "We don't need anything else tonight, Eric. I'm so very, very sorry. When you're up to it, get yourself into the office tomorrow and we'll have a chat and I'll bring you up to date as much as I can."

Mulgrew stood and walking towards him, laid her hand on Kyle's shoulder and told him, "If there's anything, anything we can do, Eric, you only have to ask."

"Thanks, Ma'am, I appreciate that," he nodded and then said, "I take it that I'll no longer be working on the inquiry?"
"No, not in light of what's occurred, Eric, but on that issue I'm officially granting you a open-ended leave of absence. I want you take the time to come to terms with your loss. Of course, that doesn't mean you're not welcome in the office, but as for working there; don't worry. We'll cope," she softly smiled at him.
He didn't reply, but simply nodded in understanding.
"We'll see ourselves out," said Miller.
Downstairs in Miller's car, Mulgrew clicked her seatbelt into place and then said, "That must have been one of the worst things I have had to do in this job, telling a colleague his wife's been murdered. Christ!"
Miller nodded as he started the engine and then almost as quickly, switched if off again. "How are we going to handle the press conference, Cathy? What do we tell the buggers?"
"Right now, all I can think about is telling them the truth, that a police officer's wife appears to be the latest victim and again appeal for information."
She didn't want to bring it up right then, but thought he should be forewarned. "There's something else, Charlie."
He stared curiously at her as she took a deep breath, preparing herself for his outrage.
"It's Freeman, he's making noises about why you haven't caught the killer yet."
To her surprise, he didn't react as she thought he might, but instead replied, "Forget him, Cathy. I'm guessing the bugger's more worried about his budget than catching a killer," and then starting the engine, he grinned at her. "We've handled worse bastards than him in our time, haven't we?"
She returned his grin and said, "Aye, we have that, DCI Miller. We certainly have."

## CHAPTER EIGHT

The following day dawned bright with clear skies. The constable standing guard at the pedestrian entrance of the underground car park under shelter from the soft, drizzling rain blew into his hands to warm them and glanced at his watch. Another twenty minutes and he'd be off shift and his thoughts turned to those of a hot cocoa and slice of buttered toast before he turned into a warm bed. He watched as the old, rusting Ford Mondeo came to a halt and parked in a bay nearby. To his surprise, the driver was Detective Sergeant Kyle of the CID and as the DS walked towards him, he saw he held a bunch of flowers in his hand.

"Morning," said Kyle and indicated the gloom of the car park beyond the blue and white tape that was stretched across the entrance. "Do you mind if I…?"

"Ah, sorry Sarge," clearly embarrassed, the young cop shook his head. "I've been instructed that under no circumstances…"

"You do know the victim…Paula. She was my wife, son."

Constable Iain Bannen was nearing the end of his two-year probation and nervously licked at his lips and then thought this was a decision better handled by his Inspector. "Can you give me a minute, Sarge?" he asked as he reached for the radio microphone clipped to his stab-proof vest.

"Look, I'm not asking much, son," Kyle interrupted, the distress clearly etched on his face. "I just want to…" and held out the flowers in front of him.

Bannen exhaled and with a quick glance about him, replied, "My relief will be here shortly, Sarge. I'm sorry, but can you be as quick as possible? I'll be right in the shit if I let anybody into the locus, even you."

"Aye, I understand," Kyle smiled with relief. "I'll be but a minute." He ducked under the tape and walked quickly towards the waste bin area where Bannen watched him stand for a minute before laying the flowers on the ground. Then turning, he retraced his steps and again ducking under the tape, clapped the young cop on the shoulder and said, "Thanks son, I'll not forget that."

Martin Craven turned slowly away from the sleeping Shelley and gently lifted her arm off his chest. The light from the street lamp outside peeked through a crack in the curtain allowing him to see and safely step over the skimpy French maid outfit that lay abandoned on the floor. As quietly as he could, he made his way to the bathroom and switched on the light, cursing the urgency of the bladder call. As he stood there peeing, he again felt the pain in his chest and feeling faint, reached out to place a steadying hand on the wall. The room began to spin and without warning, he crashed to the floor.

It was the noise of him falling that awoke her and panicked, she rushed to the bathroom

The pain had subsided for now, but Martin Craven remained sat on the cold, tiled floor with his back to the toilet pedestal and a worried Shelley, her hair dishevelled and wearing one of his old tee shirts as a nightie, crouched over him.

"Please, *please*," she pleaded with him, "let me phone an ambulance, Martin."

"No," he gasped, embarrassed at the wet stain on his short, "it would only lead to questions and I'm not ready for this." He waved a hand towards her. "I'm talking about for you and me being found together."

She squatted in the cramped space beside him and rubbed tenderly at his cheek. "Look, I don't care *what* people might think. All I care about is you and I don't want you dying on me, you stubborn old bugger. I mean, how the hell would I explain my boss lying dead on my toilet floor?"

He grinned at the black humour, knowing she was teasing him and continually surprised how even in the midst of a crisis she would joke with him. The girl was amazing, he thought.

"Stubborn old bugger, eh? So, at last you're admitting I'm far too old for you?"

"You know what I mean," she pretended to be annoyed at him.

"Here, help me up," he reached for her hand, "this cold floor is numbing my arse."

She strained to pull him to his feet and half carrying him on her shoulder, led him through to the bedroom where first gently sitting him down, then supported him as he lifted his legs and stretched out.

"Martin," she gently stroked his cheek, "you have to see a doctor. Please, if not for yourself then for my sake."

"I will, I will, Shelley," he nodded. "What if I promise to phone and make an appointment for tomorrow at Ross Hall? Will that ease your mind, hen?"

"Better than that," she replied with a frown, for he had made this promise before. "*I'll* phone when I get to the office and *I'll* make the appointment and that way I know it's done."

He smiled at her and nodded. "You're the boss, Shelley."

At his desk in the newsroom far earlier than usual, Ally McGregor hammered at the keyboard, a lit cigarette hanging from his lower lip and in complete disregard of the no smoking signs that was pinned to every wall. As he typed, he read the article on the screen monitor, every now and then back tabbing to change or amend a sentence. After almost forty minutes, he sat back and again re-read the article with a quiet smile on his face. Hitting the print button, he snatched at the two-page report and headed towards his editors office. The information from the mortuary guy was invaluable and gave the 'Glasgow News' a head start on their competitors, for McGregor was not waiting for the evening print of the paper, but was confident the editor would run with the cut hair story in the morning edition. He banged on the editors door and without waiting for a response, entered and slapped the two pages down in front of the balding man. "Read that, Larry and don't quibble about my next expense sheet," he smirked.
Sat at his desk, jacket off, tie undone and sleeves rolled back on his thick forearms, Larry McNaught was the archetypical newspaper editor. Annoyed at the sudden intrusion, he glanced at his chief crime reporter and slowly picked up the two sheets of pages. At a remarkable speed he scanned them, then throwing them back down onto his desk he asked, "What do the polis have to say about this?"
"Haven't spoken with them," replied, McGregor, then with a sneer added, "I kind of want to surprise them at their morning press conference."
"You're way out of order, you fat shite," McNaught angrily shook his head. "We stab them in the back and their media boss, Harry Downes will never speak with us again."
"That cow doesn't speak to us anyway unless it suits her," McGregor snapped back, "but you run with this in the morning edition and we're on a winner."
McNaught waved at the pages and peering at McGregor, said, "You do realise that if we use this we'll have every woman in the city peeing her knickers?"
"It's our job to report the story, Larry. How people react is up to them. Besides," McGregor tried a little soothing, "think of the papers we'll sell with this story and the follow-up. We've got the lead here, Larry. It would be foolish to let some other paper run with it and

let's face it; the cops *might* be disclosing the hair thing anyway at their conference." He shrugged. "All we're doing is getting ahead of the pack."

"What about your source. Is he or she a copper?"

"No, someone I've been cultivating," lied McGregor, "and he's costing me two hundred and fifty quid for this that I'll expect to get back in expenses."

McNaught guessed that McGregor was lying about the payment, but as a former crime reporter he himself had more than a few times exaggerated his own expenses. "But is the source credible?"

"Stand on me, Larry. He's a diamond," smiled McGregor.

Nothing would have given McNaught more pleasure than standing on McGregor and preferably his head, but instead he growled, "This headline, you've suggested. Don't you think it's a little theatrical?"

"Yorkshire had its 'Ripper'," McGregor grinned, "Glasgow had 'Bible John' and London had its 'Jack the Ripper'. Why can't the 'Glasgow News' name our very own serial killer?"

Larry frowned and slowly shook his head. "Let me think about this, Ally. Give me twenty minutes."

McGregor looked at his watch and replied, "Okay, Larry, but remember, the printers will be wanting the story to set within half an hour. Any later…"

"I'm well aware of deadlines, McGregor," growled McNaught and nodding firmly towards his office door, repeated, "Twenty minutes."

He awoke and stared for a few minutes at the ceiling. In the kitchen downstairs he could hear Moira moving around and glanced at the digital clock by his bed. Their usual routine was that he would remain upstairs until she left for work and then he would dress and have breakfast before departing for his office. She had insisted their contact be minimal though for the life of him he couldn't understand why she had made him dinner the previous evening.

Perhaps, he thought, it was some sort of olive branch. They even had a conversation of sorts. It had been going reasonably well until the doorbell was rung by that bitch Lara Quinn.

Well, fuck her, he angrily thought. If she could believe that he would shag or even attempt to make a play for the old cow, then she was sadly mistaken.

He breathed in deeply then slowly exhaled, forcing himself to be calm, relaxing his body beneath the quilt. His head turned towards the window and the radiator beneath it. He got out of bed and then reached behind the radiator, but couldn't quite grasp the handkerchief hidden behind it. His eyes flickered anxiously, but no, he reasoned. Moira could not possibly know of the handkerchief nor what it contained. It must simply have slipped down beyond his reach. He fetched a coat hanger from the wardrobe and using it, hooked the handkerchief and pushed it down below the radiator and into his hand.

The hair it contained was now dry and he held it against his nose, acutely aware of the scent of shampoo, though he couldn't identify it. Excited as a schoolboy, he fetched the plastic bag from his underwear drawer and the small bob of ribbon and nail scissors it contained. Cutting a strip of ribbon, he tied the twist of hair in a bow and adding the hair to the bag containing the other trophies, gazed in awe at his collection. He knew the urge would be on him again and, his eyes narrowed as he smiled, soon he would add more trophies.

In his office, Charlie Miller awoke, sat in his swivel chair with a crick in his neck, a mouth as dry as tinder and an ache in his bladder. He glanced at the wall clock and saw he had managed just three hours sleep and wondered how the hell he was going to get through the rest of the day.

The door was knocked and pushed opened.

"Bloody hell, Sadie," he stared wide-eyed at his wife, "what the heck are you doing here?"

Wearing a navy blue coloured tracksuit and training shoes, Sadie Miller carried a suit bag in one hand and a small holdall in the other and grinned as she replied, "That's a delightful greeting, Charlie Miller. Whatever happened to 'Good morning, darling'," and laughed as she laid the suit bag across a chair and the holdall onto the desk.

"Eh, yeah, good morning darling, but whose got the weans?"

"I phoned my mum. She's at the house now with the baby and one of the other mums will collect Geraldine and take her to school with her own kids." She smiled at him and pointing to the suit bag and holdall, added, "I've brought you your shaving kit and a clean shirt, socks, underwear, tie, your good suit and some sandwiches. I'm not having my man appearing on the tele looking like a bag of shite tied in the middle."

He moved towards her to take her in his arms, but she waved a hand in front of her face and laughing, said, "Did I mention I brought your toothbrush and paste as well?"

He laughed with her and said, "Sorry. My breath must be toxic."

"Look, I know my way around the office and after all, I *am* a serving officer, so DCI Miller, head down to the shower and I'll have a fresh cuppa here for you when you get back."

He turned to leave the room, but paused and said, "I'm guessing you know we broke the news to Eric?"

She nodded and asked, "Did Cathy go with you?"

"Aye, he took it badly," then shook his head. "What a *stupid* thing to say. Of course he's going to take that kind of news badly. I just hope…" but didn't finish and as he closed the door, Sadie wondered what exactly her husband hoped for Eric Kyle.

In the incident room in response to the murder of Paula Kyle, DI Mark Barclay was busy with his civilian analyst Melanie Clark organising fresh Actions that would be allocated to the team when they reported for duty. Already word filtered among them that the victim was a colleague's wife and the muttering had begun. Dire threats were being bandied about and the wish among the team was that each of them hoped that they would be the officer who arrested the murdering bastard.

Barclay listened, but made no comment, neither encouraging nor dissuading the chatter and made a mental note to warn Charlie Miller that the atmosphere among the team was tense. He knew from bitter experience that such an atmosphere could lead to mistakes of the worst kind and that in the past many cases had been lost or dismissed at court when in their haste to arrest a suspect, detectives made unorthodox or illegal shortcuts.

Like it or not, Miller would need to crack down on the mood of the team and remind them that they were professionals, that the victim would receive the same quality of investigative competence that was expected for any victim.

"Mark?"

He turned to find Elaine Hamilton standing beside him. "I'm taking a wee collection to buy some flowers for…well, you know. Just to take over to where she…the place where…" she bit at her lip and he could see she was trying with difficulty to maintain her composure. He stood and placing his arms around her, drew her close. "Right, get yourself off to the ladies, Elaine. Go and wash your face then take five minutes to have a cuppa and a walk in the fresh air."

She took a deep breath and managing a tearful smile, nodded and placing the plastic box of cash on his desk, made her way out of the door.

He reached behind him and drew his wallet out of his suit pocket and adding a twenty pound note to the box, glanced up to see Eric Kyle standing in the doorway.

Instinctively, he got to his feet and approached Kyle, his hand outstretched and aware that the whole room had gone silent.

"Eric, I'm…" then stopped and conscious of the team around him watching, instead, said, "We're all so very sorry about what's happened. Come away in."

Acknowledging the men and women who gently patted his back or solemnly nodded to him as he passed them by, the dishevelled Kyle allowed himself to be led by the arm to a chair by Barclay's desk where he slumped down into it. "Thanks, Mark," he said at last, then asked, "Is Charlie Miller in?"

"He's been here all night, Eric. His wife Sadie arrived ten minutes ago with a change of clothes for him. Look," Barclay placed a comforting hand on his shoulder, "hang on here for a minute and I'll see if he's back from showering in the downstairs changing room."

Showered and feeling a lot better now that he had changed into fresh clothes, Charlie Miller was wolfing down the sandwiches Sadie had brought with her while she stuffed his washing into the holdall when Barclay knocked on the door and entered.

"Sorry, guys," he nodded with a smile to Sadie, "but Eric Kyle's just walked into the incident room, Charlie. He wants to see you."

While Barclay went to fetch Kyle, Sadie took her leave of her husband, stopping briefly in the corridor outside to hug Kyle and express her condolence for his loss.

"Sit down, Eric," Miller told him and added, "You hang on too, Mark," as he indicated the chairs in front of his desk. "I'm surprised to see you Eric. I thought you might have been taking some time to come to terms with what's happened or maybe trying to contact Paula's family."

"I couldn't sleep and frankly, I don't want to get into conversation with anyone right now. I just felt that I had to come. Stupid really, but well, I left some flowers down by the waste bin…where she was...you know, where it…" he sighed, seemingly unable to form a sentence without choking, then taking a deep breath, said, "Paula's murder I mean, it was on the seven o'clock radio news this morning."

Miller glanced at Barclay who nodded and said, "Aye, we know, Eric. We have already had the media, the newspapers and the radio people on to speak with us. We're passing all their queries through to the Media Department who will for now confirm a suspicious death, but nothing more at this time."

"I suppose you'll give out details at the press conference?"

Miller nodded and replied, "It's better coming from us than having them badger you at your home."

"Fair enough," Kyle agreed, then took a deep breath and added, "The reason I'm here, Charlie is that I want to know if I can do anything? I just don't…"

He got no further, for Miller raised a hand and more sharply than he intended, said, "No way, Eric." His voice a little softer, he continued, "You've been a policeman longer than me and God alone knows how many major inquiries you've worked on. You know as well as I do that there is no way that I can have you anywhere near the inquiry. You're Paula's husband. You're as much a victim as is Paula. You have to trust us to do our job. Trust *me*," he forcefully said and beat at his chest with his fist. "I swear to you I *will* get the person who did this."

Kyle stared keenly at him, his eyes heavy with fatigue and slowly, very slowly, nodded his acceptance of a situation over which he knew he had no control. He made to rise, but Barclay placed a restraining hand on his arm. "Did you drive to Stewart Street, Eric?" he asked.

"Aye, my car's parked round in Milton Street," he sighed.

Barclay glanced at Miller who gave the slightest of nods and said, "Leave your car there for now. I'll get one of the guys to run you home."

Miller stood as they left the room and his eyes narrowed as a thought crossed his mind, but just as quickly he dismissed it.

A man of routine and an early riser by habit, Davie Craven was up and dressed and making his daughters breakfast when the childminder arrived at the door to take Elsa for her day at the nursery. He was determined that he would beat his father to the office this morning and while he would never accept his father's decision that Davie become the next MD, he would work very hard to obtain Martin's approval of his new girlfriend, Mary.

Twenty minutes later he handed the tearful and petted lipped Elsa to the childminder and mentally crossing his finger, switched on the car engine. With a smile of relief, he steered the car from the driveway of the semi-detached house and turned onto Fleurs Avenue.

Uncommonly for that time of the morning, Davie's journey from the Dumbreck area to the warehouse in Tradeston had been without encountering heavy traffic and he arrived less than fifteen minutes later, pleased to see that neither his father nor sister's vehicles were in the car park.

Switching off the engine, he frowned, for what he did see was the warehouse manager Alex Mason standing smoking with a number of other staff at an open bay door. He took a deep breath, preparing himself for the snide comments and backstabbing insults and got out of the car.

As he walked across the car park towards the bay door, he saw Mason turn from him and a few seconds later, the other staff laughed at something Mason had obviously said.

"Morning," he greeted them and was about to pass by when a sudden anger overtook him.

He stopped and turning, said, "Alex, can I have a word, please?"

Mason grinned at the others and slowly replied, "Sure, young Davie, what can I do you for?" a comment that earned a giggle from the two young women who stood there.

"Just the two of us, please," Davie politely asked and as if apologising, nodded to the others.

Mason shrugged and followed Davie into the warehouse and out of earshot of the staff.

"What's up?" asked Mason, a grin plastered to his face.

Davie inwardly took a deep breath, conscious that his knees were shaking and replied, "You know my Dad's setting me up to be the next managing director?"

Mason's eyes narrowed and with a curious expression on his face, nodded.
Emboldened now, Davie stared at him and slowly said, "Well, warehouse manager or not, I get any more sleekit looks from you or anyone else, come that day, you're the first to get your fucking books! Understand?"
He didn't wait for a response, but turned and walked away and though his stomach was churning, he couldn't help but smile.

Just over half a mile away, Shelley McPhail, modestly dressed in a cream coloured, long sleeved blouse and black trousers, her long blonde hair tied severely back in a ponytail, knelt before the seated Martin Craven as she tied his shoelaces.
"Really, hen, this isn't necessary…" he began, but was hushed by Shelley who said, "I don't want you falling over again and remember, Martin. Like it or not, I'm making that appointment today for you with Ross Hall. Promise me," she stopped tying his lace and stared up at him, "that you *will* go and get yourself checked out?"
"I promise," he replied with a nod.
She finished tying his lace and placing a hand on each of his knees, leaned forward to kiss him before pushing herself to her feet and saying, "Right, I've ordered two taxis, fifteen minutes apart. I'll take the first one and you…"
"I don't need a taxi, I'll…"
"Martin!" She scowled at him as she got to her feet. "I'm not having you driving till I know you're okay. Besides, if you had a relapse or something, you're not just a danger to yourself. What about other people on the road? How would it look if you crashed and hurt someone?"
He reached out and pulling her to him with his hands on her slim waist, smiled up at her. "When did you get to be so bloody sensible?" he asked.
She patted his cheek and returning his smile, she softly replied "When I met you."
He pulled her even closer and slid his hands down over her backside. Pushing his hands away she grinned and narrowing her eyes as she cocked her head, she continued, "I can see that glint in your eye, Martin Craven. How would it look if neither the boss nor his receptionist turn up for work today?"

"Aye, I suppose you're right. Okay then, get yourself off to work and I'll lock up here."
"And you won't drive, you'll wait for the taxi?"
With a forefinger, he crossed his heart and nodded.
"Good boy," she again patted at his cheek and bending down, kissed him on his forehead before grabbing her jacket and handbag from the chair and left the bedroom.
He heard the front door close and as he sat there, wondered once more just how long this wonderful happiness would last.

The staff were beginning to arrive in the large room of the 'Glasgow News' that was shared by the crime, features and political desks. The usual morning banter was excitedly replaced by the news that another woman had been found dead in the city centre and while the police had described the discovery of the body as suspicious, nobody in the room believed it was anything other than murder.
At his desk, Ally McGregor listened to the gossip and opinions of his colleagues, keyed up that McNaught the editor had finally agreed to run not just McGregor's story in the morning issue, but also McGregor's headline. That headline, he hoped, would finally bring him to the attention of some of the larger nationals as he believed was his right. McGregor had over the years built what he believed was a sterling reputation as an investigative journalist, wisely choosing to ignore the countless times he had fell foul of the numerous editors who frequently complained about his complete disregard for ethical reporting, as well as his numerous fraudulent expense claims. To his credit, he had outlasted most of them though he guessed this new guy McNaught was a real tricky bugger and had to be closely watched.
As he thought about his editor, he wondered if there was any dirty secrets in McNaught's past that he could exploit.
He glanced about him at the busy office, desperate to boast about his inside information, but sworn to secrecy by McNaught who knew that in the world of deadlines and journalism, not even his own staff could be fully trusted from divulging media coups to their rivals and particularly when serious money could be made.
His desk phone rung and now buoyed by his own arrogance, he aloofly answered, "McGregor."
It was the supervisor at the print room.

"Ally, this headline that's been sent down. Am I reading it correctly?"
"Oh aye, son," McGregor grinned, "that's exactly what I want you to print."

Driving in Cook Street and passing the front door of the warehouse before turning into the gate that led to the rear car park, Moira Bain was a little surprised to see her father step from a taxi. She had never known him to not drive to work, but as she negotiated her way across the concreted car park, she guessed that perhaps the night before he had imbibed a little too much wine and with the recent strict change in the drink-driving limit, likely he was taking no chances.
She switched off the engine and again wondered when it would be the right time to challenge her husband about the locks of hair she had discovered hidden behind the radiator and in his underwear drawer.
The bastard, she snarled as she tightly gripped the steering wheel. He might not be having sex with her, but that didn't give him the right to fuck anyone else!
She forced herself to be calm, slowed her breathing and glanced in the rear-view mirror. She was a good-looking woman and smart too. There was no reason why a divorce should hurt her chances with another man, but like James it would need to be someone that she could control; a man who was as good looking, but just as pliable. Unconsciously, she nodded at her reflection. That's what she would do; she would confront him and use his extramarital affairs to divorce him. He would get nothing form the divorce, for her father had ensured the house and both their cars were registered in her name.
She'd be well rid of him.
As she watched she saw two women chatting together as they walked towards the rear bay doors to commence their shift and her eyes narrowed. One of the woman, the dark haired one, she instantly recognised as Mary McLaughlin, the woman who hoped to get her claws into Davie.
Well, not if I can help it she savagely thought and getting out of the car, followed them to the bay doors.

When she passed through the doors, the elderly doorman turned away and blatantly ignored her. She was about to stop and rebuke him for not greeting her, but realised to do so would admit that she recognised his presence.

When her father finally retired, she angrily promised herself that the doorman would be another one to be dismissed.

She was about to make her way to her office, but decided first to uplift any mail from the reception desk.

Pushing open the internal door, she saw that the blonde hussy Shelley McGregor was at her desk, speaking on the phone. Ignoring the teenager, she lifted some correspondence addressed to her and was about to return back through the door when she heard her father's name mentioned.

"What was that about?" she snapped at the younger woman.

Shelley, replacing the phone into the cradle, smiled and blithely lied, "Mister Craven asked me to ensure his BUPA medical cover was up to date, Missus Bain."

Moira stared at her, suspecting there was more to it than that, then scowled and returned back through the internal door as she made her way to her office.

Shelley slowly exhaled. She didn't like Moira Bain and was certain Martin's daughter didn't like her either. In fact, she was almost convinced Moira Bain didn't like anyone, not even her own brother Davie who like his father was a good man and always pleasant to speak with. She involuntarily smiled, recalling the gossip she had heard in the canteen from the two women who worked behind the hot plate that Davie had an interest in the new girl, Mary McLaughlin.

Well, good for him, thought Shelley. From what Martin had told her, his son deserved a little bit of luck in his life.

She glanced down at the note she had made on her pad and rising from her seat, made her way to Martin's door and knocking, entered to give him the appointment news.

Steering her Lexus into a bay in the rear yards at Stewart Street, Cathy Mulgrew got out of the car and made her way through the back door into the charge bar area. Greeting the duty Inspector with a nod, she made her way to the DCI's room on the first floor and knocked before entering.

"Morning, Cathy…again," Charlie Miller greeted her as she flung her handbag down onto the floor and slumped into the chair opposite.

"Oh, oh," he stared at her. "Who's upset you now?"

She returned his stare and her eyes narrowed as she looked him up and down. "How the *hell* can you be here all night and look so bloody fresh? You've even changed your suit," she accused him.

He grinned at her anger and replied, "A loving wife who just adores and idolises her husband."

"That's not what she told me that last time we had a night out," Mulgrew cattily responded.

"Aye, right. So, what's up?"

"What's up? What's *fucking* up?" she stormed onto her feet, her hands waving about her head. "I'll tell you what's up! That dickhead Freeman! That's what's up!"

Miller raised a hand to stop her speaking and lifting the phone, dialled an internal number and when it was answered, said,

"Melanie, I've Miss Mulgrew with me. Can you oblige me, hen, and bring us two mugs of coffee and a bottle of valium tablets? No, I'm kidding about the valium; the coffee will be fine. Thanks, pal."

He stared up at the irate Mulgrew and said, "Right, Cathy. Calm down. What's he done now?"

She shook her head and exhaling through pursed lips, shook her head and lowered herself back into the chair.

"I received a phone call at home, just after seven this morning. It was Freeman's secretary, that flunky Inspector he has follow him around."

"I've seen the guy. Isn't he the young fellow he brought up from his previous Force and had him promoted as soon as he arrived here?"

"That's him. Rumour is he's some sort of relative on Freeman's mother's side. Anyway, I was called to a meeting at the Dalmarnock office with Freeman and I've just come from there. Needless to say, he's been informed about the murder of Eric Kyle's wife and he's going his dinger. Threatening to remove you as SIO and replacing you with me."

"I wouldn't have a problem with that, Cathy."

"Being removed or replaced by me?"

"Replaced by you. If he wants to get rid of me that's his call; however, you never said anything about Freeman taking over. I don't suppose *that's* in his interest?"

"Of course not," she angrily replied, but was then interrupted by Melanie who handed two mugs of coffee through the door and closed it behind her again.

"Charlie, I'm not angry with you. How could I be; I mean, you are doing everything to catch this bugger that you can with the resources you have available. As for Freeman taking over," she sighed and rubbed at her forehead, "he won't take on any responsibility that might interfere with his meteoric rise to power."

"Meteoric? That's a good word," he grinned at her.

"I'm being facetious. I heard a whisper the Chief is not enamoured with Freeman's performance to date. Anyway," she stared sadly at him, "the really bad news is he's also threatening to return you to uniform duties."

"Oh," Miller simply replied for they both knew that being removed from CID duties and returned to the same rank as a uniformed officer was more often than not a career killer.

"Well," he continued, smiling in an effort to appear light-hearted and said, "I've had a good run so I can't really complain."

"We're not done yet," she grimly replied. "After this morning's press conference…"

"That you will also attend?" he asked.

"Yes, that I'll also attend. After the conference you and I are to meet Mister Freeman at the City Chambers in George Square."

"The City Chambers? What the hell is that about, then?"

"No idea," she shook her head, "the sod wouldn't tell me, but whatever it is it won't be good news for either of us."

As she sipped at her coffee, he told her of the visit to the incident room by Eric Kyle and turning down Kyle's request to be a part of the investigation.

"Quite right. I mean, we can't have him investigating his wife's murder."

She looked thoughtful and then asked, "What service does Eric have left before his thirty's in?"

"Eh, I'm not certain, but I think it's about five or six months. Closer to five, maybe. Why, what are you thinking?"

She laid her mug down onto the desk and replied, "Well, he's just gone through the worst experience that a spouse can go through and as he's on compassionate leave…"

"Ah, you're thinking about stretching it out to cover the period he has left to serve?"

She nodded and said, "Let's face it Charlie. Even if he did come back to work in a couple of months time, his head would be up his arse so what use would he be for what…three months?"

"Point taken. How about I give him a call then I put it to him; he remains on extended compassionate leave for the time being till his ticket's punched."

"I think it's a good idea. You can let me know how you get on with that. So, anything else I should know? Nothing new come in through the night," then as if realising what she had said, put her hand to her mouth as she added, "My God, I mean apart from that poor woman's death."

"No, no new information," he shook his head and glanced at his watch. "I've set up the PM with Sherlock before the press conference, so I'm heading there now. I'm taking Mark Barclay and a couple of MIU people to deal with the evidence."

"Okay then," Mulgrew also stood and opening the door, told him, "I'll see you at the press conference at Dalmarnock." She paused at the door and turning to stare at him, said, "I take it that it's still tight about the cutting of the victim's hair?"

"Tight as a drum," he confidently replied and stood to grab his overcoat from the peg.

**CHAPTER NINE**

Mary McLaughlin wearily lifted another box of soft toys and wondered why if they were soft toys, they were so bloody heavy.

"Hi, thought you might be down this aisle," said the voice behind her. She turned to find Davie Craven holding a clipboard and smiling at her and for some reason she felt a little better at seeing him, but immediately wished her hair didn't look such a mess.

She shoved the box she was holding onto the shelf and self-consciously wiped her hands on her jeans. She didn't understand why she was so tongue-tied and heard herself say, "Eh, I enjoyed our wee chat last night."

Our wee chat? Bugger, he'll think I'm some sort of idiot if that's all I can say, she thought.

"Me too," he grinned at her then hearing two staff speaking as they walked down an adjacent aisle, glanced behind him and in a low voice, added, "Look, it's a bit difficult talking here with everybody around, so if your sure you're free why don't we meet tonight. Say, seven-thirty at Sloans on Argyle Street? You know the place?"

He watched her and for a heart-stopping few seconds and thought she was about to say no, but then she smiled and nodding, replied, "I know it. Okay then. Half past seven at Sloans."

He grinned with relief and turning, retraced his steps.

She turned to lift another box, but this time it didn't seem to be so heavy.

Chief Inspector Harry Downes kissed her husband cheerio and informing him that she might be late home for dinner, left the house to travel to her office at Dalmarnock police office. Not the most confident driver at the best of times, the heavy morning traffic took its toll on her nerves and by the time she arrived at Dalmarnock she was fit to murder any bugger that got in her way.

Pushing open the door to the Media Department, she was met by her secretary who reminded her about the ten o'clock press conference and handed her a list of vetted journalists that had so far confirmed their attendance.

"Right," said Downes, "get the passes prepared for their arrival at the front door and what have we got about the discovery of the latest victim?"

Her secretary handed her a second sheet that was a synopsis issued by DI Mark Barclay at the murder incident room and was for Downes information only.

She glanced at the sheet and her face turning pale, she stopped dead in her tracks.

"Jesus Christ, it's Eric Kyle's wife," she muttered.

Her secretary, taken aback by Downes reaction, asked, "Do you know him, Harry?"

"Aye, I know him," she quietly replied, her haste and bad temper deflated by the sad news. She exhaled and shook her head. "Give me a minute to get my head round this," she asked, wishing to God she had not given up the fags.

"Okay," her secretary slowly replied and then added, "You might want to read the rest when you're sat down, Harry and I'll bring you in a coffee."

"Whisky would be better, but coffee will do for now," she mumbled and head shaking, walked towards the glass enclosed booth that served as her office.

Martin Craven glanced again at Shelley's hand written note with the time and name of the doctor who would conduct tomorrow's examination of him the following morning at Ross Hall private hospital.

In all his life, he had never shirked from a challenge, but the thought of being diagnosed with a life threatening condition or disease was something that terrified him; so much so that he had never admitted this fear to another human being.

He had little doubt that tomorrow morning, all his worries, all his concerns would come to a head and the examining doctor would undoubtedly confirm his worst fears.

Not particularly adept at IT, nevertheless he had used his laptop to painstakingly research the pains he was experiencing and been horrified at the number of possible conditions the web had thrown up.

He sat back in his comfortable leather swivel chair and wondered how he might react to such bad news. It was the loss of control that he feared. The thought that something insidious, some disease might lay him so low that he would be unable to fight back against it, that he would be subject to the control of others.

He had so far avoided telling Davie and Moira of the chest pains and his fainting fit, the second in a month and made light of it to allay Shelley's concern's.

But this morning had been the last straw for the young woman and now, like it or not, he was going to hear tomorrow exactly what was wrong with him.

He thought again of his collapsing in Shelley's bathroom, how quickly it had come upon him and sighed.

He opened the top drawer in his desk and fetched out his personal telephone directory.

Flicking through the pages, he settled upon the number he was looking for and stared thoughtfully at it.

If he were to suddenly turn his toes up, then maybe it was prudent for him to make some proper arrangements and update his Will. After the shock of finding out about his relationship with the much younger woman, he knew that any assets or belongings he bequeathed to Shelley would enrage Moira who undoubtedly would try to claw them back in court. However, he didn't believe Davie would make too much fuss, but being Davie, he inwardly sighed, his son would likely acquiesce to Moira's demands.

His eyes narrowed. The Will would need to be drafted in such a manner that no matter what nonsense Moira tried, Shelley would not lose out.

Of course, he grinned to himself, the easy answer would be to now simply inform his son and daughter of his relationship with Shelley and for a heartbeat, he savoured the delight in coming clean about his love for the teenager.

He finally decided; if he were to live for a few more months or even a few years, it was more than possible Moira would shun him and strong personality that she was, perhaps persuade her brother to do likewise. No, he wouldn't do that for he could not dare risk losing contact with his granddaughter.

He glanced again at the name and telephone number in his directory and dialled the number.

Try as he might, James Bain was unable to find a parking bay near to his building and aware that his shift start time was nearing, becoming desperate as he threw the Fiesta round corners into narrow lanes in an effort to find somewhere to park. At last, he heaved a sigh of relief and stopped the car immediately behind a large, builders skip dumped on the pavement underneath scaffolding near to the corner of Waterloo Street. With a glance to ensure that there were no construction workers watching, he lifted two red and white cones and placed them at the side and rear of the car in the hope any passing parking attendant would assume the car belonged to whoever was working nearby with the skip. With a backward glance to ensure he hadn't been seen, he hurried round the corner into Bothwell Street and hurried towards the buildings main door. His luck held and seeing the lift was on the ground floor, he made it inside just as the doors slid shut.

It was then that he saw the only other occupant was his supervisor, Annette Bell who standing in the opposite corner of the lift, favoured him with a wide grin.

"Well, well, if it isn't my favourite latecomer, Mister Bain."

"I'm not late today, Annette," he huffily replied, conscious of the bead of sweat that was trickling down his spine. He hated confrontation of any kind and being anywhere alone with the poisonous dwarf was his idea of hell.

The old lift rattled as it approached the first floor and in a low voice, she said, "Your problems with the management could go away, you know James. All you have to do is agree to have a wee drink with me one evening. Then," in a soft voice she coyly suggested, "we could see where it goes from there."

His blood run cold for he knew exactly what she wanted from him. He stared at her, at her limp, straw like red hair, the gaudy coloured sweater she wore to hide her bulbous breasts, the make-up thickly applied in the vain hope it would hide the acne that scarred her forehead and both cheeks, the lengthy brown coloured skirt that sat like a tent on her heavy hips and he was repulsed. Never had he wanted to use his hammer on a woman as he did Annette Bell.

"So," she moved closer to him as the creaking lift moved past the first floor and towards the second floor, "how about it, then?"

Backed into the corner of the lift, she gave him no warning as she reached with her hand and gently stroked at his groin.

"Fuck off away from me!" he suddenly reacted and pushing at her, caused her to stumble back.

Furious, her face crimson with embarrassment and anger at his rejection of her, she regained her balance and was about to scream at him, but the lift shuddered to a halt on the third floor and the doors opened onto the spacious area that was the call centre.

Wordlessly, she stormed from the lift and without a backward glance made her way towards her office.

He watched her walk off and knew then that his days at the call centre were numbered.

Breathing a sigh of relief, he made his way to his cubicle. In his mind he was already trying to work out how he would explain to Moira that he'd lost another job.

In the front car park of Dalmarnock police office, DI Mark Barclay smoothly turned the CID vehicle into a parking bay and switched off the engine. Charlie Miller nodded his thanks and getting out of the car, walked towards the front door of the building. Sympathetically, Barclay shook his head as he watched the DCI walk off, acutely aware of the pressure Miller was under and using his mobile phone, called Stewart Street to inform Elaine Hamilton that he was now returning to the incident room.

"Paula Kyle's PM, Mark. Is it the same killer?"

"Aye, it is, Elaine," he sighed and glanced at the police office front door. "Sherlock will be forwarding the report post haste. I've dropped off Charlie Miller and he's just away in to the press conference to break the news to the media."

"How is he?"

"Tired and like the rest of us, bloody frustrated that we don't seem to be getting anywhere with this investigation," he replied.

"Well, I know you're tired too, Mark, so do me a favour and be careful driving back here. You haven't had that much sleep yourself in the past couple of weeks.

He smiled at the phone and quietly replied, "Thanks, Elaine, it's nice to know that somebody's thinking about me," then ended the call.

At her desk, Elaine Hamilton smiled too, wondering if Mark Barclay would be shocked if he realised just what thought she did give him.

Parked in a visitor's bay and slid down in their seats, Ally McGregor and a 'Glasgow News' photographer watched Miller walking from the vehicle and Barclay on the phone.

"Did you get some snaps there, son?" McGregor asked the youthful and eager photographer.

"Aye, Ally. A good clear shot of the big guy walking across the car park, but not much of a shot of the guy in the car."

"Forget the guy in the car, it's Miller's photo we want, but not him walking across the car park," McGregor continued to watch as Barclay drove off. Sitting upright now, he continued, "We'll give it ten minutes then head into the press conference. Remember now, when I say my piece, I want you to capture Miller's reaction when I give him the bad news, okay?"

The youth grinned and replied, "Okay, Ally."

Cleared by the commissionaire at the front door, Charlie Miller made his way to Chief Inspector Harriet Downes office on the first floor. In the large general office, he raised his eyebrows at Downes secretary who smiled and nodding towards Downes office, said, "Go right in, Mister Miller. She's expecting you."

Closing the door behind him, Miller saw Downes, dressed in a black trouser suit, was seated behind her desk while in a soft chair to one side, Janice Maxwell's father sat nursing a mug of coffee.

"Morning, Mister Miller," Downes smiled at him and continued, "Two of your team dropped Mister Maxwell off about ten minutes ago. I've just explained to him what the set-up for the press conference will be."

"Good morning, Mister Maxwell," said Miller to the older man, who rose to shake the detective by the hand. "I'm sorry that you have to endure this today, but our experience is that the family and particularly the parents of a victim might evoke some sympathy from a witness who might otherwise not come forward with information that could be vital to the inquiry. Are you still okay with being present, sir?"

"Aye, Mister Miller, I'm happy to do anything that might help," Maxwell softly replied and as he sat back down again, his hand shook slightly and he spilled some of the coffee onto his trousers. As Downes stood to hand him a tissue from a box on her desk, he waved her away and sighed, "It's an old suit anyway, Miss. I've had it for years. Weddings and funerals," he joked as he used his hand to wipe away the spillage, but then the significance of those words struck him and he turned pale.

Miller stooped over the older man and laying a hand on his shoulder, quietly said, "We'll get whoever did this, Mister Maxwell. Stand on me regarding that. We *will* get the person responsible."

Downes watched Maxwell and her professional instinct was that he would be an asset to the press conference, for if they had any information that was useful, who in their right mind could but feel for the grieving father.

"If you don't mind, Mister Maxwell, I'd like a wee word with Chief Inspector Downes," smiled Miller and indicating the older man remained seated, led her from the room into the general office.

"Right, Charlie," Downes quietly said, "it's the usual format with you in the middle, me and Mister Maxwell on either side of you on the podium. I'll introduce you both to the press corps and I'd better warn him there will be a lot of flash photography too. Is Cathy Mulgrew…?"

"Aye, she says she will attend, but likely will remain off the podium. As for questions, the PM indicated we're looking at the same killer, Harry so I'll open with admitting that we're now looking for the person responsible for four murders."

"What information can you release?"

Miller's brow knitted as he thought about it and shaking his head, he replied, "Really, there's not a lot I can say about the murders other than to issue a warning to women travelling anywhere in the city alone and in particular, the city centre. As you'll guess, I have some knowledge that I'm holding back…"

She raised her hands and interrupting, said, "On that point, these boys have been at it for a long time, be careful what you disclose."

He grinned and replied, "If I'm about to make a cod of myself, feel free to elbow me in my big mouth. Anything else I should be wary of?"

She slowly shook her head and pursing her lips, said, "You've done this before, Charlie, so nothing comes to mind."

Turning, she opened her office door and following him back in, returned to her seat.

"Just getting a few things sorted out," she explained to Maxwell with a smile.

Her thoughts were interrupted when the door opened to admit Cathy Mulgrew and instinctively, she stood up from her desk.

"Good morning," Mulgrew greeted them all and was introduced to Janice Maxwell's father by Miller.

"Right," Downes glanced at the wall clock, "if you would like to follow me, please," and led them through the general office to the room that was set aside for the conference.

The room was already busy with local TV crews and photojournalists setting up their equipment at the rear and the front seats occupied by journalists from dozens of newspapers from all over the UK, excited by the report that a serial killer was at large in Glasgow.

In the middle seat in the second row, Ally McGregor waited impatiently. He was desperately eager to challenge Miller about the cuttings of hair removed from the victims and just as eager that his fellow journalists heard him do so.

McGregor was keenly aware he was disliked by his peers, but convinced himself that the root of his unpopularity was simply jealousy. Through the years he had filed a number of gang related stories that had earned him several prestigious journalistic awards. How he obtained his information had been the subject of much discussion among his more principled peers, many of whom believed that McGregor was not a tenacious reporter, but a corrupt and devious individual who would sell his grandmother to steal a march on the opposition. That he was successful was beyond doubt, but his methods were known to be unethical and on both occasions when he had been brought before the Press Complaints Commission, lawyers hired by the 'Glasgow News' who also featured in the complaints successfully defended both the newspaper and McGregor. However, the latter complaint was the final straw for the newspaper's board of directors who informed him that one more breach or even the sniff of a complaint and he was out.

Taking their seats, Miller saw Cathy Mulgrew sidle in at the back of the room among the technical guys, none of who appeared to pay her any attention.

Seated on Millers left, Harry Downes remained standing and called for the room to come to order and remained on her feet till the noise became a quiet mumble.

"Ladies and gentlemen," she begun in a strong, clear voice, "Police Scotland have called this press conference in response to the recent murders that have occurred in the city centre of Glasgow. As you will be aware, rumours have abounded as to the similarities in these murders and as you will learn, this conference is primarily to issue an appeal for public assistance. On my right is Detective Chief Inspector Miller of Stewart Street CID, who is the Senior Investigating Officer in these inquiries. Sitting beside Mister Miller is Mister John Maxwell," she turned towards the pale faced and noticeably nervous man, "the father of Janice Maxwell, who you will be aware from our recent press release was discovered murdered yesterday in West Regent Lane."

Seated beside Charlie Miller and upon hearing these words, the older man seemed to shrink even deeper into his seat.

She paused to permit them to scribble their notes and raised a hand, cutting off questions.

"DCI Miller will provide you with an update and then there will be questions."

She sat and nodded to Miller who remained seated and clearing his throat, called out loudly, "Before I proceed with any appeal, I wish to inform you that the body discovered in the early hours of this morning has been identified as that of Paula Kyle, aged forty-two years. Mrs Kyle," he licked at his dry lips, "was the wife of a serving police officer."

The journalists were stunned into a very brief silence, but then Miller's short statement provoked a blinding flash of light as cameras captured his solemn face.

It seemed then that the whole room had leapt to their feet, all shouting out questions, but Downes was equal to them and herself on her feet, shouted, "Quiet, quiet, please! There will be an opportunity to ask questions when Mister Miller has completed his statement!"

A subdued hush crossed the room and slowly, but with extreme reluctance the journalists resumed their seats.

"As I was saying," Miller continued in an even voice, "it is my sad duty to inform you that the latest victim is a police officer's wife. The deceased's husband has been placed on indefinite compassionate leave and I urge you to refrain from attempting to contact the officer or indeed the families of any of the victims." His voice took on a harder note when he said, "Should any of you *ignore* my request I will instruct my officers to deal with you under the current legislation, Protection from Harassment Act 1997 and any other legislative act I can think of."

He paused and glanced around the room and everyone there was left in no doubt that Charlie Miller meant every word.

"Right, you are now aware that the individual who is responsible for the four murders in the city centre has struck at women walking alone in the darkness. I regret I am unable to provide you with any details or description of a suspect. I also regret that at this time my team have been unable to trace any witnesses and so I must ask that through the medium of your readership or television audience, you issue my request that I am appealing to the public for their assistance in tracing and stopping the individual responsible for these murders. I must stress that if any member of the public has the slightest inclination that they have information, no matter how insignificant, then I urge them to come forward and contact either the inquiry team on the phone numbers you will be given or if they wish to remain anonymous then contact Crimestoppers, either by telephone or via the Internet. What I must also stress to the public is do not assume we have your information. Do not assume your information is trivial. Do not assume that your information will be of little use to us. Provide the police with the information and allow me and my inquiry team decide if what you know is relevant."

He paused and glanced at Downes and rubbing at her forehead, said, "Ladies and gentlemen, this individual needs to be caught and time is of the essence. We the police will catch this person, but we really do need your help to stop this individual. I do not want to inform another family their loved one has been murdered because someone out there has not bothered to come forward with information."

He turned to Downes and nodded. On cue, she stood up and said, "Questions?"

McGregor had been waiting his moment and aware that not only his fellow reporters but that television cameras would be focused on him too and quickly rose to his feet He held up the early edition of the 'Glasgow News' for all to see.

"Mister Miller," he almost gloated, "Ally McGregor of the 'Glasgow News.' I was wondering…"

"I know who you are, Mister McGregor," Miller deliberately interrupted.

"Eh, yes," said McGregor, momentarily wavering from his prepared speech. "Ah, right. Now, the headline and lead story by me on the front page of my newspaper," he snapped at the folded paper with his forefinger, "reports that prior to today's announcement of the fourth victim, each of the three women has had a lock of their hair cut from their head. A souvenir taken by the killer, if you might. Can you confirm if the latest victim also suffered this gruesome act?"

Miller was stunned and an icy hand clutched at his stomach.

He knew! The wee fat bastard knew about the hair being cut!

The crowd of faces turned from McGregor to stare quizzically at Miller.

He glanced quickly at Cathy Mulgrew whose face was chalk white and watched as she turned and walked towards an exit.

"Mister Miller?" prompted McGregor.

A hubbub of noise and the flashing of cameras distracted Miller who could only stare stony-faced at the smirking reporter.
At last he found his voice and as calmly as he could, replied, "That is still to be confirmed."
A host of voices were shouting at him, clamouring for information about this new development, that the killer of four women was taking their hair as a souvenir.
Miller slumped back in his seat as Harry Downes jumped to her feet and waving her hands, tried to calm the almost frenzied crowd before her.
In his seat, McGregor parried the questions shouted at him, exulting in the attention that his scoop had created.
The 'Glasgow News' he had waved at Miller sat on the empty seat beside him, its headline screaming out for all to read; Glasgow's Demon Barber Stalks City's Women.

## CHAPTER TEN

Using the remote control, Sadie Miller scrolled down the list of programmes and stopped at the midday Scottish news, aware that her husband would wish to see the press conference and knowing him as she did, likely be self critical of his performance. She had already decided she would tease and mock him and looked forward to his embarrassment.
Her mother called through that the coffee and bacon sandwich was ready and ensuring the news programme was on record, followed the tantalising smell through to the kitchen.

Cathy Mulgrew waited impatiently in Harry Downes office, dismissing Downes secretary's offer of a coffee and almost immediately regretting her curt response when she saw the younger woman's expression.
The door opened to admit Downes and a crestfallen Miller who with a shake of his head, said, "Before you start, Cathy, I have no idea how he got that information."
"That's just not good enough, Charlie!" she hissed at him. "How the *fuck* could you let it happen? What kind of inquiry have you been running?"

"I don't need to tell you…" he was almost shouting back in return when Downes bellowed, *"If you please!"*

They stopped and both turned to stare at her. "For one, this is *my* office and I have staff outside who can hear every *bloody* word! For two," she held up her fingers, "accusation will get you nowhere! For three," another finger was added, "I don't know how this issue of cut hair will help or hinder the investigation, but if you *are* to catch the killer of these unfortunate women, you need to calm down and work together! Recrimination is *not* the way forward," then, her face crimson, she turned to face Mulgrew and softly added, "Ma'am."

Mulgrew turned to stare at Miller who cast his eyes to the floor and shook his head.

Acutely aware of the tense atmosphere between her two colleagues, Downes felt she might have overstepped her mark and made to leave, but was stopped when Mulgrew raised her hand and said, "It's okay, Harry, there's no need for you to go. In fact you might be of use."

She turned to Miller who had slumped down into a chair and though still angry, quietly this time continued, "Tell me again, Charlie, who knew about the cut hair? Who was in this circle that was, how did you put it again? Oh yes, as tight as a drum!"

He slowly exhaled and using his fingers, he counted them off as he replied, "You, me, Mark Barclay, Sherlock, Eric Kyle and the SOCO supervisor Jean Galbraith that took the evidential photographs at each of the PM's. Just the six of us and before you ask," he held a hand up, "I'm confident that none of us has tipped McGregor off."

"Well, *some* bugger has," she retorted.

An uncomfortable silence fell between them, but was broken when Downes interjected. "You said you thought I might be of use, Ma'am. If that's the case, how so?"

Mulgrew stared at her for a few seconds before replying, "It's your job, Harry, to know these people, the press I mean. McGregor's been around for a long time now and it's common knowledge he's not above twisting the truth to suit a storyline or bribery if it gets him information. Christ, the bugger even tried it on with me when I was a DS at Pitt Street. So my question is, what's your opinion? How would he go about obtaining information that," she glanced at Miller, "is supposed to be known by just the six of us?"

Downes took a deep breath as she thought, then shrugged and chewing at her lower lip, slowly replied, "Well, you guys are the detectives, but as Charlie is confident the leak *isn't* one of you then my first thought is McGregor has someone on the inside and I *don't* mean the police. Therefore, to me that poses the question. Other than the police office where it's likely you six discussed the hair being cut from the victims, where else would it have been discussed? It would need to have been somewhere where one or more of you were overheard. I mean, what other location outside the police office would the cut hair have been discussed?" She glanced from one to the other, surprised at their apparent bemusement. "Am I making sense here? I mean, do you follow me?"

Miller stared hard at Mulgrew, who returned his stare and almost in unison, they both said, "The mortuary!"

He rose sharply from the chair, now angry and determined that whoever had provided McGregor with the information would be hunted down.

Mulgrew raised her hand to stop him and just as sharply said, "Charlie! What's done is done and we can deal with it in due course, but right now we've an appointment at the City Chambers with ACC Freeman."

He took a deep breath, forcing himself to be calm and nodded. "Okay, Cathy, but I promise you I *will* find this bastard, whoever he or she might be and…"

"Yes, well, all in good time." She turned to Downes and said, "Harry, as always, a pleasure and accept both my own *and* Charlie's apologies for our outburst."

Miller nodded in agreement and grinned at Downes. "Thanks, Harry, about the mortuary angle I mean. Sometimes it's good to get a different perspective on things."

"Anytime," a relieved Downes smiled at him.

They travelled together in Mulgrew's car to George Square, their short argument forgotten, both comfortable in the friendship that had been forged so many years before.

Miller still found it hard to believe that the investigation had been compromised, that the single most important piece of information regarding the four murders was now public knowledge.

"You are aware that Freeman will use this against you," Mulgrew broke into his thoughts.

Miller nodded. He had already accepted that the Assistant Chief Constable, known throughout the CID by his senior officers for being petty and vindictive, would use McGregor's disclosure at the press conference as an opportunity to remove him from the inquiry.

"I assume that you will be appointed to head up the investigation as the SIO, Cathy. Just be sure you don't make a fuck up like I did," he sighed.

"Oh, stop feeling sorry for yourself, Miller!" she snapped at him. "You didn't fuck up, you were railroaded by that little shit McGregor," she sighed. "So, let's move on from that and like Harry Downes said, find the bastard who's killing these women."

He stared at her and grinned. "You know, back in the day when I was a drunk and you an ambitious DS, I thought you and I might have hit it off."

She knew exactly what he was thinking and replied with her own grin, "Perhaps if you'd grown a pair of tits and lost your other parts, we might have made quite a couple; but seriously, how could I possibly compete with Sadie?"

"Aye, you're right of course. She's without doubt the best thing that happened to me. I mean, after…"

"I know what you mean," she nodded, her concentration on the doddering old fool driving the rusting Peugeot in front who occasionally took a wee wander over the centre lane.

To her surprise, the traffic eased as she approached the city centre and she was fortunate to find an empty parking bay opposite the Carlton George Hotel in George Square.

Walking together towards the City Chambers, she insisted that no matter what Freeman might say, Miller did not react to any provocation.

He raised his hands and assured her that he would let her do the talking.

"Well, that will be a first," she cattily replied as he held open the door and they passed into the opulent entrance. Her high heels beat a steady tattoo on the tiled floor and identifying themselves to the reception staff, were informed they were expected in Committee Room One in the Councillors Corridor, on the second floor.

"It always catches my breath when I visit here," said Miller as they trudged up the wide and imposing marble stairway.

"Aye, might be something to do with you being out of shape," Mulgrew dug him in the ribs.

It was not difficult to find Committee Room One for ACC Freeman's youthful Inspector stood waiting for them outside the large double doors that led into the room, one of which was slightly ajar. Leading the way, Mulgrew was about to walk into the room, but stopped by the Inspector who nervously said, "If you would kindly wait here, Ma'am, I'll inform Mister Freeman you have arrived."

Taken aback, she first glared at the Inspector then ignored him and pushing open the door, muttered, "I don't need to be announced, sonny, so *I'll* inform him I've arrived."

Followed by Miller with the Inspector anxiously trailing behind, Mulgrew entered the large and bright room to see Freeman seated at a massive conference table between two men, both wearing suits.

"Ah, you've arrived," said Freeman in a tone that suggested he was annoyed at the unexpected intrusion. "Kindly take a seat," he brusquely nodded towards two chairs on the opposite side of the table.

Clearing his throat, his hands clenched on the table in front of him, Freeman continued, "Now, to business."

Laying her handbag on the floor beside her, Mulgrew sat upright and in a calm, formal voice, smiled and said, "I am Detective Superintendent Catherine Mulgrew. This gentleman," she inclined her head towards Miller, "is Detective Chief Inspector Charles Miller of Stewart Street CID." Addressing Freeman, she stared at him square in the eye and continued, "Perhaps, sir, you might be good enough to introduce the gentlemen who are with you."

Miller, watching the three men, caught the man on Freeman's left struggling to refrain from laughing at Mulgrew's obvious rebuke. Freeman's face turned pale, recognising her criticism at his lack of civility. He swallowed with indignation and almost snarled, "The gentleman on my right is Councillor McFadyen of the Council's Licensing Board. The gentleman on my left is Morris Thomson of the city's Publican, Brewery and Licensed Victuallers Association. Now that we've got *that* out of the way, Miss Mulgrew, perhaps we might get on?"

"Of course, sir," she smoothly replied and gave him her most engaging smile.

A pregnant pause followed her reply, then Freeman turned to Miller and asked, "Mister Miller. As likely you will have guessed, I watched your performance at the press conference on a televisions here in the Chambers and frankly, I was *not* impressed. It seems to me that you do not have a full grip on what is happening among your team and that begs the question. What progress have you made in finding this killer?"

Miller frowned before responding and staring at Freeman, said, "I don't believe I'm comfortable in providing you with an update regarding my inquiry, Mister Freeman, when I have no idea why these gentlemen are present nor what their interest is."

Freeman's face turned crimson and his eyes widened to a point that Mulgrew briefly hoped that his head was about to explode. Clenching his fists, he finally managed to restrain himself and replied, "These gentlemen represent the interest of the city's business communities, Mister Miller. Because of your lack of progress in finding the killer of these women, the public are avoiding the city centre in large numbers and in consequence, this is directly affecting the revenue generated to the business community and in turn, the city council. I am reliably informed this lack of revenue affects the business interest of these gentlemen's organisations and I need not remind you that we as the police are accountable to our public."

"The public, yes," Miller agreed with a nod and then sat forward in his chair to stare angrily at Freeman, "but I don't quite understand why we the police, as you say sir, are accountable for the loss of profit currently being experienced by these *gentlemen's* organisations. I'm intent on finding a killer and I don't really give a shit about who's making money or who's not!"

"You forget yourself, Miller!" roared Freeman, now on his feet and pounding the table with a fist.

"Sir!" Mulgrew was now on her feet, her hands raised as she tried to calm Freeman, anxious because the bloody situation was getting completely out of hand.

"I'll wait for you outside, Ma'am," Miller quietly addressed Mulgrew and pointedly ignoring the irate Freeman, pushed himself up from his chair then walked out of the door.

"Perhaps, Arthur, we might all calm down," Thomson calmly said, his hand resting lightly on Freeman's arm, but raised his eyebrows as if trying to convey a warning message to Mulgrew.

Freeman turned towards Councillor McFadyen, his face still crimson and said, "I'm so sorry about that, Mathew, but don't worry. I'll see that Miller's dealt with."

Mulgrew's face turned white with anger and she was incensed at Freeman's open threat to Miller, in particular to what in essence were two members of the public. Nor did it didn't escape her attention that the ACC seemed to be very tight with the Councillor, causing her to wonder just what the relationship was between the two men.

Freeman turned to stare at Mulgrew and his eyes narrowed. "You're dismissed, Miss Mulgrew," he curtly told her before turning to speak in a low voice with the Councillor, Mathew McFadyen.

Her fury knew no bounds, but realised that to respond to Freeman's dismissal of her would only seem to be petulant and no way was she giving the bastard the upper hand.

She leaned down to lift her handbag from the floor and as she got to her feet, she was taken aback when she saw that Thomson, with the subtlest nod of his head towards the door, indicated he would meet her outside.

In the corridor, Miller was pacing back and forth when Mulgrew exited the room, nosily slamming the door behind her.

"Cathy…" he begun, but with a raised hand, she hushed him and nodded towards the other end of the corridor.

He followed her there and turning, she angrily told him, "Before you start, you've nothing to apologise for. That ignorant bastard! Who the *fuck* does he think he is!"

He breathed a sigh of relief. At least, he thought, there was some comfort in not being the only one who had obviously fucked up.

They both turned when the door opened and saw Morris Thomson walking towards them, his hands raised as though in surrender.

Thomson, six feet tall, slim build and in his late forties with neatly trimmed salt and pepper hair, was a strikingly handsome man and dressed in what the fashion conscious Mulgrew recognised as an expensively cut, tailor made suit.

"Guys," he quietly begun with a glance about him as though fearing being overheard, "I'm sorry that you had to go through that. When I was invited to the meeting as a representative of the Victuallers Association, I thought it was to discuss how we in the Association might assist you in helping to catch the killer of these young women. I swear, I had no idea it was a witch hunt and in particular against you, Mister Miller," he nodded towards him.

"So, what exactly did you expect from the meeting, Mister Thomson?" queried Mulgrew, suspicious that this might be one of Freeman's ploys.

Thomson shrugged and sighing, replied, "I thought it might be the pubs and clubs putting up posters, watching out for any described suspect, something like that. You'll know that the pubs and clubs who are part of my Association are all signed up to a radio link, much the same as the shops already have in place to combat shoplifting, so we are in touch with each other regarding any problems that might occur and are also in immediate contact with the local police office. And of course after all, it, it *is* in my Association's interest that you guys catch whoever is murdering these women." He paused and shook his head. "Freeman was correct about that; the business is suffering because the murders are badly affecting the evening trade."

Mulgrew opened her mouth, but before she could respond, Thomson held up his hand and cocking his head, he squinted at Miller. "You know he's out to get you, don't you? He told me and Matt McFadyen before you arrived that he was replacing you as the," his eyes narrowed, "what do you call it, the lead investigator."

"The SIO?" suggested Miller.

"Aye," Thomson nodded, flashing a set of perfectly white teeth, "that's what he called you. The SIO. Said that you were getting nowhere in the case."

"Why are you telling us, this, Mister Thomson?" Mulgrew asked, her eyes betraying her suspicion.

He took a deep breath and replied, "On of the woman that was murdered, your first victim, Linda Docherty. I knew her. I owned or rather I used to have a part share in the restaurant where she worked. She was a nice young lassie, a good grafter." He stared at Miller. "I've worked in the pubs and clubs in this city for a long time, Mister Miller, so I've also heard about you from a mate of mine in the Masons, Bobby Franklin."

Miller stared in surprise. "You mean Bobby Franklin who was a DI over at the Cranstonhill office? Retired last year?"
"That's him," grinned Thomson. "Bobby and I are close friends and he's mentioned you in the passing, told me good things about you and that you have the reputation as a solid and tenacious detective, so if anyone's going to catch the bastard that killed Linda, I'm guessing it will be you."
He turned and cocked a thumb at the door of the Committee Room. "Your boss, that twat Freeman. He's trying to solicit Matt McFadyen's backing because Matt's not just the Chair of the Council Licensing Board, he's also the Deputy Chair on the Police and Fire Committee. Apparently the word is that there's some political in-fighting going on amongst your bosses and I heard that Freeman's coat's on a shaky peg with your Chief Constable, but your boss would need the backing of the Police and Fire Committee to sack him…"
"And if he signs on McFadyen to fight his corner, then Freeman has a better chance of keeping his job," Mulgrew finished for him.
"Exactly," Thomson continued, then added, "but not just his job, Miss Mulgrew. I'm hearing whispers that Freeman is extremely ambitious and he's looking to go further in your organisation, but to be honest I don't know any more details. However," he smiled, "don't worry about Matt McFadyen. Leave me to work on him. My Association is a large and influential part of the city's social structure and nightlife and where there's customers there's revenue for the city, so the council won't want to piss off my lot, if you'll pardon me, Miss Mulgrew."
"I've heard worse, Mister Thomson," she favoured him with a wide smile.
"Right, I'll head back in there now that I've been or rather, they think I've been to the loo," he grinned then winked at Mulgrew as he turned away.
Walking down the marble stairs towards the exit, Miller stuck a thumb over his shoulder and said to Mulgrew, "Thomson, he fancies you, you know."
"Don't they all," she sighed, her nose raised in mock appreciation of her popularity among men.
"Aye, and you're so modest with it," Miller retorted with a grin.

# CHAPTER ELEVEN

Sitting in her office poring over the financial pages of that morning's edition of 'The Herald', Moira Bain was half listening to the radio that played quietly in the background when the hourly news broadcast commenced with an item about the recent city centre murders. She had no real interest in such things, but her concentration was disturbed at the news the serial killer, now crudely labelled by a local daily newspaper as the Glasgow Demon Barber, had claimed another victim. As Moira listened her ears perked up when she heard the broadcaster mention something about the victims hair. Her interest was peaked and she quietly uttered an expletive at missing the full news item. Switching the radio off, reached for her keyboard.

Signing onto the company website, she was briefly annoyed at the length of time it took to connect to the Internet and at last with a sigh, clicked the mouse button to sign onto the search engine. While the PC took what seemed like forever to open the page, Moira made a mental note that when she took charge of the business one of her first decisions would be to change the Internet service provider and update the business IT. Irritated, she petulantly slapped at the side of the monitor and at last the search engine appeared on her screen. Quickly, she tapped in the 'Glasgow News' website and clicked into the report of the city centre murders by the chief crime reporter, Ally McGregor.

As her eyes danced across the screen, she took a sharp intake of breath and a chill swept through her. Unconsciously, she reached forward to read the article once more, her hands holding the sides of the monitor and her eyes narrowing as again she read the paragraph that alleged the killer of the three women had cut and removed a lock from their hair. She unconsciously raised a hand to cover her mouth when she read the reporter McGregor's opinion that the hair had been taken as a souvenir.

The paragraph also inferred that the fourth victim, not yet identified in the newspaper's morning edition report, was also suspected to be a victim of the so-called Glasgow Demon Barber. Reading the article it occurred to her there was no specifics as to how the reporter had come by this information.

Time seemed to stand still.

"Dear God, no," she muttered as the full horror of the memory of her discovery and her husband's secret now struck at her with the force of a sledgehammer.

She shrank away from the monitor, unable to breathe, her eyes widening in shock as she silently screamed into her clenched fists. She didn't realise it, but was now slowly rocking back and forth in her desk chair, her mind a maelstrom of thought.

It was him, her mind screamed at her.

It was James who killed those women!

They weren't girlfriends as she had thought…they were women he had killed!

She was married to a murderer, a man who hunted for women then killed them and cut off their hair!

Their hair!

Close to tears of self-pity and her hands trembling, she reached forward to click the mouse and returned to the start of the report.

The reporter, McGregor she read again the name, didn't identify the killer anywhere in his report as a man or a woman. Yes, the suggestion in the name 'Glasgow Demon Barber' inferred that the killer was likely a man, but nothing she read confirmed that.

Desperately she clung to the hope that the reporter had got it wrong, but almost immediately dismissed that hope for why would James have locks of women's hair hidden behind the radiator and in his underwear drawer?

The hair.

Her eyes narrowed. The hair was not the same colour; she remembered now and recalled that two of the locks of hair had been knotted with ribbon. Two locks with ribbon and one hidden behind the radiator.

Three locks of hair!

Three women murdered, no, she shook her head. Four women. She glanced again at the report on the screen. The last woman was suspected to be a victim of the same killer, she read, but no mention of the woman's hair being cut off.

Did it mean that James had not cut off the woman's hair or that he still carried it with him or even that the hair was in her home, but she had not yet found it?

Her mind was in a whirl.

What should she do…what should she do?

Her hands now tightly clenched in her lap, she again rocked back and forth on the desk chair as she wondered just what evidence the police had.

She took a deep breath and slowly exhaled through pursed lips.

She was strong.

She was bright.

After all, hadn't she as the brightest student in her year obtained the top mark in all her subjects?

Wasn't she a graduate with a First in Economics?

She would deal with this; *could* deal with this.

Calm now, she determined to think this through logically and assess how the information that she now held could be of use to save her for as far as Moira was concerned, James was now lost for she had little doubt that with all the resources available to them, the police must soon surely identify her husband as the murderer of the women. However, she was determined that whatever happened to him, whatever sentence the court might impose on James must *not* impact on her life.

Her hopes, her dreams, she glanced about her at the shabby cupboard like office. She was worth much more than this!

Christ, haven't I given so much to this bloody company, she angrily thought. Didn't I sweat blood and tears keeping it going when Dad was going through his depression after Mum died?

She was becoming angry again and banging her fist onto the desk, fought the temptation to stand, to scream and to shout and throw the chair through the *fucking* window!

Her breathing was heavy and laboured and her chest hurt so much she thought she might have a heart attack.

No way was she going to go through life tainted as the wife of a convicted killer!

With difficulty, she forced herself to again calm down and slumped into her desk chair, her manicured nails beating a tattoo on her desktop. Her pretty, even white teeth clenched tightly, she stared with narrowed eyes at the monitor and slowly the glimmer of an idea began to take shape.

For the first time since reading the report, Moira considered that there might, just might be a way out of the hellish situation that she now found herself in.

Nevertheless, she thought, she must get home before James if she was to set in motion the plan that would save her.

Climbing the stairs to the corridor that led to the incident room, Charlie Miller had come to a decision before he commenced that morning's briefing.

The cat was out of the bag as far as the cut hair was concerned even though he had no idea how the reporter Ally McGregor had come by the information. Yes, he reasoned, the likelihood was that a member of his team had tipped McGregor off, but he could not and would not reconcile himself to believe it was any of the few officers he trusted with the information. No, the suggestion by Harry Downes that someone in the mortuary was responsible was far more credible. He stopped at the top of the stairs to draw breath, aware that he was overly tired and needed to sleep and it didn't help that ACC Freeman was gunning for him too. He slowly exhaled in the knowledge that he would need to get his head down at some point, but right now he sighed, he had a briefing to conduct. He guessed the team would have watched the press conference on the television and no doubt the more shrewd detectives would realise that McGregor's revelation had to come from someone with inside knowledge of the investigation.

But this was not the time for a witch-hunt and any suggestion by him that the leak was from the team would not only be counterproductive, but would seriously impact on the team's already low morale. No, he had to go in there and regardless of how he felt, be as positive as he could be.

Bracing himself, he pushed open the door.

Martin Craven stared at the files and paperwork scattered upon his desk, idly picking up a half dozen sheets that he stared at before letting them slip through his fingers to float down onto the floor beside the desk.

This is so much crap, he thought as he forced his back into the swivel chair and realised he was worried, for his mind was occupied by thoughts of the examination he was to undergo the following morning.

Reaching for the intercom, he pressed the button for Shelley's desk.

"Shelley here," said the soft voice, "how might I be of service to you, my lord and master?"

He grinned as he always did when she teased him and said, "A massage might be nice, but I'll settle for a coffee, hen."

"One coffee, coming right up, oh mighty one," she replied.

A few moments later, the door opened to admit Shelley carrying a tray upon which rested a china cup and saucer and a plate of digestive biscuits.

He marvelled again at the tall, teenage beauty, yet still felt pangs of guilt because of the huge gap in their ages.

He forced a smile and watched as she bent to lift the sheets of paper from the floor and shuffling them into order, returned them to the desk.

"I take it you don't feel like doing any work today, Martin?" she stood in front of the desk, her arms folded and her eyes betraying her concern.

He sighed and nodded. "It's the thought of the examination tomorrow morning, hen. It's…well, to be honest I'm a bit worried about it. What the doctor will find, I mean."

"Maybe he won't find anything to worry about," she shrugged. "Maybe you've just been overdoing it. I mean…" she stopped, biting at her lip.

"What you were going to say is that it's my age."

She unfolded her arms and leaned forward onto the desk with her hands. "What I *was* going to say, Mister Smartarse, is that every time we go to bed we don't have to have sex. You don't *need* to prove to me that you're some kind of stud." She grinned at him. "I'd be happy with a cuddle now and then."

His eyes narrowed as for the thousandth time he wondered why this young woman was so intuitive and who really was the adult in their relationship.

"You'll come with me? To the hospital, I mean," he asked.

It was Shelley's turn to be surprised. Taken aback, she replied, "I thought you might want Moira or Davie to go with you?"

"No, I haven't told them about the appointment and I won't be telling them. I would like *you* to come with me, Shelley. To be there," he awkwardly finished.

Her eyes flickered and she bit at her lower lip, then not trusting herself to speak, slowly nodded.

"Good, that's settled then," he heaved a sigh of relief. Slapping his hands down onto the desk, he continued as he stood up, "Right, I can't concentrate on anything today, so I'm going home, hen. I've called a taxi to take me down to your place to collect the car. I'm having an early day to gather my thoughts and take a bit of personal time. Let Moira and Davie know I'm gone…"
"Moira's already left for home, Martin."
He stared curiously at her. "When did she leave?"
"I'm not certain, but I tried about an hour ago to put a call through to her line, but there was no reply. When I went to her office it was closed and her car's not in the car park either."
"That's not like her," his brow furrowed, but dismissed the news. "Right then, let Davie know I'm gone and that he's in charge, but not a word about tomorrow, okay?"
"Okay," she smiled and held his coat out to him.
"Oh, one more thing," she smiled seductively at him, "if you find the time to pop down tonight, we'll talk about that massage."
"The way I'm feeling about tomorrow," he wryly returned her smile, "I think that cuddle you offered is probably preferable."
Stopping for a minute at the exit door to exchange some craic with the elderly doorman, Craven bid cheerio and made his way to his car.
He felt bad about lying to Shelley, but knew that she would object to his plans for she constantly insisting that he did too much for her and including her in his Will, she'd complain, would be a step too far. That girl, he inwardly grinned as he waved the taxi forward to the front door of the building. She just could not appreciate how much he loved her; not that he would ever admit it, for to do so would place a burden upon her to respond and he knew that the difference in their ages would never allow for such an open relationship.
No, it was better that she was unaware of his plans.
Fifteen minutes later the taxi dropped him at Whitfield Street next to his car. Turning the engine on, he drove out of the street and headed towards his lawyers office in the city centre.

James Bain decided that he'd take the four hours due him and leave work early. Fortunately for him, his own supervisor Annette Bell was on a break so he was able to sign off with her deputy without too much fuss.

Now headed towards his car, he was dismayed to find the ruse of parking it by the rubbish skip hadn't worked and not only had the construction crew placed the red and white traffic cones onto the roof of his car, but a parking fine ticket was tucked under the windscreen wiper. Ignoring the jeering workers on the scaffolding above his head, he tore the ticket from the window and angrily threw it onto the passenger seat.

Just another fuck-up he seethed, in a fucked up day as tyres screeching he accelerated away from the skip.

As he raced through the streets, he could not have imagined what awaited him at home.

Eric Kyle idly stirred the coffee and come to a decision. Charlie Miller had told him there was no urgency to provide a statement, that he was to come to terms with his loss and contact the office when he was ready to be interviewed.

Well now was the time, he decided. Better to get it done and over with.

Lifting the mug, he walked through to the small lounge to fetch his mobile phone.

The briefing had gone better than Charlie Miller hoped and the news that their colleague's wife Paula Kyle was victim number four was received with anger and he believed, a renewed intensity.

What did surprise him was seeing Myra McColl and the young aide, Kevin Feeney seated among the team. While the rest of the detectives queued to receive their Actions for the day from Mark Barclay and his staff, Miller indicated that McColl and Feeney follow him from the room and led them through to his office where he bade them sit in front of his desk.

"Right, Detective Sergeant McColl," he pretended to be angry as he began and sat down, "if I'm correct, you and the young fellow here were both late shift last night till what? About three, this morning? So, what the hell are you both doing in at this time of the day?"

Feeney shifted uncomfortably in his seat, but McColl just grinned for she recognised that Miller's anger was just that; pretence.

"You need all the help you can get, boss and this bugger," she calmly replied while cocking a thumb at her neighbour, "is just too keen to stay away."

Feeney stared at her in shock, but then relaxed when he saw Miller smiling.

"Well, for what it's worth I'm glad you are both here, but the bad news is I can't pay you any overtime, so it will need to be time in the book I'm afraid."

"That'll do me fine," snorted McColl, who then grinned, "I'm saving up my hours anyway to take the last year off before I retire."

"Right then, as you pair have nothing better to do in your sorry lives here's what I need. You will have seen from the TV broadcast that slimy bugger McGregor from the 'Glasgow News' somehow or other has latched onto the fact the killer…" he raised a hand and sternly stared at them both in turn, "and do *not* refer to him or her as the Demon Barber, that the killer is taking a souvenir from each of his victims. Kevin," he turned to face the young aide, "that knowledge was restricted a very few members of the inquiry team. The fact that it's now public knowledge…"

"The hair, sir, it was the unique feature?" interrupted the eager Feeney.

Miller was staring at him in surprise when McColl interjected, "I've explained to young Kevin here, boss about the sort of thing an SIO might retain as specialist knowledge. A unique feature as it were, but not in this case about the hair," she clarified.

Miller nodded in understanding and addressing Feeney, said,

"Absolutely correct, Kevin. So, here's what I want you and Myra to do. I'm convinced that none of the officers who were aware of the cut hair being taken by the killer have divulged that information to any person. However, it was suggested that there might be a leak at the mortuary, some individual who might have learned or overheard the hair being cut from the victims discussed and in turn passed that information to the reporter, McGregor." He paused and drew breath as he continued, "Finding that individual will not solve our murders, but it will cut off McGregor's source of information and could possibly prevent any further information about future inquiries being leaked to the press. Can you do that for me? Can you find this individual?"

Watching Miller and Feeney, McColl smiled. Speaking directly to Feeney as though tasking the aide with an important assignment Miller had undoubtedly secured the younger man's loyalty and respect. It also did not escape her notice that during the briefing at no

time was Miller angry or seek to identify a scapegoat among his team. On the contrary, he made it clear he did not doubt his teams loyalty and accepted without question that the men and women working for him would not have divulged the information.
And he wonders why we came in early to work for him, she inwardly mused.

Davie Craven was working at the rear of the enormous warehouse, operating the forklift to stack large crates on the upper shelves of an aisle when Shelley McPhail called to him. Switching off the engine, he jumped from the seat and smiled at the teenager. Unlike his sister, Davie liked the young receptionist and had seen a change come over his father since Martin had employed her. Of course, he also realised that when his father hired Shelley, his sister Moira was outraged and he believed her suspicion of an affair between Martin and Shelley was simply another case of Moira's usual spitefulness. After all, he reasoned, Martin was old enough to be Shelley's father, maybe even at a pinch her grandfather.
"Your dad's gone for the day, Davie," Shelley informed him, "and he's asked you to take charge now he's away."
Davie was puzzled. "What about Moira…" he started to ask, but Shelley shook her head and interrupted him. "She's away too, so it's down to you."
"Right then," he started to pull off his working gloves and sighed, for he had been hoping to slip away an hour early to spend some time with Elsa before he had to get ready for his date with Mary. "What's to be done?"
"Nothing," smiled Shelley as she raised her hand. "I'm just letting you know in case anything crops up," and turned to go, but then stopped. Something in his voice, some disappointment had pricked at her female intuition. Turning, she stared curiously at Davie and asked, "Is taking charge for the rest of the day a problem for you, Davie?"
"Eh, aye, actually it is. I was hoping to get away a wee bit early this afternoon," then he blushed as he confided to her, "I'm seeing someone tonight."
"Oh," replied Shelley, who then wickedly grinned as she teasingly asked, "wouldn't be someone working here, I suppose?"

Davie returned her grin and with a quick glance about him, whispered, "Mary McLaughlin."

"Ah, then the rumour's true," said Shelley.

"What rumour?"

"Davie," she continued to grin, "you and Mary are the talk of the warehouse. It's an open secret you're keen on each other. Look," she leaned conspiratorially into him, "why don't you head off like you'd planned. I have your mobile number and I promise, if there's any problem, anything at all, I'll call you. It wouldn't take you any more than twenty minutes to get back here. After all, Alex Mason can lock and secure the premises as he always does. There's no need for anyone to know you're away."

He stared at her, his head reeling in indecision, but at last he nodded. "Okay then, I'll do it." He clapped her on the arm. "Thanks Shelley, I won't forget this."

Walking back to her office, she recalled the conversation she had previously overheard between Martin's daughter, Moira and the warehouse manager, Alex Mason. She did not doubt that Moira Bain wanted to get rid of the girl and from what Martin had told her about his son's past marriage failure, she thought that perhaps Moira felt threatened by the girl McLaughlin.

Well, she liked Davie Craven and the girl seemed very nice too and as all young women do, Shelley enjoyed a good romance. So she decided if the worst come to the very worst, she would inform Martin about what she had overheard and let him make the decision about sacking Mary McLaughlin.

## CHAPTER TWELVE

He was seated behind his desk, fighting the sleep that threatened to overwhelm him when the door knocked and Mark Barclay stuck his head round.

"Boss, that was a phone call from Eric Kyle. He's coming in to give us a formal statement. How do you want to handle it?"

Charlie Miller, suddenly alert, replied, "As the SIO it's my job to be objective and distanced from the statement taking, Mark. However, Eric is one of our own so I'd like him handled with some compassion. Can you take time out to note the statement yourself, please?"

"Aye, no problem. I take it you'll want to see him while he's here?"

"Yes, but do the interview first and then I'll have a word before he leaves."

Something else occurred to him and as the door was closing he called out, "Mark."

Barclay again stuck his head round the door as Miller asked, "The lassie from the drag area. Has she been contacted again about the car she saw the night Linda Docherty was murdered?"

Barclay's eyes narrowed as he replied, "Not certain, boss, but I'll get right onto it."

"Thanks, Mark. It's likely nothing, but every avenue, eh?"

Eric Kyle parked his Mondeo in a police bay round the corner from the police station and glanced at his unshaven reflection in the rear-view mirror. His reflection showed a weary eyed man who carried the troubles of the world on his shoulders.

Getting out of the car he glanced briefly across the road at the vehicle entrance to the underground car park and saw that the police blue and white tape had now been removed. With a shiver he glanced upward at the clouds heavy with rain and hunching into the collar of his anorak, made his way towards Stewart Street office.

The young civilian receptionist smiled hesitantly as she buzzed him through the security door, uncertain whether or not to offer her sympathy at his loss and watched wordlessly as he walked towards the stairs that led to the upper floors.

The phone rang on Cathy Mulgrew's desk and lifting the receiver, the security officer at the reception desk informed her that ACC Freeman was in the building and on his way to her office.

Bloody hell, she thought. That's all I need and standing in front of the mirror on the wall, checked her make-up and prepared herself for the storm that was about to descend upon her.

Knocking on the door of the first floor flat located in St Georges Road, the MIU detective was taken aback by the smartly dressed woman who opened the door and smiling, invited her in before leading the way through to the lounge. The neatly furnished room also took the officer by surprise.

"What, because I'm on the game, hen, you thought I might be living in a squat or something?" Karen Bailey grinned at the detective.
"Eh, no, of course not," blushed DC Mhari McGhee as head down to hide her embarrassment, she fumbled in her shoulder bag for her notebook.
"Right, before we start, coffee or tea?"
"Ah, a cuppa might be nice, thanks, Karen."
"Okay," grinned Bailey, then her eyes narrowed as she added, "let me get the kettle on and then I'll tell you what I've remembered about the car that I saw, the night the lassie was murdered."

Freeman pushed open the door and without invite sat facing Mulgrew, his eyes boring into her. With a wave of his hand, he refused the offer of a coffee from her anxious secretary who quietly left the room. He didn't offer Mulgrew the courtesy of a greeting, but bluntly stated, "I want Miller removed from the inquiry."
Mulgrew had already made up her mind and decided that there was little point in arguing with Freeman, that the ACC had the authority and had already made his decision before he arrived at her office. To his complete surprise, she nodded and then asked, "Who do you suggest I replace him with, sir?"
"Why, you of course, Miss Mulgrew. You *are* an experienced detective, are you not?" he replied, his voice reeking of insolence.
"Yes sir, I am," she nodded, "but I lack the experience DCI Miller has running major inquiries. My CID experience was more inclined towards anti-terrorism and upon promotion to my current rank, the management of CID resources. However, if that's what you order, then of course I will comply."
He hadn't expected it to be this easy, not after the embarrassment he had endured from them both at the City Chambers. He was irate that she did not argue with him, that his prepared rant was now of little use and felt deflated, that somehow or other that by agreeing with him she had cheated him of his anger and again gained the upper hand, but he took solace in the knowledge that Miller was gone and his final act would be to return the bastard to uniform.
"Will there be anything else, sir?" she calmly asked.
He stood and pointed a stubby finger at her as he snarled, "Just get it done and get it done today, Miss Mulgrew."

He left her office leaving the door open behind him. Her secretary appeared at the door, her pale face betraying her uncertainty. Mulgrew smiled humourlessly and told her, "Don't worry about him, but yes, a coffee might be appropriate."

As the secretary closed the door, Mulgrew sat for a few minutes and contemplated the phone call she was about to make. Her mind made up, she reached for her desk phone, but hesitated. What she intended could result in one of two things and the worst of these was the ignominious termination of her own promising career.

Still, she grimaced, she had never had a friend like Charlie Miller and lifted the phone.

Martin Craven sat in his favourite armchair in the comfortably furnished lounge, a cut crystal glass with two fingers of whisky in his hand and reflected what might become of him after tomorrow's medical examination.

He had made his decision that no matter what occurred, no matter what result was handed down to him, he was giving up the business. If nothing else, passing out in Shelley's bathroom had forced his hand. He no longer had the same drive to succeed that once drove him on. No, the business was set up and running successfully. All it needed now was a young hand at the tiller and that hand would be Davie's.

His thoughts turned to Moira. Yes, he knew she would be disappointed, even pissed at him and yes, there would be tears and anger, but the sign above the business that he had so lovingly built from scratch read 'Craven and Son', not 'Craven and Daughter.'

The business was his legacy and he did so want to be remembered. He sipped at the whisky and smacked his lips before grinning, for he guessed that doctors being doctors, tomorrow he would be told to avoid everything that he enjoyed and staring at the glass thought he might as well enjoy what might be his final glass of the golden nectar.

He glanced about him at the room, so full of memories, at the small ornaments bought here and there, some expensively and others cheaply, but once considered to all be of sentimental value.

Now, he thought, they really meant so little to him.

He remembered the first time he had brought Shelley to this lounge, her fascination at first the size of the room and then her joy and innocence, her wide eyes meeting his as she sought his approval before she run her hands across all that the room contained.

He frowned because of what he had to do tomorrow. He had asked her to accompany him to the examination, but not because he needed her company.

No, the real reason was that tomorrow he intended ending their relationship.

After the visit to Ross Hall, he would take her somewhere where he could sit with her and explain that he was finishing with the business; finishing with her.

He had already made a tentative inquiry about purchasing a house abroad, somewhere he could be alone.

The visit to his lawyer had sorted out his Will. Shelley would continue working for Davie and when the time came, she would learn that he had purchased the flat she now rented and settled a sum upon her that would see her comfortably through the next three to four years. Time enough for her to find a man nearer her own age. She would be angry and hurt, but he knew it had to be done.

He loved her too much to permit her to continue their relationship and he would not have her believe herself obliged to care for him if tomorrows diagnosis was to be as he feared.

He sipped the last of the whisky and laid the glass down onto the table.

He would not as Shelley had suggested, pop down tonight to see her. No, he would uplift her in the morning for the hospital visit and that would be their last day together.


Mark Barclay first knocked then strode into Charlie Miller's room and laid a statement form down onto his desk.

"How is he?" asked Miller.

Barclay shrugged. "He's having a coffee in the incident room with some of the team and he seems to be okay, but you know Eric. It's sometimes hard to tell what he's thinking." He took a deep breath and pointed at the statement. "I think you should read this before you meet with him. There are a few things in there that kind of took me by surprise. Page two, the second paragraph. It doesn't make easy reading, boss, and it won't be easy speaking to Eric about it, but there's a couple of follow up inquiries we will have to make and I'm thinking it might be prudent if it was me or Myra that did the Actions."

Miller stared curiously at Barclay and turning to the second page, glanced down at the paragraph and his eyes narrowed. He shot at a glance at Barclay and exhaled. "Bloody hell, Mark, this is the last thing I expected. It takes us down a road I didn't imagine we would go. I see you what you mean. Right then, you'd better ask Eric to come through and have a word."

While Barclay went to fetch Kyle, Miller was rubbing at his forehead when the desk phone rung.

"Charlie? It's me," said Mulgrew. "I've a bit of bad news. I've just had a visit from Arthur Freeman. He's ordered me to stand you down as SIO."

"Fuck!" Miller shook his head, then asked, "Effective when?"

"Effective as of today, but he didn't give me a specific time so as far as I am concerned that doesn't mean right this minute and today doesn't finish till midnight," she replied. "Is there any news, anything that might justify me in countering his order? Any breakthrough?"

"No, nothing," he slowly replied, a fleeting vision flashing before his eyes of his career sliding down the toilet bowl. "Who's to replace me?"

"That's not decided yet," she slowly replied and listened as she sighed for he could not know how uncomfortable she was lying to him. It was then he realised Eric Kyle was standing at the door. He beckoned Kyle to come in and pointed to the chair in front of his desk. "Cathy, I've got Eric Kyle with me now, so can I get back to you later?"

"Yes, of course and tell Eric my thoughts are with him," she said before ending the call.

He replaced the handset, his mind reeling and forced himself to smile at Kyle.

"That was Cathy Mulgrew. She sends her regards. Eric, thanks for coming in. This statement you gave to Mark. I have to say it took us both by…surprise. Are you sure about this?"

"That Paula was seeing another man? Oh aye, Charlie, I'm definite," he slowly nodded and related that returning home a few days earlier he had seen her kissing the driver of the red Volvo.

"This woman you mention," Miller glanced at the statement, "this Jill Hardie. You seem to think…"
"That she was aware of Paula seeing another man…or men?" he bitterly spat out. "Yes, I'm sure she knew. Look," he leaned forward, both palms on the desk, "I've been round the block a couple of times. I'm not naïve. Stupid, yes and bloody blinkered regarding what was going on under my nose, I'll give you that. But I was so much in love with Paula that I turned a blind eye to her shenanigans, never questioned where the extra money was coming from. What I *could not* admit to myself was that her so called fucking pal Jill Hardie is a real tart and I know for a fact that she has a conviction for soliciting. Did she inveigle my Paula to get into that game? Jesus Christ!"
He sat back in the chair, his hands clenched into fists as he rubbed furiously at his forehead. "I don't know for certain, but if you're asking for my opinion, then yes." He lowered his head and stared at the floor between his feet. "I think Paula was turning tricks for her mate and that's where the extra cash was coming from."
Miller stared helplessly at Kyle unable to say anything that might ease his colleague's pain. Hell, he thought, and I was worried about my bloody *career*?
He allowed a minute to pass and Kyle to compose himself before speaking. "Eric, you realise that this information will lead to at least two lines of inquiry? Interviewing this woman Hardie and tracing the driver of the red Volvo?"
His head bent low, Kyle slowly nodded.
"I'll ensure that these inquiries are kept confidential, Eric. I'll have Mark Barclay and Myra McColl attend to them. No one need know…"
"About Paula maybe being on the game?" Kyle scoffed. "Fuck, Charlie, *I* know!"
An uncomfortable silence arose, broken when Miller asked, "Is there anything that I can do? Anything that…"
"No," Kyle waved the suggestion away, "but thanks. I mean it."
He stood and reached awkwardly across the desk, his hand outstretched.
"I know that you'll be in touch if you have any information."

He stopped at the door and turning, added, "No matter what she did, Charlie, she didn't deserve to end up stuck in some rubbish bin area. That's what was the hardest thing to take."

Miller nodded in agreement, but then inwardly cursed, almost forgetting what Cathy Mulgrew had suggested.

He raised a hand to stop Kyle leaving and said, "One more thing before you go. Look, Eric, at the minute you're on compassionate leave, but the thinking is that with the short time you have left to serve you might wish to consider extending that leave into your pre-retirement leave. That would take you up to…"

"My final pay-off?" smiled Kyle. "Thanks, Charlie, I'll give it some thought," and turned to leave, softly closing the door behind him.

Miller felt disconsolate. Never in the recent past had he endured such a shitty day. With a sigh he was reaching for the phone when it chirruped.

"DCI Miller," he said.

"Boss? Myra McColl. I'm down here at the mortuary with my lad and I believe we have a result and I have to admit, it's mostly down to Kevin. Turns out he was a third year apprentice at the Glasgow Building College before the polis beckoned."

The infectious excitement in her voice perked him up slightly and he listened as she continued.

"Anyway, according to Kevin it seems that the new building is constructed with plasterboard walls that have air ducts running between them. Do you happen to know what room is located next door to the examination room?"

"No, surprise me," he replied.

"The mortuary attendant's room is right next door and guess what runs between both the examination and attendant's rooms?"

"An air duct," he grinned at the phone.

"Bang on. The duty attendant was very helpful and tells us that when he's in the attendant's room and if the extractor vent is switched off he can hear what's going on in the examination room, clear as a bell."

"Is he the…"

"No," McColl interrupted, "but he was kind enough to let us have a look at the duty log on his computer that identified the attendant on duty at the PM's for each of the three victims."

She didn't bother explaining that the bogus threat of hampering a major investigation had been used to obtain the attendant's permission.

He heard the rustle of paper as McColl read out, "Colin Napier is the name we have and we also have a home address."

"Good work to you both and be sure to let young Kevin know how pleased I am," he told her. "I take it you'll be bringing Mister Napier in for interview?"

"Oh aye, boss and depending how cooperative he is, he might or might not be going home tonight."

He returned the phone to its cradle, but then thought Cathy Mulgrew should at least know of this development and dialled her Gartcosh office number. After a couple of rings the call was transferred to her secretary who informed him that Miss Mulgrew was already on another call. He requested the secretary inform her boss that the leak had been discovered at the mortuary and stifling a yawn, added that he was returning home and if Miss Mulgrew wanted to speak with him, she would get him on his mobile.

Collecting his coat from the peg, he made his way into the incident room and beckoned Mark Barclay join him in the corridor.

"Not public news yet, Mark, but it seems that as of today, I'm being replaced as the SIO."

"What!" Barclay was astounded. "Is this that bloody idiot Freeman's doing? Has that clown…"

Miller raised a hand to hush Barclay and continued, "The new SIO has still to be appointed, but I suppose that for now Cathy Mulgrew will likely take over. Right, I'm going home. There's not much more I can do here, but the good news is that Myra's on her way to detain the leak regarding the information being passed to that wee shit McGregor. A mortuary attendant called Napier that she will be bringing back here for interview."

"Well, it's a bit like losing a shilling and finding a tanner, isn't it?" Barclay shook his head. "Fuck it, Charlie! I don't know what to say…"

He smiled and clapped Barclay on the shoulder. "Then don't say anything and particularly not to the team. They've enough to cope with at the minute. One final thing. I've spoke with Eric and assured him that you and Myra will attend to the visit with his wife's…friend and the pal, the woman Jill Hardie. It's likely if what Eric suspects to be true that Hardie will be able to provide details of the friend, the driver of the red coloured Volvo."

"I'll see it gets done, boss," replied Barclay, his anger at the unfairness of Miller's dismissal reflected on his face.

"Thanks, Mark," Miller nodded and turned towards the stairs.

## CHAPTER THIRTEEN

Cathy Mulgrew replaced the phone and blew through pursed lips. She had not expected a response to her own call in such a short time and was still mulling over the return call when the door was knocked, startling her.

Her secretary entered and said, "Miss Mulgrew, you had a phone call from DCI Miller." She glanced at her notepad and continued. "He said to inform you that the leak has been discovered at the mortuary and that he's returning home and if you need to contact him, he'll be on his mobile."

"Thanks," she smiled her dismissal and sat back in her chair, again reflecting on her phone call.

The die was cast, but what would happen now was out of her control.

James Bain turned into Dalcraig Crescent and approaching his house, was surprised to see Moira's car parked in the front of the driveway, leaving him no option other than to park on the roadway outside the house. Getting out of the car, he glanced across the road and saw the curtains in Lara Quinn's front room twitch. He ground his teeth and resisted a sudden desire to fetch the hammer from the boot of his car, break down her door and smash the nosey bitch's head in with it. Forcing the tension from his body, he quickly strode to the front door and tried the handle, but was surprised the door was locked.

Curiously, he unlocked the door and shouted, "Moira?" but got no reply.

Strange, he thought, that she should be out of the house though her car was in the driveway.

He let himself into the house and then in the kitchen switched on the kettle and was fetching a mug from the cupboard when he heard the front door close.

Moira, wearing an overcoat, entered the kitchen and stood staring at him.

"Hi," he avoided her eyes as he greeted her, "I was surprised you were home so early. Been out for a walk?"

She turned and taking off her coat, walked into the hallway to hang it on the coat stand by the front door.

"Yes and no," she replied and returned to the kitchen, her face pale and her voice stony cold. "I've been to the post box on the main road, posting a letter to my lawyer."

"To your lawyer?" he repeated, a cold shiver running down his spine. Was this about the divorce she kept threatening?

"Sorry, I don't understand."

"Perhaps you might wish to sit down, James" she said, inviting him to join her at the small kitchen table as she sat and bent to place her shoulder bag on the floor beside her.

He did not like this, did not like this at all. The boiling kettle now ignored, he slowly sank into the chair opposite her and stared at her. "What's going on? What's this about?"

She didn't reply, but reached down into her bag and withdrew an unsealed brown coloured A5 sized envelope that she placed on the table in front of her.

"What's that?" he stared at the envelope, a cold hand gripping his stomach.

She had practised this in her mind, what she would say, what she would do and how she assumed he would react. She was far stronger willed than her husband and it never entered her head that the weak and manipulative James might try something, might try to hurt her. Her face as pale as the kitchen walls, she replied, "This envelope, James, contains a copy of the letter that I have sent to my lawyer. If anything should happen to me, my lawyer has been instructed to open the letter and inform the police of the contents. It's what you might call my insurance policy. Do you understand?"

"No, not really," he shook his head, but had a sinking feeling that she was aware, that the bitch knew!

"I…I mean," he stuttered like the frightened schoolboy he once had been, "what's going to happen to you? Why…why would you need an insurance policy like that?"

"Because of this," she tipped the envelope up and falling out with the single sheet of paper was the small, clear plastic bag with the three ribbon tied locks of hair. "The letter to my lawyer, James, includes some samples of hair from your three wee bundles that you tied nicely with the ribbon and an explanation about where I found them."

He stared in horror at the plastic bag, his worst fears now realised. "What's this?" he asked, his voice low and threatening. "What the *fuck* is this!" he suddenly screamed at her, using his hands on the table to push himself to his feet, his face a mask of hatred and without warning, turning the table over with a crash onto the floor and reaching for her with claw like hands.

Never before had James even hinted at violence towards her and stunned at his sudden change from manipulated lamb to ferocious lion, she tipped her chair backwards, her head striking the kitchen wall and though dazed, raised her hands to fend him off, but he was too quick for her and his hands were around her throat.

She tried to scream, but no sound came and terror shone like a beacon in her eyes.

The weight of his body pinned her to the chair and staring into his maddened eyes, she saw the raw hatred he had for her. All the taunts, past slights and verbal abuse he had suffered at her hands were focused in the grip that grew tighter round her throat. She broke her false fingernails as she clawed at him and scratched at his wrists and his face, vainly trying to prise off the hands that were choking her. Her laboured breathing now was no more than a strangled gasp.

Then, as suddenly as he had attacked her, he released his grip and stepped back, his nostrils flaring, a thin line of saliva escaping his mouth and his body shaking with the exertion he had expended trying to throttle her.

She couldn't help herself, for all at once she was weeping and choking and gasping for air.

Her body shaking, she watched with terror as he bent and retrieving the plastic bag from the floor, righted the chair he had knocked over then sat down and then to her horror, almost lovingly rubbed the bag against his cheek before shoving it into his trouser pocket.

He's mad, she thought; he's off his fucking head!

Slowly, very slowly and unable to take her eyes from him, she pushed the chair forward onto the four legs so that her head and back was no longer pressed against the wall.

He didn't look at her, but quietly and venomously told her, "I hate you."

She stared wide-eyed at him, but didn't trust herself to speak, afraid that anything she said might provoke him to again attack her.

They sat like that for several minutes while she regained control of her breathing and though it was difficult and painful to speak, at last she managed to croak, "There is a way out of this."

He did not reply, but continued to stare at her.

"We need to talk about this," she told him, slowly rubbing at her bruised throat to ease the pain and discovered that during his attack, the top two buttons of her blouse had been torn off and the top of her brassiere was exposed.

That's when she saw him staring at her breasts.

They had not been man and wife for a very long time, not for several months before the loss of their child so why was he staring like at her like that, she wondered; and then it struck her.

He was aroused. Astounded, she glanced down to his groin and realised with a shock that the short burst of violence she had endured had aroused him.

Unable to take her eyes from him, she slowly unbuttoned the rest of the blouse and pulled the material out from her skirt to let it hang loose, allowing him to see her breasts restrained in the creamy white bra.

"Is this what you want, James? Do you want me?" she asked with difficulty, her voice husky and fighting the pain of her near strangulation yet determined to again gain control of her weak-minded husband

His head jerked up and his eyes stared into hers.

"Talk about what?"

She was startled, for he had heard her after all. Her eyes fluttering, she replied, "About how to save you."

"There is no saving me. I've done some very bad things," he replied, his voice soft, but lucid.

Her throat still hurt like hell, but she now realised that confronting him had been a terrible mistake and careful not to antagonise him again, quietly said, "James, there *is* a way out of this. All we have to do is work it out, together. You need to let me explain, to tell you how it will work."

His gaze had returned to her breasts and she saw his chest heave. Slowly while he watched, she stood and pulling the bra upwards to release both breasts, nervously moved towards him. She held her breath, hoping that he was sufficiently calm to allow her to get close. He didn't move as she stood before him and reaching her hands behind him, pulled his head onto her naked breasts.

She shivered, not with lust, but with revulsion that she was resorting to seduction. Fear urged her to continue as with one hand she gently rubbed her breast against his cheek and with the other hand reached down to massage his swollen groin.

When making love, it had always been Moira who was the dominant partner; Moira urging him to satisfy her needs, for she had quickly realised that handsome and muscular though he undoubtedly was, in bed James was dull and boring.

"Why don't we go upstairs, James. You want me, don't you," she whispered, fighting the sudden nausea that threatened to overwhelm her and resisting the desperate urge to knead her sore throat.

"There's things you would like to do to me, isn't there?"

His head arched back as he stared up at her and eyes narrowed, he asked, "What way out? What the *fuck* do you know!" and pushing her away, stood and walked to the other side of the kitchen and stood with his back to the kitchen worktop, his arms folded and head down, staring at the floor like a petulant schoolboy.

Embarrassed and a little surprised that he should reject her, she tucked her breasts back into the bra cups and stood watching him. This is ridiculous, she thought. I'm standing here half-naked trying to persuade my husband, a fucking *murderer*, to listen to me!

She glanced at the doorway and it briefly occurred to Moira that she should escape, run to the front door and scream for help, but that would hinder her plan and staring at him with sudden realisation, she knew!

He was afraid.

Afraid of being arrested or...no, she thought.

He's afraid of me, of what I know, what I can do!

Her blouse flapped loose about her waist while she bent down and with some difficulty, pulled the table back from the floor onto its legs and pushed his chair against it.

"Come and sit, James, please," she softly asked.

God, she inwardly screamed, it's like dealing with a fucking insolent child!

"You said I could do things to you," he muttered.

Momentarily confused, she stared at him and replied, "What?"

His head lifted and he stared again at her breasts. "You said I could do things to you. Well, if you want to talk to me, then we do it in bed. We'll talk after you let me do what I want with you. After you let me do it."

She shivered, wondering what kind of sexual fantasy was going through his dull and unimaginative head, but she had come too far now, risked too much to back down. If her plan was to work and having sex with James was what he wished and if it meant using her body to control him, then it had to be done. There was too much at stake.

Forcing a smile, she swallowed with difficulty as she reached her hand towards him and said, "Okay James, let's go upstairs and you can do the things you want. We'll talk after it and I'll tell you how we can save you. I'll let you do to me whatever you want then we'll talk. Anything you want, okay?"

As he took her hand and they turned towards the stairs, she could not begin to imagine how she would regret the pact she had just made with the devil.

Charlie Miller parked his car behind Sadie's and switching off the engine, sat for a moment to collect his thoughts. Eric Kyle's revelation about his wife's activities had been a shock that far outstripped his own dismissal from the inquiry. Poor bugger, he thought.

He startled when the window was knocked and turned to see Sadie standing there with a mug in her hand. She stepped back to permit him to open the door and said, "Coffee, strong, black with two sugars."

"I thought you had put me off the sugar because of my ever expanding waistline," he joked as still sat in his seat, he sipped at the piping hot liquid.

She stared at him and reached forward to stroke a lock of hair from his forehead.

"Mark Barclay phoned. Wanted to give me a heads-up in case I was standing behind the door with a rolling pin or waiting to nag you about something."
"Ah," he mentally thanked Barclay as handing her the mug, he stepped from the car. "Well, I've had a good run."
"Good run nothing, Charlie Miller," she fumed. "You've earned your rank and the only reason that…that…"
"Careful," he leaned forward to whisper, "Jellybean's watching us from the lounge window."
She turned to see their smiling daughter waving at them and forcing a smile, she returned the wave.
Walking together arm in arm towards the front door, she said, "And by the way, that press conference."
He stared down at her.
"I was mortified," she shook her head. "Imagine me letting you go on television looking like you needed a haircut."
And that's all she had to say about it.

With some difficulty, first agreeing to a take-away meal and an outrageous extra payment, Davie Bain finally persuaded Elsa's childminder to remain at the house for the evening, assuring her that he would return home no later than ten-thirty.
With an eagerness that surprised him, he showered and dressed for his seven-thirty date with Mary McLaughlin. He had briefly considered phoning Sloans and booking a table for a meal, but having made no arrangement with Mary about dinner, guessed she would have already eaten. Maybe the next time he mused, wincing as the sharp sting of the scented aftershave bit into the pores of his shaven face.
He glanced at the clock seeing he had an hour to get there, already deciding that he would forgo a drink and take the car. Besides, he hoped that bringing his car would give him the opportunity to provide Mary with a lift home.
Davie felt a little guilty kissing his crying daughter goodnight, but reasoned that one night without her Daddy tucking her in wouldn't hurt her.
Smiling at his reflection in the wardrobe mirror, he mentally crossed his fingers that tonight would go well.

The taxi was waiting for Shelley McPhail when she left the warehouse and after giving the driver her address, she sat back in the darkened cab and wearily closed her eyes.
Instinctively, she knew that Martin wouldn't come to visit her tonight and reaching for the mobile phone in her handbag, stopped. She guessed that if she called even to find out how he was feeling, he would jump into the car and drive down to the flat.
He was worried about the examination tomorrow morning, that was clearly evident, but what he didn't realise was that Shelley was equally worried.
Martin wasn't just her boss nor just her sexual partner; he wasn't just the man who paid her rent.
He was her whole life.
Regardless of their age difference, regardless of their upbringing, Shelley McPhail, a young woman who had never before experienced love, knew she would never, could never love any man as she loved Martin Craven.
He wasn't ashamed of her of that she was convinced, but correctly guessed that he was ashamed of himself, for she was certain that Martin believed he was taking advantage of her, of her youth and naivety.
He would never be so wrong about anything.
Shelley was two months short of her twentieth birthday, but the young woman had already experienced life as few others had. Orphaned at six years of age and placed by an underfunded and overstretched social work department with her mother's childless sister and her husband, Shelley did not at first understand the kind and benevolent uncle who by day was a pillar of the community and God fearing church elder, while at night as she lay in her bed, he would fondle and molest the child placed in his wife's care. Her fear of his threats that if she told she would be taken from her aunt and put into a Dickensian type workhouse kept her silent. It was only when Shelley reached the age of ten years that she came to understand her aunt was aware of her husband's nocturnal molestation of the little girl.
Even at that tender age Shelley was a bright and articulate child and one dark, winter night when the uncle climbed into her bed and his rough hands began to caress her, she whispered the carefully constructed lie that she had written a letter to the police that was now

in the care of Shelley's school friend. So frightened had he been he stayed away from her after that night.

But that didn't stop the physical abuse, the occasional slaps from her aunt or the poor food and the stony silence when she was around them.

With no other relatives and nowhere else to go, Shelley lived in their home, but apart from them. The part time job in the local grocery had come to a sudden end when the middle-aged shopkeeper had attempted to force himself upon her.

That incident had decided her and the one-way train ticket to Glasgow with the half-promise of accommodation with a former school friend had been a spur of the moment decision, but one that she would never regret.

Since leaving her aunt's home, there had not nor would there be any further contact; no one in Cawdor would be looking for her and no one would miss her.

Her thoughts again turned to Martin. She had never told him of her love for him for she feared that to do so would require him to commit to her and that, she knew, might wreck the relationship they currently enjoyed.

No, if their time together must continue to go on as it did without their relationship becoming known to anyone else, then she would gladly resign herself to that for all that mattered to her was that Martin was in her life.

The taxi arrived at Whitefield Street and leaning forward, she paid the driver through the window before exiting the cab.

She glanced up at the darkened flat and shrugged.

One day, she mused, perhaps Martin might be standing there, waiting for her to come home.

She sat in pain on the edge of the closed lid of the toilet seat in the en suite, still shivering in terror, her arms about her as she rocked back and forth and softly wept, her dressing robe pulled across her shoulders to hide her nakedness while next-door James snored in the double bed.

With misplaced confidence in her own supremacy, she had led him by the hand upstairs to the bedroom and with reluctance prepared to give herself to him for his cooperation with her plan, but when she pushed open the door, from that moment she lost control to him. He had given her no opportunity to tell him of her plan or even speak with him for as soon as they had entered the room, he slammed the door closed, grabbed her by the hair and to her astonishment slapped her face and pushed her backwards onto the bed. To her shame, she had been so surprised and terrified she had offered him no resistance as pushing and pulling at her and calling her by every vile name he could think of, he literally tore her clothes from her.

She gently massaged her breasts and nipples, certain they would bruise where he had roughly squeezed and bitten them while she cried out in pain. Her wrists were beginning to bruise where he had held her pinned to the bed while he forced himself upon her. Her head hurt after he had turned her over and with his fingers entwined in her hair, painfully jerked her head back as forcing her to crouch naked on the bed on her hands and knees, he ignored her tears and pleas while he savagely thrust into her. The memory of him pulling her by her hair from the bed and forcing her to the carpeted floor on her knees to kneel before him, caused her to retch. Both hands clutching at the sides of the toilet bowl, she vomited, her body heaving until there was nothing left to throw up but a yellow coloured mucous that dribbled onto her chin and stained the enamel bowl. Shuddering, she flushed the toilet and wiping her mouth with the back of her hand, sat exhausted with her back against the bath. With her legs curled beneath her on the bathroom floor, tears of angry shame flowed freely at the thought of his final indignity, when using the weight of his body to subdue her used the most vile language while demanding that she repeat back to him what he was doing to her.

During his assault, she had been terrified and compliant because she believed he meant to kill her and realised now she had been a fool to think that in his heightened state of arousal she could control him as she had planned. After confronting him in the kitchen, she now realised the barbarity of his attack upon her should have alerted her to his unpredictable savagery.

Sitting there, remembering the pain and brutality he had visited upon her, Moira correctly guessed his rape and assault upon her had not been to satisfy any sexual need, but was his way of dominating her; a need to restore his pride, to physically revenge himself and punish her for what he believed she had made him suffer.

She despised and hated him as surely as she knew he hated her.

She forced herself to be calm.
He would not, could not break her, she snarled for she was stronger than him.
Her eyes narrowed. In time, she would get over that last, horrific half hour and soon, she told herself, it would simply be a horrible memory.
Her plan was everything and while she had no concern for his freedom, she knew if she was to go ahead with her plan she risked her own freedom, so it *had* to work.
She stood awkwardly, using the rim of the bath to pull herself to her feet, grimacing against the pain of her injured body and slipped the robe off. Still hurting, she reached to turn on the shower.
The hot water eased some of the ache and washed away the bloodstains from where she guessed she must be internally torn, but it would heal though presumed it would be several days before she felt any real relief.
She soaked under the shower for almost ten minutes and when at last her tears subsided, turned off the water and listened carefully until she was sure she could hear him snoring.
She dried herself and then stared into the mirror. Her cheek bore the imprint of his fingers. Tentatively, she rubbed a moisturiser into the skin to dull the redness. A silk scarf would hide the marks on her throat, but there was little she could do about the marks on her wrists other than to wear long sleeves. Fortunately, no one would see the teeth marks or bruising on her breasts.
She took a deep breath and slipped on the robe, tying the cord tightly about her waist.
Opening the door, she slipped into the bedroom and arms folded across her aching breasts, stood over him. The bedding was in disarray, her ripped blouse and torn underwear and skirt lying discarded on the floor where he had thrown them.
His eyes closed and hair dishevelled, he looked nothing like the raping monster he had been for almost a full thirty minutes.
She stared at him with dead eyes and wondered; what she had suffered, was it worth it.
Her analytical mind balanced the short time of pain and degrading humiliation against a lifetime of future success.
There was no doubt in her mind, yes, and when the time was right, she would find a way to get rid of the bastard!

But first though the thought revolted her, she needed him. Her plan depended on his cooperation.

"James!" she snapped at him.

Slowly, his eyes flickered open and lying there on his back, he stared up at her.

She wanted nothing more than to lift the metal bedside lamp and smash it down onto his open-mouthed face, but instead she hissed, "You did it, everything that you wanted to do to me! You've had your…your pleasure, now it's time for you to *listen*! To do as *I* say!"

Still blazing mad at her husbands unfair dismissal as SIO, Sadie Miller was stirring the pasta while her daughter Geraldine worked at her homework on the coffee table in the lounge. Ella the baby was snoozing in her pram at the back door and her husband, now changed out of his good suit and into his gardening clothes was coming to terms with his bad news and trying to relax by potting some plants in the garden shed.

He had been home for over an hour and it surprised her that he hadn't spoken of his sacking from the inquiry, but she wouldn't press him, deciding instead to give him some time to think things over. There would be time enough this evening when the kids were in bed

She startled when she realised that she was stirring the pot so furiously the water was spilling over onto the cooker.

"Bugger," she muttered, reaching for a cloth to wipe the spillage.

The doorbell rung and glancing at the wall clock, wondered who would be so insensitive as to visit at dinnertime.

Turning the heat down under the pot, Sadie wiped her hands on her apron and passing through the hallway to the front door, waved the curious Geraldine back to her homework.

Pulling open the door, her eyes widened in surprise. Though Sadie had never personally met the man who stood there, he was instantly recognisable, all six feet five inches of him and in particular, the squashed nose that was so favoured by the Scottish media cartoonists and advertised his love of rugby.

Wearing a navy pinstriped suit, crisp white shirt and striped navy tie, Martin Cairney smiled at her and said, "Good evening, Sergeant Miller. I apologise for calling unannounced at your home." He turned towards the gleaming black coloured Rover V8 that sat on the roadway across the driveway entrance where the uniformed driver was unfolding a newspaper and pointing to it, said, "I trust parking the car there won't be a nuisance?"

"Eh, no, of course not, sir," she shook her head, confusion evident on her face.

"Well, is that the kettle I hear boiling?" he continued to smile at her.

"Oh, forgive my manners," she blushed and stood to one side, "please come in."

He strode past her and stood respectfully in the hallway. "Is your husband at home? I haven't missed him, have I?"

Pulling her apron off, Sadie replied, "He's in the garden, sir. I'll fetch him if you'd like to wait in here," and showed him through to the lounge where Geraldine turned from the dining table to stare curiously at the smiling giant who was interrupting her homework.

Charlie Miller was wiping his hands on his old trousers when Sadie came rushing through the shed door, her face crimson.

"You'd better get up to the house, love," she gasped.

"Is something wrong?" he frowned

"No, well to be honest, I don't really know," she shook her head, "but you have a visitor."

He sighed and said, "Okay, let me guess. Cathy has come over with a bottle that you and her will drink to help me get over my disappointment."

"Eh, not quite. It's the Chief Constable. It's Martin Cairney."

"You're kidding," he grinned, but the grin quickly faded when he realised Sadie was serious. "You're not kidding. Bloody hell," he muttered and rushed past her to the path that took him through the kitchen door.

Grabbing a tea towel, he began to wipe the dirt from his hands as he walked through to the lounge to find Cairney and Geraldine both kneeling by the table and huddled over her homework book.

"Aye, seems I'm wrong and you're correct," he heard Cairney say. "Seven nines *are* sixty-three," then turning, winked at Miller.

"Mister Miller," he rose to tower above the little girl who stared at him with a wide smile and extended his hand to her Daddy. "Like I told your lovely wife, I apologise for calling at your home unannounced." Smiling down at Geraldine, he then asked, "Is there somewhere we might have a chat? I don't want to disturb this young lady's homework and," he reached down to pat the little girl on the head, "I think we have the makings of a real mathematician here."

"Of course, sir. We can sit through in the conservatory, if you'll follow me, please."

Comfortably seated in the wicker chairs with a small table between them upon which Sadie placed two mugs of coffee before she left the room, Cairney glanced at his watch and said, "Forgive me if I'm blunt. I have a meeting in half an hour at the Paisley Town Hall, so I will cut to the chase. This meeting we are having will be known to five people only. My driver who delivered me here and who I implicitly trust, your wife, you, me and Cathy Mulgrew who called me earlier today. No one else must know of this meeting and what I am about to say is completely confidential and anything that passes between us will remain *strictly* between us. Is that clearly understood?"

"Yes sir, of course," nodded Miller.

"I'm aware that Mister Freeman has dismissed you as the SIO in the ongoing city centre murder inquiries. He is after all the Assistant Chief Constable (Crime) and it is his prerogative to appoint or dismiss his staff as he sees fit. That said your dismissal today as the SIO was an operational decision that was made by Mister Freeman without recourse to any other advice. However, it is my intention to rescind that decision and as of tomorrow, I am reinstating you as the SIO. I make this decision based on the extremely high opinion Miss Mulgrew has of you as well as my own knowledge of your career." He paused and his brow furrowed. " You may not know this, but several years ago while working within the Counter Terrorism Unit, I was the Detective Chief Inspector who seconded Cathy Mulgrew to work with you at Stewart Street police office when you hunted the bugger who was responsible for killing the wee girl in the city centre fire. A lawyers office, if memory serves me correctly."

"That's right, sir," Miller slowly nodded.

"That inquiry in turn resulted in you and Mulgrew solving a case that impacted upon an inquiry being covertly conducted by my own department, the CTU, though regretfully it resulted in you being injured when the bloody car exploded."

Miller unconsciously traced a finger across the scar on his cheek and smiled. "I thought I was a goner that day, sir."

"So did many of us, Mister Miller, but fortunately you recovered and subsequently your tenacity and many successes as an investigating officer has not gone unnoticed, not least by me."

"Thank you, sir."

"You must understand my decision will not in any way reflect badly on Mister Freeman or his decision making," but here he hesitated as though seeking the right thing to say, then to Miller's surprise, leaned forward and continued. "The Force is receiving bad press about our inability to catch the bugger murdering these young women, Mister Miller. I *need* a result and I need it soon. Are you the man to get me the result?"

Miller took a deep breath before replying, "You're asking me to catch a killer, a serial killer sir, with no witnesses coming forward and who so far has not left anything of evidential value at any of the locus to identify him or her, who randomly picks the victims, presumably based on their vulnerability and though you haven't given me a time frame, you want it done yesterday. With respect, you're asking a lot, sir," he stood and rubbed at his brow with the heel of his right hand, inadvertently leaving a smudge of dirt on his forehead. "Without proper resources and funding, my guys have worked their arses off trying to catch this bastard and often worked long hours without payment." He exhaled and slowly sat back down. "I appreciate what you're trying to do for me, sir…"

"I'm not trying to do anything for *you*, Mister Miller!" snapped Cairney. "What I am doing is getting you back working as the SIO because according to Cathy Mulgrew and what I know of you, you are our best chance of catching this individual. There is no question of a time frame, but to quote you; yes, catching this bastard yesterday would serve both the community and me well. Without going into too many details, I need this individual caught for reasons other than the murders committed or might be committed. The question remains, Mister Miller. Can you do it? Can you find me the killer?"

"Will I be able to call upon extra resources?"

"No," Cairney shook his head, "I regret that is something I cannot provide. You must also understand that I have to be seen to be completely transparent in supporting my senior staff. Reinstating you is about the only move I can make without alienating my Deputies and the rest of the Assistant Chief's. If I were to interfere in

Mister Freeman's budgetary decisions to secure extra funding for you it would completely undermine him and I really cannot afford to have any dissension among the senior staff." Almost under his breath, he added, "particularly at this time."

The throwaway comment caused Miller to suspect there was more going on than Cairney was disclosing and the remark made by Morris Thomson, when he and Mulgrew visited the City Chambers, that there was political in fighting among the police senior management, sprung to mind.

"What you also need to understand, Mister Miller," continued Cairney, "is that Mister Freeman will undoubtedly be extremely annoyed with me for interfering in his area of responsibility, but that is something that I will deal with," he sighed. "I also regret that your reinstatement as the SIO might cause some difficulties for you and likely you might find some of the MIU currently attached to your investigation will be operationally diverted to other inquiries." He glanced again at his watch and standing, continued. "In short, Mister Miller, you will need to catch this killer with the resources available to you and possibly even less so when Freeman finds out," he muttered. "So, I've set you not just the impossible task, but the damndest task. I'm asking you while having one hand tied behind your back to catch the killer and Mister Miller," he smiled humourlessly, "I suggest when you report tomorrow morning at Stewart Street police office you wear your issued stab-proof vest because quite frankly, there will be knives drawn and *you* will be the target."

He turned and followed by Miller, strode into the hallway while calling out, "Missus Miller, thank you for the coffee," and as he passed by the lounge, waved to the smiling Geraldine.

At the front door, Cairney turned to shake Miller by the hand and said, "Even in my so-called exalted position, Mister Miller, I have to mind my P's and Q's, but that said, Cathy Mulgrew has my personal number. Goodbye," he hesitated and then with a soft smile, added, "and good luck."

Watching Cairney walk down the driveway, he sensed that Sadie was behind him and without turning, said, "The good news is that as of tomorrow morning, I'm reinstated as the SIO in the inquiry."

"And the bad news?" she placed her arm comfortingly around his waist.

He sighed before replying, "The bad news, if I'm correct in what I'm thinking, is that if I fail to catch the killer then we might lose Martin Cairney as our Chief Constable."

In the large open office on the fourth floor of the building that housed the 'Glasgow News', Ally McGregor smiled with pleasure at the prints lying on his desk. The young photographer had done a good job, he thought as he stared at a photograph he held in his hand that showed a dour faced DCI Charlie Miller walking towards the front door of Dalmarnock office.
McGregor did not like Miller. In fact the truth be told, he did not like any of the fucking polis he had to deal with. Overpaid tossers, the lot of them!
Grinning, he lifted the early edition of the newspaper with the bold headline 'Glasgow's Demon Barber Stalks City's Women' and his name prominently published underneath. If that and his scoop about the hair being cut from the victims did not attract interest from the major UK dailies then something was badly wrong, he thought. He glanced at his desk phone. When the television stations broadcast their evening news programmes, his headline would go viral and he expected by tomorrow morning, his phone would be ringing constantly with, he fervently hoped, better job offers. He sat back in his chair, his hands behind his head. The evening edition of the paper had been a follow-up article to his scoop and hadn't taken him but thirty minutes to type. He burped as he grinned. Maybe he would leave a little early, head down to the pub in George Street for a couple of halves and on the back of his success, see if that young copy typist with the big tits was there. If she was it could prove to be an interesting evening.
"Mister McGregor, sir?"
He turned to see one of the apprentice juniors hired by the paper for a pittance to fetch and carry and do all the shirty jobs. "Aye son, what can I do you for?" he quipped.
"Eh, you're wanted down at the reception desk, Mister McGregor. Two polis. Detectives. A man and a woman. They're asking for you," the lad gasped.
"Oh aye?" he grinned and pushing himself to his feet, asked, "Did they say what they wanted?"

"No," the lad shook his head, "only that…" He stopped, clearly embarrassed and licked at his lips.
"Only that what?" McGregor's eyes narrowed.
"They said…the woman I mean. I think she's the boss. She said…well, she told me to tell you that you were to get your arse down there pronto or she would come up here and fetch you herself."

## CHAPTER FOURTEEN

The waitress smiled as she delivered the glass of chardonnay and the soda water and lime to the nice couple at the table, pleased when Davie Craven waved away the change and left her with a generous tip.
"That was nice of you," smiled Mary McLaughlin, lifting her glass as she watched the waitress walk off. "Good tips help with the wages in some of the pubs and restaurants these days. I know that I certainly appreciated it," she added.
Davie shrugged with a smile as Mary leaned forward and asked, "So, no trouble getting a baby-sitter for your wee girl then?"
"Ah, no," he blithely fibbed, thinking that he would have paid the childminder double or even treble if it meant he could spend time with Mary.
Their conversation so far had been general; about work, their families and now their respective child. Keen as he was to know more about Mary he did not wish to seem too nosey and besides, Davie was the first to admit he had no real experience of women for his previous few relationships and in particular, his marriage to Jean had all ended disastrously. This time though, he was determined that he would do better.
What he could not know or even suspect was that he didn't need to try too hard, for Mary liked him a lot, recognising Davie to be a decent and honest man who epitomised the old Glasgow adage of what you see is what you get.
She herself had led a quiet life with few friends and even fewer boyfriends, her one lasting relationship that had ended so badly when Marcus, the father of her son had sailed with his ship without being aware of her pregnancy and with no interest in returning or contacting her again. It had been a hard time for Mary who shy by

nature, had endured scorn from her family and but for the support of her widowed mother, believed she might not have endured as she did.

Sitting there together, comfortable in their closeness, they chatted about trivia but neither bored by the other. At last, glancing at his watch, Davie realised that if he was to drop Mary off and return home in time to relieve the childminder, it was time he made a move.

Mistaking his glance for his desire to leave, she felt a little hurt, but when he said, "I've got to get back by ten-thirty or the childminder will go nuts, so can I drop you home first?"

She nodded, but her insecurity still caused her to wonder; was it a lie he was telling to end a boring night or did he really have to be home for that time?

"I can get a taxi, if you're in a hurry," she suggested.

For his part Davie's heart sunk a little as his insecurity kicked in and he wondered, does she not want a lift? Is she already bored with me?

"Oh," he simply replied, but some instinct told him to go on and he added, "I'd really like to take you home. Only, if that's okay with you though?" he shrugged.

It was something in his eyes, she thought, something about the way he asked that made her say, "Yes, I'd like that if it's not too far out of your way?"

"No," he smiled, a smile that made her catch her breath, "it doesn't matter where you live, Mary. It's not too far."

He had parked the car in a bay in the nearby Queen Street and as they closely walked together, she decided to take a chance and slipped her arm through his.

They turned from Argyle Street in Queen Street and he stopped, emboldened by her nearness.

Turning towards her, he said, "I really like you, Mary. Would you come out with me again? Maybe next time for dinner or a film or something?"

She didn't reply, but reached forward to touch his cheek and with her heart beating a drum tattoo in her chest, leaned forward to kiss him on the lips.

Surprised at her own boldness she began to apologise, but he didn't listen. He stretched both arms about her and drawing her close returned her kiss.

"Hey you two, get a room," a drunken teenager called to them from across the street.

Grinning, Davie waved at the girl and whispered to the embarrassed, but giggling Mary, "Maybe we'll consider that once we've had a couple of dates, eh?"

Sitting in the darkness of his car, James Bain glanced out at the group of prostitutes gathering together on the corner outside the former Anderston bus station, his face expressionless. She had forbidden him to kill any more women, any of the bitches because it would ruin her plan and that infuriated him, but after reading the copy of the letter she had sent to her lawyer with the strands of hair, she left him in no doubt that if he wanted to stay out of prison, he must do exactly as she said.

He hated her, hated it that once more she had him by the balls. Bitch!

He saw the women separate, walking off alone or in couples, waving and calling out to each other, though he couldn't make out what they shouted as they made their way to their favourite pitches in the nearby streets. How he would love to grab one of them off the street and take her somewhere quiet where he would…

His breathing was becoming rapid and he felt himself become aroused. His thoughts turned to Moira and what he had done to her, what she had made him do.

Christ! He had not thought himself capable of it, of standing up to her like he had done.

He had hurt her, had taken pleasure in slapping and biting and forcing himself upon her like he did, making her do and say the things that he had once only imagined doing to her. Humiliating her just like he had always dreamed of.

But it was all her own fault! If she wasn't the way she was, hadn't treated him like she had, he would never have had to…to rape her.

Yes, he unconsciously nodded, that's what he had done, he had raped the bitch; just like she fucking deserved!

It was her fault; she had brought it upon herself.

She was to blame!

He hammered with both hands frustratingly at the steering wheel.

He shook his head, still finding it difficult to believe that after finding the hair, his souvenirs and sending that letter, the bitch still controlled him.

How could he have been so *stupid* to leave his souvenirs in his drawer and behind the radiator?

His breathing calm now, he continued to watch the women until they were out of sight and then reached down to switch on the radio. Shit, the static reminded him he still hadn't replaced…

The knock on the window startled him and he turned to see a policewoman staring curiously at him, her gloved finger making a circle in the air to indicate he lower his window.

"Eh, hello officer," swallowing with difficulty he managed a nervous smile, now aware that a second policewoman stood slightly behind the first officer.

"Do you have some purpose for parking here, sir, or were you just having a wee fly look at the women?" she asked, her voice calm and monotone and her head level with his as she had an obvious sniff of his breath.

"The women?" he replied, now conscious the other policewoman was at the rear of the Fiesta and hearing her speaking on her radio.

"Let's just say we meet a lot of voyeurs round this area, sir. You know what voyeurs are, don't you? They are the men that like to stare at the girls, the prostitutes. You know," she smiled companionably, "the guys that like looking at the short skirts and the long legs, that kind of thing. Maybe have a wee wank while they're sitting in the darkness in the car," and leaned her head forward to deliberately glance down at his crotch to ensure his trousers were not unzipped. "So, I'll ask you again, *sir*, what's your purpose for parking here? Is it for a wee bit of sexual gratification, have a wee play with yourself while you're watching the ladies across the road there; something like that or what?"

He could hear her partner sniggering behind her and teeth clenched, he replied, "I work round here, in Bothwell Street. I was supposed to meet a colleague here for a drink."

"Bit late for meeting somebody for a drink, is it not?"

"Well," he hesitated, the lie coming quickly, "it's a female colleague. We don't really get much of a chance when we're working, if you get my meaning, officer."

"Oh really," the constable pretended surprise and glancing at his hands gripping the steering wheel, the knuckles white with tension, she added, "and is your wife aware you're meeting a female colleague this evening, sir?"

"My wife?"

"I see you're wearing a wedding ring, sir."

"Oh, ah, no. My wife doesn't know," he shook his head.

"Right then," the constable wearily sighed. "I'll take it as you've been sitting here for over twenty minutes now that your…what did you call her, you *colleague* did you say?" her voice dripping with sarcasm. "It appears that you've been given a dizzy and that she doesn't seem to be turning up, so perhaps you might consider going home to your dear wife, eh?"

"Yes, constable, that sounds like a good idea," he stammered and switched on the engine.

Driving off, he glanced in the mirror, but the two cops had turned away and were walking off in the opposite direction.

He couldn't believe he had gotten away, had thought for those few, awful moments that he was going to be arrested.

His hands shook as he steered the car and then with relief, he remembered.

There was nothing in the car that could incriminate him, for after telling him of her plan Moira had insisted that she take the hammer and wrapped in its bloodstained towel, it now rested in the boot of her Audi.

Tapping the keyboard of the laptop, Eric Kyle searched for the bank's Internet address, furrowing his brow in concentration when the search engine provided him with the contact web address. If what he had been told were true, opening an account with the bank that had its head office in the Republic of Ireland would mean his final lump sum and pension could be transferred there without any problem and his ferret-faced ex-wife would not be able to touch the money, even if she applied to a Scottish court. His eyes danced across the screen as he read the details, smiling when he saw that the tax laws were more favourable than those of the UK and opening a contact box, typed in his current banking account details with the request that an account be opened in his name and transferred one hundred pounds to open the account. He had already decided it was worth a few quid to get the Irish account set up in preparation for the lump sum he would receive when he was officially retired.

He sat back and sipping at the glass of whisky, considered what Charlie Miller had told him. He had to admit it was decent of Cathy Mulgrew to suggest he remain on compassionate leave until such time his official retirement date arrived. Traditionally there would be a pay-off party, though after Paula's murder it could be that his colleagues might instead believe he would prefer a quiet drink somewhere. No matter, he had no intention of attending any sort of function anyway.

He drained the last of the whisky and set the glass down. Thoughts of Ireland reminded him of the sunny holiday he spent there as a youth with his parents, the rolling hills and the camp site a few miles from the Drombeg Stone Circle. He smiled when without difficulty he recalled the face of Marie-Rose, the red-haired, freckled faced girl who he loved for most of the two week holiday and to whom he wrote twice, but never received a response. He remembered at the tender age of thirteen, his introduction by some local lads to Guinness behind Flaherty's pub and the rollicking he received from his mother when he staggered back to the tent, the worse for wear after almost two pints while his father outrageously winked at him behind her back.

The memories decided him and once more he tapped the keyboard for the search engine page, but this time typed in 'cottages for sale, Cork, Ireland.'

Sadie Miller answered the phone in the kitchen and called through to the lounge, "Charlie, phone call."

He smiled and ruffling Geraldine's hair, he picked himself up from the floor and told the little girl, "One more game and then bed, young lady."

"Aw, Dad..." she started to complain, but he was already out the door and heading for the kitchen.

Sadie handed him the phone as he mouthed, "Cathy?" but she shook her head.

"Charlie Miller," he said.

"Charlie? It's Liz Watson. Sorry to call you at home..."

"That's okay, Sherlock," he interrupted, "What can I do for you?"

"Well," she drawled, "I'm not really certain if it's you I should be calling. I heard today that you might be not be returning to the inquiry."

It doesn't take long for bad news to get about he thought, but replied, "Bit of a misunderstanding, Sherlock. I'll be at Stewart Street bright and early tomorrow. So, what's up?"

"Look, I'm sorry to call you at home, Charlie. Maybe it can wait till…"

"Sherlock, if you called me at home it must be something that's troubling you. Shoot."

"Right then, well, it's Paula Kyle's PM. I've just had the Forensic results e-mailed to my business web address. There's something that doesn't quite fit with the previous PM's, something that concerns me, Charlie."

He could hear the uncertainty in her voice and knowing Watson, Miller did not doubt if it was an issue troubling her enough to call him at home, it was worth the time to speak with her.

"Where are you calling from, Sherlock?"

"Eh, I'm at home."

"Alone?"

"Yes, of course. Why?"

"Right, we've the kids to settle down and then Sadie and I will have our dinner, so you're only just over ten minutes away. Pop round and join us for something to eat and we can chat then, okay?"

"Charlie, you're very kind but I couldn't possibly…"

He turned toward Sadie and asked, "Is there enough dinner for Sherlock to join us, hen?"

"Course there is," she smiled, then added, "but tell her to come in a taxi. That will mean I'll have someone to share a bottle of red with."

"Did you hear that?" he asked Watson.

"Yes, I heard, but tell Sadie I'll bring the wine. Say thirty minutes?"

"See you then," he agreed and replaced the phone.

He stared thoughtfully at his wife and said, "It's not like Sherlock to be unsettled about a PM."

"Well, there's no point in you worrying your head about it either, so you get Jellybean upstairs and into her pyjamas and her teeth brushed. I'll see to Ella and when they're in bed, I'll finish making dinner while you can set the table in the kitchen and that means you and Liz can use the dining room later, for your chat."

"Right, boss," he grinned then surprised her when he folded his arms about her and tightly held her close. "Thank God I have you," he quietly told her, but his thoughts were elsewhere, in a place that he really did not want to go.

Ally McGregor was not a happy man, not happy at all. In fact, he was fucking livid.
That he should be taken from the newspaper offices, bundled into the back of a CID car and treated like a common criminal!
Bastards!
Now here he was, pacing back and forth in a smelly detention room at Stewart Street police office.
Him!
The 'Glasgow News' top reporter!
Who the *fuck* do these people think they were dealing with?
Pacing up and down the small room, his rage knew no bounds.
It was jealousy, he thought; jealousy and petty revenge because he showed these polis bastards up, showed them to be the bungling arses they are!
It was his headline that did it, his scoop. They couldn't handle the fact that he had his finger on the pulse, knew where the real story lay, the story he would write when he was released; the story of their incompetence.
That's what it is, he told himself and he didn't miss the sniggers or the smirks of his so called colleagues either while they watched him being manhandled into the car by that cow, Myra McColl.
Fucking detective?
She would get hers, he promised himself.
He would make sure of it.
He would destroy her in print!
The door opened and McColl stepped into the room.
"Mister McGregor," she smiled, oozing the charm of a premenstrual Cobra. "If you would care to follow me, sir?" and then turned in the certain knowledge he would trip along after her.
"Where are we going?"
She stopped and turning, continued to smile as she replied,
"Interview room number two. It's my favourite place. I just *love* the ambience it offers."

"Are you winding me up, you fat cow?" his eyes narrowed in suspicion as he followed her along the narrow corridor.

"Now, now, sir," she pretended to be hurt by his comment. "That's no way to speak to a lady, is it?"

They passed through the main entrance and into the ground floor corridor that housed the CID offices where McColl stopped at an open door and indicated with a wave of her hand that McGregor enter the room.

The room was just as he had seen on multiple police programmes on the television, a small room with just a table and three chairs, one of which was on the other side of the table. He saw that the chair nearest the door was occupied by the young detective who had accompanied McColl when she had detained him. On the table was a tape-recording machine, but it looked to McGregor to be switched off.

"Take a seat please, Mister McGregor," said McColl from behind him as she closed the door.

He moved to occupy the seat that faced them both and sat down, his arms folded and his face like fizz.

"Right, I'm saying fuck all to you people till my lawyer gets here and then when I'm back at my desk, I'll be writing an article about police harassment and I swear that article will tear you pair of bastards a new one!"

"Tut, tut, Mister McGregor," smiled McColl. "There's really no need for you to say anything at all, unless you wish to respond to the charge I am about to libel against you."

"Charge? What fucking charge! I've done fuck all!" he screamed at her, pushing himself up onto his feet, an action that caused Kevin Feeney to rise from his own chair and lean threateningly towards the older man, who faced with the much younger and athletic detective, hastily sat back down.

Taking her time and enjoying every second of McGregor's bewilderment, McColl reached down into her handbag and fetched out her police notebook. Opening the book, she then theatrically licked the end of her pencil and began to write in it.

"What are you doing, what are you writing?" he thundered at her.

"The charge, Mister McGregor, the charge," she smoothly replied.

He knew he wouldn't win with rage and instead decided to try some charm.

"Look, hen…I mean, officer. I have no idea what you believe I've done, but this is all a mistake. Can you not explain…tell me, what this *bloody* charge is that you're talking about? I mean, I'm feeling a wee bit anxious here, a wee bit hurt that the polis should consider me to be anything but one of their biggest supporters."

McColl stopped writing, her face blank and stared at him before she said, "Kevin, could you fetch me a glass of water, please, there's a good lad."

Puzzled though he might have been, Feeney did not reply but stood and left the room, closing the door behind him.

A few second passed before McColl, with unexpected speed for a woman of mature years, leaned across the desk and grabbing McGregor by the hair, pulled him across the desk so that their noses were almost touching.

"Listen to me, you weasel! You've had a good run so far, but it stops here today. You have stabbed too many police inquiries in the back for me to have any consideration for your feelings, so here's why you're being detained. For purchasing information from your tout, Colin Napier."

He would have shouted with joy, but for the fact McColl was still twisting his hair round in her stubby fingers. Buying information? Fuck, is that all they had? Didn't she realise that was standard practise in the newspaper industry?

McGregor grinned cockily at her and as she released her grip to permit him to sit back down, sneered, "You can't do me for that, you stupid cow. So what if I gave Napier some dough for a wee bit of gossip. Reporter's privilege. No judge will convict me for that, so charge me if you dare. You'll get laughed out of court."

She smiled and slowly shook her head. "You don't know, do you? You never gave it a thought, did you?"

She was too confident, too sure of herself and some feeling of apprehension crept across his chest. What had he missed, he wondered.

The door opened to admit Feeney, who handed a paper cup of water to McColl before he resumed his seat.

"You'll have guessed that Mister Napier has provided us with a statement," she said.

"Aye," McGregor nodded, "so what? I'm not denying that I paid him for some information."

"Yes, a hundred quid it was in a brown envelope that bears your initials and is currently being fingerprinted and will, I am confident, have your fingerprints upon it. I will also be taking a DNA sample from you and we'll compare that to the saliva that sealed the envelope."

"You're going to a lot of bother for nothing, hen. You'll never convict me," he grinned, but still that queasy feeling stuck with him.

"Mister Napier," she returned his grin, "as you already know, works within the mortuary at the new hospital."

"So?" he shrugged.

"Do you know who employs Mister Napier?"

"Why the *fuck* would I be interested in who employs him?"

She smiled and though he did not know why, his stomach lurched and his bum cheeks twittered.

"Let me explain in lay man terms, *Mister* McGregor. Colin Napier is a local council employee and of course as a council employee working within an environment like the mortuary, has signed a non-disclosure agreement not to divulge any personal details of the deceased who pass through the mortuary. Therefore, any information that is learned by him in the course of his profession about the deceased and passed or sold by him to a third party for pecuniary purpose or some other purpose, is illegal. Perhaps if Napier had some sort of pang of conscience and believed by telling you about the cut hair he was performing a public service, the Procurator Fiscal might not pursue you, *Mister* McGregor. But that's not what happened, is it? You *paid* Napier for the information, didn't you?" She smiled and added, "That is why you are here, *Mister* McGregor. You will be charged with bribing and corrupting a council employee. You are to be reported to the Procurator Fiscal and will at a later date stand before the Sheriff Court where with Napier you will face a charge of colluding with him to procure information. The evidence, quite apart from Napier's confession that implicates you, is the money you sent him in the envelope that bears your prints and as I am sure our laboratory guys will confirm, will include your DNA that adhered to the sticky part of the envelope when you licked it."

"Now," she opened her notebook again and smiling at the open-mouthed McGregor, added, "While I continue to write the charge down here, perhaps you might like to consider some smart-arse wisecrack as a response?"

Sitting curled upon the armchair in the lounge of her home and dressed in a loose fitting, yellow coloured cotton tracksuit, her hair still damp and tied back with a bobble and her hands wrapped around a mug of coffee, Moira Bain reflected on the evening. Still aching, she had popped four Paracetamol from the blister pack and with complete disregard for the printed instructions, downed them together. She would cope with her sore throat and neck and the discomfort in her breasts and wrists, but if the vaginal pain persisted, she feared that embarrassingly she might have to attend her GP. Bastard! She still could not believe how stupidly naïve she had been leading him into her bedroom like that. What had she been thinking! She sighed for she knew exactly what she had been thinking. She had believed she could control him, that she was brighter and smarter than James.
Yes, she *was* intellectually superior to him, but it was he who was physically stronger and that's where she had made such a stupid blunder.
She slowly sipped at the scalding liquid.
After he had dressed and followed her downstairs, it had taken her a full twenty minutes to explain her plan and still, even after almost two years of marriage, she could not believe how stupid her husband really was.
Or, she wondered, was it she who was really the stupid one for putting up with him?
He had cried like a baby, sobbing as he begged her forgiveness for the terrible things he had done to her, promising that he would seek help.
Watching him weep she had heard, but not listened. It did not matter to her if he sought help or not, for he would never again lay a finger upon her. Their life as a couple was completely over. She already planned that for the foreseeable future they would share the house and appear to be happily married; maybe even for as long as a few months after her plan had worked. Then without fuss she would quietly instruct her lawyer to force him to leave and find somewhere else to live.
At an appropriate time she would file for divorce and be rid of him. He had been gone now for over two hours, hurrying off like a thief in the night.

Bastard!

She sipped at her coffee and glanced at the phone number on the slip of paper in front of her. She suspected when she made the call it would be recorded, though ironically her sore throat would mask her voice for she did not intend leaving any details of how she might be traced. Better the police believe her to be a distraught girlfriend with a grudge than who she really was.

Draining the mug, she placed it on a side table and stared again at the phone number on the scrap of paper.

She would make the call tomorrow, after she had visited his house. There would be no problem getting his house keys, for the personal lockers were seldom secured and besides the company regulations were that no personal property belonging to the staff including bags, coats or jackets was permitted in the warehouse. It would take her less than twenty minutes to get to his home, five minutes there and twenty minutes back, but she would allow herself an hour so that in the unlikely event that anyone should ask, she would explain her absence as her lunch break. However, she was confident that no one would miss her from the office for curiously, her father had arranged to take the day off. Her brow knitted as she remembered that Shelley McPhail, his tart of a receptionist was also taking the day off, but suspicious though she was at the coincidence she dismissed it from her mind. She had far more important matters to concern her. Ironically, with her father and the wee tart McPhail absent from the office, it helped with her plan.

Yes, she smiled without humour to herself; nothing would go wrong. It would begin tomorrow.

"Right you two," Sadie Miller stood up from the kitchen table, "I'll clear away here if you guys want to head through to the dining room and have your chat. And Liz," she grinned and cocked her head to one side, "don't be finishing that bottle of red without me."

Watson returned Sadie's grin and carrying her glass while Charlie Miller carried both the bottle of wine and his coffee, followed him through to the dining room and lifted her briefcase from the hallway as she passed by.

Miller pulled out a chair for Watson and sat opposite her. "Okay, Sherlock, what's so important that you want to discuss it with me right away?"

Placing her glass down onto a mat, Watson sat her briefcase upon her knee and opening it, withdrew a brown coloured cardboard folder that she placed on the table.

"Well, let me begin by saying that I wasn't too comfortable bringing this to the office tomorrow morning and of course I'm delighted that you are to remain on the case, regardless of what I had been told." She paused to draw breath and continued, "Like I said on the phone, Charlie, I had the Forensics e-mail the results of the PM on Paula Kyle and frankly…" she bit at her lower lip. "Look, I could be wrong."

"Well, if you are, that'll be a first," he smiled encouragingly at her.

"Yes, well, the thing is Charlie…"

"Liz," he leaned across the tale, "just tell me. Please."

She stared at him then her professionalism kicked in. "You know from the many PM's that you have attended with me and other pathologists that we all have different ways of conducting our examinations, of doing things. One of the methods I favour when examining the deceased and where a weapon has been used to puncture or in some other manner cause injury to the body is that after the initial examination, I have the wound shaved of any head hair or surrounding body hair so that I might be able to fully examine and measure the wound without hindrance. I also instruct that the wound be measured and photographed and these photographs become part of my record of the examination. The photographs also assist me at subsequent trials or Fatal Accident Inquiries when explaining the injury or wound to a jury or a Sheriff."

"I get that, Liz," he held up his hand.

Her brow furrowed and again he saw her chew at her lower lip. "The thing is, Charlie, while I am almost certain that the weapon used to murder your four victims was a carpenter's claw hammer, I'm not so certain that the fourth victim, Paula Kyle was murdered by the same weapon."

He sat back in his chair, stunned for a few seconds before he asked, "How did you arrive at this… this uncertainty?"

"Well," she fished in the file for A4 sized colour photographs and laying them out on the table facing towards him, said, "here are our victims starting on your left with Linda Docherty, then Allison McVeigh, thirdly, Janice Maxwell and lastly Paula Kyle. Each photograph shows the wound on the back of the head after the hair has been shaved off."

"I see that," he peered at the photographs, "but to be honest, all the wounds look the same to me."

"Ah, but that's where the Forensics come in," she pushed a printed sheet of paper across the table to him. "If you look at the diameter of the wounds on the first three victims, they are almost the exact same. However," he noted a touch of excitement in her voice, "Paula Kyle's wound is clearly five millimetres larger."

"I am going to be the Devils Advocate here, Liz, but couldn't the extra five mil be caused by the hammer going in at a different angle? It's hardly evidence of a different weapon, is it?"

"That's what I argued when I read the report," she replied, "the wounds are almost circular, like you would find on the head of a carpenters hammer, Charlie, but the five millimetres seem to suggest the head of the weapon that killed Paula is of a different hammer. Yes," she nodded, "while I suspect it *is* probably a carpenter's hammer, on this occasion I am almost certain a different carpenter's hammer was used. On the back of the e-mail I received from Forensics, I phoned and spoke with a friend of mine, Davie Smillie, who has done some work for me replacing my kitchen and other things about the house. Davie tells me that basically there are two type of hammer heads on carpenters hammers; a twenty millimetre head and a twenty-five millimetre head and of course there are different weights for hammers depending on what they are used for. The larger twenty-five millimetre head is for a heavier hammer, such as the type used on building sites when driving in thicker nails. However," she became more animated, "the point is that the hammer used to kill the first three victims was almost certainly twenty millimetres wide whereas the hammer used to kill Paula Kyle, and I'm almost certain about this Charlie, was a twenty-five millimetre wide head."

She stopped and sipped at her wine and then reminded him, "Do you recall when we had the meeting in your office and I mentioned the seminar I attended regarding serial killers?"

"I do," he nodded, "and to be frank, what you told us worries me no end."

"Well, this new issue of the different sized hammer heads has raised the question, Charlie. Is your killer changing tactics or…" she shrugged, seemingly unwilling to continue.
A cold shiver run down his spine and though he already knew the answer she would give, he had to ask the question anyway.
"So, Liz, what does this information lead you to conclude?"
She stared at him as she slowly replied, "I'm sorry, Charlie, but it leads me to conclude that either our killer of the first three young women used a different hammer to murder Paula Kyle or as I strongly suspect, she was murdered by someone else; someone who must have had information about the previous three victims having their head hair cut from them after their death. It seems, Charlie, that you might have a copycat killer on your hands."

## CHAPTER FIFTEEN

Charlie Miller was first into the office that morning, greeting the weary-eyed cleaners as they went about their labours. The young civilian analyst in the incident room, her feet raised to sit upon another chair and her long red coloured coat covering her like a blanket, was dozing in the chair behind her desk when he entered. She came awake with a start when she saw the DCI tiptoeing towards the table that was crowded with a kettle, mugs, coffee and tea.
"Oh, good morning sir," she jumped to her feet, instantly awake.
"Hello there, I'm sorry if I disturbed you," he smiled at her, inwardly cursing that he could not recall the young lassie's name. "Quiet night then?"
"Ah, yes sir," she hesitantly replied, resisting the temptation to rub at her eyes. "No phone calls through the night, sir, and no new information."
He could see the young woman was fighting sleep and lifting the kettle, shook it and found it full before asking, "What time does your shift officially finish, hen?"
"Ah, at eight-thirty, sir."
He glanced at his wristwatch. "That's just gone seven the now. Right then, you are relieved young lady, so get yourself up the road and thanks for your input last night. I'm sure it must have been boring

for you, but I'm glad you were here to man the office and the telephone. One thing though, are you driving?"

"Yes, sir," she stared at him slight confused by the question.

"Well, be careful. You look half asleep and I don't want you having an accident, okay?" he smiled at her.

Her eyes widened and she returned his smile in gratitude before replying, "Thank you, sir."

The girl grabbed her coat and handbag and was gone in record time. Grinning at her haste, Miller plugged the kettle into the socket and was spooning coffee into a mug when the phone on the departed girls desk rung.

Striding across the room, he lifted the phone and answered, "Incident room," but got no further when a young woman's voice abruptly said, "Get me that young lassie who's supposed to be manning the incident room hotline and now, please!"

The one thing that always set Miller's teeth on edge was bad manners and he decided that the woman was not being assertive, but just plain rude. He guessed that whoever she was she did not expect to be speaking to anyone but the young civilian nightshift analyst.

"Who's calling, please?" he politely asked.

"It doesn't matter who the fuck's calling," the woman sharply replied, "just get me that wee girl who's supposed to be there on the phone, doing her job!"

"Oh, I'll ask again. Who's calling, please?"

There was an exasperated, snorting sound before the woman hissed, "It's DC Fraser at Crimestoppers. Now, are you getting me that wee lassie or what!" thundered the voice.

"Actually, she's gone home," Miller calmly replied.

The pause led him to believe that Fraser did not expect that response and she answered, "Who the *fuck* let her go early and by the way, who are you?"

Miller inwardly grinned, then replied, "It was me who let her go early and eh," he paused, savouring the moment, "I'm Detective Chief Inspector Charlie Miller. So, DC Fraser from Crimestoppers. What can *I* do for you?"

He could almost hear the sharp intake of breath and imagined the woman wilting. In a more subdued voice, she replied, "Ah, sorry sir. Eh, yes, well, it's about the ah, murders, sir."

"The murders," he calmly repeated. "Yes?"

"Eh, it's just to inform you, sir, the incident room I mean, that we've had a number of phone calls through the night recorded on our tape machines regarding the hair cut from the victims. Callers firing in suspects names and eh, bit and pieces of information."

"So, these bits and pieces of information, DC Fraser, will be collated and forwarded to my incident room. Is that correct?"

"Yes sir, this morning, sir. I'll see it gets done, sir."

"But I'm assuming that if you have already sorted out the wheat from the chaff, there's really nothing of particular interest in the information Crimestoppers received, for if there was you wouldn't be on the blower harassing some young civilian analyst, but bringing the information over here yourself. Correct again, DC Fraser?"

"Sir," was the quiet response.

"Thank you for your call, DC Fraser, and if I might be so bold as to offer you some advice?"

"Sir?"

"I've found that courtesy costs nothing and goes a long way when seeking cooperation from a colleague, regardless of that colleagues rank or position in the police. Enjoy the rest of your day, DC Fraser," he ended the call and then he shook his head. No matter how long he had served in the polis, there was always some arse trying to make a name for himself or herself at the expense of others. He thought about what Fraser had told him and sighed. It had started. Ally McGregor's revelation at the press conference had opened the floodgates. The nutters and every bampot in Glasgow was now coming out of the woodwork, claiming to have some knowledge about the cut hair.

"Morning, boss," said the voice at his back.

He turned to see a grinning Mark Barclay hanging his coat up on a wall hook and narrowed his eyes. "Somehow you don't seem to be surprised to see me here this morning, Mark. A wee birdie been whispering in your ear?"

"Actually, a good looking raven haired birdie with a fabulous figure and a better salary than me," grinned Barclay as he made his way to the kettle. "Ma'am phoned me last night at home with the good news and on that point; as far as I'm aware none of the team know about you being dismissed, so it's a moot point about you being reinstated. Ma'am also said to tell you that if she can she will pop by later, but she's away this morning to Cumbernauld office. Something about

the DI there having a bit of a problem regarding two families and allegations of abuse with some weans. Sound nasty," Barclay shook his head as he poured the boiled water into a mug.
"Aye, you're right. Anything involving child abuse is nasty," Miller agreed as he sipped at his coffee, then smacking his lips together said, "Right, first thing's first. Any updates?"
"You know that Myra McColl got a result regarding the mortuary?"
"Yeah, but I've still to hear details."
"I'll get her to come and see you when she gets in," Barclay told him, then added, "Apart from that and a number of Actions still outstanding, not a lot doing I'm sorry to say."
"Well, for my part I've a couple of things for you that will require Actions being allocated. A DC Fraser from Crimestoppers will be sending some information over regarding calls received since McGregor disclosed to all and sundry about our victims' hair being cut. Likely they'll all be the usual nutters, but we still need to make the inquiry," he sighed.
"That's going to cause a few Actions. And the other thing?"
"Sherlock called by my place last night. She has some interesting info that I'd like to share with you, Elaine Hamilton and Cathy Mulgrew, but if Ma'am isn't here till later this morning, I'll speak with you and Jean when she gets in."
"She is in," Hamilton called from the doorway.
"Morning, Jean," they both said in unison as they turned and greeted her.
"I was saying to Mark that I'd like to speak with you both, when you're ready," Miller told her.
"Anytime, sir," Hamilton nodded with a smile, but Barclay frowned and staring pointedly at Miller said, "No problem, but I'll be heading out after that. I've allocated myself an Action to track down and speak with Paula Kyle's pal Jill Hardie, the woman that Eric thinks might have been exerting some kind of eh," he glanced quickly at Hamilton before replying, "inappropriate influence over his wife."
"Okay," Miller realised that Barclay might not wish Hamilton to know of Kyle's suspicions about his wife and added, "well, if you have that Action to deal with, we'll maybe wait till Cathy Mulgrew gets here and that way I won't have to repeat what Sherlock told me last night."

Both agreed and he turned to head into his office, quietly pleased that he was still there as the SIO and not a carrying a cardboard box to pack his things away.

It had been his lifetime habit that Arthur Freeman always arrived before eight am at his office and this morning was no exception. Unfortunately for his staff officer and secretary, they were expected to commence work before their boss and were at their desks when he thundered through the door like a runaway steam train. They both stood respectfully when he entered, but the expression upon his face indicated the kind of day they expected to have and their hearts sank. "Get me the Chief Constable on the phone," he snapped his fingers at his secretary as he passed her by and slammed his office door behind him.

Now seated behind his desk, he impatiently drummed his fingers while he waited on the call being put through and was about to bark out at the intolerable delay, when his phone rang.

"Please hold for the Chief Constable," the female voice politely said. Almost a full minute passed and his rage at being kept waiting grew. At last, Martin Cairney calmly said, "Good morning, Arthur. How are you today?"

"Good morning, Chief Constable," he coldly replied. "I'm calling about a decision I made regarding one of my DCI's. A decision that I have learned this morning was overturned sir, by you!"

"You mean DCI Miller. Yes, Arthur, I did rescind your decision and for that I apologise; however, I had my reasons."

Freeman was furious, but fought the anger that threatened to spill over and forcing himself to remain calm, icily asked, "Would you care to disclose those reasons, sir?"

"My decision, Arthur, was based on the operational morale of the officers currently involved in the investigation regarding the murders of four young women in Glasgow city centre. I believe that it would be highly detrimental to the morale of the inquiry team to have their SIO dismissed at such a crucial time and the backlash from the media would undoubtedly be critical of your decision to appoint Mister Miller as SIO in the first place."

Freeman was stunned and stammered, "But I didn't appoint Miller as you well know. He just happened to be the senior divisional CID officer in situ who quite naturally took the case on."

"Yes, Arthur, *we* both know that," Cairney smoothly replied, "but of course the media would not be interested in the natural order of our rank structure. No, they would be seeking someone to lambast, a scapegoat as it were for our failure to detect this individual who is murdering these women. Naturally Miller would be their first choice, but I firmly believe *you* would also be caught in the backlash."
Freeman turned pale and ground his teeth, his knuckles white and his fist threatening to crush the plastic handle of the phone as he listened to Cairney's bullshit. He had been stymied and shafted, good and proper. To complain now would seem petulant and in particular as Cairney was taking the line that his decision was for Freeman's own good. His instinct was to rage at Cairney, to call him the backstabbing bastard that he was, but instead he evenly replied, "Thank you for your consideration, Chief Constable."
"No problem, Arthur," Cairney politely replied and then to Freeman's outrage, added, "I like to keep abreast of what's happening with my ACC's and consider their welfare and ambition as much as I'm certain they consider the welfare of the officers under their command. Good morning, Arthur."
He was still holding the phone to his ear after the call had ended and wondering, was that a veiled threat? Did Cairney suspect or God forbid, know that he was soliciting the backing of the other ACC's and some of the councillors on the Police and Fire Committee to usurp Cairney from his position as the Chief?
Was it possible that somehow or other, Cairney had learned of his own ambition to be recommended for the post of Chief Constable? His stomach tensed for political animal that he was, he was now almost certain that Cairney was aware of the moves his ACC was making to get rid of him.
That was it, then he decided; the gloves were off.
Now he had two bastard's careers to ruin.
Cairney's *and* Miller's.

After a sleepless night, Martin Craven arose early and took a leisurely shower before dressing and going downstairs where he made himself a light breakfast.
He continued to worry about the medical examination he was to endure later that morning and almost accepted that whatever was

wrong with him would be life changing, while privately praying it was not life threatening.

He glanced at the wall clock. Shelley had suggested getting a taxi to his home and travelling from there with him in the taxi to Ross Hall, but instead he insisted he pick her up in his car and made her smile by intimating it would give him that little more time to spend with her.

He decided there was time to phone his son and remind him that his father was taking the day off, but if there was any need for Davie to contact Martin he would have his mobile with him.

He smiled when Davie answered the call, hearing the strain in his son's voice as he spoke with Martin and tried to feed a whining Elsa.

"You in the middle of it, son?"

"Aye, Dad. The childminder's running a bit late because of an accident on the M8 and this wee one doesn't want to go to nursery today, do you pet," Davie's voice faded as he turned his head away to speak with his daughter. "Don't worry though," he was back on the line, "I'll still get to work on time and I'll be sitting in the big man's chair today," he laughed.

Martin was puzzled. Davie sounded quite chirpy considering that he hated being in charge and curiosity getting the better of him, he asked, "Everything okay, son? I mean, you feeling all right?"

"Great Dad, I'm feeling great."

Some unexplainable instinct kicked in and eyes narrowing, Martin asked, "You seeing someone, some girl?"

"Why'd you ask?"

"I dunno, it's just, well, you sound…happy, son."

He heard the intake of breath and tensely, Davie replied, "Yes Dad, I'm seeing someone. Just be pleased for me, eh? Please, this once, be happy for me."

But Martin was not pleased.

Martin was worried though this was not the time to tell his son that. "Okay Davie, look, why don't we get together, like a family; you, me and the wee one and you can tell me about this girl, this woman I mean. We'll go out and have a slap up meal, maybe McDonalds? You know how I'm really into them happy meals and the plastic toys you get with them."

Davie softly laughed, the tension in his voice now eased and he replied, "Okay Dad, sounds like a plan. So, why the day off? What you up to, you old rogue?"
Caught off foot, Martin stammered, "Oh, just a bit of this and that, you know?"
"I suppose it's just a coincidence that Shelley's off today, too?"
"Shelley? Oh, aye, of course it is. What are you suggesting, son?"
"Nothing Dad, nothing," said Davie, but Martin could hear the fun in his voice. "But if by any chance you should bump into her, tell her I owe her one and I'm really grateful. I like Shelley, Dad. She's a cracking lassie."
Martin was confused. What the hell was Davie talking about, he owed her one and he was really grateful? And that comment about liking Shelley and her being a cracking lassie. Was his son giving some sort of veiled permission for Martin's relationship with the young woman?
"Well," he carefully answered, "I can't think *why* I'd bump into her on her day off, but if I should, I'll pass your message on."
"Aye, Dad, you do that," and as he ended the call, a red-faced Martin could almost swear that above Elsa's crying, he could hear Davie laughing.

Mark Barclay stopped the CID car and pulling into a parking bay in Dumbarton Road, again checked the Glasgow A to Z map. Jill Hardie's home address hadn't been hard to find. According to the numerous entries on the PNC, Hardie was known to the police for minor drug dealing, shoplifting, breach of the police and minor assault as well as importuning. Surprisingly though that having accrued a number of fines, she had never served a custodial sentence. It occurred to him it might have been wise to bring Myra McColl with him, but she was engaged in other duties. Besides, he knew that Charlie Miller wanted Eric Kyle's suspicion of Paula's soliciting to be kept as tight as possible for it was bad enough the poor guy's wife was murdered. The last thing Kyle needed was gossip that his wife was prostituting herself.
According to the map, Hardie's flat was another hundred yards in front and off to the right, so checking his way was clear, he pulled out and less than a minute later was parking in Drysdale Street. The recently built flats seemed to Barclay to be a mixture of council and

privately owned and from memory, the area had come upmarket since he had been a young DC working in the Partick sub-division. Not that he was overly familiar with the area, but he had on occasion attended inquiries in the nearby streets.

He glanced up at the flat listed for Hardie and saw a woman's face duck away from the window. Well, he thought, at least someone is in.

Making his way to the door he suspected she must have been standing behind it for he had barely knocked when it was pulled open.

The woman stood there, blonde and heavyset and wearing a stained nightdress and in her bare feet, her heavy bosom hanging and clearly without a bra, looked like she'd been dragged backwards through a hedge.

She stared at him and he thought her baggy eyes was likely the result of a drinking binge if the smell from her was anything to go by.

"Miss Jill Hardie?" he politely asked.

"Who are you," she slurred.

"My name's Mark Barclay, I'm a Detective Inspector with the CID at…"

Curiously, he got no further as angrily she tried to slam the door, but Barclay had been to too many doors in his time and already he had a foot jamming it open.

Realising that the door would not close, Hardie snarled, "Have you got a warrant?"

"Do I need a warrant to ask you about your friend, Paula Kyle," he politely replied.

To his surprise, Hardie's eyes watered and blinking back tears, she turned wordlessly and beckoned he follow her through to the lounge.

The place was a mess with empty beer cans and spirit bottles lying about and the odious smell of cheap wine, cigarettes and cannabis hanging in the fetid air.

Hardie slumped down into an armchair and indicated he sit on the couch.

"Do you want a drink?" she slurred.

"A bit early for me, Jill. Can I call you Jill?"

"Whatever," she waved a hand at him and reached for a glass on a table by her arm, though what the clear liquid was he could not guess.

"You mentioned Paula. It's true then, she's really dead?"

"Oh aye, Jill. Murdered like three other young women in the city centre."

"Stupid cow, I told her she should have come to the casino with me," her lips trembled.

It took him over half an hour to elicit the story of Hardie and Paula Kyle meeting in Lauders pub, of attending the show at the Pavilion and of parting outside; Hardie to wander down to the casino where she met with a male friend and Paula Kyle to the underground car park in Cowcaddens, where she met with her death.

It took another half hour of patient questioning for Barclay to learn that Jill Hardie had a number of men friends who worked on the oilrigs and who on their shore time, liked the sexual company of women without the hassle of the women being wives or girlfriends. At no time would Hardie refer to these men or the circle of women she knew as anything but 'friends' and Barclay knew that while Hardie was obviously the contact between the men and women, the Madam as it were, proving it would be difficult. Besides, he reasoned, he was more interested in identifying the male clients than prosecuting bored or penniless housewives for prostitution.

"Tell me about the guy that Paula might have been seeing, the man who drives a red coloured Volvo. You do know what type of car that a Volvo is, Jill?"

"Course I do, I'm not stupid," she sleepily snapped at him.

He let her calm down and was about to prompt her when she said, "Chris. He's the guy with the big fancy red car. Chris Martin that works on the rigs off Aberdeen, I think it is."

"Chris Martin," he slowly repeated. "How close were Paula and this guy Chris?"

She stared at him as if he were stupid. "Close? He was shagging her, that's how close they were," she giggled.

"I mean, was it a…"

"Was he paying her? Course he was," she scoffed, "and good money too. Paula was popular with the men. A lot of them wanted to contact her when they come ashore from the rigs."

Barclay felt his stomach knotting. This was turning out to be a can of worms. If Eric Kyle discovered this; Jesus, it would tear the poor guy apart.

"Can you tell me the names of the men who Paula was seeing?"

She shook her head. "I'd get phone calls and then I'd text Paula with an address, usually a pub or a hotel. I didn't always get their second names either."

"But you're certain about Chris being Chris Martin?"

"Aye, that's for sure," she said and he realised her voice was becoming more slurred, that she was not far off sleep.

"Do you have any more details for Chris Martin, Jill? Where he lives or anything?"

"No, and there's no use in looking at my phone," she added. "Once I get the call and pass the information on to my friends, I always delete the number." She cocked a finger against the side of her nose and grinned. "Just in case you bastards come calling, pardon my French," she giggled again.

He checked her phone anyway and she was correct. There was no incoming calls listed.

"See, I told you," she sneered then said, "He's offshore. I'm sure he told me that he wanted to see Paula before he went offshore. Aye, I remember now. He's away for three weeks."

He realised he would get nothing further and telling her that he might come back again, left her ready to drop off to sleep in the armchair.

It was as he prepared himself to leave that Hardie crooked a finger and licking at her dry and cracked lips, said in a low voice, "There's something else you should know."

He stared at her and guessed she wasn't too keen on imparting the information, but decided not to ask, just wait for her continuing.

"Sometimes there were bruises. On her arms and her tits, I mean. Not all the time, but sometimes."

His eyes narrowed. "Was this from the clients…I mean, the men friends or are you telling me that Paula's husband…"

"No, I'm not saying it was him. Christ, the number of men she shagged it could have been any of them," she sniffed, her eyebrows raised in what Barclay assumed was her private opinion of the male gender.

"What I'm, saying is that he *must* have seen the bruises, do you understand? If it wasn't him and he must have been shagging her as well," she tapped the side of her nose with her finger, "do you not think her man must have wondered how she got them?"

"She never told you who did it, then; who gave her the bruises."

"No," Hardie shook her head. "I knew there was bruising because sometimes she got changed into her other clothes here at my flat before she went out to meet the clients…I mean, the gentlemen friends, so occasionally I saw her undressed, but she wouldn't talk about it."

Closing the front door of the flat behind him, Barclay took a deep breath and shook his head.

Jill Hardie was a piece of work and her information would need to be followed up, but worst than that he had a feeling in his gut that he had just come to a dead end, that while Paula Kyle might have been prostituting herself with oilrig workers, it took them no further in identifying her killer.

As it happened, Cathy Mulgrew arrived at Charlie Miller's office just as he was receiving the report from Myra McColl about her detention of the 'Glasgow News' reporter, Ally McGregor. Slipping through the door, she waved them both back to their seats and listened as Miller asked, "I take it he was released for report, Myra?"

"Correct, boss. The duty Inspector agreed that detaining him in custody was unnecessary and he was released on an undertaking. That will give me time to have the DNA evidence returned from the Lab and available when I compile a report to the Procurator Fiscal."

"Not a happy man, I suppose," grinned Miller.

"Not happy at all," McColl shook her head and then added, "and he will be a lot unhappier when he reads the rival newspapers this morning."

"Oh?"

"Aye," she wheezed as she adopted an air of innocence. "It seems that some bad bugger anonymously phoned a couple of local news desks last night to let them know that Ally McGregor of the 'Glasgow News' was arrested by the polis on corruption charges. I don't expect his boss at his paper will be too happy to learn that," she waved the forefinger of both hands in the air, "His chief crime reporter is the front page news in the rival editions."

Miller stifled a grin and as procedure dictated, asked, "You'd know nothing about that I suppose, Detective Sergeant McColl?"

"Nothing at all, sir," she cheerfully lied.

From behind her, Mulgrew grinned. "Ah, well Myra, what is it they say? What goes around, comes around?"

"Something like that, Ma'am," agreed McColl, "though if I'm really honest with you, when I send my report into the PF there's a likelihood that he'll put his pen through it. You know what the Fiscal service is like; they do not want any trouble with the media and chances are that both Napier and McGregor will be lucky to get warning letters, let alone a court date. That said, it will keep him worrying for a couple of months while the PF makes his mind up."
"Serves the bugger right. He has caused a lot of damage to police inquiries in his time and was not beyond lying either. However, the sad truth is the bugger did some damage to our inquiry before we caught him, though," sighed Miller. Then he explained, "Mark Barclay's dealing with at least a dozen Crimestoppers reports that came in through the night, each of them requiring Actions. Crimestoppers has previously been a great help in a number of inquiries I've been involved in, but there's always some idiot phoning in with information that tends to divert the course of the inquiry until the information is proven to be a totally false or a malicious lead."
"Well, with not a lot to be going on, if nothing else it will give your team something to do in the meantime, Charlie," suggested Mulgrew.
"Will that be all, boss," asked McColl, rising from her chair.
"Yes, thanks, Myra and be sure to tell that lad of yours, well done to you both."
"On that point, boss," McColl hesitated, on hand on the door, "I know he's only been with the department for a few months now, but I think young Kevin's a keeper."
"For the department or you, Myra," Mulgrew saucily grinned.
"Need to be the department, Ma'am," McColl returned the grin as she went through the door. "The poor wee soul wouldn't last five minutes with me on top of him."
"Hoy, I'm sitting here, you know," complained Miller, shaking his head in pretend disgust. "Honestly, you two are giving me a red face," then almost as an afterthought, added, "Myra. Ask Mark and Elaine Hamilton to come in, please."
Occupying the chair McColl just vacated, Mulgrew stared at him and smiled. "And it *is* nice to see you sitting there, Charlie."
He stared at her and simply said, "Thanks, Cathy."

She nodded, both knowing that nothing else needed to be said, that had the tables been turned her best friend Charlie Miller would have done the exact same for her.

"Right," she took a deep breath, "now that we've got *that* out of the way, what's the latest on the murders?"

"Hang on a bit please, Cathy, I'm waiting on…" but just then the door opened to admit Barclay and Hamilton who slipped into the room. However, as the two pulled out chairs to sit down his eyes narrowed at the look of anger on Barclay's face and he said, "What?"

"Sorry to tell you this, boss, but I had a phone call a minute ago from the Detective Superintendent in charge of the MIU. He sends his regrets but has to inform you that he's been instructed to deploy extra officers onto a Greenock murder inquiry." Barclay paused and with a quick glance at Mulgrew who was slowly shaking her head, he continued. "I know him, boss. He's a good man and he wouldn't mess you about. He also told me on the QT that there is no real need for extra officers down at the Greenock office, that it looks like a domestic beating that got out of hand, but that it was ACC Freeman who called him personally and instructed his guys were to be re-deployed to there. He asked that I let you know his hands are tied."

Miller glanced at Mulgrew who simply shrugged her shoulders for the message was clear; cutting down Miller's resources was Freeman's way of sticking the knife in.

"No matter, we'll get by," said Miller cheerfully, but that wasn't how he was feeling. "Right, guys, before I gather the team together for the morning briefing," then wryly added, "or what's left of them anyway, I have something to tell you. As usual, it's privileged information, so let's keep it tight. I had a visit last night at home from Sherlock," he begun and over the next few minutes, proceeded to relate the pathologist's findings and suspicions.

Of course, there were questions, but all Miller could do was repeat Watson's observations and what she had learned about the difference in the wounds suffered by the first three victims and latterly, Paula Kyle.

Elaine Hamilton, her eyes narrowed and biting at her lower lip, said, "What I don't understand though, sir…"

Miller stared at her, his eyes coaxing the question from her.

"What I *don't* understand," she slowly repeated, "is if Doctor Watson thinks the killer of Paula Kyle is a copycat killer and her body was discovered *before* the reporter Ally McGregor disclosed the cut hair at the press conference..."

"Aye, that's right, Jean," he slowly nodded.

"Okay, so at the time of Paula's murder, when the killer removed her hair it was not public knowledge. How then would a copycat killer know to cut off and remove Paula's hair?"

So there it was, he inwardly shivered, the elephant in the room. The unspoken suggestion that he had been trying to push to the back of his mind; if Watson was correct and it *was* a copycat killing, then the killer must have had prior knowledge of the victims hair being cut. He stared wordlessly for a few seconds at the civilian analyst with that same old feeling, like a long forgotten friend; the feeling of a cold chill running down his spine.

As if reading his mind, Cathy Mulgrew interjected and said, "Perhaps before you consider a *second* killer, Charlie, you might concentrate your inquiry on finding the killer of the first three victims." She shrugged as if dismissing the possibility of a second killer and continued, "It's more than likely that for some reason known only to himself or herself, the killer used a different hammer. I would urge you to concentrate all your effort and resources on the killer of the first three women and I'm certain the murder of Paula Kyle will fall into place."

He glanced at her and recognised the steely-eyed Cathy Mulgrew of old.

Do not get ahead of yourself, her stare told him; do not go off on a tangent. One hurdle at a time, but unaware that she in turn had seen something in his eyes. Charlie Miller had a suspicion and now wasn't the time to discuss it.

"Perhaps you're right, ma'am," he slowly replied then as if perked up, added, "That's what we'll do. In the absence of any further information, at this time we're looking for one killer. Agreed?"

It did not escape his notice that Barclay and in particular, Elaine Hamilton were a little ill at ease and slow in agreeing.

"Well, now that's settled," he attempted a little cheerfulness, "if you guys don't mind, I'll have a word with Ma'am."

When the other two had left the room and before he could speak, Mulgrew raised a hand to stem any protest and sharply said,

"Charlie! I can guess what's going on in that head of yours! You know it's not like me to pull rank and I certainly don't want to do it today with you, but I insist, I categorically *insist*," she slapped a hand down hard onto his desk, "that you concentrate on finding the killer of the first three victims! When that is done and you have the killer in custody and if there is *any* dubiety about Paula Kyle's murder, we will concentrate together in solving it. Clear?"
He took a deep breath and nodding his head, said, "Clear."
"Right then," she stood up from her chair, "before I head back to Gartcosh, let's go together and brief your team and do what you do best," she smiled grimly at him. "Motivate people."

Ensuring that Cathy Mulgrew was gone, Mark Barclay met with Charlie Miller in the DCI's office and closed the door.
"I tracked down Paula Kyle's friend, Jill Hardie. A real piece of work," he shook his head. "Much as I hate to tell you this, it seems if Hardie is to be believed and to be honest, I've no doubt she was telling the truth, then Paula *was* prostituting herself.
"Just as Eric suspected," muttered Miller. "Is there anything that you learned that might help us?"
"Well, the guy that Eric saw leaving in the red coloured Volvo seems to be a man called Christopher Alexander Martin, aged forty-three with a home address in East Kilbride. My inquiries revealed that Martin is currently working a three-week shift on an oilrig off the Aberdeen coast and has been since the evening of the day Eric saw him. Martin's married with kids and when he's ashore, found an excuse to meet with Paula for…" he hesitated. "Well, let's just say Paula wasn't the faithful wife she might have been and was earning extra money on the side. The short story is Martin was travelling off-shore when Paula was attending the theatre, so he has a rock solid alibi."
"Was he the only man she was seeing?"
"According to Hardie, no, but she hasn't got a list or full names. Does all her contacting by mobile phone and erases the numbers when the contacts are passed on."
Barclay shook his head and continued, "Look, boss, for what it's worth I think we're chasing a dead end here with how Paula was earning her money and if we continue down this road it will not just deflect the investigation from the real killer, but open a can or

worms that we'll never be able to get the lid back on." He sighed and added, "Apart from that if it becomes an open inquiry it will utterly destroy Eric Kyle's memory of his wife and might reflect badly upon him, too."

"So Eric, you're suggesting that the line of inquiry regarding Paula prostituting herself isn't worthy of investigation?"

Barclay stared tight-lipped at Miller before slowly nodding. He knew that his reputation as an investigator with over two decades of experience was at risk, but he had made hard decisions in the past and replied, "I'd stake my career on it. It's just too coincidental that one of Paula's…clients, would murder her with the exact MO as the previous three murders. No, boss, I don't think it's worth pursuing; at least not at this time."

To his relief, Miller replied, "Well, Mark, if I can't trust your judgement then it's a sorry day. Right then, here's what we'll do. Put your visit down onto a statement form with a summarised conclusion that I agree with your opinion and we'll file Paula's extra-curriculum activities for now. If the very worst happens and the shit hits the fan, then you and I will again raise the inquiry regarding Paula's clients and take our smack on the arse. Okay with you?"

"Okay with me, boss," nodded Barclay, pleased that Miller was openly backing his DI's conclusion, then added, "There's one more thing that you should know. Jill Hardie told me that on several occasions she had seen bruising on Paula's arms and her breasts. When she questioned her about the bruises, Paula refused to say how she had come by them. I asked if she thought it might have been Paula's husband, but she didn't know, though she did remark that he couldn't have failed to see the bruises. When you were at the PM, did you see any bruising on her body?"

"No, I can't recall that," he reached into his basket and retrieved a sheaf of paperwork from which he selected a report. "This is Sherlock's PM result." He quickly glanced through the paperwork and then shook his head. "As I thought, nothing about bruising, but curious that Hardie mentioned it, eh?"

"Aye, and even more curious that Eric Kyle didn't," muttered Barclay.

Turning to leave the office, Barclay could not know that his boss had unconsciously discounted Paula Kyle's clients as suspects and would have been shocked to discover what was really going through Charlie Miller's mind.

It had been a regular complaint of hers, that her office window that faced into the rear car park was far too narrow to allow sufficient sunlight into the small dark and drab room, but today she had no complaint for standing by the window, she was able to see him when he arrived in his car.
She watched as he locked the car and waved to someone who was out of her sight and presumably at the rear staff entrance to the warehouse. It would take him but a few moments to get his jacket and keys into his locker and then start work in the warehouse. Impatiently and a little nervous, she waited for a full five minutes and was about to leave her office when the internal phone rang.
"Hello?"
"Hi sis, it's me. You probably know Dad's taken the day off?"
"Yes, I *am* aware, Davie, though God knows what he's planning to do. He never takes time off from the business," she replied and suspiciously again wondered at Shelley McPhail also being off.
He was used to her insolence when addressing him so her attitude washed over him. "The thing is Moira, he's asked me to sit in at his desk, so if there are any problems that arise…"
"Yes, yes, I'll be here for most of the day," she replied, her free hand idly playing with the silk scarf about her neck that hid the finger marks upon her throat. Hastily she added, "Unless of course I'm having lunch."
"You can have lunch with me in the canteen," he suggested with a grin, knowing how she would respond.
True to form, Moira, her voice dripping with sarcasm, sneered, "And sit downstairs with those morons discussing last night's soaps on the TV? Really? No, thank you. Now, was there anything else?"
"No, not that I can think of," but she had already ended the call.
He shook his head at her abruptness. Moira had never changed since they were children, always the one who had to have the last word. Now, standing in his father's office, he glanced about him. Yes, he could cope for today, but this was definitely a short-term thing. He would never reconcile to the idea of assuming control of the business when his father…stepped down? Yes, he would prefer to think of dad stepping down, rather than the alternative. He walked round to

the other side of the desk and slowly sank into the padded luxury of the swivel chair.
One day, yes; he could cope with one day.

She stared at the handset and taking a deep breath, steeled herself as she grabbed her handbag and left her office before making her way unseen down to the staff locker room.

He parked the car in a bay outside the entrance, but before he got out of the drivers seat, Shelley reached across and squeezed his hand. The canopied entrance to Ross Hall Hospital, built to connect the red-bricked former baronial mansion and the new, state of the art steel and glass construction, beckoned the reluctant Martin Craven to its doors. Walking at his side, her hand clasped in his, Shelley carried a small holdall he had packed in the event he might be admitted for observation.
Embarrassed that anyone seeing them should wonder at the middle-aged man and the tall, pretty, teenager holding hands, he had suggested that if asked, she say she was his daughter.
She did not protest, but simply replied, "Whatever makes you comfortable…Dad," and caused him to nervously laugh.
The smiling receptionist noted his name and asked them to take a seat in the pleasantly furnished waiting area.
They had been sitting for no more than a few minutes when the attractive doctor, no more than in her early thirties he guessed, arrived and introducing herself as Doctor Singh asked him to follow her. Turning, he gave Shelley a nervous smile to which she responded with a thumbs-up.
Doctor Singh led him to a white painted examination room where seated behind a desk, she took notes as she rattled off questions to Martin regarding his family history, his current symptoms, his diet, his lifestyle, his profession, his leisure activities and a number of other questions that he could not later recall.
His admission that he was prescribed no medication other than Viagra was dismissed by Singh with a shake of her head as irrelevant to his condition. There followed a short, physical examination that included his blood pressure being noted, his eyes and hearing examined, being asked to sit then stand repeatedly before his blood pressure was again taken. The entire procedure lasted no more than

forty minutes and all the while he could feel his heart race as he awaited what he knew to be bad news.

It was in anticipation of this bad news that caused him to be visibly surprised when Singh smiled at him.

"Mister Craven, these symptoms you have described. The dizziness and light-headedness, unsteady on your feet after rising from your bed or a chair, the occasional blurred vision and general feeling of weakness and nausea. Without extensive tests that I believe would be a waste of both your time and money, you are a middle aged man and in my humble opinion, demonstrating the conditions that are symptomatic of high blood pressure."

"High blood pressure," he quietly repeated, then added, "Is that all?"

"Mister Craven, high blood pressure should never be ignored," she smiled tolerantly at him. "However, with a strict regime of the proper diet, exercise and medication and regular health checks, there is no reason for you to concern yourself as undoubtedly you have done." She peered at him through narrowed eyes. "I'm guessing that prior to today's consultation, you imagined all sorts of things wrong with you, is that correct?"

"Yes, Doctor Singh," he sheepishly admitted, fighting the urge to stand up and hug this woman who in one fell swoop removed all his doubts and fears. High blood pressure? Bloody hell, he wasn't going to die after all!

"Well, you foolish man," she playfully wagged her finger as she gently chided him. "My advice is cut down on your workload and importantly, attend your GP on a more regular basis. I would also urge you to follow the regime that I will cause to be posted out to you. I also intend lettering your GP who I am certain will prescribe you with medication that will help and which you *must*," again she wagged her finger, "ensure you take regularly. Failure to keep to the medicinal regime I will set down could make you susceptible to more serious issues such as a stroke. Do I make myself clear?" she smiled at him.

He slowly nodded, not trusting himself to speak.

"Mister Craven," she paused and stared thoughtfully at him, "from what you tell me of your business and the hours you work I suggest cutting down on your workload and by that, I don't mean working a few hours less." She paused again and her brow furrowed. "You tell me that you are currently prescribed Viagra so I will assume that your life is being shared, yes?"

"Yes," he replied, his voice almost a whisper.

"Would I be correct in also assuming by the young woman who I met you with in the reception area and who looked anxious as she sits waiting for you?"

"Yes," he replied, conscious that he was blushing.

"Well," Singh hid a smile, "I suggest that you sit down with your…friend and discuss your health for I am certain if she cares for you she will want you to continue to, how can I put this," she wagged her pencil in the air, "lead an active life?"

"Yes, doctor," he quietly replied.

"However," she stared intently at him, "this Viagra you are taking, Mister Craven. I cannot dissuade you if you believe you believe you must take such medication, but you have to realise that you are a relatively young man for such medication. It is my opinion that once you have settled into a more relaxed lifestyle and you are less stressed, you will undoubtedly feel better and fitter and likely," she paused and with a gentle smile added, "nature will resume."

Her brow furrowed as she glanced down at the notes she had written and then shuffling the paperwork into a neat pile, lifted her head to stare at him.

"Mister Craven, you seem to me to be a man of some means and from your response to my profile questioning you have worked very hard from an early age to achieve the status you now enjoy. Has it ever occurred to you that if you are on sound financial footing and able to do so, that you consider early retirement and enjoying your life?"

He took a deep breath.

Retirement, the very thing he had considered. Now that in his mind he had been given a second chance at life, it was more than just a consideration and so replied, "It's something that I will certainly discuss with my… with my friend, Doctor Singh."

"Then, Mister Craven," she stood and smiling, extended her hand, "I suggest you give it a *lot* of thought."

The note had been on the desk at his workstation when he arrived and clutching it, made his way to the manager's office.

"Come in, James, come in," the manager beckoned him through the door. Seated on a chair with her back to him, Annette Bell ignored him as entered the glass cubicle that served as the manager's office. He guessed that she had raised yet another grievance against him, but this time he was still so very angry with his wife Moira's blackmail of him and had no interest in defending himself against Bell's petty complaint.

The manager sat back in his comfortable chair and staring at him, took a deep breath as though what he was about to do weighed heavily upon him. James knew it was a front, that the manager was indifferent to his staff's welfare and had little doubt that just like every other bugger who worked in the call centre, James would simply be another faceless employee who passed through the shithole and would be forgotten five minutes after he left.

"James," began the manager, "it is with regret that I have to…" Never before would he have had the courage to speak up, to complain or rail against a manager or supervisor or anyone in authority, but what he did to Moira, his assault upon her, had exposed him to a strength and anger he had only before experienced with the carpenters hammer clutched in his fist. Now, staring at the lack of interest that was pasted on the manager's face, he moodily snapped and shouted, "*Fuck* you and your wee arse licking cow here!"

Stunned, the manager was about to protest as Bell, rising from her seat, her face chalk white, was turning towards him when he sneered at her, "Why don't you tell him how you tried it on with me in the lift, you smelly, fat dwarf!"

Now on his feet, the manager was nervously reaching for his phone with one hand while with the other, trying to calm the irate James as he called out, "I think you had better leave, Mister Bain before I have the building security…"

But, before the manager finished, he was already turning away towards the door, shouting over his shoulder, "Shove your fucking job!" while a hysterical Bell, at last finding her voice, screamed after him, "Fuck you too, you poof!"

His shouts and Bell's screaming been heard throughout the large room and shaking with unbridled rage, he quickly made his way to his cubicle to grab his jacket from the chair, tears of impotent rage burned at his eyes and bad-temperedly he shoved the chair with a loud crash onto the floor. Ignoring the wide-eyed stares of his now former colleagues he headed towards the lift.

He knew it had to happen. The sacking was just a matter of time, but inwardly he was glad and convinced himself that he was leaving under his own terms.

The lift took an eternity to arrive and he knew without turning around that dozens of pairs of eyes were silently watching him. At last, the lift shuddered to a halt at his floor and pulling at the automatic doors he stepped in, but his grand exit was foiled when the lift doors slowly closed and instead of travelling to the ground floor, it began to rise.

Shit! he thought and had to endure almost five minutes of the lift stopping at each of the upper floors before it travelled downwards and once more stopped at the very floor he had entered. As the doors hissed open, he saw to his dismay the call centre staff with Annette Bell at the forefront had gathered to wave and jeer at him as he passed by.

His cheeks burned a bright red as the guffaws and laughter followed him downwards.

Seated at his desk, Mark Barclay pored over the incident reports that had been dispatched to the incident room by DC Fraser of Crimestoppers and sighed. Of the dozen or so reports, perhaps one or two were worthy of serious investigation while the remainder were clearly motivated by malice or just plain time wasting. However, like all leads brought to the attention of a murder incident room, each report had to be followed up by a detective and so he began the laborious task of raising Actions to have them checked out. He had no complaint against Crimestoppers for they were merely doing their job and was aware that on numerous occasions information received by the charitable organisation was responsible for the successful conclusion to a number of major inquiries.

"Coffee," said the voce at his elbow. He turned to see Elaine Hamilton lay his favourite mug on the desk beside his elbow.

"Why don't you take a break, Mark, and let me deal with these?"

He pushed backwards into the chair and arched his back before glancing at his watch and made a decision that was long overdue.

"Here's a better idea," he replied. "Why don't we skip coffee here and we'll both take a fifteen minute break. I'll get young Melanie

Clark to hold the fort while you grab your coat and we'll walk round to the wee delicatessen in Port Dundas Road. I'll treat you to a latte. How about it?"

She smiled tightly, but her stomach was clenching, and carefully replied, "Yes, I'd like that, but give me a minute till I pop to the ladies and I'll meet you out front."

Less than five minutes later she joined him on the front steps of Stewart Street office and surprised, he saw that she had taken the opportunity to apply a fresh coat of lipstick.

Together they walked at a leisurely pace towards the Deli.

"So, how are things?" he asked.

"Well, we're keeping on top of the reports, though there are a number of outstanding Actions to be returned and the MIU Actions that were not completed before they left have to be distributed among…"

"No, Elaine," he stopped and turning towards her, raised his hand and smiled, "I meant, how are things with you?"

"With me?"

"Personally, I mean."

"Oh," she stared at him, a little taken aback and her face reddening. "Well, you know, so and so."

"How about socially. You seeing anyone right now?"

"Seeing anyone? Me? No! I mean, no Mark," she was fully blushing now, "I'm not seeing anyone. Why?"

He took her by the elbow to steer her around the corner from Milton Street towards the Deli and taking a deep breath, said, "Well, I was wondering, eh, if you like and you've nothing else on, I mean. How about maybe you and me getting a meal out one night. Nothing fancy, just a…"

She stopped dead and staring at him, said, "Yes, I'd like that."

"Oh, right," he was taken aback, but curiously pleased by her sudden acceptance and with a nod of his head, continued, "Well, we'll talk about that and come to some arrangement, but first Miss Hamilton, let me treat you to a takeaway latte."

She turned into the driveway and sat for a moment, her eyes darting back and forth to ensure that none of his neighbours were watching, but then thought why should it matter? After all, even if they do see and recognise me I've been to the house on a number of occasions anyway.

With more confidence than she felt, she got out of the driver's seat and made her way to the front door then with shaking fingers, used his house key to get in.

Closing the front door behind her she listened, but of course as she already suspected, there was no one at home.

Quickly she made her way upstairs to his bedroom and just as she had in James room, pulled open the underwear drawer. From her large shoulder bag she lifted out a pair of thin leather gloves that she pulled on then carefully brought out the clear plastic bag that contained the three twists of cut hair. She guessed the police would check the bag for DNA or whatever tests they made and disposing of the original bag used by James, had replaced it with a new bag.

Closing the drawer, she sighed with relief. The first part of her plan was complete, now for the second part. Making her way downstairs to the bottom hallway and through the narrow door under the stairs that led into the attached garage, she saw an old, wooden bench with two drawers set against the back wall. Opening a drawer that was stiff with age and dampness, Moira saw it contained some rusting tools and small jars of screws. Nervously, she fetched the carpenters hammer from the shoulder bag. Her nose twitched at the faint, but nauseous sweet smell of dried blood and placed the towel wrapped hammer at the rear of the drawer. She had already examined the hammer and if the Internet page was accurate, confident that the police would not be able to obtain any fingerprints from the moulded rubber handle.

That done, she returned to the hallway and glancing about to ensure that she had left nothing behind, made her way through the front door, locking it behind her.

With a sigh she returned to her Audi and reversing from the driveway, braked hard and almost collided with an elderly woman walking a small dog who glared angrily at her. Waving her hand and smiling an apology, she mouthed the word 'Sorry' and waited until the woman was well away before reversing into the road and driving off.

That's when she noticed the slight tremor in her hands, but nevertheless could not refrain from smiling. It had gone exactly as she planned.

Turning from Fleurs Avenue into Nithsdale Road, she stopped the car outside a large, detached mansion with a high hedgerow that hid the house from her view. From her handbag she fetched the mobile phone and the slip of paper. Glancing at the number, she took a deep breath and slowly exhaled, preparing herself to dial the phone number written on the paper. When the number connected, she listened to the recorded message before reciting the information she had practised that included her own little twist that made her smile. Less than a minute later she finished and ended the call. Almost immediately she removed the SIM card from the small, ten-pound phone she had purchased that morning and with a little difficulty broke the SIM card in two. The small, plastic phone she would later dispose of into a bin.

Satisfied that her plan was now fully in play, she was grinning now as she drove off and headed back towards the warehouse.

## CHAPTER SIXTEEN

Stepping off the bus, for the first time in a long while Mary McLaughlin was looking forward to work that day, even though she normally dreaded the late shift. Her keenness was all to do with last night's date with Davie Craven. It had gone far better than she had anticipated and sleep that night had been hard to come by for her thoughts and imagination were filled with waking dreams, imagining a life with the very nice and she fervently hoped, trustworthy Davie. On the way to drop her off at her home he had insisted that she bring her son Mickey on their next date and he would bring his daughter, Elsa. "Maybe take them to a McDonalds, just to let them get to know each other," he had suggested.

To Mary, that inferred Davie was more keen on her than she realised for after all she reasoned, why else would he bring his child with him.

The down side was when Davie asked that for the moment they kept their relationship between themselves. He had seen her face fall and explained that his father was not yet fully supportive of Davie seeing other women. A little embarrassed he further explained that his father believed Davie was too open, that his son wore his heart on his sleeve and that he worried about him.

Shyly she had touched his arm and told him that she would keep their secret, all that mattered to her was they continued to see each other.

Upon arriving at her home he had got out of the driver's seat and gallantly insisted on opening her door, extending his hand to help her from the car.

They had stood close to say goodnight and she blushed, recalling the awkward moment when he leaned forward to kiss her as she did him, only for them to bump noses.

They had giggled like school kids and then he had kissed her goodnight.

She knew without turning her mother was watching them from behind the curtain at the lounge window.

Stepping through the large gates into the warehouse car park she met with some of her fellow employees and listened to their moans about working late shift. She knew they would be surprised that Mary instead felt like skipping towards the rear staff entrance.

Driving his Fiesta along the M8 towards his home in Blantyre, James Bain was still so very, very angry at the humiliating manner in which the staff of the call centre had jeered at him as he left the building. Angry enough to kill some bitch!

But he could not, for his very own *bitch* Moira had taken his hammer and made him swear that he would not hurt any more women, that if he did as she told him she would make arrangements so that he need not worry about the police catching him and arresting him for the murders, that she would sort things out.

She refused to tell him exactly *how* the fuck she intended doing that, but promised that if he said and did as she told him, he would have nothing to worry about.

All he had to do for now was be her fucking lackey; to do as she said and more importantly, not touch her, not speak to her and to stay away from her, even if they were in the house together. They were to have what she called the minimal contact unless there were other people present and that's when she completely contradicted herself. She had told him that if they were to go out as a couple to any event, he must act as though they were happily married, that she wanted him to be seen to be all over her, that there was not to be even be a hint that they were anything but crazy for each other, that not her family or her friends were to suspect that they hated and despised each other.

Happily married? Crazy about each other?

How the *fuck* was he supposed to do that?

He had asked why the charade only for her to scowl and tell him he did not need to know why, just to do as she said because it was part of her fucking plan!

As he drove he remembered what he had done to her, how he had degraded her, but as much as he would wish to do it again, to hurt and…he shook his head and snarled at the thought.

Yes, not just cut her hair, but scalp the bitch. Use a razor to cut *all* her hair off but knew that if he even looked at Moira the wrong way, it was over. The letter and hair strands she had sent to her lawyer for safekeeping ensured his reluctant cooperation. Hating himself for it, he knew he had no choice but to do as she wanted. He was nothing but a dancing puppet on a silver chain.

He unconsciously nodded as he drove tears of rage smarting at his eyes; he was nothing but the bitch's dancing puppet.

He reached forward to switch on the radio, but then loudly cried out, "Fuck!", for he had again forgotten to get a bloody replacement from the Internet and switched the static off, not interested in listening to the same bloody CD's repeatedly.

Right now, wound up as if he was, he wanted nothing more than to hit out at some woman, smash her head to a pulp and take her hair!

He smiled evilly, recalling the headline he had read.

He was Glasgow's Demon Barber, the stalker of bitches!

He turned off into the carriageway that led towards Uddingston and drove towards Blantyre Farm Road.

He briefly glanced at the pretty, dark haired young woman driving the Micra as he overtook her car in the outside lane and a fleeting vision of her blood-soaked head came to mind.

Pity, he thought, for right now killing bitches was no longer an option.

Well, he smirked; not for a while anyway.

He had decided that he and Shelley would celebrate his good news, his reprieve he inwardly thought and drove towards a restaurant in Fenwick that he had read was receiving good reviews.

"Are you sure you want to be seen with me in public," she playfully pouted at him, caught up in his good mood.

"Well, why not," he turned briefly to grin at her. "I mean, it will do my morale the world of good being seen with you."

"So," she slowly asked, "you *won't* be pretending I'm your daughter?"

"No, I won't pretend you're my daughter," he smiled as he shook his head, then added, "What I will do is let you take my arm when we get there so that people can stare at us and be jealous of an old guy like me taking a good looking young woman to lunch."

"Old guy," she playfully dug him in the ribs then leaning towards him, softly whispered, "You're not such an old guy when you're taking me to bed, Martin Craven."

He shook his head again. Shelley had only to sexily lower her voice to arouse him and right now, he felt himself being aroused. He shifted uncomfortably in the driving seat and aware of what was happening to him, she giggled before reaching across to gently stroke his groin.

"Hey, cut that out when I'm driving," he laughed at her.

She laughed as she ignored him and continuing to stroke him, asked, "Can you wait till later or do you want to pull in to one of these lanes we're passing? I'm sure I can handle that bump in your trousers for you," she coyly told him.

"Much as I'd like to stop right here on the carriageway and let you handle my bump, young lady," he continued to laugh, "we'll get something to eat first."

Shelley withdrew her hand and a moment later, his voice now sombre, he said, "Besides, there's something I want to discuss with you."

"Oh, is it important?"

"Yes, I think so, hen. It's something we need to sort out, something between me and you."

She felt a cold shiver wash over her and a tightness in her chest. Staring at the roadway ahead, she slowly nodded. "Okay then, Martin. Let's eat and then you can tell me what's on your mind."

Standing at the counter in the delicatessen waiting on their food order being organised, Myra McColl and Kevin Feeney were surprised to see Mark Barclay and Elaine Hamilton join the end of the lengthy queue. Giving the pair a nod, McColl suppressed a smile. If she read the situation correctly, Mark had at last got off his arse and with a bit of luck was now commencing a courtship with Elaine. If she *was* correct and her suspicions were confirmed it wouldn't be long before the office gossip would soon kick in.

McColl liked Mark Barclay; well, in actual fact was fond of the old bugger, but in a sisterly way. He had been her tutor detective in the Partick CID a number of years previously when she was an aide and always been a thoroughly decent man. After her appointment to the CID they had remained as neighbours and developed a good working relationship. Like the married Barclay, back then she had also been married to Donnie. However, within a year of their nuptials McColl's marriage had fallen apart after the young, probationary cop called one night at their door to confess to her about Donnie's adulterous relationship.

The last she heard was Donnie and the lassie, now both resigned from the police, were still together.

It had hurt that he had cheated on her and if she was honest, sometimes it still did. Astute as she stupidly believed she was, she just never saw that coming.

Of course, she had been in a few relationships of her own since then, but never with anyone who was married or involved with another woman. No, that just wasn't her style. Still, she lived in hope.

"Here we go, two chicken rolls and a tuna pasta salad," the assistant broke into her thoughts.

She was reaching for her purse when Feeney tapped her arm and said, "My treat, Sarge," as with a smile he handed the notes to the assistant.

"Thanks, Kevin," she smiled at him and passing Barclay and Elaine as they left the shop, favoured them with another nod.

Maybe it was the memory of learning her trade with Barclay. Maybe it was because the young man impressed her. She just couldn't be sure, but reaching the CID car parked outside, she stopped at the passenger door as Feeney rounded the car to the drivers door and called out to him, "Kevin."

"Sarge?"

She slowly grinned and pulling open the door, winked and said, "Seen as how we're neighbours and you've treated me to lunch, why don't you drop the 'Sarge' and call me Myra."

Charlie Miller picked up his desk phone to find Cathy Mulgrew on the line.

"Anything new?" she asked.

"Nothing so far," he replied.

"Well, I had an interesting phone call a few minutes ago," she said and he could almost hear the laughter in her voice.

"Okay, shoot."

"I had a call from our Mister Thomson, you know…"

"The guy at the City Chambers that fancies you. Yes, I remember him. What did he want?"

"Well," she slowly drawled, "he wanted to take me out to dinner and a drink after that."

"Ah, you did explain that…"

"I'm gay and in a relationship? Yes, of course I did."

"Well, what did he say to that?"

"Told me he was married and that if I didn't mind him being married he didn't mind me being gay and we could, ah, how did he put it? Oh, yes, we could work something out."

"Cathy, you're kidding!"

"Nope, honest to God, but that said, he was very charming about the whole issue and asked me to consider his proposal. Told me he knew of a lovely hotel in Lanark that he sometimes visited for dinner and asked if I'd be interested in joining him one evening."

"Aye, right, so you will," Miller laughed. "Was that all he called about, then?"

"Not exactly. He also wanted to let us know that he had spoken with the councillor, the guy McFadyen and reminded him that if McFadyen was to give support to Arthur Freeman's campaign to oust the Chief, then…"

"Whoa, wait a minute. Back up there, Cathy. Oust the Chief? You mean that sleekit bastard Freeman…"

"Is currently behind a campaign to undermine Martin Cairney's position as Chief Constable. According to Thomson, the rumour is that Freeman has already signed up a couple of Police and Fire Committee councillors, a Deputy Chief and two Assistant Chief's, who coincidentally were brought in from Forces down south at the merger of all the Scottish forces into Police Scotland. That said, there is a couple of other ACC's who also arrived from England that knocked Freeman back and completely support Cairney, so it's not a nationality thing. Freeman is apparently promising his council and police backers that if he *is* appointed as Chief Constable, those individuals who support him will have his complete backing should that be for council decisions or if they are currently Deputies or ACC's, any career move they choose to make."

"Call me suspicious, but what does Thomson get out of this, providing you with the information I mean?"

"I asked the same question, Charlie, and he told me something I was unaware of. Apparently besides being an out and out bastard, Arthur Freeman fancies himself as a bible thumping Christian who strongly condemns the consumption of alcohol and has radical views about the licensing laws that are currently in force in Scotland. If he *does* acquire the top job, then Freeman's appointment will commence with him moving to drastically reduce licensed opening hours and this will adversely affect the licensed trade who of course are represented locally by Thomson."

"Maybe not a bad thing," mused Miller, contemplating just how alcohol contributed to much of the level of crime in Scotland's cities.

"Okay, yes, I agree in principal," replied Mulgrew, "but Freeman's proposed policies wouldn't end there. Thomson has also learned Freeman intends reducing the complement of the CID and appointing uniformed officers to investigate *all* crime, including capital crime."

"You mean murder?"

"Aye," she sighed, "right up to murder."

"No harm to our uniformed colleagues, but they're already under enough pressure coping with the governmental cuts and shift changes without having to deal with reported crime for which very few have received specialist training."

"Charlie, if Freeman is appointed as the Chief they might not have a choice in the matter," she quietly said and continued. "To top it all, he intends a further budget shake-up of the Force and is committed to reducing numbers again. Apparently he has convinced a number of councillors he can save a fortune by getting rid of more officers."

"Does Cairney know about this coup that Freeman's trying to organise?"

"Oh aye, he's not daft is Martin Cairney and has his own sources in the council. He is well aware of what is going on, but unlike

Freeman, he's not a backstabbing bastard and has to be seen to do everything above board. And that," she sighed, "is why he needs a result in your case in particular and, much as I hate to say this, as soon as possible. Thomson told me that one of Freeman's ploys is to blame Cairney for his lack of foresight in choosing or keeping in position senior CID officers who are not up to the job and these officers, believe it or not, are directly contributing to the crime numbers by their failure to detect offenders."

"By these officers, you mean me?"

"Among others, I mean you *and* me. Thomson says I'm on Freeman's target list too."

Miller was stunned, but before he could respond, his door was knocked and then opened by Mark Barclay whom he could see was holding a notepad in his hand and was more than a little animated.

"Cathy," he stared curiously at Barclay, "something's come up. Can I call you back?"

"Sorry, boss," Barclay closed the door behind him, "but I thought this was too important to wait."

He dragged up a chair and sat down opposite Miller before he begun. "I'd just come back from a break and took a call from a DC Fraser at Crimestoppers office."

"She wasn't on to make a complaint about me, was she," Miller joked.

"What? No," Barclay shook his head, slightly confused and dismissing Miller's question, continued. "She was listening to a call that had just been recorded," he waved the notebook and added, "I've got the details here."

Glancing down at his notes, Barclay said, "According to Fraser's initial profile of the caller, it was a woman who identified herself as Mary, no last name, probably aged between mid twenties to mid thirties. The woman, according to Fraser, perhaps deliberately made her voice sound husky to disguise it. A local accent and by that Fraser means Glasgow or close by, properly spoken and no local slang words were used. The woman spoke a little slowly, but was also clear and concise and Fraser thinks that she had probably rehearsed what she said. The call lasted a mere, let me see," he glanced down the page, "thirty-three seconds. No background noise that could be discerned and nobody heard in the company of the woman. Fraser admits she's out on a limb here, but thinks the woman might have made the call from a car."

"That sounds pretty detailed for a thirty-three second call," muttered Miller.

"These guys at Crimestoppers, boss. They're listening to this type of call all day and because its tape recorded, they can listen and re-listen and hear things that you and I might miss."

"I suppose so," agreed Miller, "but what about the information the woman Mary passed?"

"Ah, well, the gist of it is and by the way," he glanced up from his notes, "I've DC Fraser hot-footing over here with the tape; the information is that this Mary is a friend of a man called David Craven who lives in Fleurs Avenue in Pollokshields. Mary says that Craven asked her to fetch something for him from a bedroom drawer and when she was doing that, she saw a small plastic bag with hair in it. She thought at first it might be his daughter's hair, sort of like a keepsake, but it was three different little tied locks of hair and three different shades. When Mary saw the article on the TV about the hair being cut from the dead woman, she says she panicked and decided to phone because she's worried that this guy Craven might harm her too."

He took a breath and said, "That's it, boss. The call ended with nothing about who Mary is to this man Craven and…"

The door knocked and Elaine Hamilton stuck her head round the door. "Sorry, sir," she said to Charlie, then addressing Barclay told him, "The voters roll for that address in Fleurs Avenue checks out, Mark. There's a David Craven listed on the roll, but no other person listed as resident there. I'm having Melanie run a check on the PNC to see if there's a David Craven of that address known to us."

Barclay turned towards Miller. "This woman Mary said Craven has a daughter, but if she's resident there, boss, she could be under the voting age. The voters roll might not be that accurate either."

Miller stroked at his chin as he stared thoughtfully at Barclay before replying, "What's your take on it, Mark?"

Barclay blew out through pursed lips and said, "It's the best lead so far, boss. The bit about the three different colours of the hair seems to me as if this Mary perhaps has seen the hair. I don't recall anything about the victims' hair colouring being disclosed by that idiot McGregor. Granted, it could be this woman is guessing that the hair colouring of the victims *was* different. I suspect we'd never get a warrant on the information as it stands, but it might be worth chancing our arm and calling upon this guy Craven to see if he'll permit a search of his house."

Miller was more than a little angry. If Ally McGregor had not publicly disclosed the victims hair being cut and taken by the killer, the information from Crimestoppers would have surely have earned them a Sheriff's search warrant, but ironically, the information only came in *after* McGregor's disclosure about the cut hair. Sod's law, he slowly shook his head.

"Right, here's what I suggest," he said at last. "I'll give Susie Duncan at the Fiscal's office a phone and run it by her and cross my fingers to ask if she can drum up a search warrant for us, though to be honest, Mark, I agree with you and I can't see it happening. In the meantime you organise a couple of the team to go out to the address and watch the house for any sign of movement. On no account," he firmly stressed, "are they to knock on the door or in any way whatsoever declare themselves as polis to anyone in the vicinity and particularly, Craven's neighbours. Make that *very* clear to them, yeah? I do not want this guy Craven getting spooked. It wouldn't be hard to dispose of three of locks of hair and there goes the evidence. If a nosy neighbour gives them the onceover, they are to bugger off sharpish and on that point have them monitor the local division's radio net. It wouldn't do for somebody to see them and think they're suspicious sitting about there in their car then having our Govan colleagues turning up to ask what the hell they're up to."

"So, you're running with this?"

"What else can we do," shrugged Miller.

The door knocked and again it was Elaine Hamilton who informed them that DC Fraser had arrived.

"Bloody hell, that was quick," commented Barclay.

"Ask her to come through please, Elaine," smiled Miller.

A moment later, the door was knocked and DC Fraser, a young woman in her mid-twenties with short, dark hair, silver-rimmed spectacles and wearing a black skirted suit and carrying a battery operated tape recorder in a strong plastic case, entered the room.

"Mister Miller, sir," she nervously asked.

He stood and smiling, greeted her. "Hello there, DC Fraser. This is Mark Barclay, my DI. What's your first name?"

"Eh, it's Lynn, sir. Lynn Fraser."
"Right, Lynn," he said, "let's hear what you've got, pal."
She took just a moment to set up her equipment and they listened to the recording four times with Fraser pointing out her observations at the end of each turn of the thirty-three second call.
At last Miller was satisfied he had heard enough and turning to Barclay, said, "Okay, Mark, let's run with this." He then turned towards Fraser and smiling, said, "Lynn, good piece of work. We'll keep a hold of the tape and the recorder meantime if you don't mind. Any problems about that have your boss phone me. Thanks for coming over and I'll ensure that you are informed if this should pan out for us. You did well, Lynn, and I'll not forget your contribution." Blushing at the DCI's gratitude, the young woman stood and left the room as Miller said to Barclay, "Time I made a phone call."

Lifting her handbag from the floor, Procurator Fiscal Depute Susie Duncan, a frizzy haired woman in her mid-thirties standing just under five foot tall and wearing Harry Potter style glasses, was about to head out of the door for home when the phone rung. Groaning, she bad-temperedly lifted the receiver and snapped, "Yes!"
"Hello to you too, Susie," grimaced Charlie Miller. "Catch you at a bad time?"
"Charlie Miller, long time no speak. How are you doing, doll? I was almost out the door on my way home. One of the wee buggers has fallen down the stairs and the childminder can't stop him crying."
"By wee bugger, I take it you mean a beloved child?"
"Some might call him beloved, to me he's just a noisy, attention grabbing wee shite like his father."
"Where does he come in the pack then?"
"He's number three of four and guess what."
"Aw, Susie, not another one."
"Aye, due in July."
"Are congratulations in order, then?"
"Not if you want to remain on the Christmas card list they're not," she sighed. "So, DCI Miller, what can I do you for and make it short. I was due home five minutes ago."
"Sorry, Susie, it might take more than a couple of minutes to explain."

"I knew I should have ignored the fucking phone," she sighed miserably as dropping her handbag onto the floor, she slumped down at her desk.

Less than five minutes later, she began to laugh and said, "Charlie, you're at the madam. How the *hell* can I justify applying to a Sheriff for a warrant based on a Crimestoppers call? You have no physical evidence, no named informant, the guy's not even a known criminal; you have nothing. For fucks sake, I can't work miracles you know!"

She listened as he audibly sighed and in a low voice, told her, "I knew I was probably wasting your time, Susie, but to be honest, this is the best lead we've had so far. Is there *anything* you can do?"

"Charlie, the last time I went out on a limb for you it cost me a bollocking from my illustrious arse of a leader, dickhead that he is."

"Aye, but I sent you a bottle of the hard stuff as compensation," he reminded her, to which she angrily replied, "Oh, aye, I remember. Bad enough I'd to give up the fags, but then the whisky you sent over was drunk by my sod of a hubby because I was bloody *pregnant* with my fourth!"

"Oh, sorry about that."

"Right then," calm now, she said, "give me five minutes, but *do not* hold out any hopes. I mean that, Charlie. I can only ask and if I get a knock-back..."

"I can't ever imagine *you* getting a knock-back, Susie," he interrupted.

"Flattery, Charlie? That's going to help you win me over? Have you seen me recently? I look like a wee beached whale with glasses wearing a small tent."

"But lovely with it, hen."

"Five minutes," she firmly repeated, then with a shake of her head and grinning at Miller's cheek, ended the call.

Back in her office, the keys returned to the locker, Moira Bain sat behind her desk nervously drumming her fingers on the desk and wondered how long it would be before the police acted upon her information? How long did it take them to check their bloody recording machines? Her eyes narrowed and brow furrowed. What if they didn't act on the phone call? What if they thought it was a hoax?

Unconsciously, she chewed at her long false nails, working her fine, white teeth along the edges until the harsh taste of her polish caused her to realise what she was doing.

She glanced at the clock. Should she wait at the office or go home? No, she'd go home. She could not afford for anything to go wrong, for any suspicion to fall upon her. She had to be seen to keep to her routine. Standing, she lifted her handbag and collected her jacket from the hook before glancing through the window.

Davie's car was still parked outside and it occurred to her to say cheerio, to tell him she was leaving for home, but she had never bothered before and it might seem odd if she were to do so now. No, she would leave and drive straight home and hopefully if not tonight, by tomorrow morning she would hear good news.

They both refused dessert and settled instead for coffee.

"So, that's the meal done, Martin. What is it that you want to discuss with me?"

"Well, on the back of the good news from the doctor and the apparent fact that if I take care of myself and do what I'm told regarding health issues, then it seems I still have the capacity to enjoy life so," he paused, carefully choosing his words. "I'm considering taking early retirement. What do you think?"

She stared at him for a moment, a moment that gave her time to consider the enormity of what he was suggesting before she replied, "I think it's a great idea. I think that you have put so much working time into your life, the long hours and the pressure to build up the business that it's about time you gave some thought to yourself. My only concern," she reached across the table to wrap her fingers in his, "is what about us?"

"Us? Well," he sighed and gently squeezed her hand, "that would depend on what you want, Shelley. I've said it a hundred times, I'm far too old for you. You need a younger man, someone who will be there for you to spend your years with. Someone who will give you children, a home and…and…"

"And what?" she snapped, withdrawing her hand and clutching it with her other hand on her lap beneath the table. "Has it occurred to you that I might have a say in what *I* want, Martin! Do you think I have stayed with you for what…a job? For money to pay my rent? What the hell…" she leaned across the table, her eyes fiery and voice now raised, attracting the attention of the few other couples who sat nearby. "I'll decide what I want and *who* I want in my life!" she hissed at him.

He was taken aback by her response, never before having seen her so angry and quietly said, "Well, what *do* you want, Shelley?"

"Thank you, at last you're letting me make a decision about *me*," she snapped, but quieter and turning her head, her glance dared the other diners to continue staring at her, but they all turned away to suddenly concentrate on the food in front of them.

She took a breath and calm now, swallowed hard as she told him, "What I want, Martin Craven, is for you to forget the age difference between us, but to see me as the woman that I am. I've loved you almost from the moment we met when you saw me that day, standing alone and vulnerable. Do not think I have forgotten that or ever will. I have loved you because you have made me feel that I'm not lost and I'm no longer alone. I have loved you because with me, you are gentle and caring and you worry about me. I've loved you because you told no one about us, not because you are worried about what people might say about you, but to protect *me*, *my* reputation." She took a breath and then continued, "Those are some of the reasons I loved you, Martin and because of those reasons, I *do* love you now and I always will. I've never asked you to love me in return," she shook her head so fiercely her unbound hair whipped across her face, "never demanded anything of you, so do not presume to tell me who I should love or care for, because Martin, it's *you* that I love."

He stared at her, his throat dry.

"Oh, my," he simply replied, then forcing a cough to hide the tears that threatened to spill from him, took a deep breath and slowly exhaled.

"Shelley, I'm sorry. Sorry for being such a…" he was about to say old, but instead smiled and said, "…fool." He held his hand across the table and waited until at last, she placed her own hand in his and he continued, "This retirement I'm thinking about. Would you consider spending it with me?"

"For how long?" she asked, still slightly suspicious of him.

"How about, my darling, sweet girl…how about forever?"

She slowly smiled and biting at her lower lip to stem her own tears, softly replied, "I think I could get used to that; yes."

James Bain sneaked a look through the curtained window and saw Moira's car turn into the driveway. He made his way into the kitchen and though she had insisted that they not spend any time together in the same room, she had to be told that he had lost his job, though now he really didn't give a shit what she might think about that.
He heard the front door open and then close and a few seconds later, she walked into the kitchen, but stood at the door waiting for him to leave the room.
"I'm making tea, so I thought I'd make you a cup too," he began, then added, "I need to tell you something."
Still wary of him, she continued to stand at the door as he said, "I've lost my job. One of the supervisors, a hatchet faced wee cow, had it in for me so she turned the management against me and I was sacked."
Moira suspected that there was probably more to his dismissal than that, but simply nodded and replied, "Well, for the time that we remain together, I'll see that money is paid into your account to cover your living expenses. As for the other thing, I've set it in motion so from now on we have to be seen to be together as a couple," she almost spit the word out, "so you cannot do anything, anything at all that might bring any police attention to you. Do you understand, James? Nothing at all."
He was about to reply, to thank her even, but she turned away and he heard her walk into the lounge before the door closed with a bang. Turning his face to the ceiling, he wanted to scream, to follow her and shout at her, to hurt and humiliate her, but forced himself to remain calm.
Her time would come, he promised himself and then she would be sorry.
So very *fucking* sorry!

## CHAPTER SEVENTEEN

Charlie Miller snatched the phone before it had even stopped its first ring.
"Yes?"
"Charlie, it's me," said Susie Duncan, then added, "the bloody miracle worker."

"You got a warrant," he stated, his voice betraying his surprise mixed with relief.

"Aye, and it wasn't easy; so pal, you owe me big time and I mean, big time."

"How did you manage it, Susie?"

"Sheer bloody luck, if I'm honest. I don't know if you're aware, but Sheriff Cooper-Smith retires at the end of this week, so this being his last week he's presiding over the two o'clock custody court. I gave him a bell and explained the circumstances and he agreed if I get the warrant typed up here and you can get someone to collect it and take it up to him before he leaves his chambers, he will and I quote here, 'Give the matter some sympathetic consideration.' For what it's worth, when I mentioned your name, he knew who you are and I think that's what swung it."

Miller smiled. The elderly Sheriff, one of the Glasgow Sheriff Court's most respected judges, was known by both the accused and the police officers who presented evidence in his court to be a fair and just man.

Miller's association with the Sheriff occurred many years previously when quite unexpectedly, Cooper-Smith had attended the funeral service when Miller's first wife and child had been killed in a road traffic accident. It was a kindness that Miller did not forget and distraught as he was at the time, he wrote and thanked the Sheriff for his thoughtfulness. Since that time both men had a passing acquaintance when Miller was attending court to give evidence and if they met in the court corridors, Cooper-Smith always took time to stop with the detective and chew the fat.

"Aye, he's a good man," Miller replied, lost in thought and promised himself he would have a card and a bottle delivered on the Sheriff's last day.

"So, who will you send to affirm before the Sheriff?"

"It will be Myra McColl and her aide that I'll send, Susie. I'll get her to hotfoot it up to you…"

"The typing pool, Charlie. She's to attend at the typing pool. I'm out of here, remember?"

"Aye, right," he grinned at the phone, "and Susie, thanks again."

"Yeah, well if there's a bottle in it, wait till after I drop this new bugger in July before you send it."

"Will do," he replied and ended the call.

Springing up from his desk, he went to hunt for the location of McColl and her lad, Kevin Feeney.

Mary McLaughlin glanced around to ensure there was nobody near her and then waved shyly towards Davie Craven. Carrying a clipboard, Davie was pretending to check the stock in the adjacent aisle and slowly moved towards her.
"I had a really good time last night," he whispered to her.
"Me too," she replied, a little anxious lest anyone see them together. The noise of two women gossiping as they pushed metal caged trolleys in a nearby aisle caused Davie to intently peer at his clipboard while Mary reached up and was to all intent and purpose occupied pushing cardboard boxes together.
The women passed by, glancing first at Mary then seeing Davie, before both burst out laughing as they continued on their way.
Dave grinned at Mary. "I think the word's out," he said.
"I think you're right," she returned his grin.
"If you're not doing anything later…"
"I'm late shift," she grimaced.
"Well, I could pick you up after work, if you like?"
"What about your wee one?"
His brow furrowed. "I think I'll see if my dad's free for a couple of hours," he nodded.
"Okay," she smiled. "I'll see you at eight, then."
"Okay, eight then," he agreed as he turned away to head back towards his fathers office.

Things were beginning to move quickly at Stewart Street incident room.
Mark Barclay learned from Elaine Hamilton that the two detectives dispatched to Fleurs Avenue were parked close by the house and had seen a woman and small child arrive in a car that was now parked in the driveway.
Hamilton caused the vehicle's registration number to be checked on the PNC and discovered it was registered to a woman with an address in the nearby Penilee area. A further check disclosed the registered keeper, presumably the female driver was not known to the police other than for a speeding conviction some years previously.

Myra McColl and her aide, Kevin Feeney had by now collected the warrant from the Fiscal Typing pool in Ballater Street and were en route to the nearby Sheriff Court to depose before Sheriff Cooper-Smith that the information contained in the warrant was true. This was what concerned Miller who acutely aware of the vague and uncorroborated information, worried that Cooper-Smith might think twice before appending his signature and despite their preparations, the whole thing would fall flat.

Anxiously, he waited in his office to hear from McColl.

At Miller's instruction, Mark Barclay made arrangements for the SOCO team led by Jean Galbraith to travel to the Govan office and standby should the application for the warrant be successful and entry to the house gained.

A team of detectives had been gathered in the incident room and waited patiently for if the information from the woman calling herself Mary proved to be truthful, a number of Actions would be immediately created to cover all eventualities that included door-to-door inquiries with the suspects neighbours.

Everything hinged on the warrant.

"Boss," Mark Barclay burst through Miller's door, "that's the two guys up at Fleurs Avenue phoned in to inform me that there's another car appeared in the driveway. A guy got out and went into the house. The car's plate is registered to David Craven at that address."

Miller took a deep breath. Their suspect, if indeed he really *was* a suspect, was now at home. Barclay was about to turn away when Elaine Hamilton appeared beside him to inform them both that the first car and the female driver was now leaving the driveway, but without the child.

"Nanny?" suggested Miller.

"Possibly," agreed Barclay.

The phone rung and Miller darted a glance at them both before picking up the handset. They saw him frown then grinning with relief, give them the thumbs up.

"Myra's got the warrant and is now heading towards the house," he wheezed.

"I'll get Jean Galbraith and her SOCO team on their way," Barclay said over his shoulder as he rushed back to the incident room.

"Elaine," Miller turned towards her and forcing himself to be calm, "My rank as SIO means that I've the unenviable job of sitting here waiting for information as it comes in rather than doing what I'd like to do, get out there and turn the house over myself."
He sat back in his chair, his hands clasped behind his head and stared at her. "The slightest update, anything…"
"You'll be the first to know, sir," she interrupted and smiled encouragingly at him as she closed the door behind her.
"Aye, well I'll just wait here then," he sighed at the closed door and slowly exhaled.

Sitting the laptop and a tumbler of whisky on the small table that ate his meals from, Eric Kyle tapped in the password that opened up his e-mail account. He smiled, for there were three new e-mails that included a response to the inquiry he had made with the Irish bank and another from the estate agent in Cork.
The third e-mail was from the funeral director.
He opened the banks e-mail to discover that he was now an account holder and that his new cheque card and other information had been dispatched to his home address.
The second e-mail responded to his inquiry about a two-bedroom cottage in the sailing village of Crosshaven. As he peered at the attached photographs, his smile broadened. The estate agent had obviously taken the colour photographs in blinding sunlight and showed the renovated fisherman's cottage at its most attractive and was reflected in the price of one-hundred and thirty thousand Euros. Quickly, he found a search engine that converted the Euros to Sterling and saw the price to be just a little over ninety-seven thousand pounds, a sum that was easily manageable with his final payout from the police and caused him to smile. Taking his time, he typed in a response confirming his interest in the cottage and the proposal he fly over sometime in the forthcoming week to view the property.
At last and with a little reluctance he opened the e-mail from the funeral director that contained all the details for Paula's funeral service and cremation, but decided it might appear a little unseemly to reply on line and instead would do no harm to call in personally and speak with the director about the arrangements.

He lifted the whisky and nursing it in his large hand, sat back from the table and thought about the forthcoming service. Likely there would be a large turnout by his colleagues, though suspected that it would be more to support him that to grieve for Paula.

He was aware that his wife was unpopular with his colleagues and since the incident at the Divisional Christmas Dance in the Thistle Hotel he had avoided taking her anywhere his colleagues socialised. Of course, she had constantly whined and complained, but the truth was he just could not trust her when she was drinking. Not only would she become confrontational, but flirtatious too and that *really* needled him.

Thoughts of Paula being flirtatious led him to think of the man in the red coloured Volvo and again Kyle wondered who he was. He imagined himself tracking the man down to interrogate him and to ask why he had kissed Paula. In his heart he already knew the answer, but it hurt to even contemplate what she had been up to. Sipping at the tumbler of whisky he again opened the e-mail from the Cork estate agent and as he slowly looked through them, nodded with pleasure at the photographs of the property that he hoped would soon be his.

Assistant Chief Constable Arthur Freeman, dressed in his best uniform with a small bamboo swagger stick under his arm, his briefcase in one hand and slapping his brown leather gloves against his thigh with the other hand, waited impatiently for his driver at the main entrance of the Tulliallan Police College situated on the edge of the small Fife town of Kincardine-on-Forth. At last, the red faced Traffic constable arrived and jumping from the drivers seat of the gleaming, black coloured Range Rover, held open the rear door and saluted Freeman who glowered and pointedly glanced at his watch. Once seated in the rear of the vehicle, Freeman fetched his mobile phone from his briefcase and dialled a number he frequently used.

"Councillor McFadyen," he pompously snapped at the telephonist and a few seconds later, was put through to McFadyen's office.

"Mathew, it's me," he said, "I'm on my way through to a Rotary dinner in Motherwell and then should be free for our meeting some time after nine. Are you available to meet me?"

"Ah, no, I'm afraid not Arthur, not tonight. Sorry," was the response and almost immediately, he detected a note of hesitation in McFadyen's voice.

"Is everything all right, old man? You don't sound yourself," Freeman's eyes narrowed, suspicious that McFadyen was fobbing him off.

The pause before McFadyen replied convinced him that something was wrong.

"I'm sorry, Arthur, but I've had a change of mind. I won't be backing your play."

A cold sweat enveloped Freeman that quickly became anger.

"Why not?" he coldly replied.

"Arthur, you must understand I have responsibilities that…"

"Don't fuck with me, Mathew," snarled Freeman, suddenly sat forward on the edge of his seat only to be restrained by the seatbelt. "You've been got at. Who was it? Who has been talking to you? What were you promised?" he demanded in a rush.

"Arthur, I really think you should calm down…"

"Calm down? Calm *down*!" thundered Freedman. "Let me inform you that I have recorded the meetings we had where you declared your support for my application as the Force's next Chief Constable and you are tell me to *fucking* calm down?"

"What do you mean," came the nervous reply, "you've recorded our meetings? Arthur, you *shit*; are you trying to blackmail me?"

"What I'm doing, Mathew, is reminding you that you promised your support and now you're are reneging on that promise! Why?"

"Because my support for you was based on the supposition that you *might* be selected as the future candidate for the Chief's position, but your candidacy is not set in stone, Arthur. What *is* set in stone is the political backing that I can count on from the Brewery and Licensed Victuallers Association who contribute heavily to my electoral campaign and will continue to do so when I put myself forward for election to the post of Lord Provost of Glasgow. So, I have a choice to make. You and your *fucking* obsessive belief in yourself or my political career that, might I remind you, also provides me with my income!"

The call abruptly ended and Freeman was left staring at the mobile phone in his hand.

His fury knew no bounds and teeth gritted, he suddenly threw the mobile into his open briefcase and catching the drivers eyes in the rear-view mirror he loudly growled, "Forget Hamilton! Take me home!"
The driver gave the slightest of nods to acknowledge the command and inwardly smiled. Finally, after months of driving the pompous bastard about he now had something of apparent significance to report.

Davie Craven was literally dancing on air. The first tentative steps in his new relationship with Mary McLaughlin was working out and happily he now he had a second date. But first, he remembered, he had better phone his father to ensure that Martin was available to child mind Elsa that evening.
He patted his pockets for his mobile then shook his head, recalling that the phone was still plugged into the USB socket in his car. Making his way to the front door, he pulled it open, but was surprised to see a burly woman, her dark hair tightly wound into a bun on top of her head and young man stood there, the woman with her fist raised and just about to knock upon his door.
"Can I help you?" he smiled at them.
"Mister David Craven?"
"Aye, that's me," he stared a little uncertainly from one to the other.
"My name is Detective Sergeant Myra McColl from Stewart Street CID. I wonder, sir, if my colleague and I might come in and have a wee word with you?"
Taken aback, Davie could only nod his assent and stood to one side to permit McColl and Feeny to pass by into the hallway where they respectfully stood. McColl smiled and asked, "Are you alone in the house, Mister Craven?"
It occurred to him then even though they were already across his doorstep that he really should have asked for some identification and now did so, when he asked, "I'm sorry, do you have your, I dunno what you call them and…" his face registered his puzzlement, "why are you here?"
McColl continued to smile as she produced her leather wallet bearing her photographic Warrant Card from her handbag and showing it to him, replied, "We have information, Mister Craven, that you have items in this house that are part of on ongoing murder

inquiry. Now again, is there anyone else in the house…"

"Daddy," said the small girl behind them. They turned to see three-year-old Elsa, a doll hugged to her chest, staring wide-eyed at the two strangers.

Davie moved to lift her into his arms. "This is my wee girl. There's only her and me in the house. Now, what's this all about, what murder inquiry?" he asked, his throat feeling tight and now a little afraid that things seemed to be spiralling out of his control.

McColl, instinctively realising that Craven did not pose any immediate threat, turned to Feeney and raising her hand, said, "Get onto the boss and tell him that we're with Mister Craven and his daughter and that apparently there's nobody else in the house." Turning back to the bewildered Davie, she smiled and said, "Mister Craven. Do you have any objection to a search of your home?"

Elaine Hamilton knocked on Charlie Miller's door and without waiting to be invited, said, "Sir, that's Myra and young Kevin in the suspect's home. Myra's just about to call the SOCO team in now."

"Good," he nodded, mentally crossing his fingers and his toes too.

"But I don't understand," Davie Craven, sat in his lounge with a burly detective stood impassively by the door, shook his head while his daughter quite oblivious to her father's confusion, played at his feet with her doll. Seated across from him, Myra McColl smiled tightly at the wee girl and thought that either Craven was telling the truth, that they had made some horrible mistake or he was a definite candidate for the next Hollywood Oscar.

Upstairs in his bedroom, Jean Galbraith, like her team dressed in a Forensic white boiler suit and wearing a mask and cover shoes on her feet, pulled open the bedside drawers and began to rummage through the socks and underwear she found within. It was then her eyes opened wide and she quietly said, "Oh, my," before turning and with her hand beckoned forward the team video photographer.

Excited now, Elaine Hamilton arrived at Miller's door and said, "They've found something."

The little girl was hysterical when the young, unformed police officer had to literally tear her from her father's arms. Softly crying,

Davie Craven tried to reassure his daughter that it was all right, that they were just playing a game, that Granddad would soon be along to get her and she was to be a good girl and go with the nice lady. Myra did not want to distress the child any more than necessary and stood patiently with Davie until the little girl was taken away in a marked police car to the local office at Pollok until such times her grandfather could be contacted. When the child was driven out of sight, Davie was handcuffed then bundled into the rear of a CID vehicle and driven by the stony-faced Detective Constable's Willie McGuigan and Kenny Ross to Stewart Street police office.
As McColl watched the car drive off, Jean Galbraith, the SOCO supervisor beckoned to her from the open door of the garage. "Myra, there's something here I think you should see," she called out, her face flushed beneath the mask.

"So, what have we got so far?" Miller glanced at both Mark Barclay and Elaine Hamilton, who held a notebook in her hand.
"A small clear plastic bag containing locks of hair that was discovered in a bedroom drawer, just as described by the caller Mary," she replied, "and a bloodstained hammer wrapped in a towel that was found in a drawer in the garage. Both items are now en route to the Forensic laboratory at Gartcosh for examination."
"On the back of Elaine's information from the house, I've been on to the Lab," continued Barclay, "and following my request they await the arrival of these materials against that of our victims DNA, boss."
"Is there a time frame for the Lab result?" asked Miller, trying to keep the edge of excitement from his voice.
Barclay shrugged and answered, "I've instructed the items be taken directly to the Lab and I'm told that when they arrive, we should have a result within the hour whether positive or otherwise."
"Well," Miller tightly replied, "let's keep our fingers crossed we get a positive result, eh?"
His desk phone rung and with a nod, he dismissed the other two while he lifted the receiver.
"DCI Miller."
"Charlie, its Cathy. Don't ask me how he found out, but Freeman has been on the phone asking if you have a result for the murders. He seems to think you have someone in custody."

"He's almost correct. I was gathering up the information so that when I called you I'd have all the facts at hand, but here's what I do have," he replied and informed her of the circumstances so far.
"So, this man Craven is now en route to your office?"
"He's being brought in by two of my team and is currently detained prior to interview under Section 14. Myra McColl is at the house supervising the SOCO team and the rest of the team is engaged in door to door inquiries with neighbours."
"Right, so who do you intend conducts the interview?"
"As the SIO, as you are well aware, it's my job to be objective and collate all the evidence to present to the Crown Office, so I'm not convinced I should conduct the interview or whether I'll have Mark Barclay and Myra McColl do it."
She heard the slightest hint of uncertainty in his voice and suggested, "Look, why *don't* you do the interview? That way you can report exactly what is required. I mean, it's not unknown for an SIO to participate in an interview."
"I'll consider it," he sighed, then asked, "Did Freeman say anything else?"
"Nothing specific, but then he asked me a curious thing. He reminded me about the day that you and I visited him at the City Chambers and wanted to know if I had any further contact with either the councillor guy, McFadyen or the other man, Thomson who we met that day. Of course, I told him I didn't have a clue what he was on about and asked him why he thought I be in touch with either of them, but as you can guess he didn't say."
"Anything else?"
"No, that's it. Right, I'll let you get on, but keep me apprised of any developments," she said before ending the call.
The door knocked and the civilian analyst Melanie Clarke stuck her head round to breathlessly inform Miller that Chief Inspector Downes of the Media Department had called regarding the arrest of a suspect in the murder inquiry.
"Bloody hell," he shook his head, "word gets out fast, doesn't it?"
"Shall I ring her back , sir?"
"Do that please, Melanie and tell Harry, I mean the Chief Inspector, that as soon as there is a result I'll phone her. Thanks, hen." He dismissed the young woman who had no time to close the door before Mark Barclay pushed past her to say, "That's the suspect

arrived downstairs, boss. He's going through the book at the minute. Do you want him to be taken to an interview room right away?"

"No," Miller shook his head and glanced at the clock. "I'd rather have the Forensic result in my hand before he's interviewed, so put him into a side room and contact Sherlock and ask her to get in here pronto. Before we speak with him I want the suspect medically examined to ensure he's fit to be interviewed and his clothing seized. Get him photographed as well, Mark, for any scratches, bruises or whatever then I want him dressed in a Forensic suit. In addition, Mark, see that the officers doing that don't speak with him, nothing at all. I do not want him concocting some sort of defence before he's interviewed."

"On that point, who will conduct the interview?"

"Let me think about that," replied a thoughtful Miller.

He drove the Range Rover back to the police garage and after refuelling and driving it through the car wash, parked it in the designated bay before walking into the Traffic Department office where he collected his civilian jacket from his locker and then with a cheery wave to the duty constable, signed out for the night. Whistling tunelessly, he returned to the enclosed yard and his own car and got into the driving seat. Opening his mobile phone he scrolled through the directory and finding the number he was looking for, pressed the green button then listened until a moment later the line connected.

"Good evening, sir," said the Traffic constable, aware that he need not give his name. "That's me just got back from dropping Mister Freeman home. Yes, sir," he unconsciously nodded, "I'm here at Helen Street sitting in my own car."

He smiled as he continued, "Well, you might be interested in hearing that…"

Davie Craven was a mess. Neither the detective driving nor the officer who sat next to him in the rear of the CID car had spoken and refused to answer his questions during the drive into the city and his arrival at Stewart Street police office had been greeted with a scowl by the Inspector on duty, who typed his name and personal details into a computer.

"But I don't know what's going on," he had wept then asked, "Why am I here?" and almost fainted with shock when the Inspector told him, "Mister Craven, you are a suspect for a number of murders." Now sat alone in a graffiti scarred detention room, his head held in his hands, he thought of his daughter and in all his life had never felt so helpless or so alone.

## CHAPTER EIGHTEEN

With Shelley beside him, Martin Craven had driven the Mercedes to his own home and now, after a frantic two minutes of laughing and unbridled passion trying to make it upstairs while they tore at each other clothes, they rested entwined in his bed.
He was happily dazed that his morning which begun so worryingly had ended with him at last making the commitment to Shelley that he should have made months before. That he loved her was beyond dispute and that she loved him, well, who would have thought he sighed as curled against him, she gently snored.
He heard the muted sound of his mobile phone ringing, but decided to ignore it then thought better of his decision. If it was Davie needing advice, he had better answer it. Slowly, he edged from the bed, ignoring his usual modesty and trying not to laugh at his nakedness. However, disturbed by his movement of the quilt cover, Shelley's eyes opened and she smiled sleepily at him.
"Where are you going?"
"Hang on, love. I thought I heard my phone ringing," he replied as he lifted his trousers from the floor and searched the pockets. Pressing the button to switch the phone on, he saw he had a voicemail message and lifted the phone to his ear to listen.
As Shelley watched, she saw his face change from a smile to shock, then disbelief.
"What's wrong," she asked, her brow furrowed.
Wide-eyed, he turned to stare at her and almost with disbelief, said, "That was my lawyer. He's been contacted by the police. Our Davie's been arrested on suspicion of murder!"

Moira Bain sat on the comfortable chair in her bedroom, her feet resting on the low padded stool and idly glanced through the fashion magazine. Her mobile phone rested on the bed beside her as nervously she waited on the call that she fervently prayed would come from her father. The bedside radio was tuned to the local station and she glanced at the clock, impatient for the hourly news broadcast to commence and that she hoped would announce the arrest of her brother. She could hear James downstairs in the kitchen making his dinner. When he was finished and out of there, she would nip down and make herself something to eat, a light snack she thought for she was sure that tense as she was her stomach would not cope with a heavy meal.

She turned the page, but her mind was distracted. Had she forgotten anything? Was there something she had failed to do, something that would indicate to the police that she had planted the evidence? If they took her call seriously, they undoubtedly would find the bag of hair and the hammer and she bit anxiously at her lower lip.

Still, she shrugged, there was little she could do now but wait.

The call came to Mark Barclay's desk phone when he was out at the toilet and was answered by Elaine Hamilton. As the caller spoke, she stretched across the desk and quickly scribbled the details onto Barclay's pad that lay before her.

When the call finished, she stared at what she had written and then saw Barclay entering the incident room.

"What?" he asked.

He had made his decision and was preparing the groundwork for the interview when the door opened. Mark Barclay with a smile, said, "That was the Lab. The three locks of hair and blood staining on the hammer match the first three victims."

"Thank God for that," Miller slowly exhaled, raising his arms above his head in a victory salute and almost immediately feeling the weight lift from his shoulders.

But then narrowed his eyes as he added, "What about Paula Kyle?"

Barclay shook his head. "Sherlock might have been correct, boss. It could have been a different hammer."

"Yes," Miller thoughtfully replied as he reached for the phone, "it could have been."

Chief Constable Martin Cairney was about to sit down to an appetising dinner with his wife and teenage daughter when the phone rung in the hallway.

"Sit," his wife commanded him with a raised hand as she rose and walked from the dining room table.

Courteously he intended waiting on her return before he commenced his meal, but she was back in a heartbeat, her hand protectively at her throat, said, "Martin, that's Miss Mulgrew on the phone. I think its news about those awful murders in Glasgow."

He pushed back his chair and entering the hallway, pulled the dining room door closed behind him, but not before asking that his wife and daughter go ahead and eat.

"Cathy."

"Sir, sorry to call you at home, but…"

"Don't worry about that," he hastily interrupted her, "but I trust or rather hope its good news?"

"Yes sir, it is. DCI Miller has a suspect in custody and he has just informed me that items of positive evidential value have been discovered at the suspect's home address. The interview should be commencing any time now."

"Good, good," he took a deep breath and was grinning now, much relieved that his faith in Miller was now being justified. "Right, I'm at my dinner so I'll get all the news in the briefing report tomorrow when I'm at my desk. However, Cathy, two things. Please have a private word with DCI Miller and inform him how pleased I am and secondly, that issue with Mister Freeman sacking Miller; on the QT I would like you to tell the DCI that is an issue he need no longer worry about. He'll know what I mean. Good evening, Cathy."

The SOCO supervisor Jean Galbraith finished supervising the packing up of the van and nodded cheerio to Myra McColl, who stood at the entrance to the driveway with Kevin Feeney and a half dozen detectives gathered around her.

"Right, lads and lasses," she said, "there's nothing more we can do here this evening. The local cop shop has agreed to maintain a uniform presence outside the house through the night, just in case the DCI wants something further done tomorrow. In the meantime you guys have done well, so get yourselves back to the office and in the

absence of any further Actions at the minute, I suggest you all sign off and get home and I'll see you in the morning."
She turned to Feeney and was about to tell him to fetch the car along when her mobile phone rung.
"Myra? Mark Barclay. The boss asked if you would get yourself back here as soon as possible. He's got a wee job for you."
Barclay grinned when he heard her sigh and guessed she was about to complain that she'd had a long enough day, before he continued, "He wants you to neighbour him when he interviews the suspect, Davie Craven."
She beamed, for it was a rare opportunity that a detective got to sit in when a serial killer was interviewed. "Half an hour, maybe forty minutes with traffic, Mark and I'll be there and tell the boss *not* to start without me!"

Sitting at his desk in the semi-darkness of his study, ACC Arthur Freeman banged the phone down into its cradle. This had been the second disastrous call of the evening.
The first call thirty minutes earlier from a fellow Assistant Chief Constable, informed Freeman of her withdrawal of support for his bid to be selected as the frontrunner for the position of Chief Constable. He had listened in silence before angrily slamming the phone down on her. And now the second call from a city councillor who stuttering throughout the call, likewise withdrew his support. Without dignifying the councillor with a response, Freeman also cut short his call.
It was over.
Somehow or other Cairney had learned of his bid to usurp him as the Chief and used whatever influence he had among his own supporters to undermine those who had initially backed Freeman. He snarled for his first thought was revenge, but no action he could take would now unseat Cairney for the bastard held sway over him; effectively his future as an Assistants Chief Constable and thus his career was in the palm of Cairney's hand.
He was too old to seek a senior managerial position with another Force and knew that even if he did he would never receive the backing of the Chief Constable or Police and Fire Committee that he believed he so rightly deserved.

No, there was nothing else for it for if he was to retain his dignity, he had no option other than to resign. Better to go now than to suffer the indignity of being at the beck and call of Cairney.
Pale faced, he turned to his desk and switching on the overhead desk lamp that shone brightly onto the keyboard, turned to glance and ensure that there was paper in the printer.

Both interview rooms at Stewart Street police office, located on the ground floor corridor of the CID suite, are claustrophobically small and almost boxlike. The walls are painted a dull green and being windowless, the rooms have a distinctive smell, usually emanating from the rubbish bin that daily overflows with stained paper cups or the remains of a fast food takeaway.
Each room normally contains a table and three or four chairs, dependant on how many persons will be present at the interview. Upon the table is the standard twin cassette tape recorder that is screwed down to prevent it being prised off the table and used by suspects as a weapon. There is usually a scattering of A4 sheets of paper lying on the table that interviewers will sometimes use to take notes or upon which a suspect will be asked to draw a rough map or sketch to explain a statement. Affixed to the back of the door or on the wall is the printed declaration that informs the suspect of his or her legal rights, but are seldom read for most of the interviewees who are brought to these rooms are often accompanied by a lawyer or occasionally and disdainfully refuse legal advice.
At DCI Miller's request, DS Myra McColl first obtained two blank cassette tapes from the duty officer, both of which were recorded as issued to her and then had the turnkey and a uniformed constable bring Davie Craven, now dressed in a white Forensic paper boiler suit, to the interview room where she and Miller stood waiting. Dismissing the turnkey and constable with a nod, Miller led the slighter built Davie into the interview room where McColl closed the door behind them.
Inviting Davie to sit down, Miller said, "Mister Craven, I'm Detective Chief Inspector Charlie Miller and this lady who you've already met, is Detective Sergeant Myra McColl. Let me ask you, have you been formally interviewed before by the police?"
"No, never," replied Davie, his throat painfully dry and almost choking with fear.

"Myra," Miller turned in his seat towards her, "could you fetch Mister Craven some water, please?"

He smiled at Davie, but said nothing until McColl returned to the room and handed Davie the paper cup of water that he swallowed in one gulp, some of the water dripping down his chin and onto the paper boiler suit.

"I understand that Doctor Watson examined you Mister Craven and you're well? You're not taking any medication or anything like that, are you?"

"No…no, sir," he corrected himself with a shake of his head.

"So, you are fit to be interviewed; that's correct then?"

"I don't know what's going on. Why I'm here. Am I not supposed to have a lawyer here with me, to explain what's going on?" Davie bleated.

Miller glanced at McColl, who replied, "A representative of the law firm that you indicated represents your father has been informed of your detention Mister Craven and I assume is en route here now, but under the rules of evidence we can proceed with the interview until such times your lawyer attends the office. Do you understand?"

"Yes," he replied in a voice so low it was almost a whisper.

Before he begun the formal interview, Miller took a few moments to explain the cassette tape machine, how the interview would be conducted and asked if Davie first needed the toilet, but the younger man declined; just sat there, his head bowed and his arms wrapped tightly about him.

He could not explain why, but Miller had the strangest feeling in his gut and glancing at McColl, realised that the normally placid detective also looked uncomfortable.

Switching on the tape machine, Miller went through the formality of introducing both detectives and the suspect before reading Davie the common law caution and ensuring the young man understood the caution.

The next five minutes was spent by Miller posing simple questions designed to put Davie at ease; his marital status, his employment, his family, but this question caused him to become almost hysterical when he stood and demanded to know where his daughter was and if she was being properly cared for.

Miller, himself now standing, eased the young man down into his chair and turned off the machine, explaining that DS McColl would leave the room to confirm that little Elsa Craven was well for he realised that the suspect would pay little attention to the questions if he remained in an agitated state.

A short time later McColl returned and before the machine was again switched on, told Davie, "Your wee girl has been collected from the Pollok office by your father and his partner. She's taken the wee girl to your father's house for now and he's on his way here, okay?" she finished with a reassuring smile.

Much relieved, Davie nodded, then narrowed his eyes at McColl and asked, "My Dad's partner? Who is that?"

McColl shrugged and replied, "I didn't get a name. The lassie I spoke with on the phone said it was a young, blonde girl, very striking in appearance."

Even with all that was going on and the nightmare he found himself in, Davie slowly smiled. It seemed all along he had been right about his Dad and Shelley McPhail.

"Thank you," he simply replied to McColl.

The interview continued, but it was when Miller mentioned that the information received that caused the search of Davie's house had come from a woman calling herself Mary, that Davie's head shot up.

"I only know one Mary," he replied. "Mary McLaughlin and she's my…she's my girlfriend."

"Can you provide us with Mary's address?"

"Yes, I mean I know where she lives because I dropped her off there, but I don't know the house number or the road name. She directed me to the house," he explained with a shrug, then added, "but my sister will have the address in the personnel file. Mary works at my Dad's company too."

A thought struck Miller who asked, "But Mary has also visited you at your home?"

Davie stared at him, then shook his head. "Mary's never been in my house. Well," he softly smiled, "not yet anyway."

"Never been in your house," Miller softly muttered and he wondered, yet the information from the woman calling herself Mary was quite specific as to where the evidence could be found and he concluded that Mary must therefore be a pseudonym.

"Mister Craven, the locks of hair that were found…"

Davie raised both hands and interrupting, said, "I have no idea where they came from. I know nothing about them. This lady," he pointed to McColl, "also said there was a hammer in my garage. I don't even *own* a fucking hammer…" by now he was again standing, his hands clamped to his ears as though to shut out the allegations against him and almost near hysterical.

"Calm down, Mister Craven!" Miller thundered at him, then as the younger man resumed his seat, in a quieter voice added, "Please sit down, Mister Craven. It helps no one if you get too agitated. You have to remain calm and we'll get this sorted out, I promise."

There was a pause while Davie sat down, tears now dripping down his cheeks and falling from his chin onto the table.

"Do you want a wee break, son," McColl kindly asked.

He shook his head and his head flopped down onto his arms that lay across the table as he cried, "Why won't you believe me? I do not know anything about this, I promise you. Nothing."

"Who else has keys to your house, Mister Craven?"

He raised his head and stared at Miller as he shook his head. "Nobody, no, wait. The childminder and my Dad have a set each, but that's it. Nobody else." He continued to stare at Miller and then shaking his head, added, "No, they wouldn't leave those…those things in my home. No way," he repeatedly crossed his hands over and over. "The childminder, Missus Ferguson, she's a nice lady and dotes on Elsa. And my Dad, he loves me. There *must* be another explanation. There has to be."

Miller was feeling uneasy. This was not as straightforward as he had hoped it might be. Yes, he expected that if Craven was the killer he would deny the murders and the evidence discovered in his house, but Miller had a feeling there was more to it than that.

He glanced at McColl who returned his stare and with the subtlest shake of her head, she shrugged that she too was not happy with the way the interview was proceeding.

The mobile phone lying on the double bed chirruped. Moira Bain saw her father's name on the screen and forcing her voice to be calm took a deep breath before answering, "Dad, how are you? Had a good day off?"

"Moira, I'm at Stewart Street police office. Davie's been arrested for…" but his voice failed him and rubbing at his forehead, he continued, "Look hen, can you get yourself into the city and meet me at the police office? I really need you here with me, right now."

"Arrested, Dad? Whatever do you mean? Why has he been…" but she got no further, for her father interrupted and said, "Look, hen, just come to Stewart Street police office. I'll explain when you get here. Please!"

"I'm on my way, Dad," she hurriedly assured him, her voice now oozing sympathy and concern and ended the call with a satisfied smile. Taking a deep breath, she carefully checked her makeup in the dressing table mirror before opening the wardrobe sliding door to find a suitably conservative trouser suit that would impress upon the police she was a young businesswoman who should be taken seriously. Her father would be distraught at his son's arrest and she would take charge, ask the right questions and demand of them that they tell her father and Moira exactly what Davie was charged with, what evidence they had and ensure that Martin would see her as the capable woman she is.

Smirking, she could not help but think that the business was now hers.

She took her time changing into the suit then from the top of the stairs, called down, "James. That was my father. We have to go now. I am low on petrol, so we will need to take your car. Get ready, I'll be down in five minutes."

In the lounge, James Bain switched off the television and sat fuming. She had explained her plan at length, that they would travel together to whatever police station Davie was being held in and insisted that when they arrived there, he become the conscientious husband. She demanded that he was to say nothing unless spoken to and even then, to keep his replies short. In other words, he seethed; he was to keep his fucking mouth shut.

He was to be the bitch's lap dog, the bitch's patsy!

Rising quickly from the couch, he went to the hall cupboard to grab his coat and slamming the cupboard door, shouted, "I'll wait in the car!"

Based on the damning items discovered at his home and subsequent comparative DNA evidence that indicated these items were related to the deaths of Linda Docherty, Allison McVeigh and Janice Maxwell, the interview concluded with DCI Miller and DS McColl having little option but to charge the weeping Davie Craven with three counts of murder.

Standing at the charge bar with the sobbing prisoner between them, why then, thought Miller as he glanced at the solemn faced McColl, do I feel so uncomfortable?

## CHAPTER NINETEEN

In accordance with the Force's Standing Operational Procedure, David Craven who was no longer a suspect but now an accused person, was placed on suicide watch that meant for the duration of his confinement at Stewart Street police office he would be constantly monitored by a uniformed constable who sat on the other side of the door to the cell with the instruction that every ten minutes, the officer would glance through the open hatch to ensure the prisoner had not harmed or at worst, killed himself.
It was a boring and tiresome duty for the officer delegated this watch and in particular because throughout the night, the prisoner would not stop sobbing.

Returning with McColl upstairs, Charlie Miller was surprised and touched to find that not one member of the investigating team had left the office for home, but all stood and applauded him when he and McColl pushed through the door into the incident room.
Slightly embarrassed by the attention, Miller waved them off with the cry, "You buggers get yourselves away up the road. If you're waiting for me to stand you a round of drinks, then that will be tomorrow," and was jovially jeered as the team collected their coats and en masse made their way out of the room.
That's when he saw Cathy Mulgrew sitting by a desk at the far end of the room, smiling at him. She stood as he approached and nodding at him, said, "Got your man, then?"
But his face registered that he was not happy and her shoulders slumped as grimacing, she added, "What?"
He turned and beckoning Myra McColl to follow them led her and McColl through to his office where he sat behind his desk and indicated they both sit.
"I can't speak for Myra, but I'm not happy," he shook his head. "The Crimestoppers information from this woman Mary, the exact location of the hair, the…the…"

"It's your gut, isn't it boss?" interrupted McColl, who turned towards Mulgrew and shaking her head, said, "Ma'am, it's too fucking easy, too…God, I don't know how to explain this, but I think that wee lad downstairs is being set up."

"For heavens sake, Charlie, Myra," she glanced at them both in turn. "What the *hell* are you two thinking? The evidence tells us it's him, doesn't it? You've arrested a killer of four women…"

"Three women," said Miller. "I didn't charge him with Paula Kyle's murder."

"What? Why ever not?" she was bewildered.

"Because there is no evidence linking David Craven to Paula's murder, Cathy. Yes, the circumstances and MO indicate that the same killer might be responsible…"

"And that killer is locked up downstairs!" she argued.

"We *don't* know that for certain, not without hard, physical evidence," his voice rose as he forcefully counter argued. "When I send the report to Crown Office, if they decide to proceed with a fourth charge then it's down to them, their prerogative."

McColl sat silently, watching them debate and waiting for an opportunity to speak.

"Okay then," Mulgrew abruptly asked, "Tell me why you don't think that David Craven is the killer?"

"I can't give you a definite answer to that and yes," he reluctantly agreed, "the evidence suggests…"

"Suggests? Fucking *suggests*?" she was livid now. "Charlie, the dead women's cut hair was found in his underwear drawer! The hammer with the victims' blood adhering to it was discovered in his garage! How much more evidence do you need? For fucks sake!"

"Ma'am," McColl quietly said, "I hear and understand what you are saying and yes, you're correct. The evidence is indisputable."

Mulgrew stared at her and slowly replied, "But what?"

"But I agree with the boss. I think there is more to this than what we are being told by this woman Mary. I have the gut feeling…"

"Here we go again," Mulgrew angrily shook her head, "this *fucking* gut feeling you both have…"

Determined not to be silenced, McColl gritted her teeth and continued, "…but I have a *gut* feeling that David Craven is being set up. This woman who calls herself Mary, where exactly does she fit in? Her information to Crimestoppers describes herself as Craven's friend, that at *his* request she went to the drawer," she stopped and staring unbelievingly at Mulgrew, wagged both forefingers in the air and added, "his *underwear* drawer no less, to fetch something for Craven. I mean, how many men or women do you know would ask a friend to fetch something from their underwear drawer? A spouse or a lover, maybe. Yet, when we asked him about Mary and *if* he's to be believed, the only woman he knows called Mary is a girlfriend who works within the same company and who he tells us has never visited his house. You have to admit, Ma'am, this girlfriend," she glanced at her written notes, "this Mary McLaughlin needs to be interviewed and soon to determine if she was the caller or to eliminate her from the inquiry. Now, given the boss's extensive experience and my own experience, are you prepared to dismiss our gut feelings? Besides, even *you* must admit there is some strong dubiety about the information received by Crimestoppers from this Mary woman," her voice rose as she continued. "So, because we have a fucking man locked up downstairs and it makes it easy for everybody to conclude the inquiry, we simply accept what we have at face value and bugger the fucking truth!" she hissed, her face red and eyes blazing and ready for confrontation.

So thick was the atmosphere in the room now it could almost be tasted.

But then the woman that was Cathy Mulgrew, the woman who was at heart a seasoned investigator, the woman who throughout her career had fought and railed against gender and sexual bias, the woman who through tenacity and determination had earned her current rank, stared at them in turn and shook her head as she replied, "No, Myra, I'm not about to dismiss either of your experience or your gut feelings," then turning towards Miller, calmly said, "So Charlie, you've got yourself a real dilemma here, but what I'd like to know is, what's your next move?"

Mark Barclay was the last to leave the incident room and seeing Elaine Hamilton walking with Melanie Clark in the corridor, called out, "Elaine, wait up."

Both women turned and Clarke, with an intuitive smile placed a hand on Hamilton's arm and quietly told her, "I'll see you tomorrow then," before walking on.

"Mark," Hamilton greeted him.

"Eh, that meal we discussed. If you're not heading straight home, I was wondering…"

"Yes, why not?" she smiled at him.

Together they headed for the stairs and stepping into the front foyer of the office, saw a good-looking young woman and strikingly handsome man push their way though the glass doors into the station. Passing the young couple, they saw the woman greet an older man who had been sitting on a bench in the foyer and watched him hug her to him.

Pushing open the door to permit Hamilton to pass by, Barclay offered her his arm and asked, "What do you fancy? Chinese, Italian or what?"

"Oh, I think that nice Italian restaurant down in John Street near the City Chambers would…"

She stopped dead, her eyes narrowing as she stared at a car, a silver coloured Ford Fiesta.

"Elaine? Are you okay? What's wrong?" asked a puzzled Barclay.

She turned to him and thoughtfully replied, "If you don't mind, Mark, can we do this another night? There's something I have to do back at the office."

He stared curiously at her. "Will it take long?"

"No, something I have to check," she shook her head.

He took her by the arm and said, "Well if it won't take long, then why don't we go back and check it together, then we can go and get that bite to eat."

Moira Bain was distraught or so she seemed to her equally distraught father, Martin.

"But that's impossible," she forced a tear, "our Davie couldn't do something like that. I mean, could he?" she added, deliberately sowing the seed of doubt.

"No, of course he couldn't," her father shook his head. "My God, Davie couldn't kill anyone, let alone three women!"

James Bain sat quietly watching them both, reluctantly admitting to himself that Moira's performance surprised him. The front door opened and the same couple who had just left re-entered the foyer, the woman giving him a glance as they passed by and headed towards the stairs.

Probably just gone out for a fag, he thought.

"How long before they tell us anything?" he heard Moira ask.
Martin shook his head. "The man in charge will have a word with me later, but the detective I spoke with on the phone told me that Davie has been charged and he'll appear tomorrow morning at the Sheriff Court, then he'll be remanded and probably spend time in the jail till the trial."
"Has he seen a lawyer yet?"
Martin nodded. "The guy who deals with my business affairs sent one of his associates here, but by the time he arrived the interview was over and Davie had been charged, so he told me there is nothing he can do till he meets with Davie tomorrow at the court."
"Dad," she hesitantly asked, "did Davie confess?"
Her father stared at her as though she were mad. "Confess to what! Have you not been listening, Moira? He didn't kill anyone!"
James stood and though he knew she'd be angry for opening his mouth, thought he'd better defuse the situation and asked, "Where's Davie's wee girl, Martin? Where's Elsa?"
He shook his head and said, "At my house…with Shelley."
Moira turned pale. "Shelley? Do you mean Shelley McPhail, Dad?"
"Yes," he irritably replied, "Shelley McPhail."
"Why would…"
"Because Shelley and I are a couple," he pre-empted her next question.
"Dad!" she stepped back from him, outrage written on her face.
"Don't start, Moira," he raised a hand to warn her off, "We've a more important issue here to deal with."
"For heavens sake, Dad! Shelley McPhail? She's young enough…"
"I know her age, Moira," he snapped at her, "and right now I've enough to worry me without you going on about your bloody embarrassment about what your father gets up to!"
She was raging, angry enough to walk out of the fucking place and let the old fool deal with Davie's arrest himself, but forced herself to remain calm. This was not the time to lose her head, she told herself and was about to tell her father that he was right of course, at a time like this…but she never got the chance, for just then a tall, stocky man with a scarred face that was almost as well worn as the suit he wore arrived down the stairs. Walking towards them, he addressed her father, and asked, "Mister Craven? My name's Detective Chief Inspector Miller."

Elaine Hamilton switched on her computer and impatiently waited the half minute it took to power up.

"Do we have time for a coffee, I could put the kettle on," asked Mark Barclay, still bemused by her sudden desire to return to the office.

"Eh, if you like," she absentmindedly answered over her shoulder. He walked off, but distracted by his question she failed her log in and quietly muttered, "Bugger." Successful on her second attempt, she signed in and scrolled down the screen to the statements folder, then typed in 'Ford Fiesta.'

Four statements featured either the word 'Ford' or the word 'Fiesta', but it was the statement of Karen Bailey that she highlighted. Biting at her lower lip, Hamilton quickly scanned through the statement and nodded as she smiled.

She was correct.

So engrossed in what she was doing, she startled when Barclay placed a mug of coffee down on the desk beside her.

"There we go. Now, what is it that we're checking here?" he asked.

"First things first," she replied and turned to the phone to call the PNC operator downstairs.

"Hi, it's Elaine Hamilton, here. Yes, I know, but I'm working on a wee bit later," she hurriedly explained and added, "could you do a PNC check for me, please?"

She narrowed her eyes and concentrated on recalling the registration number as she dictated the digits to the operator and then said, "Yes, that's correct, a Ford Fiesta." She was writing the details on the pad in front of her when the operator replied, "Elaine, this car was the subject of a PNC check the other night by two beat cops working down the Drag area. Do you want the details, hen?"

"Yes, please," she replied, her face flushing with excitement. Staring at the pad, she smiled.

"Is that something that can keep till tomorrow?" asked Barclay. Hamilton thoughtfully nodded before replying, "I think it might have to, Mark. I don't know if the boss will be ready for it and besides," she shrugged, "I'm not certain if it will be as useful as I'm hoping."

"Right then, if it'll keep lets you and I make tracks to that restaurant and you can tell me what you *think* you've found," he grinned.

On the drive home, they did not speak.

He guessed she would be angry with him, that he had butted in when she had challenged her father about Davie confessing and after she had clearly told him not to say a word.

Well, fuck her, he thought. If he hadn't asked after Davie's wean she wouldn't have bothered her arse either. Not that he had any particular liking for the snotty nosed wee bugger, but maybe it made Martin think that he did care about the child, that he wasn't as stupid or uncaring as he had always thought James to be.

Not that it really mattered, he sighed at he turned onto the motorway slip road. He knew that when Davie was convicted and Moira had no further use for him he would be out on his ear, but not without some recompense. He grinned to himself, for if she thought she was dumping him without a penny she would be sadly mistaken.

She might have her insurance in an envelope in her lawyers office, but he realised she could not use it without implicating herself for not only was it her plan to steal Davie's house key and plant the stuff, but how would she explain to the police being in possession of such damning evidence without turning it over to them?

He risked a quick glance at her pale, drawn face.

No, Moira did not hold all the cards in this game, as she thought.

She had waited alone in the dark for almost forty minutes outside the warehouse and it was evident that Davie wasn't coming.

Disappointed and a little hurt that he had let her down without even a phone call, head down she began to trudge towards the bus stop, picking up her pace as she strode along and ignoring the taunts of the two drunks who stood smoking outside the seedy pub.

Inwardly she argued that there must be a good reason, convinced that Davie would not have led her on and persuading herself that he definitely liked her as much as she liked him.

Arriving at the bus stop, she shook her head as if to clear her thoughts. Yes, she was positive that something had come up, that there was a good reason Davie had not arrived to give her a lift.

The bus arrived and stepping onto the platform, her mobile phone activated.

**CHAPTER TWENTY**

After a sleepless night that saw him rise at four in the morning to creep downstairs and make a pot of tea, Charlie Miller had remained in the kitchen and left the house at six-thirty to head into the office. If he was asked to explain his feelings about the apparent guilt of David Craven, he would not be able to give a valid reason why he believed the young man to be innocent nor would he be able to justify any other course of action than arresting Craven for murder and submitting a case to the Procurator Fiscal.

It did not help knowing that if Craven *was* being set up for the three murders then the real killer was still free and likely to again commit murder.

Driving on the rain swept roads to Stewart Street, he thought of the previous evening's conversation in his office with Craven's father, Martin Craven.

Of course, like any parent he refused to believe his child capable of such monstrous crimes and extolled his sons virtues as a man and a father. The young woman who had waited downstairs with the younger man, he explained, was his daughter Moira and her husband James Bain and passionately added neither of whom would believe his son to be capable of the murders.

Through subtle and patient questioning, Miller learned of David Craven's dismal record with women, of the breakdown of David's marriage and of the ex-wife who Martin regularly paid off to avoid any court dispute that might lose David his daughter Elsa; the toddler that both father and grandfather doted on. He did not tell Martin Craven that admitting his sons failure with women could without doubt be manipulated by a skilful prosecutor to suggest that David Craven hated women and infer to a jury that that this supposed hatred was a probable reason for the murders.

He learned of Martin's very recent decision to retire from the successful business he run and of his plan that his son inherit the business and continue as the MD.

Miller was about to ask about the daughter, but stopped when Martin Craven added "…of course, Moira would also be involved in the business as well, though it will be Davie who will run things."

When asked if the name Mary meant anything to him, Martin Craven admitted he had through the years known a number of Mary's and that there were some Mary's employed by his company, however, to his knowledge the only Mary personally known to his son Davie was

a young woman called Mary McLaughlin, an employee who worked in Craven's warehouse. He believed his son seemed to be keen on the woman and that if Miller needed it, Davie would have the woman's phone number and likely could be obtained from his sons phone directory; a phone that was now in the custody of the police. It was unfortunate, but helpful though Martin Craven was nothing he told Miller could absolve his son of the charges of murder and so promising to keep him updated with any developments in the case, Miller led the increasingly distraught father back to the foyer where he was curiously taken aback, though he could not understand why, to discover Craven's daughter and son-in-law had already departed. Judging that the older man was too upset to drive safely, he arranged for two officers to convey the badly shaken Martin Craven home. Now here he was back at the office, weary from the previous evening and with the lack of sleep lying heavily upon him. Parking his car in the rear yard, he pushed through the rear door that led to the charge bar and was about to head towards the stairs when he was beckoned over by the nightshift uniform bar officer who said, "Sorry, sir, I know you're on your way upstairs, but there was a telephone message left late last night for the incident room from the Forensic people. Do you want to take it with you or shall I wait for…?"
He was about to ask why the duty individual manning the incident room during the nightshift hadn't taken the message, but remembered with the case apparently solved he had instructed there was no longer a requirement for anyone to monitor the phones. Another ACC Freeman initiative, a saving in overtime he bitterly thought.
"Yeah, just give it to me, please," he nodded.
His eyes narrowed as he read the message and then he frowned. If he had been uncertain about David Craven's guilt before he arrived at the office he was even less convinced now and thanking the bar officer, made his way upstairs to the incident room.

Martin Craven had slept badly. He awoke from a nightmare where his son Davie was hanging by his fingers from a cliff top screaming for help, but no matter how fast his father run towards him, he did not get any closer as Davie continued to slip over the edge. The

feeling of helplessness was so overwhelming that when he finally opened his eyes it was to discover his cheeks wet with tears.
He lay still, staring up at the ceiling and wondering how he would cope with the day. He heard a loud knock and turning his head saw Shelley, her hair tousled, wearing one of his shirts as a nightie and standing in the doorway while a small, fair-haired bundle run towards the bed and clambered up beside him.
He forced a smile and enveloping his granddaughter in his arms, said, "Good morning, princess. How are you today?"
"She's fine, now," smiled Shelley, as she strode across the room, "though she's had a bit of a restless night and nearly kicked me out of the guest bed, didn't you, you wee toe rag." She reached across to tickle the giggling child under her arms. "More to the point, Martin," she softly asked as she sat on the edge of the bed and stroked gently at his forehead, "how are you?"
He sat up and shook his head, too afraid to speak. Sighing heavily, he replied, "I can't believe this is happening to us. Just when we were sorting out a life together and I was talking about retiring."
She smiled, for he had said 'us' and 'we' and he could not know how much it meant to her that even in this the darkest of times, she was included in his life.
She decided it was time to do what she did best. She knew he had to be motivated, that he must get up and out of bed and so took charge and said, "Right, Grandpa Martin, let's get you out of bed and downstairs for some breakfast." Turning to the wide-eyed child, she whispered, "Shall we tickle Grandpa out of bed, Elsa?"
"Yes!" cried the little girl, her bewilderment and sorrow for the moment forgotten as with the help of Auntie Shelley, she attacked her grandfather.
He played along with the pretence and slid from the bed, then carrying the laughing child in his arms followed Shelley out of the room and downstairs.

The early edition headline of that mornings 'Glasgow News' informed their readers that the 'Glasgow Demon Barber' had been arrested, that a man was in custody and would in due course appear before the Sheriff Court charged with multiple murder, though it did not state how many murders.

While the newspaper was more than happy to run with Ally McGregor's descriptive title of the killer, curiously Mister McGregor's name did not feature in the story nor in any other story in the newspaper.

Cathy Mulgrew had been at her desk for almost twenty minutes when the phone rung and the Chief Constable's secretary informed her to hold for Mister Cairney.
Less than a minute later, Martin Cairney greeted her with, "I hear congratulations are in order, Cathy. It seems that our faith in DCI Miller was justified."
"Yes, sir," she slowly replied, then paused.
He was no fool and picking up on her hesitation, suspiciously asked, "What?"
She took a deep breath and choosing her words carefully, bluntly told him, "I regret to inform you, sir, that DCI Miller is not convinced of David Craven's guilt. Certainly," she hurriedly continued before he interrupted, "as a consequence of the evidence discovered at his home, Craven has been charged with three of the four murders, but Miller is quite categorically convinced at this time there is insufficient evidence to charge him with the last murder, that of Paula Kyle."
"But the other three murders? You say that Miller's not happy he has arrested the guilty man?"
"No sir, he's not at all happy. He is of the opinion that there might have been some collusion by an individual or individuals unknown to plant the evidence at Craven's home for us to find."
This time it was Cairney who paused before he asked, "What's Miller's justification for this belief?"
How the *fuck* am I going to explain a gut feeling, she hurriedly asked herself, then replied, "His instinct and there is some dubiety about the information that was received that led us to the evidence discovered within Craven's house, sir."
"His instinct," Cairney slowly repeated, then continued, "and what's *your* instinct, Cathy? Is Miller's instinct worthy of your backing?"
She took a deep breath and said, "I trust him implicitly, sir. If Charlie Miller thinks that the evidence or how it was obtained is tainted, then I believe that given his fine record of successful

investigations we should consider letting him have some leeway, some time to confirm or negate Craven's innocence."

"But he won't release the accused, this man Craven unless there is overwhelming evidence to suggest Craven's innocence?"

"No, sir, not at all. Craven will remain in custody as the accused until such times his guilt is proven or disproven. What I'm instructing Miller to do is to continue the investigation, to try and trace the informant who led us to Craven and of course, there is still Paula Kyle's murder to be solved."

"So, as far as the media is concerned," Cairney slowly said, "we *have* solved at least three of the murders and are concentrating on solving the fourth murder, yes?"

"Yes, sir, exactly."

"What's his thoughts on the fourth murder, that of Paula Kyle?"

She hesitated before responding, "There is a possibility, not a strong possibility but nevertheless it exists, that her murder *might* be the work of a copycat killer. My instruction to Miller was that he concentrate on detecting the killer of the first three victims and he appears to have succeeded. However as I said, Miller now doubts Cravens guilt and believes another individual or individuals are responsible for the three murders. If indeed he is correct and neither Craven nor these unknown individual or individuals committed the fourth murder, he will investigate Paula's murder as a separate inquiry. If indeed it should prove that this man Craven or the individual or individuals *is* responsible for all four murders, all well and good."

"Hell, I think I'd need to be a Philadelphia lawyer to sort that one out," he sighed. "Okay then, Cathy, keep me apprised of everything and I *mean* absolutely every aspect of Miller's ongoing investigation. We have already taken a hiding from the media about these murders and given the recent situation that I found myself in with…" he stopped, unwilling to even discuss the internal strife that almost saw the hierarchy of the Force tear itself apart. "In short, I do not want to get caught out and I *definitely* don't want any surprise headlines that we messed up, okay?"

"Of course, sir."

He paused the continued. "You do understand there is more than just our careers riding on Miller's instinct, Cathy. If as he suspects he has arrested the wrong man, this could have a devastating effect on not

just the morale of the Force, but open the floodgates for numerous appeals by those already serving sentences and would in turn, overwhelm the judicial system. Our courts could not hope to deal with such a large number of appeals. There would be utter chaos."
"I understand, sir," she quietly replied, but could not prevent the gut wrenching spasms in her stomach as she inwardly prayed that her dogmatic support for Charlie Miller was not unduly influenced by their strong friendship.

Curiously, Moira Bain had slept well. That said, however, she awoke with a slight headache, but nothing two Paracetamol could not cure and before showering, was pleased to see the bruising and bite marks were fading and the vaginal ache had all but ceased. At her dressing table as she applied her make-up, she considered what her day would bring. She assumed after the shock of discovering his son was charged with three murders that her father would not be attending the office. With a smile at her reflection, she envisioned herself sat behind his large desk, issuing instructions to…but of course, it was also unlikely Shelley McPhail would be at work. No doubt her father would need Shelley to help him care for Davie's brat.
Her thoughts turned to the child and she wondered what would become of the little girl for under no circumstances was auntie Moira stepping forward. No, as far as Moira was concerned, Elsa could be handed back to her mother and goodnight Vienna. With the child gone there would no longer be a need for her father to keep milking the company profits to pay off Jean Anderson. Two problems solved, she grinned.
Her brow furrowed. Not unless her father had some notion of keeping the brat and raising her himself. Well, him and his tart Shelley.
A middle-aged man, a teenage gold-digger and a snotty nosed toddler.
The perfect happy family.
As for Shelley, she smacked her lips against a tissue; well, it was obvious she was shagging her father because of his money and what she could get out of the relationship, but one thing was absolutely certain.
The old man could have his fling with the blonde bitch, but Moira would make damned sure that Shelley McPhail would not be another

Jean Anderson and definitely would not get her mucky little hands on any of the company profits.

After a troubled nights sleep, Myra McColl could bear lying in bed no longer and a full hour before her shift commenced, found herself pushing through the doors into the foyer of Stewart Street office. The young dark haired woman sat on the seat in the foyer glanced up as McColl passed by and she was about to acknowledge the bar officer when he called her over and said, "Morning, Myra. That lassie's been sitting here for nearly an hour. Says she got a text message last night that she was to contact the incident room. I think it's for a statement. There's nobody upstairs yet except DCI Miller, but I didn't want to disturb him to take a witness statement." He lowered his voice and added, "The lassie seems a wee bit upset. Can you deal with it?"
McColl nodded and approaching the young woman, nodded to a polystyrene cup at her feet.
"Somebody see you all right there?" she smiled.
The young woman stood and nodding, anxiously replied, "Yes, Miss. The man in the office there, he gave me a cup of coffee while I was waiting for the CID. Is that you?"
"Aye, my names Detective Sergeant McColl and you are?"
"Mary McLaughlin, Miss. I got a text message from a DCI Miller to contact Stewart Street CID, but it was late last night when I received the text and…"
"Don't worry about that, Mary," McColl smiled at her nervousness. "Right then, let's me and you go upstairs and we'll find two fresh cups of coffee. After that we'll have a wee chat and I'll tell you why you were asked to come to the office, eh?"

Arriving upstairs at the incident room corridor, Mark Barclay caught sight of Myra McColl leading a young woman into an interview room and with his hands, made a T sign to McColl who instead mouthed the word, "Two coffees" and gave him a thumbs up. Making his way into the incident room, he was taking off his overcoat and whistling tunelessly as he made his way to the table with the electric kettle. The door behind him opened to admit Elaine Hamilton and two of the inquiry team.
"Kettle's just going on," he cheerfully called out.

The two detectives glanced at each other, wondering what had come over the DI for Mark Barclay was not known for his cheeriness first thing in the morning, but rather his brusqueness.

Her face deadpan and discreetly ignoring Barclay, Elaine Hamilton made her way to her desk and switched on her computer, taking off her jacket while the machine warmed up.

The door to the incident room opened and Charlie Miller greeted them before saying, "Mark, when you've grabbed a coffee, can you come through to my office, please."

"Will do, boss," he replied, then turning to one of the detectives, instructed the woman, "Can you do me a favour and make two coffees and take them through to Myra McColl and her witness in the interview room, please."

Elaine Hamilton sat at her desk and watched Barclay stirring sugar into his mug, then seeing he was about to leave the incident room, quickly pressed the print button and stood to collect the paperwork from the machine before calling out to Barclay, "Wait for me, Mark. If you don't mind, I'll come through to see the boss with you."

Back seated at his desk, Miller looked up when the door opened to admit Barclay and to his surprise, Elaine Hamilton. He saw she carried some paperwork and indicated they sit down. Without any preamble, he begun, "There was a message through the night from the Forensic people through in Gartcosh," he held up the note he had collected from the uniform bar and stared at Barclay when he asked, "If you had placed three cuttings of hair into a small, plastic food bag, Mark, what would you expect a Forensic examination to find on the bag? Particularly if you didn't expect anyone else to be in contact with the bag."

Barclay frowned, then replied, "My fingerprints, of course."

"Indeed. So then, why is it that the bag examined by the Forensic had no fingerprints upon it and in fact, no smudging, nothing to suggest the bag had been wiped clean, but is in all likelihood a brand new bag."

"Surely if Craven opened the bag to place the hair cuttings inside, he wouldn't have bothered with gloves," said Barclay as he shrugged. "I mean, what would be the point if he then stashes the bag in his bloody underwear drawer?"

"Yes, that's what I was thinking," mused Miller. "He takes the precaution of using a brand new plastic bag to avoid his prints getting on it then leaves a bloodied hammer wrapped in a bloodstained towel lying in a drawer in his garage. It doesn't make sense, does it? In fact, it completely contradicts the two pieces of evidence."

"Not if the evidence was planted," Elaine Hamilton softly interjected.

A palpable silence fell, broken when Hamilton continued, "The reason I came with Mark to see you, sir, is because of this," and placed the printed paper onto the desk in front of Miller. "That is the statement of Karen Bailey who you will recall was the woman…the prostitute who was working in the Drag area the night that Linda Docherty was murdered."

Miller lifted the statement and his gaze returned to Hamilton. "Go on."

Hamilton leaned forward, her eyes bright as she said, "Last night when Mark and I were leaving the office…" her eyes widened as she blushed and hastily added, "with everyone else, I mean. I saw a car parked in a visitor's bay outside the office, a Ford Fiesta. A silver coloured Fiesta. Anyway, the point is the Fiesta took my attention because of this," she leaned across the desk to lift Bailey's statement from Miller's hand and jabbed a finger onto the page. "Bailey recalled that on the night Docherty was murdered, she had seen a light coloured Ford Fiesta being driven round the Drag area and noticed the car because the aerial was missing from the roof. She's apparently into cars…"

"And has her own vintage Ford Capri and attends motoring events, yes," nodded Miller, "I recall reading her statement."

Hamilton also nodded and a little excited now, continued, "Mark and I returned to the office and I had the registration number checked on the PNC and the car belongs to a James Bain, who is the brother-in-law of the accused, David Craven."

Miller's head snapped round to stare at Barclay, but Hamilton was not finished. "That's not all, sir," she nodded with quiet excitement to Miller. "There is an entry on the PNC that indicates a couple of nights ago, the car was seen in the Drag area again and the driver spoken to by two uniformed officers."

"Did the entry say if it was David Craven or James Bain who was in the car?"

"No sir," she shook her head.

"Mark," Miller turned to the DI, suddenly animated, "get those two cops up here for a chat. In fact, speak with them yourself and show them the photograph of our suspect that was taken here at Stewart Street after his arrest. We need to find out who was driving the car at the time it was seen in the Drag and we also need to have the witness Karen Bailey back in for another wee chat. I know her statement says she isn't certain she can ID the driver when she saw the car, but if she is as good at spotting vehicles as she thinks she is, she might be able to ID the car. However, don't let her see Craven's photograph. If I'm wrong, I don't want to compromise any future identification parade by letting her have a look at the accused."

To Hamilton he said, "Good work, Elaine. Now, find out what you can about this man Bain and Elaine, I mean everything."

"What do you intend doing?" asked Barclay as he stood up from his chair.

Miller breathed in deeply and then slowly exhaled before answering, "What I intend doing if he's up for it, is having a word with Martin Craven, the father. I'm hoping he might be able to give us some background information on his son-in-law." He glanced at Barclay and Hamilton in turn. "I know what you're thinking, but if he wants to help his son, then he won't have any choice but to speak with me."

"But sir," Hamilton was aghast, "you can't admit that you believe there is a likelihood David Craven might be innocent, not after you've charged him with three murders! His father will have a fit and demand his son's release!"

"Yes, I know, Elaine, so I'll just have to be as careful as I can in what I say to him, won't I?" he smiled at her.

After returning to the incident room, Mark Barclay discovered the two constables who were recorded on the PNC as having stopped and checked out the registration number were both off duty. However, he decided the issue was too important to delay and caused them both to be contacted and instructed to attend the office as soon as possible.

He had just returned the phone to its cradle when Myra McColl returned to the incident room, a statement form in her hand.

"Morning, Mark," she smiled at him and added, "Thanks for the coffee."

"Who was the woman I saw you interviewing," he asked as she handed him the statement.

"Mary McLaughlin. A nice young lassie who works in David Craven's warehouse and has been out on a couple of dates with him. In fact, she was waiting for him to pick her up last night and when he did not show, was very disappointed. Thought he'd maybe had second thoughts and given her a dizzy."

"Mary," Barclay glanced at the statement before repeating, "Not Mary…"

"No," McColl shook her head. "Not *our* Mary the mysterious caller. In fact, she was utterly devastated when I told her about her boyfriend being arrested. She can't believe him to be guilty of such a thing and believes we've made a huge mistake."

"Where is she now?"

"She told me she's never visited David Craven at his home, but she's willing to have her fingerprints taken for elimination purposes, so the bar officer has her downstairs doing that now. Do you want a word with her before she leaves?"

"No," he shook his head, "I'm thinking you'll have covered everything in the statement, Myra."

He glanced up at her. "She's never been in his house, then?"

"No, never."

"Do you believe her?"

McColl thought about it for a few seconds before slowly nodding. "She comes across as quite creditable young woman, brighter than she probably credits herself and considering she's only been going out with David Craven or Davie as she calls him, for a few days, she's quite loyal to him."

"What do you mean, loyal to him; you think she'd lie for him?"

"No, I'm not suggesting she'd lie for him. What I mean is she does not believe him to be guilty. Quite the contrary," she sighed. "She thinks that someone has it in for Davie, that he's being set up."

"Did she offer up any suggestions as to who?"

"She didn't or wouldn't say," McColl shook her head, "but I think she does have someone in mind."

"Oh? Do you think there's any value then in me having a word with her, try to coax a name from her?"

McColl stared down at the seated Barclay and slowly began to grin. "The boss has sold you on our suspicions then, Mark."

"Not just that," he glanced around him to ensure he was not being overheard. "There's some dubiety about the plastic bag that the cut hair was discovered in. There's no fingerprints or even any smudging on the bag. Nothing at all."

McColl seemed puzzled. "No prints? That doesn't make sense, a complete absence of prints or smudging. Why would he…" then the penny dropped. "Somebody's transferred the cut hair into the bag, but from what? From something else that just *might* have someone else's prints or DNA on it?"

"It's a theory, Myra, but not fact. However, the boss wants it kept tight for now. Can you imagine if the papers got a hold of our suspicions?"

"That after giving us a doing for the past six weeks and urging us to find the killer, we've arrested the wrong man," she nodded and added, "No wonder the boss wants it kept tight."

Pointing to Mary McLaughlin's statement, she asked, "Do you want me to inform him that the caller Mary is not the girlfriend after all?"

"No, I'll get him on his phone and let him know. The boss has gone out on a wee visit," he explained.

She understood from Barclay's reaction that she need not ask where Miller had gone to, but replied, "Okay then, I'll pop downstairs and see if the lassie is finished providing her prints then I'll see her off the premises."

Sat behind the large desk in Martin Craven's office, her palms flat on the surface, Moira Bain smiled with self-satisfaction. She had already convinced herself that her father would not return to work, that the shock of discovering his son was a multiple murderer had been so great that it had completely shattered him. No, she would now pick up the reins and manage the business, just as it should have been.

She glanced at the walls, deciding that one of the first actions she would take would be to brighten up the room, bring in a professional decorator and…

The door knocked and was then opened to admit Alex Mason, the warehouse manager who carried a file in his hand.

"Oh, sorry Moira. Shelley's not at her desk and I thought that Martin would be here."

"Shelley's off today, Alex," she smiled winningly at him, while privately deciding if she has her way the money-grabbing bitch might not be returning, "and my Dad's…unwell."

"Oh, I hope it's nothing too serious," he approached the desk to lay the file flat before her. "It's just I need a signature," he explained.

"Well, I *am* after all a company director," she smiled as if reminding him of her status and with a flourish, signed the document where he indicated. "Will there be anything else, Alex?"

"Eh, no Moira," he shook his head as he lifted the file from the desk. She couldn't help herself, her excitement overcoming her previous good sense, for as he walked to the door, he stopped when she said, "You will have to get used to seeing me sitting here, Alex, so perhaps it might be prudent that we set some ground rules. From now on, I believe Missus Bain might be the proper way to address me."

Taken aback, he could only nod and left the room, but as he closed the door behind him, he wondered just what *was* wrong with Martin Craven.

Staring for a few seconds at the closed door, Moira then turned to switch on the desk computer and while it booted up, idly considered if she might hire a male secretary.

Charlie Miller slowly drove along the narrow driveway and stopped the CID car at the imposing arched entrance to the large, Victorian manor house and switched off the engine. He reached into the backseat of the vehicle and grabbed at the plastic carrier bag and then stepped from the car.

The front door was opened by a tall, strikingly good-looking young blonde woman he guessed to be in her late teens or early twenties, her hair piled untidily up on top of her head and dressed in a bottle green tracksuit top, blue denim jeans and her arms wrapped around a toddler who rested on her hip.

"Mister Miller?" she called out and greeted him with a cautious smile at him while the toddler, a little girl wearing a Disney 'Frozen' dress, stared curiously at him.

"That's me," he nodded and held the door ajar while she let the child down onto the floor, then taking the little girl by the hand, she said, "Please follow me. Martin's in the front lounge. Can I get you a coffee or a tea?"

"Coffee would be grand," he replied and thought he detected a faint Northern Scottish accent in her voice.

She opened a door that led into a large room filled with natural light from the huge windows and furnished with solidly built, dark wood furniture.

Martin Craven, casually dressed in a pale blue shirt, Chino's and brown leather slippers on his feet, stood up from an armchair to greet him.

"Please come in, Mister Miller," he beckoned towards the opposite armchair as the door closed. Miller thought Craven looked tired and worn out, but not surprising he told himself, considering the mans son was awaiting trial for multiple murder.

As Miller sat down, Craven said, "I was a little surprised to receive your phone call and particularly when you told me that your visit was to be…how did you put it? Unofficial?"

"Completely unofficial, yes, Mister Craven," Miller stared directly at him to reinforce the appeal. "Firstly though, how are you this morning? I was a little concerned that…well, obviously you took the news about your son badly, but I don't suppose there really is any other way to take that sort of news."

"No, you're quite right of course," sighed Craven. "When yesterday began it had been, personally for me I should say, a very good day. A day I had come to a decision about my life and then to receive the news that Davie was charged with…with those killings. It was awful."

He glanced sharply at Miller. "I assume that your visit is not to tell me that there's been a dreadful mistake, nothing like that?"

Miller forced himself to remain calm and shook his head. "No, Mister Craven. Your son remains the accused for the three murders; however, as I told you last night I do not like to leave any stone unturned and it is my duty as well as my conscience to investigate *all* aspects of the inquiry." He took a deep breath and continued. "By that I mean your son David…Davie," he corrected himself with a soft smile, "has categorically denied any knowledge of the murders, but with such overwhelming evidence discovered in his home…well, I had no option but to libel the charges."

He leaned forward and staring Craven in the eye, said, "But the fact that Davie was charged does not close the inquiry. Your son did not admit his guilt and so I am both legally and morally obliged to continue to ask the question; could some other individual be responsible for these murders? That in turn begs the question, why would such an individual cause us, the police I mean, to search Davie's home? Does your son have an enemy so devious that this unknown individual would devise a scheme to trick the police into believing your son is the culprit?"

He watched as Craven's shoulders sagged and the older man sat back in the armchair to rub a weary hand across his brow.

"Mister Miller, I cannot for the life of me think of anyone who would do this to Davie. As far as I am aware, Davie has no enemies in the world, there is nobody…"

He stopped and bit at his lower lip.

The hesitation was not lost on Miller who seized upon it by immediately asking, "What? What are you thinking, Mister Craven?"

"You asked last night if Davie knew a woman called Mary. Are you able to tell me what the significance of that name is?"

Miller knew the danger of providing evidence to any individual outwith a courtroom for such an act could not only cause Miller to lose his job and all the benefits that went with it, but might even result in him being liable to prosecution and a worst case scenario, imprisoned. However, he had considered all the risks and figured that if he was correct, it was a necessary risk.

Taking a deep breath, he committed himself and begun, "We received information about the evidence being in your son's home from a woman calling herself Mary, who contacted the Crimestoppers information hotline. I have been informed that my colleague has spoken with and eliminated Davie's friend, Mary McLaughlin, but so far we have not traced this woman who calls herself Mary. However," he reached down to the plastic bag at the side of the armchair and lifting it, placed it upon his knee and said, "I have a recording here of her voice. If I were to play this recording, Mister Craven, I would be in breach of the Laws of Evidence and if this became known that I let you hear this recording, it could go very badly for me."

Martin Craven had been in business for over three decades and during that time had dealt with not just reputable businessmen, but also less scrupulous men too. The very fact that DCI Miller was about to disclose evidence that had led the police to arrest his son surprised him, for he recognised that by doing so Miller was trusting him to maintain the confidence of what he was about to disclose. It also indicated to Craven that Miller was true to his word; he really did mean to seek the truth about Davie's plea of innocence.

"Play your recording, please," he replied.

Miller, leaning forward, removed the tape recorder from the plastic bag and placed it upon a low table between the two men. He was about to depress the play button when the door knocked to admit the blonde girl, carrying a tray, and the child who carefully carried a plate of biscuits.

"Mister Miller," Craven stood to take the tray from her, "this is Shelley McPhail, my partner."

If Miller was surprised, he did not show it and nodded with a smile in greeting to the young woman, who blushed furiously. "And the wee girl?" he asked.

"Davie's daughter, my granddaughter, Elsa," replied Craven with the smile of a proud grandparent.

After setting the tray with the two mugs onto the same small table between them, the men watched as Shelley and Elsa left the room, with the small girl shyly waving to them as Shelley closed the door.

"The recording, Mister Miller," Craven reminded him.

Miller pressed the play button and listened as the woman calling herself Mary spoke for thirty-three seconds. At the end of the recording, Miller asked, "Would you like to hear the recording again, sir?"

Craven turned his pale face to stare first through the large window then slowly turned his head to stare at the detective. It seemed to Miller that in the last half minute, the man had aged ten years.

"No, Mister Miller," he slowly exhaled and spoke softly, his eyes brimming with tears, "there's no need for me to listen again. You see, I recognise the voice. I know who your woman Mary is."

## CHAPTER TWENTY-ONE

Locking his front door, Eric Kyle whistled as he descended the stairs from the flat and headed for the front close door. His appointment with the undertaker was due at eleven and as was likely expected of a grieving widower, he'd decided to dress appropriately in a dark suit and black tie.

It took him barely fifteen minutes to drive to the Co-operative Funeral premises and after a short, sombre meeting with the undertaker, all the arrangements had been made.

His next stop was his bank in Victoria Road where he made arrangements to close his account and transfer the few pounds that remained to the Irish bank account.

Returning to the fresh air, he breathed deeply, glancing about him as if taking in the sight of the area for the last time.

He was looking forward to his two-day trip to Crosshaven to view the cottage. Making the flight arrangements on the Internet had been easier than he anticipated and his departure date was arranged for the day following Paula's funeral.

His next stop was to a local garage in Shawlands where he negotiated the sale of Paula's Range Rover. He had rightly guessed there was no need for the police to keep the car and his phone call to Mark Barclay had agreed the vehicle would be released to him when he was ready. His explanation to the manager for the sale provoked some professional sympathy for his loss, but did not deter the greedy salesman offering a price that Kyle knew was lower than he might obtain from other garages. However, as far as he was concerned, the cash was a windfall that he hadn't anticipated so he didn't quibble. Besides, he argued, he didn't intend hanging around trying to save himself a few hundred pounds when he had so much money coming his way. In the end, they agreed a price subject to him delivering the vehicle to the garage before he left the country for Ireland.

Yes, he thoughtfully smiled as he made his way back to his car, after all that he had recently endured things were finally working out nicely.

Sadie Miller was worried about her husband. She had anxiously waited for him arriving home the previous evening and sat with him while he poured out his concerns and worries that he had arrested an innocent man, that he believed his suspect was being set up to take the fall for three murders. He had told her of the problems he might encounter if he followed his conscience, of the real possibility of a threat to his career if he refused to support the charges he had been obliged to libel against the accused man.

She had listened patiently, but been unable to offer any advice other than to remind Charlie that no matter what decision he made she would always support him and had hugged him tightly before taking him to their bed.

She had pretended to be asleep when earlier that morning he had arisen, suppressing a giggle as he quietly collected his clothes and tiptoed about the room trying vainly not to waken her, for she knew that he needed the time alone to think and that if she followed him downstairs he would be upset, believing he had disturbed her sleep. She had heard him drive off far too early for work, but guessed the time in his office would also give him the opportunity to reflect on what decisions he had to make during the day.

Now here she was sat in her kitchen, a pile of clothes on the floor waiting to be placed in the washing machine, the dishwasher to be emptied, a greeting faced Ella in her high chair demanding to be fed, the beds to be made and the house to be Hoovered.

Bugger it, she thought and decided the wean came first. She stood to switch on the kettle and that done fetched her daughter out of the high chair. Loudly singing a popular children's rhyme, she placed Ella on the floor to crawl about while on her hands and knees, pursued the giggling child round the kitchen.

Sitting facing Martin Craven and anxious as he was to know, Charlie Miller decided he would wait and let Craven tell him in his own time whose voice he recognised on the tape recording.

He could clearly see the man was distraught and asked, "Shall I fetch you a glass of water or something, Mister Craven?"

"No, I'll be fine," Craven waved a hand and shook his head. "I'm sorry, it's just that…well, it's such a shock, hearing her voice."

"Whose voice, Mister Craven? Whose voice have you recognised?" Miller patiently asked.

Almost a full minute passed, a minute that stretched Miller's nerves, but then Craven took a deep breath and told him, "My daughter, Mister Miller. You have a recording of my daughter Moira's voice."

Miller sighed and then slowly said, "Was that your daughter who was with you last night at the office or do you have another daughter, sir?"

Craven shook his head. "I have just one son and one daughter, Mister Miller and you must understand that I love them both. However," he sighed, "I am conscious of their individual strengths and their failings, but as their father I have learned to accept and occasionally tolerate their…" he hesitated, then continued, "their flaws for they are two completely different people in both their character and personality."

"You do realise that by identifying your daughter as the woman who contacted us and told us where to find the evidence that was in your son's home, it infers that your daughter had knowledge of the location of the evidence and libels her to suspicion of committing or having some complicity in the murders."

"Yes, I understand," he slowly replied, his breathing tight as though a steel band was being wound round his body and with one hand absentmindedly rubbed at his chest.

"Tell me, Mister Craven, do you believe it possible it was your daughter who placed those items where we discovered them?"

Craven stared at him, the tears now flowing down his cheeks as he slowly nodded.

Miller realised that the shock of discovering his daughter's betrayal of her brother must be tearing the older man apart. Had he denied recognising the voice on the tape recording, his son would undoubtedly continue to be the man accused of three murders, but by identifying his daughters voice Craven had the most horrendous decision to make; save his son by accusing his daughter of the murders or at least knowledge of the murders.

"I'm sorry to keep pressing, Mister Craven, but I have to know. Why would your daughter identify her brother as the murderer?"

Craven tilted his head back to stare momentarily at the ceiling, before lowering it again to stare at Miller.

"If I may, Mister Miller, let me take a little time to tell you about my life and you might then understand my children."

He withdrew a handkerchief from his pocket and wiping at his eyes, returned the hankie and then reached forward to lift the mug of coffee from the table. Hands shaking a little, he took a sip then replaced the mug on the table and licking at his lips, begun.

"I didn't have a formal education, but through hard work and good fortune, built up a successful business that I run today; a business that operates both here in the UK and in Europe. I also married young and some might say, I married a woman from a better…" he sought the word, then shrugging settled for, "background than I came from. When I married my wife, God rest her soul, like everyone who enters marriage I believed I had wed the most wonderful of women. Unfortunately, as time went on I realised my wife was not the nicest of individuals and her public persona was a complete façade, that she was in fact an out and out snob. Though on the surface we had a happy marriage, my home life was not so happy. You see, Mister Miller, my wife turned out to be a woman who wanted the best in life and while you might agree there's nothing wrong with that, she drove me to succeed where I might have been tempted to relax and enjoy my success."

Miller could see that Craven's confession was difficult for him to admit.

"She was manipulative and scheming and part of the reason I built up such a successful business was that I was never at home, for I was always working." Curiously, the more he spoke the more the tightness in his chest eased. He rubbed at his brow with the heel of his hand and continued. "The simple truth is that I had no desire to be at home with my wife and the preferable choice was staying at the business and to work late hours and so, I drove myself on. The only real success from my marriage was my children, Davie and Moira. However, while I am confident Davie has turned out to be much like me, my daughter has paralleled my wife in many ways and like my wife, is determined to be a success in everything she does."

"She's married, your daughter I mean," interjected Miller.

"Yes, but let me explain her marriage. Moira could have had any young man she wanted for she's a smart and bright individual, a graduate from the Strathclyde Business School where she earned herself a First in Economics. I'd like to say she has my business acumen, but she has gone beyond my expectations for she is also a very calculating and ruthless young woman," he sighed, "a gene I believe she inherited from her mother. Unfortunately, she also inherited her mother's snobbery and though it pains me to admit this, Moira is not a very nice young woman. During her late teenage and university years, there were a number of young, suitable boyfriends, but for some reason known only to herself she chose the man she married, James Bain." He shook his head as if in disbelief. "They had not been together for any length of time when she announced she was pregnant with Bain's baby…" he hesitated and first took a deep breath before he stared tellingly at Miller, "or at least she said it was Bain's baby. Either way and to my shame, I encouraged her marriage for I did not want her to be the mother of a child and unwed. I was thinking of her future or so I told myself," he again shook his head as though he did not believe his own statement. "Regretfully, the child died in the womb and so, if I read the signals correctly, the marriage also died that day."

"Tell me about James Bain," Miller asked.

Craven's eyebrows raised and he stared at Miller, a slight suspicion creeping across his face. "Why the interest in my son-in-law, Mister Miller. Do you suspect…"

Miller raised a hand to interrupt Craven and calmly said, "At the minute, sir, I'm just trying to get a background on your daughter."

"Oh, right then," he replied, but though he did not question the detective further, he suspected Miller was holding something back.

"Well, James is a very handsome young man and the first impression one gets of him is that he is most appealing to the female gender. However," he tapped at the side of his head with a forefinger and added, "Unfortunately he is not the brightest of men and what little sense he has I fear, is almost childlike. He can be very petulant and there is no doubt he is completely under my daughter's control." At this, he smiled as he added, "What we in Glasgow would describe as henpecked, eh?"

He paused and took another sip of coffee then continued, "To be frank, I neither like nor trust him. To my knowledge, he has an extremely poor work ethos and that does not sit well with my daughter. Morally, I believe him to be weak and lacking in self-confidence. As far as I'm aware and what little I know of it, he had a bad upbringing with a domineering mother and no male role model in his life. I gather he and his mother are no longer on speaking terms or perhaps, even in touch with each other for she did not attend the wedding ceremony. Though I was never directly informed as such, I suspect that she was not invited."

He held Miller's gaze and then shook his head. "I met the woman only once, when for some reason known only to themselves, they invited her to the house here," he waved a hand about him and sighed, his eyes narrowing as he recalled the occasion. "It was *not* a successful visit. His mother is the sort of woman I believe I would gladly murder and bury on Eaglesham Moor without any second thought," and smiled softly at his own joke. "I will also share this with you. As a wedding gift I purchased my daughter and her new husband's house and also her car. My mistrust of James is such that I ensured both the house and the car were registered in Moira's name and owned by her for I did not expect the marriage to last and certainly did not want James Bain to walk away with more than he deserved. That might make me sound callous, but my primary concern was and remains my daughter's welfare."

"That said, Moira is a very strong character and as I told you, quite openly and publicly dominates her husband. To be frank, Mister Miller, I am surprised the marriage has lasted this long, but then again it is in my daughters nature that she must always be in control and if that means a husband she can also manage then that is probably why they remain together. Though as I said he is undoubtedly handsome, James is what I might describe as a cardboard cut-out, someone that she can bring out for events or functions and show off when the need arises."

As he listened Miller nodded, mentally building a profile of Moira Bain, the woman who called herself Mary and who now was increasingly becoming his number one suspect. However, he still needed more information and asked, "You said Davie is much like you?"

"Yes," Craven smiled grimly, "but not as driven or as obsessive. Unlike me, Davie prefers to enjoy life and would much rather finish work at the allotted time so that he can travel home to spend time with his daughter while I was more…" he shrugged, "willing to work on. Like I told you, Mister Miller, I really had nothing to go home to."

He paused and took another sip of his coffee before continuing. "I have…no, I *had* expectations that having built the business up to its current success Davie would continue in the role of MD when I decided to retire, however, he has other ideas."

"Other ideas?"

"As I've said, he isn't as motivated as me and would much prefer…" he stopped and seemed bemused before adding, "To be honest, Mister Miller, I've never really asked Davie what he would prefer doing. How strange."

An inkling of a suspicion was forming in Miller's head when he said, "How did your daughter figure in the plan you had when your son assumed the position of MD?"

"Moira? Well, of course she would be appointed as the deputy director and support Davie during the transition period. I wouldn't dream of not involving her in the business."

"Did it occur to you that from the way you have described your daughter, she might not be satisfied with the deputy position, but perhaps coveted the MD position?"

"But Davie's her brother," he smiled tolerantly at Miller as though explaining to the detective, "She would understand that the name Craven must continue…"

He stopped and stared with sudden realisation.

"Oh my God, how could I not have seen this," his voice dropped to a whisper. "That's why she phoned. That's why she must have…" He closed his eyes against the sudden throbbing in his head. "She was jealous. She wanted to get Davie out of the way. Moira wants to be the MD; she wants the business. That's it, isn't it?"

"Does your daughter have a key or access to your son's home, Mister Craven?"

"I don't know. Certainly, she has visited Davie's house, we all have at some time or other, but a key?" he shook his head. "I don't know for certain."

"I can't make any promises, sir, not at this time, but the information you have given me causes me to suspect that your daughter Moira has vital information about the murders of the three young women. I must ask you to keep this to yourself meantime and the reason I ask is that if you believe your son Davie to be innocent of these murders, then any phone call to alert your daughter to my suspicion will enable her to formulate an alibi when I question her. That in turn will be detrimental to your sons defence. Do you fully understand what I'm asking of you, Mister Craven?"

He turned to stare at Miller, his eyes again wet with tears and unable to trust himself to speak, nodded.

Miller stood and wanted to say more, to tell this man that the promise he had just agreed would help his son, but equally the same promise would likely condemn his daughter.

Instead, he chose to say nothing and with a final nod turned towards the door.

He had driven just a few hundred yards before he found a safe and quiet place to stop and park. Fetching his mobile phone from his pocket, he dialled the number for the incident room and before speaking, took a deep breath then said, "Mark, it's Charlie Miller. I've an update for you, so here's what I need."

Cathy Mulgrew was vexed. Pulling her car into the back yard at Stewart Street police office she got out and acknowledging the greeting of two passing cops, hurried towards the rear door and made her way upstairs towards the incident room.
She had hardly slept at all with Charlie Miller's suspicion that he had arrested the wrong man keeping her awake all night; so much so that her partner Jo had irritably taken her pillow and moved into the guest room. As she walked up the stairs, her conversation with the Chief, Martin Cairney, still worried her. 'More than just our careers,' he had said. She turned from the top of the stairs and was almost bowled over by Myra McColl, who caught her by the arm and grinning, said, "Sorry, Ma'am. Nearly knocked you flying there."
"What's going on," asked Mulgrew, her brow furrowed as she stood back against the wall to permit at least half a dozen of the inquiry team to hurry downstairs past her.
"Can't stop, Ma'am," McColl cheerfully called out over her shoulder as she followed the detectives downstairs, "but if you head into the incident room there, DI Barclay will give you an update."
She watched McColl and her young aide disappear from sight then a with curious flutter in her stomach, made her way into the incident room.
Mark Barclay was on a call and beckoning her over to his desk, pointed to the chair in front of it while he spoke on the phone.
"Yes, Missus Duncan," she heard him say and didn't miss the excitement in his voice, "and I'll get someone up to you as soon as possible." She watched as he put the phone down, but before she could speak, he raised a hand and called across the room to a young civilian analyst, "Melanie, get on the blower and divert one of the team to meet with Susie Duncan at the Fiscal's office in Ballater Street. She's getting a warrant typed up for a house search, so it has to be collected from her and taken to the Court to be signed by a Sheriff. She has all the details, so it's a straight collection and then when it's signed, the warrant to be taken to the team heading to the house in Blantyre."

That done, he sighed and turning towards Mulgrew, said with a smile, "Sorry, Ma'am. Bit of a rush on there."
"I'm hoping you have good news for me, Mark?"
"Better news, I'd say," he rose from behind his desk, "but before I begin, can I get you a coffee because to be honest, *I* really need one."

Shelley McPhail and Martin's granddaughter Elsa, who stood upon a chair, were both covered in white flour as was the kitchen table and a sizeable portion of the floor about it. The misshapen buns lay upon their baking trays waiting to be placed into the oven. The little girl squealed with delight as Shelley pasted some sticky white icing onto Elsa's nose and grabbing Elsa by the shoulders to hold her, bent down to lick it off the giggling child. From the doorway, Martin Craven smiled at their antics, but his mind was elsewhere.
Had he been wrong to identify Moira's voice? Should he have denied knowing who the woman Mary was he wondered again, but to do so would have surely condemned Davie who he knew in his heart to be innocent of these dreadful deeds; the murder of the young women.
He also knew that Moira could not have been guilty of the murders either and his brow creased.
The detective Miller had also expressed some interest in James, Moira's husband. Could it be that James is the man the police are looking for? Could James be the killer? His mind raced with a number of possibilities.
He could not understand why if as he suspected James *was* the killer, why Moira would shield him and instead cause her brother Davie to be implicated.
He had always thought that Moira would seize any opportunity to get rid of her lazy husband, though of course his first inclination had been by divorce.
His eyes narrowed as he watched Shelley and Elsa and thought if James Bain *was* the killer then by simply being married to him…he sighed, for he realised now why his daughter would protect a man she no longer loved.
It was simply business.
Mister Miller had been correct when he inferred Moira might not be satisfied with the Deputy MD position.

She was not protecting James Bain, she was protecting herself.
It would be far easier to gain control of the company if Davie was no longer around and besides, her business reputation would remain intact; she would not be known as the wife of a killer for it would be far easier to disown a brother than a husband.
"Granddad? Granddad!" called the shrill voice. Turning, he saw Elsa, her small hands covered with sticky flour, grinning at him as she offered him some icing. Upset as he was, he forced a smile and took the bait, slowly approaching the small girl who laughingly pasted some icing onto his nose.
"Right then, princess," he grabbed the squealing girl off the chair and whirled her around, "Let's you and me and Auntie Shelley bake some buns!"
Watching him, Shelley had one hand on her throat for she could only guess at the effort it took for Martin to pretend to his granddaughter that everything was all right.

Mark Barclay glanced up as the two women, both casually dressed with one holding the hand of a small boy, hesitantly entered the incident room, then seeing him at his desk strode towards him.
He smiled at the two off duty constables and said, "Sorry girls, I didn't recognise you with your clothes on."
"Aye, very funny sir," replied the woman with the child who then stared curiously at him. "We got your message that you want to see the two of us?"
"Yes," he nodded, "and thanks for coming in. I'll see you get some hours in lieu for it. Now, the reason you're both here is about a stop that you did in the Drag a couple of nights ago, a Ford Fiesta you checked out on the PNC."
He sat back in his chair and smiling, indicated they both draw up a chair and grinning, handed the wee boy a pencil and notepad as he glanced at the two officers and added, "Tell me *all* about it."

Moira Bain had worked through several files and glancing at the clock, was about to send Shelley McPhail out to collect her a sandwich when she remembered, the slut was off today and more than likely playing house with her foolish father and Davie's wee girl.

She laid her pen down onto the desk and sat back. She really was peckish and decided that she'd go out herself, take half an hour for a break.

Collecting her handbag from the floor, she stood and was lifting her jacket from the back of the chair when the door knocked.

"Enter," she called out as she slipped the jacket on.

Alex Mason pushed the door open and was followed into the room by a woman and a young man.

"Missus Bain," he nervously begun, "these people are from the police, the CID. They said they want a word with you."

Quickly she formed the opinion it must be something to do with Davie, some kind of statement they needed. Quite deliberately she audibly huffed and sat back down, conveying the impression that she was being inconvenienced by the visit.

"Yes, how can I help you?" she snapped.

The woman walked towards the desk and replied, "Missus Bain, I'm Detective Sergeant McColl and this is Detective Constable Feeney..." but before she could continue, Moira sharply called out, "Alex, I'll deal with this, if you don't mind!"

Mason hurriedly left the room, closing the door behind him.

She turned to the older woman and with a steely glint in her eye, continued, "I gather this will be about the arrest of my brother Davie Craven. Now, this is all rather inconvenient for I am quite busy. So, if you would like to make an appointment..."

"No, I don't think an appointment will be necessary, Missus Bain," McColl coldly smiled at her. "You see, we're not here to interview you. We're here to detain you for questioning about the murder of three women."

## CHAPTER TWENTY-TWO

When he returned to his office, Charlie Miller found Cathy Mulgrew sitting at his desk reading a file.

"My God, Miller," she shook her head, "you don't do things by half, do you?"

Hanging his overcoat on the peg he narrowed his eyes questioningly, but before he could speak, she continued. "Your team have brought in a James Bain and apparently Mister Bain didn't come quietly. According to Mark Barclay, he was screaming blue murder and your guys had to handcuff him to get him here. Myra McColl phoned and is on her way here with a Moira Bain who Mark tells me is the man's wife and that they are both detained under Section Fourteen in connection with the three murders. So," she sat back and stared at him, a smile playing across her lips, "what the *hell* is going on, Charlie?"

He raised a forefinger and with a grin, replied, "Can you hang on for a minute or two while I fetch us in a coffee? I'm absolutely gagging."

She did not have time to reply for he turned and was out the door and gone. Three or four minutes elapsed before he returned to hand her a mug and sat down in the chair opposite her.

"It seems, Cathy, that regretfully I did arrest the wrong man, but" he held up his hand before she could speak, "there is extenuating circumstances that I'm certain won't cause any problems for us regarding his arrest. You see, David Craven wasn't the only person set up; so were we."

"Explain," she sipped at her coffee."

"Well, Craven's sister Moira Bain and perhaps her husband James are possible suspects for the murders. Difficult as it was for him, Craven's father Martin identified his daughter's voice as Mary, the woman who phoned Crimestoppers and told us where to find the evidence in David Craven's home."

Her eyes opened wide and her face fell as she stared at him.

"Charlie! Don't tell me you let the accused mans father listen to the tape! Fuck, you know the Rules of Evidence…"

However, she got no further for he waved away her complaint and said, "It was a decision I took for the greater good and," he grinned, "it paid off. Like I said, Mister Craven recognised his daughter's voice…"

Caught up in his excitement, Mulgrew interrupted, "…which would infer that either she planted the evidence or was told by the individual who *did* plant the evidence that it was there." A little more excitedly, she continued. "And her knowledge of where the evidence was to be found in turn infers that she must be the killer or is aware of who the real killer is!"

"Exactly," he smugly agreed, sipping at his coffee and exhaling with pleasure as the caffeine kicked in.

"Bloody hell, Miller," she shook her head, "how the hell do you get away with it? You should put a lottery ticket on tonight with the luck you're having."

The door knocked and was opened by Mark Barclay who said, "Bit of news for you, boss. The team that brought James Bain in are telling me that when they arrived at his house to detain him, Bain went nuts and tried to run off and began screaming like a madman and he had to be wrestled to the ground."

"Yeah, Ma'am here told me about his refusing to come in quietly…" he nodded towards Mulgrew.

"Aye," interrupted Barclay, "but I've also just learned from the guys that brought him in that apparently he was shouting that his…" he paused as he grinned, "and I quote, 'bitch of a wife' has betrayed him, that it was her idea to set her brother up, that he isn't going to prison alone."

"Oh, now that *is* good news. I take it the detaining officers have noted all this?"

"Oh, aye," Barclay continued to grin, "all noted and written up and can I also add the guys suggest that with the mood he's in, Bain be interviewed on tape as soon as possible before he has time to think about what's he's said."

"Right then, Mark," nodded Miller, suddenly anxious to get the ball rolling, "organise an interview room and tapes and then you and I will conduct the interview. Give me a shout when you're ready."

"Boss," Barclay acknowledged with a nod and closed the door behind him.

"Anything I can do to help?" asked Mulgrew.

"To help?" he smiled and stared thoughtfully at her before he replied. "Cathy, I went against the evidence, acted on my gut instinct when it would have been so much easier to just charge David Craven and let the Crown Prosecution Service take it from there. I've risked not just my own career, but counted on the close friendship you and I have to support me and you did, even though you knew if I was wrong it would drag you down as well and likely your career would be finished too. You want to help?" He shook his head. "You have no idea how much you have already done for me. I know how difficult these last few days must have been for you and I can only guess at the pressure you must have been under not just from Arthur Freeman, but likely the Chief as well to countermand me and to insist I went with the evidence. You have to know that without your support, without your friendship, I could not have lasted the pace. I know I can be a pain in the arse sometimes…"

"Sometimes?" she snorted.

"…but, because of your help an innocent man will not go to prison. Cathy," he leaned forward and slowly shook his head, "where the *fuck* would I be without you?"

She grinned at him and sighed. "Probably out of a job, you idiot. Now, I have a request of you."

He was taken aback. "And that is?" he slowly drawled.

"It's been quite a while since I was involved in a suspect's interview. Would you mind if I sat in when this woman, Moira Bain, is being questioned?"

"I was thinking of letting Myra McColl and her aide conduct the interview, but if you like, you can neighbour Myra."

"Yes, I think I'd like that," she grinned at him.

His clothing was seized and now dressed in a white coloured paper Forensic suit, James Bain could not prevent his legs shaking. Standing with his forehead and his hands pressed against the cold wall of the detention cell, his mind was a flurry of thoughts, not least being that Moira the bitch had changed her mind, that she had after all fired him into the police as the killer.

The door opened and two burly detectives he recognised as among those who had been at his house when he was arrested, stood there with the uniformed turnkey.

"Mister Bain," said the older detective, "we're going to walk you through the office to an interview room. You have two choices, sir. You can go there in handcuffs or walk calmly and civilly with my partner and me, but I am warning you; if you try to kick off with your nonsense like you did at your house, I'll be the first to pummel you to the ground. So, what's it to be…sir?"

He stared at the detective, at the man's misshapen nose and the broad shoulders and knew that even if he had been foolish enough to contemplate tackling him, he could not overcome him let alone three of them.

"I'll walk without the handcuffs and I'll not give you any trouble," he quietly replied.

Walking between the detectives with the turnkey trailing behind, he was led to a corridor on the other side of the building and directed into a room where two middle-aged men both stood. The door was closed behind him and a man he had seen before when he had accompanied Moira to Stewart Street, the man with the facial scar wearing the rumpled suit told him, "Mister Bain, I'm DCI Charlie Miller and this is Detective Inspector Mark Barclay. Take a seat there, sir," and pointed to the chair that was on the other side of the desk.

When all three were sat down, Miller said, "Just to remind you, Mister Bain, you are detained at this office under Section Fourteen regarding your involvement in the murder of women in the Glasgow city centre. This was all been explained to you when you were brought in, wasn't it?"

He nodded, his hands clenched under the desk and his knees tightly drawn together to stop his legs from shaking.

Miller droned on about his rights, the function of the tape recorder that was bolted to the table, but he heard none of this for all he could think of was that his life was over. It did not matter that he might lie or plead or sob or whine or tell them that he didn't really mean it. They had caught him and he was going to prison for a very, very long time.

"Mister Bain? Do you understand, sir?"

His head jerked up and not trusting himself to speak, he nodded.

"Mister Bain! James! Have you heard anything I have said? Were you listening?" Miller asked, his face betraying his annoyance that Bain didn't seem to be paying attention.

"I'm fucked, aren't I?" he turned a pale face towards the two detectives.

Miller's instinct wanted to seize upon what sounded like the beginning of a confession, but his professionalism took over and almost through gritted teeth, he replied, "Mister Bain, I have to remind you that you are being recorded. Can you explain that comment for me, please?"

He did not immediately respond, but lowered his head and stared at the table.

"Mister Bain?" Miller prompted him again.

He raised his head and slowly shook it, then said, "She told me that if I did as she asked, did like she would tell me, then Davie would get the blame. But she lied, didn't she? The bitch lied!" he venomously spat out.

"Who is the woman that you're referring to, Mister Bain? Who told you Davie would get the blame? Who is the woman you are calling a bitch?"

"Her, Moira, my fucking so-called wife! She said when you found the hair and the hammer that she put in Davie's house, he'd be the one who would be blamed…" he was crying now, tears running down his cheeks, his lips quivering as his shoulders heaved. "She told me that the letter with the bits of hair she sent to her lawyer would protect her. That I couldn't hurt her because of it." He paused then sniffing, wiped the mucous from his nose on his sleeve as he evilly grinned at the memory of her humiliation. "Well, I *did* fucking hurt her, didn't I?"

Tears still flowed, but his legs no longer trembled and his sorrow now turned to a venomous hatred for his wife.

"You're saying that your wife, Moira Bain, planted the hair and the hammer in her brother David Craven's house. Is that correct?"

"The hair, my hair, it belonged to me, but she took it from me," he snarled as he beat at his chest with his fists. Seated across the table from him, Mark Barclay inched his body a little closer to the wall. He sensed a change in Bain's demeanour and feared that if the bugger launched himself across the desk, he was hitting the alarm button affixed to the wall.

"What do you mean, the hair belonged to you?" asked Miller.

He stared at the detective as though Miller just was not grasping what he was saying and replied, "The hair. It was my trophies, what I'd taken from the bitches."

"By the bitches, you mean…"

"For fucks sake, why are we even here! You already know, don't you!" he screamed, suddenly now on his feet and his fists pounding at the desk.

Both detectives jumped to their feet and the door swung open to admit the two burly detectives who had stood outside the room.

"Mister Bain!" shouted Miller, his hands raised. "Calm down and sit down! *Now*, Mister Bain!"

A sudden silence fell upon the room, broken when Miller turned and nodded to the two detectives that they were dismissed.

The door was closed as they left the room and slowly, Bain and the two detectives sat back down.

"Now, Mister Bain," Miller calmly repeated, "Who is it that you mean by the bitches?" then almost as an afterthought, his eyes narrowed as he added, "And what do you mean when you say that you hurt your wife?"

She had already decided that she would not reply to any of their questions. To do so would simply give them the opportunity to trick her and she was far too bright for that.

They just did not know whom they were dealing with.

The journey to Stewart Street police office had been made in complete silence with the young detective driving while the middle-aged hag, what was her name again…McCool or McColl or something like that, sat beside her. A couple of times she had caught the drivers eyes on her in the rear-view mirror and she knew exactly what was going through his head.

He fancied her, of that she was in no doubt.

And why wouldn't he, she inwardly smiled as she turned her head to stare out of the window.

The procedure she endured at their office where her name and personal details were taken by the Inspector was embarrassing, particularly when the matronly woman they called the turnkey or something stupid name that, searched her. Discomforting though it was, the woman's body odour would have knocked over a horse and her absurd attempt at pleasantry when she run her hands across Moira's body was almost laughable. I mean, she thought, where the hell do they *find* these people?

Then, the ultimate disgrace of being forced to wear this ridiculous paper coverall or whatever they call it.

As if that was not bad enough, to suffer the indignity of sitting for almost an hour in a smelly, graffiti ridden room before bringing her here. She cast a glance about her at the sickly green painted walls, the desk with the tape recorder and the two empty chairs opposite. How long must she tolerate this, she wondered as she idly tapped her fingers on the desk.

But calm though she tried to be, she could not hide the sense of paranoia that tapped at the back of her mind.

What had caused them to suspect her of being involved in the women's murders? Ludicrous that it was she had absolutely no knowledge of the murders, had no interest in asking James to explain them, so no matter what tricks they employed she could truthfully tell them no, I have no idea what you're talking about.

How could they think that she would help Davie…but it was not Davie, she reminded herself; it was James who had killed those women. Even so, how could they think that she would know anything about the murders?

She inwardly smirked. No, all she had to do was keep her mouth shut. They could not know it was she who made the phone call, but an acute sense of apprehension now gripped at her stomach.

Could they?

No, how could they. She took a deep breath and unconsciously sat upright in the chair as she focused on a damp patch on the opposite wall and mentally tried to reassure herself.

The door opened to admit the detective woman McCool or McColl, she just couldn't remember her name and another woman, a tall rather striking looking woman with copper red hair wearing a black, skirted suit and cream blouse, who closed the door behind her.

"Missus Bain," said the older woman as with her hand she indicated the redhead and said, "This is Detective Superintendent Mulgrew."

She watched as both women sat and listened as McColl, she remembered her name now, went through some sort of procedure about the tape recorder, but she hardly listened for after all they would soon discover their mistake, so it seemed pointless paying attention.

"You do understand, Missus Bain?" asked McColl.

"Yes, of course, now can we get on with this please," she impatiently demanded.

"Right then," smiled McColl. "You are aware from the procedure at the bar when the Inspector explained your rights that you can have a lawyer present?"

"There's hardly any need, is there?" she stiffly replied. "I mean, it's all a huge mistake. You have arrested my brother for the murders of these women. Why should you think I would have any knowledge about them?"

"Yes, well, it seems that the information I have is that your brother is not the individual we were looking for, Missus Bain."

Her stomach knotted and she forced a humourless smile.

"What? You are telling me you have made a mistake? My brother is to be released? Well, that is good news, isn't it? So again, *why* am I here?" she hissed at McColl.

She watched as McColl turned to glance at the other woman, the one called Mulgrew before McColl replied, "You are here, Missus Bain, regarding a phone call you made to the Crimestoppers hotline purporting to be a woman called Mary and because the information you provided to the police in that call indicated you had specific knowledge of certain items of evidence that are related to the murders of three women. Do you deny…"

"Of course I deny making the call!" she snapped. "I have absolutely no idea what you're talking about!"

"Perhaps, Missus Bain," McColl smoothly replied, "I should make you aware that prior to coming into the room, the Detective Superintendent and I were briefed by my boss, DCI Miller regarding an interview he conducted with your husband, James Bain. As a result of that interview, some of my colleagues are en route to your lawyers office where they will present to your lawyer a Sheriff's Warrant that will entitle them to seize a dispatch sent by you that allegedly contains items of evidence and a letter, apparently in your handwriting, that identifies your husband as being responsible for the murders. I believe the dispatch and the items it contains were referred to by you as your insurance policy. Now, does that ring a wee bell, Missus Bain?"

She felt the blood rush to her face, her throat was unaccountably dry and she imagined she was about to faint.

He had confessed, told them about what he had done.

What *she* had done!

There was no other explanation.

She had to think…had to think…to think!

At last she managed to speak and in a faltering voice, said, "He threatened me. Told me to do it. I was in fear of my life. He…he raped me, too. I had no choice. You can't imagine how violent he is!"

"Who was it who threatened you and who raped you, Missus Bain? I need you to tell me the name."

"My husband, James. James Bain. It was him. He's the killer!"

"So, you admit that you made the call?"

"Yes," she tightly answered, her head down as she stared at the scratched and scored desk.

"And the dispatch to your lawyer. What does it contain?"

"Some strands of hair I found in his drawer, his underwear drawer," she quietly replied.

"What about the hammer and the rest of the hair?"

"He forced me…" she swallowed with difficulty, "forced me to take them and hide them in Davie's house. I did not want any part of it, not at all. I only did what he told me," she whimpered.

"I see. The hair that you hid in your brother's house. What was the hair contained in?"

She gulped, the words sticking in her throat. "A plastic bag, a food bag."

"Where did you hide the bag of hair, Missus Bain?"

She slowly exhaled and glanced at the ceiling, curiously wondered why the bulb was encased in a wire cage.

"Missus Bain?"

"Yes, the bag of hair," now she stared at McColl, fighting the tears that threatened to spill from her. "I hid the bag in Davie's room, in his underwear drawer," she wheezed, "just like I'd found it in James's drawer."

"What did you do with the hammer, Missus Bain?"

"The hammer," she shook her head and sniffed, the tears now biting at her eyes. "I hid the hammer in the garage, in an old unit. A drawer in the unit."

McColl turned towards Mulgrew and asked, "Ma'am?"

Mulgrew stared at the young woman and with a shrug, quietly replied, "I think we have enough, Myra."

"Yes, Ma'am," agreed the solemn faced McColl, who in a fixed voice, formally cautioned and then charged the shocked Moira Bain.

It was Shelley McPhail who answered the house phone while Martin was in the shower; a shower she insisted he take, which gave her the opportunity to make the beds and generally tidy the house.

In the lounge and within Shelley's hearing, Elsa played happily in front of the television watching her favourite children's show, Waybaloo.

"May I speak with Mister Craven, please? It's DCI Miller," said the voice.

"Eh, he's in the shower. Mister Miller. It's Shelley here, his…partner," she said at last, the word 'partner' sounding strange upon her lips.
"Ah, Shelley, right. Look, there has been a development. Can you get him to phone…?"
"Who's that," said the voice behind her. Turning, she saw Craven coming down the stairs, wrapping his dressing gown about him, his face pale and wet hair slicked back.
"Hang on, Mister Miller, he's just here," she said, handing the phone to Craven.
"Mister Miller."
"Mister Craven, I have some news for you."
She watched as for a few moments, he listened and saw him wipe his free hand almost disbelievingly across his face. Reaching out to him, she thought he was about to collapse, but he steadied himself by leaning against the wall. At last he replaced the phone and turned towards her.
"Martin," she moved into his arms, "tell me. What's happening?"
"Moira's been arrested. Moira and James. It was them, Shelley," the tears begun. "They did it. They tried to get my Davie sent to prison."
She did not need any further explanation, but then he added,
"Davie's being released from custody. Miller told me that he's been on to the Procurator Fiscal and requesting something called a Fiscal's release, so once the paperwork's completed he should be out of Barlinnie within an hour or two."
"I'm sorry about Moira," she said, but felt a little guilty because her heart was truly not in the sentiment.
She hugged him tightly to her and stood back to look into his eyes as she continued. "Get dressed, Martin. Look, your car is still parked at Stewart Street, so you'll need to get a taxi. If Moira has been arrested there will be nobody at the office so here's what we'll do. We'll share a taxi to the warehouse. I will take the wee one with me to the office and you go on to get your car and then collect Davie from the jail. We can't have him coming out of that place and nobody there to meet him, can we?"
"No, we can't," he agreed. "My God, Shelley, where would I be if you weren't here with me, keeping me right?"
"Aye, well that's my job now, darling, and what I do best," she grinned at him and then added, "so get yourself going, Mister

Craven and I'll organise the princess. Besides," she cocked her head to one side as a thought struck her, "there's something else you need to do at the office."

Charlie Miller thought that though on one hand he was delivering bad news about Martin Craven's daughter, on the other hand he felt a deep satisfaction that David Craven, or Davie as his father called him, was to be released.

Three murders solved and one to go, he thought, but the same thought made him feel uneasy and deeply apprehensive.

Getting to his feet, he made his way through to the incident room where he saw Cathy Mulgrew going round the detectives and civilian staff, speaking to each member of the investigation and he smiled. It was what made Cathy such a good boss for it was her style not to pass her congratulations on via the SIO, but to ensure that each individual would be told how pleased she was.

Catching his eye, she smiled and toasted him with the mug she held in her hand.

He made his way to where Mark Barclay sat at his desk with Elaine Hamilton standing beside him, one hand proprietarily resting on his shoulder as she gazed fondly at him and for the first time, Miller thought he detected a spark between the two of them. Of course he had heard rumours, but never taken them seriously and now here they were, eyes only for each other.

With a polite cough, he interrupted them and handing Barclay a notebook page, said, "Sorry to barge in guys, but I was wondering Mark if you could do me a favour."

Hamilton blushed and turned away towards her own desk while Barclay stared at the page. Miller jabbed at it with his forefinger and asked, "Can you find out what shift was on duty on this night and in particular, what officers were assigned this location."

Barclay's head snapped up and he begun to say, "Is this to do with…" but Miller raised a hand and added, "I'd be grateful if you make the inquiry yourself, Mark. Keep it between us, if you don't mind."

"No bother, boss," Barclay nodded. "I'll get right onto it. What about you, are you staying on?"

"Aye, I'll need to get the report done for these two buggers appearing tomorrow at the Sheriff Court and likely that will take a few hours."

Barclay waved the page at him and asked, "When I get this information for you, do you intend following it up today?"

"No," Miller shook his head, "it can keep till tomorrow. I want to discuss it with Cathy Mulgrew first and I'll need her to be here when…well," he took a deep breath and almost immediately exhaled as though expelling a great burden. "If it pans out the way I believe it will, I'll need Cathy here with me when I act upon it."

"Okay, boss. Give me ten minutes and I'll let you know how I get on," replied Barclay as he got to his feet. "I'll head downstairs to the Inspectors room. I'm sure I'll find what I need there."

## CHAPTER TWENTY-THREE

Sat in the cold chill of the cell, her arms wrapped about her knees that were drawn up under her with her chin resting on them, Moira Bain could not believe that it had gone so wrong. The plan had been perfect or at least, so she had thought.

But now James was charged with the murder of the three women and she was charged with aiding and abetting him to falsely accuse her brother Davie, as well as some bloody thing called perverting the course of justice. Her lawyer, the useless shit that he is she snorted, had tried to explain what it all meant. All she wanted from him was to get her out of this *fucking* place, but he could not even do that!

To her surprise her complaint of rape against James had been treated seriously by the police who brought in a doctor, a middle-aged woman called Watson who examined her while a female officer had photographed her bruised body. Following the examination, the detective called McColl had taken a statement from her and told her that while she could not be certain that he would be convicted, she would ensure that James would be charged with the rape and the prosecutor informed of the circumstances.

Like that's going to fucking help me now she had bitterly complained as teeth gritted, she shook her head.

Her thoughts turned to the interview. It was obvious to her now that neither of the two detectives, McColl or the redheaded woman had believed Moira's tale of being forced to plant the evidence in

Davie's house. Her tears and sobs had not been as convincing as she had expected. Her eyes narrowed. How could they have known it was she who had phoned Crimestoppers? She had not even told James about the phone call, yet McColl had *known*!

She shook her head to clear it of all other thoughts, trying to work out how the police had discovered it was she who had phoned and used the name Mary.

In her head she went back over her actions that day, beginning when she purchased the ten-pound phone from the city supermarket. The assistant had not requested any personal details, so it was unlikely the police would trace her through the mobile phone that she destroyed after she had made the call. The message she left was simple and straightforward and…recorded!

She remembered when making the call it had been a recorded voice that answered the call!

Her eyes blinked rapidly. She had not thought they would record the call, but now realised the police would have her voice on tape, albeit she had tried to disguise her voice.

On tape, she thought; so who would have heard her voice, who would the police have permitted to listen to the tape?

Her heart sank, for now she knew.

Her father had heard the tape. The police must have let him listen to the tape and he had recognised her voice.

It was Dad who had known it was her voice, had told them it was his daughter; he *fucking* told them and sacrificed her to save Davie!

Her lips begun to tremble. She wrapped her arms about her head and in a fit of self-pity, burst into tears.

Shelley's suggestion that after dropping her and his granddaughter Elsa off at the warehouse, Martin would have the taxi to take him to Stewart Street police office to collect his car from where he had left it was a good idea. Upset that he was, he inwardly thanked her for her sound common sense. Now here he was standing outside the smoke glass entrance to Barlinnie Prison waiting impatiently for Davie to appear.

Two young women, both painfully thin with cropped outrageously dyed hair and dressed in brightly coloured tracksuits and training shoes, leaned against the silver painted metal railings. Blatantly ignoring the sign attached to the brickwork, they stood smoking while they loudly opinionated about the prison service in general and one officer in particular. As he listened to the women's piercing and colourful language, Craven stifled a laugh as the teenage women reviled the officer's parentage, seemingly because the officer had the audacity to catch one of the women's boyfriend or brother or whoever the prisoner was, with some drugs. It almost caused Carven to laugh aloud when one women screeching loudly and waving a fist at the prison entrance protested the seized drugs were "…purely for personal use, ya bastards!"

He glanced at his watch, suddenly realising that he was tense and anxious. It was just then, when he looked up at the sliding doors, they opened and Davie walked out carrying a small white coloured plastic bag in one hand and the other raised as he blinked against the bright sunshine.

"Davie!" he cried out and rushed to greet his son with a bear hug. The two women nudged each other and watched in amusement as Craven, emotional now and unable to prevent the tears flowing, continued to enfold his son in his arms.

Davie, also weeping, wrapped his arms about his father and simply said, "Dad."

At last they parted and with his arm about Davie's shoulder, he led his son to the visitor's car park.

It was as they approached the car that Craven said, "I brought someone with me. I hope you don't mind. Eh, it was Shelley's idea," he beckoned towards the car.

Davie glanced up as the passenger door was opened and Mary McLaughlin stepped out, one hand on the top of the door and the other by her side, her eyes bright, her cheeks wet with tears and her lips trembling as she tried to smile.

Sitting reading that morning's edition of the 'Glasgow News' at the bar in the pub in Victoria Road, Eric Kyle fetched the ringing mobile phone from his pocket and staring curiously at the screen, he answered, "Mark, how are you?"

"Fine, Eric fine. Eh, I'm on to ask if you can call into the office tomorrow. Cathy Mulgrew and Charlie Miller would like a word." He did not wait for an answer, but carried on, "I understand that you've been offered the opportunity to remain on extended compassionate leave?"

"Yeah, that's what the boss said. Told me there's no rush to get back to work," he cautiously replied.

"Aye, well it must be something to do with that. Likely there will be paperwork or something to complete. Anyway, what time would suit you?"

"Well, morning would probably suit. Say eleven if that's okay with them."

"I'm sure that will be fine and I'll let them know. Right then, see you at eleven, Eric," Barclay brightly replied and ended the call.

Kyle stared at the mobile and his eyes narrowed. That must be it he thought, paperwork to sign and sipping at his pint, returned to reading the newspaper.

Charlie Miller stared at the shift sheet and glancing at Barclay asked, "You're certain this was the shift and it was this guy in particular?"

"Certain," he nodded. "I spoke with the shift Inspector and I called the shift sergeant at home and they both agree it was him. I don't personally know him, but by all accounts a fairly decent young guy and he's never given his bosses any reason to think otherwise. He's due to finish his probationary period next month and they don't foresee any difficulty with him getting kept on."

"Is he on shift now?"

"Starts late shift at four o'clock, boss. I've asked the Inspector to send him up to see you when he gets in."

"And neither the Inspector nor the sergeant know why you were asking? They weren't suspicious?"

Barclay pursed his lips and shook his head, before replying, "I thought it better to give them a story than tell them nothing, so I told them that you were drawing up a plan of the location and you needed to know where everyone was at a particular and material time, that all you were doing was being specific in your report." He grinned as he added, "I told them you were a pain in the arse when it came to paperwork, so they were happy with that. It doesn't do any harm to complain about the management now and then."

"Good. Thanks Mark," Miller returned his grin.

Davie had elected to sit in the back seat and as they travelled back to his father's house, he opened both rear windows to permit a draft of air to circulate in the car. Sitting in silence the front seats, Martin and Mary both felt the draft of air, but neither complained.

When the Remand Wing officer entered his cell to tell him that he was being released, the officer had been not just vague, but completely indifferent so there had been no explanation and he still could not understand why he had been let out. The process of paperwork he had to undergo took longer than he would have liked, but the important thing was he was free and gulped another breath of fresh air.

Free.

He caught his father glancing at him in the rear-view mirror and knew his Dad was still smiling. He switched his gaze to the back of Mary's head, her hair tied back and still wearing her warehouse overalls. Even dressed as she was and though crying, he had never thought her so lovely and was so very pleased his father had thought to bring her and promised himself he would not forget to thank Shelley for influencing the old man. He had started to ask why he had been released, but Dad had told him in the car park that there was plenty of time for explanations, that the first thing was to get him back home to his fathers house and that Shelley, who was clearing up things at the office, would meet them there with Elsa. It did occur to Davie to ask why Moira was not at the office dealing with the business, but his father was too intent on ushering him into the car and getting away from the prison car park.

He closed his eyes and wriggled into the comfortable upholstery, his head forced back against the headrest and wrinkled his nose. The prison smell was not just on his clothes, but in the short time he had been remanded he felt as though it had ingrained into his very skin and looked forward to a long, hot shower.

"Nearly there, son," his father called out from the front of the car with forced cheerfulness.

Davie hadn't realised he had been dozing and opening his eyes, stared out of the window and saw that they had now arrived and were travelling along the driveway.

Mary turned her head and stared curiously at him, her eyes expressing her surprise at the large detached property.

He smiled and winked, his expression reassuring and conveying to her that she was not to worry, that it was only a house; that what mattered was the people who lived there and not what they owned or how affluent they were.

She shyly smiled back and reached across the seat for his hand, but the car came to a halt at the front door and his father switched off the engine and almost guiltily, she quickly withdrew her hand.

"Mary," his Dad turned towards the young woman, "I'll need to have a word with Davie. There are some things he has to know. I don't think Shelley and the wean have arrived yet, so if you wouldn't mind maybe sticking on the kettle?"

"Yes, of course, Mister Craven," she nodded, but to Davie's surprise his father shook his head and reaching across the seats, gently placed his hand on her arm and replied, "No, hen. It's Martin. The last few days have made me realise that there is going to be a lot of changes in our lives, some good and some not so good and if you are going to be part of our lives as I believe you will be," his father turned to smile at Davie, "then it's Martin. Are you okay with that, Mary?"

She nodded, not trusting herself to speak as his father opened the driver's door and then turning as Davie got out of the car, said, "You head into the house, son, and I'll show Mary where the kitchen is then I'll meet you in the lounge."

Seated at the reception desk, Shelley McPhail quickly scanned the mail, creating a small pile of correspondence as she decided what was worthy of being immediately dealt with while a larger pile was judged to be not so important.

The door from the warehouse opened to admit Alex Mason, who glancing at the child playing happily on the carpeted floor, strode over to Shelley's desk where he planted a bum cheek on the edge.

"So, what the hell is going on then, Shelley?" he brusquely asked.

"Going on, Alex?" she stared up at him, her eyes widening and recognising him for the bully he was, pretended surprise at his question.

"Aye, you *do* know the CID were here earlier today and lifted Moira right out of Martin's office, don't you?" he stared quizzically at her.

She slowly shook her head and narrowing her eyes, replied, "No, never heard a thing about it. Mister Craven asked me to child mind his wee granddaughter there, didn't he princess," she called across to the smiling child and turning back to Mason, continued. "Then he instructed me to come in a bit later to deal with this correspondence," she pointed to the mail. "I'm afraid that's as much as I know, Alex, but I'll tell you what," she adopted an air of innocence as she reached for the desk phone and continued, "I'll give Mister Craven a call at home and tell him that you're keen to know what's going on, shall I?"

His face turned red and he stood up from the desk. He was certain the bitch knew exactly what was going on, but she wasn't telling.

"Aye, very good, hen. Just remember we had this conversation when Moira takes the reins. You might not be so fucking cocky then, eh?" he sneered at her as he walked towards the warehouse door.

She refrained from smiling, but thought that when the truth of this day became public, Alex Mason might not be so cocky himself.

He was halfway through preparing the formal report of the arrests when his door was knocked by a uniformed constable who said, "Constable Bannen, sir. I was told by my Inspector that…"

"Come in, son, come in," Miller waved him into the room and pointing to a chair, added with a smile, "Sit yourself down. Iain, isn't it?"

It was clear to Miller the young cop was nervous, particularly when he asked, "Am I in some sort of trouble, sir?"

"Why would you think that, Iain?"

"Well, the Inspector told me that you wanted to see me about where I was stood that morning. You know, when…" he hesitated and then swallowing with difficulty, asked, "I mean, getting called up to see the DCI, isn't that a bit unusual, sir?"

Miller placed his pen down onto his desk and sat back, his hands clasped behind his head.

"When I joined the polis, Iain, I had an old Inspector who was a former member of the City of Glasgow Police and who was long in the tooth; due to be retired, in fact. A right strict bastard, if you excuse my French. He told me as he did every other probationary cop, something that I have always abided by. He said that there are three definite things that will get you the sack in this job; getting involved in theft, assaulting somebody that does not really deserve it and the third thing was lying to cover up a crime. Now, I can quite truthfully tell you I have never stolen anything," he smiled, "other than a woman's heart. I have never handed out a bleaching to anyone who didn't deserve it and more importantly, I have never, ever lied to cover up a crime. Now, would you agree with those three wise words of wisdom, Iain?"

"Absolutely, sir," agreed the pale faced Bannen.

"As for your question, Iain, I don't believe you *are* in trouble, but you *might* be if you don't tell me the truth. Do you understand, son?"

"Yes, sir," replied the increasingly nervous young cop, now sitting bolt upright in the chair, his eyes wide as he stared at Miller.

He wasn't a bully by nature and truth be told, Miller disliked the bullying that he occasionally had come across when serving in the police, but he had to make the young cop understand and so said, "Loyalty to ones colleagues is a good and commendable thing, Iain and I'm sure that there has been times when you believe that what you did or what was asked of you was being loyal. However, sometimes loyalty can be misplaced when a colleague might ask something of you that you know to be wrong, put you in a position that to refuse might infer you were being *disloyal*. Do you understand, Iain?"

"I think so, sir," Bannen hesitantly replied.

"Let me explain. A colleague who asks you to do something that you know to be wrong puts you in a very bad and vulnerable position and a colleague who does that, Iain, is being selfish by placing you at risk to further their own end." He took a deep breath and softly said, "Sometimes you can be asked to do something that is wrong, but you believe you are agreeing for the right reason. Equally, sometimes it is difficult owning up to a mistake, but like I said earlier, lies eventually catch up with you and you're old enough to know there is a huge difference between making a mistake and lying."

Bannen continued to stare at Miller for now he knew why he had been called to the DCI's office.

Miller sat forward, satisfied that his questions would be truthfully answered.

"Now, Iain, the night that the body of Paula Kyle was discovered, you were on night shift. That's correct, isn't it?"

Bannen nodded, his mouth too dry to respond.

"Right then," Miller leaned towards the young cop and stared at him as he said, "tell me *exactly* what occurred while you were stood at the pedestrian entrance to the underground car park."

Chief Constable Martin Cairney's surprise visit to Gartcosh that afternoon caused the civilian security supervisor to be completely bewildered. Cairney's visiting had not previously occurred without some official notice or at least a tip-off from his own office. Striding after the tall, burly man, the supervisor almost barged into him as Cairney strode to the lift that would take him to the upper floors.

"If there's anything that you need, Chief Constable," whined the portly man.

"Maybe you could arrange for a tray of coffee and biscuits to be delivered to Miss Mulgrew's office," Cairney replied with a smile. "I'm partial to a chocolate digestive," he added with a wink.

Mulgrew's secretary was equally taken aback when Cairney strode into the outer office and politely suggested she inform Miss Mulgrew that he was there.

The inner door opened almost immediately and Mulgrew stood smiling, inviting Cairney through.

"Sorry to arrive unannounced, Cathy," he cheerfully said as he removed his cap and lowered his bulk into the leather sofa that was against the wall. "I thought I'd come and see you personally, catch up on what's going on with our Mister Miller. Oh, and I've arranged for coffee and a wee biscuit, so it should be on its way," he grinned at her.

She politely returned his grin and returned to her chair behind her desk, but her stomach was knotted.

"Chief Constable," she formally begun, "regarding the ongoing inquiry into the murders of four women in Glasgow city centre, I'm pleased to report that DCI Miller has arrested two individuals, a husband and wife, who will appear separately tomorrow before the Sheriff Court in Glasgow."

"Separately?" his eyes narrowed.

"Yes, sir. The man, James Bain will be charged with three murders and also with the rape of his wife, hence the separate appearance as the PF believes it would be inappropriate for them to appear together. DCI Miller is of the opinion that the Crown is unlikely to proceed with the charge of rape for there is neither corroborative nor Forensic evidence to substantiate her allegation, though I do understand there is some physical evidence to indicate the wife has suffered a beating and presumably if she is to be believed, from her husband. After Bain's appearance, his wife will appear before the

Sheriff charged with aiding and abetting her husband by colluding with him to falsely cause her brother to be accused of the murders as well as an additional charge of attempting to pervert the course of justice. I'm also pleased to tell you that there have been corroborative admissions on tape from both accused and a there is strong probability that at their appeal hearing, there's the likelihood of some sort of plea."

He took a deep breath and run a hand wearily across his brow before he stared at her, as though contemplating his response, then quietly asked, "So, this man Bain is to be charged with three murders, Cathy. What's the hiccup about the fourth murder that I'm guessing I *won't* enjoy hearing about?"

Davie Craven still could not take it all in. His sister had set him up to take the blame for three murders. He quickly stood up from the chair and paced the room for a few seconds before standing in front of the panoramic window, his hands on the sill as he stared out to the well-tended lawn. He shook his head disbelievingly and turning, said, "What will happen to her, Dad?"

Still seated, his father shook his head. "I don't know, Davie; that will depend on what the court decides. As far as James is concerned," he sighed, "I don't think he'll be seeing daylight for a lot of years to come…if ever again. DCI Miller told me Moira's not charged with the murders, but it's more than likely she will serve a custodial sentence for her part in blaming you and trying to cover up for James. What that sentence will be…" again, he shrugged and shook his head.

Davie turned back to the window. "I always knew she disliked me, but to do that to me? To my daughter…" He turned again to face his father and grimfaced continued. "And you think it was all about her jealousy, that she thought I'd be the next MD, that it was because *she* that wanted the job? Bloody hell Dad," he snapped, his hands outstretched, "how many times did I tell her that I didn't *want* the bloody job! It was hers for the asking! All I ever wanted to do was…"

He paused, because he had never had this conversation, never disclosed to either his father or Moira or anyone for that matter what his real ambition was.

The door knocked and was opened by Mary who held a tray with two mugs on it.

"I thought you might like some refreshment," she said, hesitating at the door as if waiting to be invited in.

Davie strode quickly across the room to take the tray from her and smiled. "Thanks, love. I'm sorry, you probably heard me shouting…"

"Well, if anybody has a good reason to shout, Davie Craven, it's you," she handed him the tray and smiled.

Watching them, Martin suddenly realised she was correct; his son had every reason to scream and shout at the unfair way he had been treated and not just by his sister or the police. No, the unfairness had begun with his father who never once thought to ask, what do you want to do with your life, son? His father who had selfishly and mistakenly made the decision that Davie would follow him into the family business. Continuing the Craven name had been his own egotistical ambition, not Davie's.

Well, he had just yesterday made a life changing decision about his own future and now it was time that Davie made a decision about his.

"Mary," he called out, stopping her as she turned to go, "get yourself a coffee and come and join us. I think Davie has something to tell us both."

## CHAPTER TWENTY-FOUR

The following morning dawned with rain clouds hanging over Glasgow and beyond. Turning his collar up against the slight drizzle, Mark Barclay glanced at the grey sky and locking his car, strode towards the rear entrance of Stewart Street police office.

He had just stepped into the rear doorway when he heard his name called.

"Morning, Mark," Charlie Miller greeted him. "How are you today?" Taking off his overcoat, Barclay shook the drips from it and replied, "I'm feeling a lot better now that we've got those two buggers locked up," he nodded towards the lift that was used to convey prisoners to the cells on the first floor. "I'll organise two teams to get them to the court this morning for their appearances this afternoon."

Walking together towards the stairs, Barclay asked, "How are you feeling about this morning? Eric Kyle coming in, I mean? How are you going to break the news to him?"

"Cathy Mulgrew will be here about ten o'clock and then we'll discuss how we're going to handle it," Miller said, his voice tense. They reached the first floor landing, but before turning into the incident room, Barclay said, "You must know that when the reporters who cover the story at the court hear that James Bain has been charged with just three murders, there will likely be questions about Paula Kyle's murder. Any thoughts on how you're going to handle the media on that one?"

Miller shook his head. "To be honest, it's kept me awake most of the night and I'm hoping that Cathy might have some idea about that. I'm also going to give Harry Downes over at Dalmarnock office a call. She will probably be the media's first point of contact when Bain's murder charges are read out in court, so I'm sure she'll appreciate the heads up. Besides, Harry's the best placed person to give us advice on how we respond to the media's queries."

"I can phone Harry, if you want."

"Yes please, Mark, and you can let her know that I'll give her a call later this afternoon and explain the situation in more depth."

"Okay, boss," Barclay nodded and turning into the door of the incident room, stopped and asked, "What about Moira Bain's father, Mister Craven. Do you want me to give him a call and ask about his son? We'll need to get a statement from David Craven about his arrest and his relationship with his sister."

Miller's brow furrowed and he shook his head, replying, "Leave that with me. It's only fair as the SIO that I give the family a call. In fact, if I get the opportunity later today, I'll take a turn out to their house, maybe take Myra McColl with me and she can note Davie's statement."

"Okay, well, I'm in here," he nodded towards the room, "if you're looking for me."

"Thanks, Mark," smiled Miller and made his way to his office. Hanging his coat on the peg, he sat down behind his desk and rubbed at his eyes.

No matter what happened today, he thought, it was definitely a day he would never forget.

Shelley McPhail had lost the argument. Martin Craven, dressed for work, had firmly decided he was going in to the office.

"Well, I'm coming too," she told him and lifting her jacket from the coat stand in the hallway, marched out towards his car.

He grinned as he locked the door behind him and replied, "Like I could stop you?"

They were no more than five minutes into the journey when she asked, "How will you deal with the questions? People are bound to know that something's wrong, particularly when Moira was taken away yesterday by the CID."

He did not reply immediately, but then shrugged and said, "I'll call a meeting for the staff that is on duty and tell them the truth, that she and her husband have been arrested."

He paused then added, "Then I'll tell them I'm selling the business, that I'm retiring, but that I'll make sure the new owners keep on the workforce."

"So, you will go through with it, Martin? You *will* keep your promise?"

"To you *and* to Davie," he nodded, then almost under his breath, added, "It's the least I can do for my son, after what he's been through."

"What about her court appearance, today? Do you think you will go to see Moira?"

He did not immediately answer, but then slowly shook his head. "It's not because I don't want to, but Mister Miller suggested that as I'm to be a witness in the case it might be prudent to avoid going to the court. No, I'll pay for Moira to get the best representation, but…but I do not think I can face seeing her just yet, not after what she has done. Her actions did not just affect Davie. Her actions rippled right through our family, affecting wee Elsa, me and by association, you too. Even that young lassie Mary that Davie's so keen on."

He turned with weary eyes to Shelley. "Does that make me an uncaring father?"

She did not reply, but leaned across to lightly lay her hand comfortingly on his arm.

Traffic was light and he made good time, arriving at the warehouse just over half an hour later. Turning into the car park at the rear of the premises, he was surprised to see his son's car already parked there.

Pulling up along side it, he told Shelley he was going to find Davie in the warehouse and asked if she would go to his office and attend to the mail.

Nodding a greeting to the old doorman, Craven found Davie within a couple of minutes, issuing instructions to some staff.

"I thought you were taking the day off?" he stared quizzically at him.

Davie nodded in greeting and lowering his voice, replied, "I thought I'd come in, show a united front, Dad. I called the childminder last night so she has Elsa for the day. I'm trying to keep things as normal as possible for the wee one. Besides, I felt you needed some support today; you know, with Moira going to court and that."

His father inhaled, his face registering his surprise at his sons thoughtfulness.

"What," Davie continued to grin, "you think I'd let you go through this yourself?"

He clapped a hand onto Davie's shoulder and replied, "It's not that, son. It's just that I wish I had been as good a father as you have been a son."

"Ach, you're getting too sentimental for me," Davie teased him and added, "Now, if you don't mind buggering off, boss, I have work to do."

"Aye, right. I'll be in my office if you need me…for anything."

After his shower, Eric Kyle ironed a clean shirt and laid out his best suit. He had already decide to accept whatever offer Cathy Mulgrew would make about his retirement and considered this to be likely the last time that he would attend Stewart Street office. Then, once Paula's funeral service had ended, a new life beckoned and glancing at the cupboard, smiled when he imagined getting rid of the old, worn suits and purchasing a new wardrobe for himself.

He wondered if he should maybe take a bottle of wine into the meeting to celebrate his pre-retirement. He knew Charlie Miller no longer took drink, but Mulgrew would likely take a glass. Maybe he would also follow the age-old tradition of splashing out and buying a large box of cream cakes for the office. If he took a bottle of wine in, he thought, he had better take a taxi to the office. Would not do to get done for drunk driving days before he was so close to leaving the country, he grinned.

He closed the cupboard door and turned towards the full-length mirror, buttoning the crisp, white shirt to the neck and choosing a brightly coloured tie, but then remembered. He was supposed to be in mourning, so instead swapped it for a more sober, navy blue striped tie and then dressed in his suit. Satisfied with his appearance, he checked the time on his wristwatch and decided that he would have some breakfast and walk to the local supermarket for his purchases before calling a taxi to take him to Stewart Street.

She was about to leave her office when Cathy Mulgrew took a phone call from the Chief Constable. Again she assured him that when she had met with DCI Miller and DS Kyle, she would immediately call Cairney to inform him of the outcome of the meeting.
Informing her secretary that any messages should be directed through to the incident room at Stewart Street, she made her way through the building towards the car park.

Carrying a large and full plastic bag in each hand, Eric Kyle had the taxi drop him at the front door of Stewart Street. He shouldered his way through the front doors and was almost immediately surrounded by the duty bar staff who with sympathy for his loss, good-naturedly bombarded him with questions about how he was keeping, how he was coping, was there anything he needed. With a forced smile, he accepted with good grace the kisses on the cheek from the women and pats on the back from the men. It was there surrounded by the officers and staff from the uniform bar and control room that Kyle was taken aside by the duty Inspector and learned in a whisper that the team upstairs had caught the man who had murdered all the women; a man called James Bain. The Inspector added the bastard was appearing with his wife that afternoon at the court. It was unfortunate that in his haste to be a smart-arse who liked to believe he had his finger on the pulse, the Inspector neglected to mention that James Bain had been charged with three murders, not four.
At last Kyle tore himself away from his well-wishers and with his mind racing and a curious sensation in the pit of his stomach, made his way to the incident room where again he was welcomed by the officers and civilian staff on duty with the same questions and sombre greetings. Laying the plastic bags on the coffee table, he turned to tell the civilian analyst Melanie, "Cakes for everybody,"

and drew a small cheer of thanks as he shrugged off the handshakes and quickly strode towards Mark Barclay.

"Good to see you, Eric," Mark Barclay smiled as he shook his hand. "I'll see if the boss is in his office." he turned to go, but was stopped when Kyle took him by the elbow and said, "I heard from the Inspector downstairs he's been caught, Mark. The killer. Paula's murderer."

Barclay stared at him and slowly nodding, replied, "I think the boss wants to tell you himself, Eric. Wait here and I'll let him know you have arrived."

He returned a couple of minutes later and told Kyle, "The boss says to go through when you're ready."

"Right, thanks Mark," Kyle nodded and his face expressionless, took his leave of the crowd and made his way along the few steps in the corridor to Charlie Miller's office. Knocking on the door, he was called in to find Miller sat behind his desk and Cathy Mulgrew sitting in a chair in the corner, her legs crossed and hands clasped on her lap.

"Come in, Eric," Miller waved him to the chair in front of the desk and watched as Kyle eased himself down into the chair and placing a bottle of red wine onto the desk, clasped his hands to his chest.

"Thought we might have a wee drink to celebrate my early retrial," he explained and waited expectantly for Miller to formally break the news of the arrest.

Charlie Miller stared coldly at him before raising his hand and replying, "I might as well get right down to business, Eric. I've called you in today to inform you that with the authorisation of Detective Superintendent Mulgrew, I am invoking The Police (Scotland) Regulations 2004 and giving you notice that I am officially suspending you from duty…"

It took a few seconds for Miller's statement to register and it did not just confuse Kyle, it shocked him into hissing, "You're fucking what!" as he leapt to his feet.

"Sit down, Detective Sergeant Kyle" snapped Miller as he stared up at him. "You're histrionics will get you nowhere! Now, sit down!"

Slowly, his face beetroot red, Kyle sunk into the chair as he stared menacingly at Miller.

In the corner, Mulgrew had uncrossed her legs and if need be, readied herself to tackle the livid Kyle.

"What the *fuck* is this all about?" snarled Kyle, snatching a glance at Mulgrew.

"This is about you murdering your wife, Eric. That's what this is all about," Miller coolly replied.

"You're insane! *I* didn't kill Paula! That bastard you've got locked up, that guy Bain, he did it!"

"No, Eric," Miller slowly shook his head, but his eyes never left Kyle. "James Bain readily admitted to the murders of the first three women and I am satisfied he told the truth when he denied killing Paula."

"So, what makes you think *I* did it?"

Miller took a deep breath. "You've been a detective for a long time, Eric. You have been involved in a number of murder inquiries so you know the system, probably even better than I do, but you're not perfect. You *didn't* commit what you thought was the perfect murder."

Kyle, smiling now, but without humour, replied in a soft voice, "Tell me how I'm supposed to have killed my wife then, Charlie and let's be detectives, eh? Let's apply MAGICOP here. What was my motive?"

"If you didn't know for certain, you must have suspected Paula was cheating on you. Worst, you also suspected that she was prostituting herself and that's how she came by her extra money; money that she couldn't truthfully account for."

"What makes you think she was prostituting herself?"

"We have a witness statement…"

"Jill *fucking* Hardie," he guessed correctly and nodded as he laughed out loud. "How can you believe *anything* that tart tells you?"

"Well, I'm sorry to have to tell you this, but our inquiries have revealed that Hardie *is* telling us the truth, Eric."

He took a deep breath than carefully said, "So, you're suggesting my motive was jealousy about other men or even anger at what Paula was up to. What about the guilty intent, then?"

"Your guilty intent was to silence her, get her out of your life. I believe that Paula had proven to be an embarrassment to you, both socially and economically. You never made any secret of the fact that you are in debt, that your former wife will screw you for more than half your pension and currently receives a goodly portion of your monthly salary. When the opportunity for getting rid of Paula arose, when she told you that she was meeting her friend Jill Hardie that night, the likelihood is you reasoned that with Paula out of the way not just your own social life, but your income would improve and your debts might not be so crippling."

"Yes, well, I'll admit Paula could be a bit of a tart with the men when she set her mind to it and yes, every penny I made or what was left of it after my ex-wife had her chunk of it was squandered by Paula. But you're forgetting the preparation and my supposed conduct after her murder. I mean, are you actually suggesting I *planned* this whole thing, her murder?"

"No, Eric," Miller shook his head. "I don't think you had considered it for any length of time, but it was more of an opportunist crime. On that night when you knew that Paula would be in the city centre and you knew where she parked her car, it occurred to you to take advantage of an ongoing situation. With three unsolved murders being investigated, you thought that murdering Paula would simply be labelled the work of the killer of the first three victims. To be frank, you probably hoped we might not catch the culprit and even if and when we did make an arrest, we would not believe that Paula was not the work of the same killer. I believe it was a moment of madness on your part; an opportunity had presented itself and you took it, nothing more."

"And how exactly am I supposed to have murdered her when her murder had all the characteristics of the same killer, this guy Bain?"

"Well, as a senior member of my investigative team, Eric, you were privy to certain confidential information about the murders of the first three victims. This information included the use of a carpenters type hammer as the murder weapon and the removal of some hair from the victims. You agree?"

"Aye, of course I agree, but I wasn't the only person who was in the know," he cautiously replied, choosing each word carefully, his eyes never leaving those of Miller.

"That's correct, there were more than you who knew about this privileged information, but you made the mistake as I did in thinking all carpenters hammers were the same. It was one of those strange circumstances, a fluke you might say, that Sherlock discovered the hammer head used to kill Paula had a slightly larger circumference than those used in the first three murders."

"And you think I have that hammer?" he stared at Miller as though daring the DCI to contradict him.

"I have absolutely no doubt that you no longer have the hammer, Eric and I'm also certain that I will never recover that hammer. The hammer and the hair you removed after you murdered your wife will likely have been disposed of, never to be found again." He smiled and added, "After all, who knows better than an experienced murder detective how to dispose of incriminating evidence."

"So," Kyle spread his hands out wide, inwardly fighting the urge to sneer at Miller, "You have no murder weapon for your preposterous allegation."

"No, no murder weapon," agreed Miller with a shake of his head.

"And that's your case?"

"Not quite. You referred to MAGICOP. Well, you had ample opportunity that night and were ideally located to kill Paula that night. Myra McColl and her neighbour place you in the office here just before the time that Paula was making her way to her car. That's fact, Eric. Paula's car was parked in a car park close by in an area that you are familiar with and where you knew she usually parked each time she visited the city centre. You told us that yourself, remember?"

"That's not evidence, but sheer coincidence and remember, Charlie, I was at my place of work that night, somewhere I was supposed to be. The timing was also coincidental."

"I'll grant you that," sighed Miller, "and I agree. It's not evidence, but the timing and location *does* place you in the neighbourhood when your wife was murdered."

Kyle forced a smile, but his stomach was knotting. He knew Miller and his reputation, a reputation built on tenacity and dogged determination. With a cold feeling creeping along his spine he realised that the DCI would not be telling him this unless...unless he had something!

"So, what else have you got that causes you to think I killed Paula?"

"After her body was discovered, Cathy Mulgrew and I attended at your flat to...well, as we thought at the time, to break the news."

"So?" he shrugged.

"We sat with you when Cathy told you about Paula being murdered, do you recall?"

"Yes, of course I do," he snapped.

"You were upset at our news. Do you recall that?"

"Yes! Why wouldn't I be upset?"

"To save you any further pain or so we thought, we didn't tell you where Paula's body had been found. Cathy and I had already agreed that to tell you she had been dumped in a waste bin area might have been further upsetting for you."

"What's that got to do with it?" Kyle shrugged.

"Later that morning when a young cop, constable Iain Bannen, was on duty at the pedestrian entrance to the underground car park round the corner, you arrived with some flowers that you wanted to lay at the spot where Paula had been discovered. It's become a common thing these days; a mark of respect to a deceased person and you being Paula's husband, it would seem quite natural for you to pay your respects where your wife was discovered dead."

"I don't understand where you're going with this," he almost sneered and added, "Laying flowers? What was wrong with that?"

"You arrived just before Bannen went off shift. Do you remember?"

"Yes," he slowly drawled.

"He's a bright young lad, is Bannen," Miller half-smiled. "Almost through his probationary period now, but still at that stage of his career to be in awe of a grizzled Detective Sergeant like you, particularly one who has seen and done what you have in your career and who seemed so upset that morning. So when you persuaded Bannen to let you into the locus to lay the flowers down, he did not have the nerve to say no and though he was very reluctant to let you through into the locus in case he got into bother from his bosses, he also felt sorry for you and permit you through anyway. Then he watched you walk straight to the waste bin area where her body had been discovered. A straight line, no deviation, no question as to where she had been found."

Kyle's face turned white and he swallowed with difficulty.

"Nobody told you where Paula had been found, Eric," Miller shook his head. "Not Cathy Mulgrew nor me nor constable Bannen nor any member of the inquiry team," Miller slowly continued. "You went straight to the waste bin area because after dragging her there, that's where you struck her with the hammer and battered her to death, isn't it?"

"You believe the word of a rookie cop over me? That's your evidence?"

"Bannen might be a rookie cop, Eric, but he's a rookie cop who is a very, very credible witness and besides like I said, nobody told you where Paula had been found. You already knew about the rubbish bin area because you murdered her there."

"That's total shite and you know it, Charlie! You don't have enough to charge me and I'm not saying another word," Kyle retorted.

Miller did not immediately reply, but then slowly said, "Perhaps not, but like I told you, you are now suspended from duty pending my report to Crown Office that will name you as the murderer of your wife, Paula Kyle. If Crown Office wish to proceed…"

"You think they'll go for that…that fucking *fairytale!*" he did sneer this time.

"I agree, the evidence isn't enough for me to go ahead and charge you, Eric and I really don't know if Crown Office will pursue the murder charge against you, but what I *do* know is that the Chief Constable has been informed of all that I've told you and agreed that your suspension is valid. I must add the suspension is without pay. I am also instructed to inform you that should you seek legal action against Police Scotland, the Chief Constable will defend *any* action by you in *any* court to prevent you recouping any pension or salary from Police Scotland. In essence," he spread his hands wide, "even if the Crown Office do not pursue you in court for the murder charge you can say goodbye to your pension and any future salary. One further thing, Eric. For as long as her murder inquiry continues, Paula's vehicle will be retained as a production and the Range Rover will not now be released to you."

"You'll never get away with this!" he snarled and turned to Mulgrew, adding "Cathy, for fuck's sake! I've served loyally for almost thirty years! You know I'm being screwed over here! For fucks sake, tell him!"

"I agree with Mister Miller, Detective Sergeant Kyle, that you *did* murder your wife," she replied, her face pale and now on her feet, "and if *I* had my way you would be charged and locked up downstairs. Now, as you are suspended I require your warrant card," she held her hand out.

He stared dumbly at her, then from the inside jacket pocket withdrew his black leather bound police wallet and flung it to the floor. Standing now, his breathing heavy and rapid, he stared at them in turn and in a voice filled with venomous hate, battered a fist down onto the desk in front of Miller and said, "You won't get away with this, Miller! I'll have you for this, you *bastard*! You'd better watch your fucking back! And I'll have you in court."

His glance fell upon Mulgrew, "both of you *and* that bastard Cairney too! You tell him," he wagged a forefinger at them in turn, "you tell him I'll fucking have the Federation onto him! You two bastards as well! All you all!"

He turned and snatched the door open before storming out of the room.

Miller turned to stare at Mulgrew and slowly exhaled.

"Well," he blew out through pursed lips, "it seems we might have hit a wee nerve there, eh?" Then his brow furrowed as he added, "Do you think we should call him back to collect his wine?"

While Cathy Mulgrew used his room to call the Chief Constable, Miller sat on Mark Barclay's desk, gripping the edge and his legs slightly clear of the floor. He beckoned the inquiry team to gather round and to grab chairs and relax, that he had something to tell them.

With Mulgrew's approval, he had decided there was little point in holding back the details from the team and after instructing them that they considered what he was about to tell them as extremely confidential, took almost ten minutes to set the scene, first explaining the situation and the circumstances that led him to believe that Eric Kyle had murdered his wife, Paula Kyle.

He explained that while he was convinced the evidence was insufficient to arrest Kyle, his report to Crown Office and the flimsy evidence would reflect his belief in Kyle's guilt.

He intimated that the Chief Constable had been fully aware of the issue and was now being updated by Cathy Mulgrew regarding Kyle's interview and denial of the murder. He assured them that the Chief fully supported Kyle's suspension, but refrained from telling them of the financial circumstances that would deny Kyle his pension and his income.

He had thought that at the outset there might have been mutterings of discontent, had believed that Kyle was popular and that some of the team would consider that he had erred, that Eric Kyle was not capable of committing such a dastardly crime. To his surprise, when he finished his briefing he saw many shaking their heads in disbelief and heard mutterings of "Bastard!" that were directed towards the errant Kyle.

While the team dispersed about the room, muttering to themselves about Miller's revelation, Mark Barclay excused himself and went to find a phone, telling him, "I'll give Harry Downes that heads-up now, boss."

"What do you think Crown Office will decide, sir?" asked Elaine Hamilton, her arms folded across her chest.

"No idea, Elaine," he shook his head, "but I suspect they won't proceed on the poor evidence that we have. As far as Paula Kyle's murder investigation goes, it will remain an open case. However should some other evidence arise at a later date that either conclusively identifies Eric as the murderer or exonerates him, which I believe is unlikely, he will remain listed as the primary suspect."

She placed a comforting hand on his arm and said, "It can't have been easy for you, any of you. Knowing Eric like you did, I mean."

He was grateful for the support and placing his own hand over hers, gently squeezed as he replied, "Aye, you're right, Elaine. I have never had to deal with a colleague who I know to be a murderer and please God I will not have to again."

He could not know then how prophetic those words would be.

In Miller's office, Cathy Mulgrew sat at his desk, briefing the Chief Constable Martin Cairney. When she had finished, he asked, "So, what's your thoughts on the matter then, Cathy. Should Miller have made the arrest and requested the court seize his passport in the event Kyle tries to flee the country?"

"The sad truth is, sir, that both DCI Miller and myself believe it's unlikely the Crown Office will proceed with the charges. There just isn't enough evidence to support a court case and lets face it, prosecuting a murder is an expensive business and if Crown Office don't believe they can win the case, they will not go ahead."

"But there's no doubt he will fight the accusation?"

"None at all, sir. He was quite vehemently angry when he left the office. Threatened all sorts of legal actions against Miller, me and of course your good self."

"Aye," he absentmindedly replied, "the burden of being the top man I suppose."

He paused and she thought he was about to end the call, but then he said, "It comes to mind that perhaps Mister Kyle is angrier than we think, Cathy. From what you tell me he's apparently no other financial resources other than his salary and some of that is diverted to a former wife. That's correct, yes?"

"As far as I'm aware, yes sir," she agreed.

"His state of mind when he left Miller's office. How angry was Kylie? Was he *very* angry?"

"Mainly with Miller, yes sir, though of course both you and I were caught in the crossfire" she slowly replied, attempting to lighten the situation but wondering where this was going.

"You are at Stewart Street right now?"

"In Miller's office, yes sir."

There was another pause, then Cairney said, "Cathy, meet me at Dalmarnock office. I'll be there in…say one hour, depending on the traffic. There is something I believe we should discuss. And Cathy, I'd prefer you did not tell Miller where you are going or why."

"Of course sir," she replied, curious as she thought *I know where I'm going, but I have no idea why*.

## CHAPTER TWENTY-FIVE

He was beyond angry.

Spits of saliva dribbled from his mouth as he cursed and vented his hatred as expletives poured from him in the loudest voice.

He did not remember the journey home, had paid no attention to the angry blasts of car horns as almost in a frenzy he sped through the city traffic. His fury caused him to be oblivious to his speed as he raced his car along the road, narrowly missing other vehicles.

Traffic lights were ignored, pedestrians crossing the road unseen.

He was completely unaware of the raised fists, the screams of abuse, the shocked expressions of shoppers as his Mondeo weaved back and forth along Victoria Road.

He had been driven by the urge to get home; he had to get back to the flat to think, to work out his next move.

It was all Miller's fault, he snarled. He would have gotten away with it if it had not been for Miller, the backstabbing bastard!

He shoved the door of the car open and getting out, made his way towards the close door, convinced now that it *was* all Miller's fault!

So irate was he that he fumbled with the key in the lock, viciously kicking at the door in his rage before finally getting it open and slamming it behind him.

He stumbled upstairs to his front door, his legs shaking and his breathing coming in short gasps, the pain in his chest was almost unbearable and he thought his heart might stop at any second; the shock of the meeting and Miller's accusation finally hitting home.

*Bastard!*

In the kitchen, he scrabbled at the cork from the bottle of whisky and finally twisted it open to pour four fingers into the china mug. In his haste he spilled some onto the worktop then tilted the mug back and threw it down, retching as the fiery liquid hit the back of his throat and droplets trickled down his chin.

He coughed deeply, his hands clenching the edge of the worktop, almost bent double and slowly lowered himself to his knees, his tears falling like raindrops.

He did not know how long he sat there, his body wracked with sobs of self-pity.

It had all come apart, his hopes, his dreams; all because of that righteous fucker Miller!

The Federation would not help, not if he was the subject of a murder charge and he was certain the useless bastards would not want to piss off Martin Cairney.

He guessed that even though he was suspended, he was still technically employed by the police so would not therefore qualify for Legal Aid. No reputable lawyer would take his case pro bono and the disreputable ones were even less likely to; at least, not without a large backhander up front.

And thanks to Miller he now had no income, no money for even that!

He took a deep breath and struggled to his feet, wiping his running nose and eyes on his jacket sleeve.

Because of Miller, damn him, there would be no Irish cottage, no new life, no quiet retirement. The bastard had even ensured that Paula's Range Rover was no longer an option for him to sell!

Once it became known he was being reported to the Crown Office for Paula's murder, his reputation would be finished. Friends he had made would certainly abandon him and the Police Discipline Code would ensure that none of his former colleagues would be permitted to associate or maintain any contact with him, even if they wanted to.

He had given almost thirty years of his life, thirty years of punishing shift work, thirty years of dealing with the city's scum and for what; for this?

He glanced around at the narrow, squalid kitchen and teeth gritted, took a deep breath as he fought the frustrated scream that threatened to erupt from him.

Now his life was over; no pension, no income and facing more debt, more threatening letters from his ex-wife.

Miller!

His breathing became more rapid as thoughts of vengeance filled his mind.

He *would* get even, he promised himself.

Sadie Miller was looking forward to Charlie coming home early for the first time in weeks and decided to treat her husband to a quiet night. Waving cheerio to her daughters, she watched her mum set off down the driveway in the car. Sitting beside Ella, Geraldine twisted round in the booster seat to grin at her mum and wave, all promises not to eat too many sweets forgotten the minute the car turned into Westbourne Drive.

With a satisfied shrug, Sadie watched the car out of sight, then sniffed at the stain on her top, her nose wrinkling at the failed attempt to scrub Ella's milk smelling saliva from the material. She glanced at her watch. With a sly grin, she decided there was plenty of time to prepare a meal then take a long, lazy bath, sip a glass of red wine and a change into something slinky before Charlie got home. Her eyes narrowed.

Maybe something that he can easily slip off her.

Bugger the cooking, she thought. It'll be a takeaway for tonight and with a smile full of anticipation, she headed back into the house.

Arriving at Dalmarnock police office, Cathy Mulgrew was informed by the young civilian bar officer that the Chief Constable had requested she wait for him in the conference room and with a smile, added that a pot of coffee was already there waiting for her.

It was almost a full thirty minutes before Martin Cairney arrived, accompanied by Detective Chief Superintendent Jacqueline Ross, the frosty-faced Deputy Head of the Operational Support Division and current head of the Tactical Surveillance Unit. Watching the tall and willowy, dark haired Ross enter the room, Mulgrew took a sharp intake of breath as she suddenly guessed why she had been summoned to the meeting.

"Thanks for coming over, Cathy," Cairney greeted her as he removed his cap and invited both women to sit and then ever courteous, moved towards the side table as he added, "First things first. Let me get you ladies a coffee."

Settled a few minutes later, Cairney opened the meeting by asking Mulgrew, "How did DCI Miller perceive the threat made by Kyle? I do not mean the possibility of court action, I mean the physical threat. Did he take it seriously?"

Mulgrew shrugged and replied, "You've been there, sir. You know how it is when a suspect threatens you. On most occasions it's just hot air. In my experience I have only ever known one occasion when a suspect actually stalked the detective who arrested him and that was almost eight years later, after the suspect had been sentenced and served his time. Even then, the man simply hung about outside the office where the detective worked, nothing more."

"Yes, I can appreciate that Kyle was probably upset and likely his threat was more verbal anger than intent, but all the same I don't like it when my officers might be at risk," he shook his head. "Kyle might just be a *little* different from the incident you speak of, Cathy and I'm guessing he's focusing all his anger on what he believes to be the root cause of his problems; our DCI Miller. Remember, we're not simply sacking the man, we're accusing him of murder, stopping his income and threatening to take away his pension and lump sum. That's a hell of a shock to the system, you would agree?"

"Yes, sir," she glanced briefly at Ross, "so what exactly are you thinking?"

"What I'm *considering* is bringing Miss Ross's mob into the equation, Cathy. What you might call…" he smiled, "our insurance policy."

He turned to Ross. "How soon can you muster a team, Jackie? A team that would include AFO's?"

Ross stared back in surprise. "I can get a team briefed and in the field within an hour, sir, but may I ask why you believe they need authorised firearm officers with them?"

He did not immediately respond, but chewed at his lower lip as though deliberating before answering. Finally, he stared at them in turn and said, "I don't believe we would achieve anything by conducting a surveillance operation against Kyle. According to his personnel file, the man has been round the block more than twice so he will probably expect that there is the possibility a surveillance operation could be conducted against him. If we were to mount a surveillance against him and God forbid your team lost him, Jackie, and he *did* commit some assault against DCI Miller…" he shook his head and continued. "It's just not worth the risk."

He paused as though deliberating then said, "What I'm proposing is that for now we take seriously the threat made against DCI Miller and thus we *can* lawfully justify a protective surveillance for him. As for the inclusion of AFO's in the surveillance team, I do not believe we can properly assess the threat against DCI Miller, but if as we suspect Kyle is a murderer, I believe we must assume against any threat against Miller to be extreme. In short and strictly between us in this room, I have had the opportunity to peruse Kyle's personnel file and I am not happy with what I read. Cathy," his eyes narrowed, "are you aware that within the last five years Kyle had three assault complaints lodged against him? Once by his former wife and two by suspects he interviewed. I am rather ashamed to admit that it seems to me that at least two of the assaults, and I include the domestic assault, appear to have been genuine complaints. However, it is also apparent to me our former Complaints and Discipline Department failed to properly investigate these two complaints," then almost under his breath, added, "or chose not to."

"I wasn't aware of the alleged assaults, sir," she shook her head, annoyed at the oversight of not checking Kyle's personnel record herself.

"Well, no matter. All it does is lend strength to my belief that DCI Miller should be afforded some degree of protection against *any* threat; at least for the foreseeable future. Do you agree, ladies?"

Ross nodded and drumming the nails of her right hand upon the tabletop, said, "I see no harm in providing a modicum of security for Miller. My only concern, sir, is that I have a number of major ongoing inquiries that require the services of my surveillance teams and so I would be grateful if you might consider reconvening next week to re-evaluate whether or not Kyle does in fact present a threat. After all, we can always review our decision at that time."

The drumming of her nails was beginning to annoy Mulgrew. Cairney's brow furrowed and then he simply replied, "Agreed."

Ross narrowed her eyes and asked Cairney, "Is it your intention to inform Miller about the surveillance?"

"Cathy?" he turned towards Mulgrew.

She unconsciously bit at her lower lip as she gave it some thought, then shook her head. "Knowing Charlie, he'd be livid at the thought of being babysat. No sir, if Jackie believes her guys can conduct the surveillance without showing out to Miller then I think we should keep it in house meantime." She smiled as she said to Ross, "Just tell them to be careful. He's a fly bastard is Charlie and though he seems to be a big, lumbering type of guy, he's a sharp bugger. If he even suspects that someone is following him, he'll drag them out of the car window for a quiet chat."

"Don't worry," she returned the smile, though Mulgrew suspected there was a slight sneer behind it as Ross replied, "my guys are good. Now sir," she turned to Cairney, "I'm up to speed with all the details you have provided so if you don't mind, I'll head back to my office and get it set up. I assume that authorisation for the AFO's will come directly from you?"

"I'll have the authorisation directly messaged to you within the hour."

When Ross left the room, it seemed to Mulgrew that Cairney visibly relaxed and catching her eye, he smiled. "I have to confess that Miss Ross does tend to keep me on my toes, Cathy." He leaned forwards, his hands clasped on the table and in a moment of confidence told her, "She was a strong supporter of Arthur Freeman and I believe she rather hoped that if as he thought he were to be chosen as the next Chief Constable, she'd be appointed as the new Assistant Chief Constable in charge of the Operational Support Division. A good and competent officer, but very, *very* ambitious," he smiled and she wondered if there was some sort of veiled warning behind his statement.

"Now, unless you're in a rush to get away I was wondering if I might take you into my confidence."

"Sir?"

"Let me begin by stating that I was very impressed by DCI Miller's arrest of the two suspects in the city centre murder, the so called," he waved his forefingers in the air and grinned, "the 'Glasgow Demon Barber' case."

"Please sir," she groaned and shook her head, "don't let Charlie hear you use that term. Whether you're the Chief Constable or not I think he'd go berserk."

"And rightly so," he laughed. "Well, what I'm getting at is that despite the evidence that might have indicated this man David Craven committed the murders and was probably the killer of the fourth victim Paula Kyle, Miller didn't trust the evidence and indeed went against it. Through his own determination, his persistence and dogged belief he proved Craven innocent of the killings and indeed arrested the true killer James Bain and his accomplice. Impressive in itself alone, but he then went further and then identified our DS Kyle as the individual who most likely is responsible for murdering his own wife. Your friend is pretty impressive, Cathy and I won't forget that you supported him throughout when you could have so easily turned away."

"Thank you, sir, but I'm guessing this is leading somewhere?"

He took a deep breath and arching his back into the chair, clasped his hands behind his head. "I need a good man to run the Detective Course at the Scottish Police College in Tulliallan. Someone who is an experienced detective and capable of teaching our future CID officers to think outside the box; to teach our detectives to think like your Charlie Miller. How do you feel about Miller being that man? It would mean a promotion to Detective Superintendent."

She breathed in and slowly exhaling, thought of the lost and drunken Detective Sergeant she had first met so many years before. The man who had risen from the pit of despair, who had lost one family and found another and whom she was privileged to call her friend.

She smiled and replied, "I couldn't think of a better candidate, sir."

Davie Craven could not explain why he needed to be there and did not dare tell his father for fear of an argument, but quietly slipped away from work. He did not bother with the car, but instead walked the short distance towards the city's Sheriff Court.

He did not know if he would be permitted entry to the custody court, but thought he had to try. Making his way to Carlton Place, he entered the Courts main door and followed the signs to the custody court. Mingling with the large and noisy crowd he soon realised that the majority of them were reporters, some of whom he recognised from the local television news programmes.

The seating in the public area of the court was soon filled and he sensed a buzz of excitement, hearing the odd comment of 'Glasgow's Demon Barber' being bandied about. Spotting an unoccupied seat, he managed to squeeze in between a heavy-set woman whose body odour caused him to wrinkle his nose and a thin, grey-haired hatchet faced man who smelled strongly of cigarette smoke.

Glancing about him he saw that there were a large number of uniformed police officers standing guarding the doors as well as some uniformed court security in the court who clearly were there to monitor the unusually large crowd.

Almost dead on two o'clock the clerk of the court, a bewigged man dressed in a black robe, called those in attendance to rise and with the rest of the public, Davie shuffled to his feet.

A door opened and a muted silence fell over the public benches as the elderly Sheriff walked stiffly to the bench below the huge Royal Seal that was affixed to the wall and took his seat. Nodding to the clerk, permission was given for those in attendance to sit.

For the next hour, Davie watched as a number of men and women appeared before the Sheriff charged with varying crimes that included assault and theft; some of whom pled guilty and were summarily dealt with while others were either released on bail or remanded in custody meantime.

During the proceedings, one man, a short weedy, balding individual charged with the theft of a large sum of money from a neighbour was remanded in custody. The Sheriff's decision caused the woman seated beside Davie to loudly mutter, "Bastard!", before she arose and hurriedly made her way from the court, but whether her comment was directed at the accused or the Sheriff, Davie was uncertain.

He could not explain why, but his throat tightened and a shiver of dread crept down his spine as he remembered the fear he felt when he had also appeared before a similarly attired Sheriff, but on that occasion charged with murder.

Glancing about him he experienced a growing sense of anticipation from the public benches as the time approached for James Bain and Davie's sister Moira to appear.

When Bain was called forward and appeared through from a side door, handcuffed and led to the dock by two prison officers, the reporters in the court began to scribble furiously in their notebooks. Bain, pale-faced and haggard in appearance, hung his head low as the charges were read out; three counts of murder, perverting the course of justice and the rape of Moira Bain, his wife.

It was the final charge that shocked and caused Davie to swallow hard.

"…the rape of Moira Bain, his wife", the court official had read out. An overwhelming urge to jump up from his seat and rush to the dock and take Bain by the throat seized Davie, but his legs were shaking with fury and he knew that any attempt to disrupt the court process would liable him to not just being evicted from the building, but probably result in him also being arrested.

He watched in silence as Bain's lawyer made no plea on behalf of his client who was remanded and led from the court. A moment passed then Moira, not handcuffed but accompanied by a uniformed female prison officer, was led by the arm to the dock.

Like her husband, pale-faced but with her head held high, Moira seemed to Davie to be enjoying the attention her appearance provoked from the assembled media.

Charged with aiding and abetting James Bain to liable David Craven to prosecution and perverting the course of justice, she did not wait for her lawyer to plead on her behalf, but loudly called out, "Not guilty!"

The Sheriff, his head bowed as he made a notation on a pad in front of him, glanced sharply at her before beckoning forward the Fiscal Depute and Moira's lawyer. The court watched as a subdued, but brief conversation took place, before the Sheriff with a wave of his hand sent the Depute and Moira's lawyer back to their respective desks and called out, "Remanded meantime."

"For what!" screamed Moira. "I'm innocent, you fucking moron!" she screamed at the Sheriff and continued to screech as she waved her arms about her. The prison officer struggled to control her and was pushed almost out of the small space of the dock and suddenly the public area was filled with noise as the reporters stood or tried to push their way to the front benches to record Moira's outburst. The Sheriff's gavel was repeatedly thumped down onto his desk while he shouted for order, but so loud was the racket from the dock that he was ignored. Within seconds two male police officers had bounded across the court and with their assistance, the prison officer began to drag the hysterical and violently struggling Moira down the short steps from the dock towards the exit that led to the cell area. Unaccountably, Davie found himself on his feet and it was just before she went through the door and as she turned her face towards the public area that she saw him. Her face, the image of vitriolic hatred for the man she believed was to inherit what was rightfully hers, turned beetroot as she screamed at her brother, "It's all your fault!"

Shocked and more than a little depressed, Davie could hardly breathe as he stared helplessly back, watching as Moira was pulled from the courtroom and the door slammed closed.

Beside him, the thin grey-haired man nodded towards the closed door and turning to Davie with watery eyes, said over the hubbub around them, "I don't know who she is to you, pal, but for your sake, I don't think you should lose any sleep over her."

The man shook his head. "She seems like she is one bad bastard, that lassie, so she is."

Charlie Miller gave a long, tired sigh as he placed his pen on the desk. He had now edited the report twice, adding or deleting as he did so and was finally satisfied that it made sense.

Lifting the report, he left his room to walk the short distance along the corridor to the IT section and spoke with the supervisor, requesting that she herself type the report and thereafter e-mail it across to the Fiscal's office in Ballater Street.

"Treat it meantime as extremely confidential, please Liz," he told her with a tap on her shoulder.

That done, he made his way to the almost empty incident room and flopping down into a chair at Barclay's desk, almost with regret informed him that it was done. The report naming Eric Kyle as the murderer of his wife, Paula Kyle was now completed and would soon by arriving at the Fiscal's office. Once there it would be assessed by the PF himself before being forwarded for the consideration of prosecution to the Crown Office at Chambers Street, in Edinburgh.

"What's your thought on the time frame for something like this?" he asked Barclay.

Barclay inhaled deeply, then blowing through pursed lips replied, "I'm guessing they'll take at least a month to come to some sort of a decision, but we both now it's unlikely to be in our favour or I should say, in Paula's favour." He shook his head and added, "I don't think Crown Office will proceed with a prosecution, boss."

"How do you think they'll handle it?"

"In my humble opinion I think they'll send Kyle a letter informing him of the allegation against him and that if any further evidence should come to light, they *will* proceed with a prosecution. I really can't see them doing anything other than that, can you?"

"No, you're probably right. I just hate to think of him getting away with murder. It is more than that, Mark. It's a complete betrayal of everything we do as well as a betrayal of us, his former colleagues I mean."

Barclay arched his back to ease the ache before asking, "What do you think drove him to it?"

"Who know what goes through someone's head," Miller slowly shook his head. "Eric wasn't shy about his financial difficulties, telling anyone who would listen about how much money his ex-wife was screwing him for. That and remember how he would moan about Paula running around in that big motor of hers and giving up her job. It also must have occurred to him that knowing what she was like, particularly with a drink in her with the men, that she was probably cheating on him too. I think in the end he looked about the office and saw that his younger colleagues were all doing that wee bit better than he was; most settled happily with families, most with their own homes and running cars that weren't held together by sticky tape and super-glue. Probably he realised that he was middle-aged and coming to the end of his career with bugger all to show for thirty years other than one failed relationship and one failing relationship, a lot of debt and probably the strain proved too much. When the first three murders were committed he decided to take the chance to ease his problems; the main problem being Paula. Get rid of her, take his pension and lump sum, fuck off somewhere and start afresh."

"You know," Barclay's brow furrowed, "I really don't know whether to condemn the man or feel sorry for him. The Eric Kyle I knew was a good, hardworking detective." He glanced at Miller and added, "But then again, that was the guy I worked with. Who knows what goes on behind closed doors or as you said, in somebody's head. Early in my career I worked in the Shettleston office with a DC who like me, was just starting off in the CID. Him and his wife used to socialise with my wife and me and I thought they seemed to be a happy, contented couple," his eyes clouded over at the memory. "Then one night I was late shift and got called to the casualty at the Royal Infirmary and there was my mate's wife, battered and bruised. Seems when he got a good drink in him she became his punch bag." He looked a little embarrassed at repeating the story and finished, "Suffice to say, it wasn't long after that he got his books. I haven't heard anything of them since or whether or not they're still together," but under his breath fervently hoped they were not.
"Right then," he stared brightly at Miller, "isn't it about time you had an early night? You've been punishing yourself with these murders for weeks now. The report's finished, the murders are cleared up, so why not get home to Sadie and the weans and have some time with your family, eh?"
Miller got to his feet and wagging a forefinger at Barclay, winked as he replied, "Great idea. I'll see you in the morning," but before turning away, asked, "I take it you'll not be long behind me?"
Barclay returned his grin and said, "I'm waiting on Elaine finishing a bit of paperwork then her and me are going to dinner. Some swanky place down in John Street. We tried to get there the other night, but the bloody place was closed."
"Well," Miller said, curiously cheered by the news that Barclay and Elaine Hamilton were at last getting round to seeing each other, "have a good night and I'll see you in the morning."
In his office he collected his overcoat and with a final look around, switched off the light and made his way through the office to the back door, calling into the bar officer that if there was any calls he would be at home.
Waving a cheerful goodnight, he walked towards his Volvo and glancing up through the falling darkness at the clouded sky, threw the coat onto the passenger seat before getting in and switching on the engine.

He ensured the road was clear before pulling out of the rear yard into Maitland Street and taking his usual route home.

The driver sitting low in the dark coloured vehicle saw the Volvo exit the car park exit onto Maitland Street. He watched it drive the short distance towards Milton Street then when it turned out of sight, pulled the seat to the upright position and switched on the engine.

## CHAPTER TWENTY-SIX

It had been Shelley's idea, meeting in Davie Craven's house. It had also been her idea to forego cooking and instead she had ordered in a takeaway meal for all of them. Now sat around Davie's dining table with little Elsa in her high chair, they decided to eat before commencing their discussion. Shelley knew that Mary McLaughlin might be feeling a little uncomfortable for not only she had been going out with Davie for just a few days, but now here she was sitting with him and his father in Davie's home.

"Mary," Shelley smiled at her, "I understand you have a wee boy? What's his name?"

"Mickey, his name's Mickey," she shyly replied, curiously thinking that even though she was older by a decade or more, she wished she had the confidence and self-esteem of Shelley McPhail.

"Will we get to meet this wee chap, Mary?" Martin Carven asked as she shovelled the last spoonful of rice into his mouth.

She glanced nervously at Davie and with a half smile, replied, "I hope so Mister…I mean, Martin."

"Okay then, is that everyone finished then?" he said, glancing at each of them in turn before tickling the giggling Elsa under her chin. "Right then, Davie and I will clear the table away and then we'll get on with it."

While the two men were in the kitchen, Shelley reached across the table to hold Mary's hand and said, "You like him, Davie I mean?"

"Very much," Mary quietly replied, still taken aback that this young, perceptive woman could be so commanding.

"Well, if you like him that much, don't let anything stand in your way. I mean it, Mary. Davie is not like his sister; he's not as confident as Moira and will need someone to trust; someone who can be honest and supportive of him. Is that you, do you think?"

She did not get the opportunity to reply, for the sound of raised voices from the kitchen was followed less than a minute later by both men returning to the table, their faces grim and clearly showing the argument they had just had.

"Well," Shelley crossed her arms and sat back, staring at them in turn. "Do you want to tell Mary and me what's going on or is it a guessing game now?"

Martin huffed before replying, "Davie went to the court today. To see Moira being arraigned."

"Arr…arranged?" Mary asked, clearly puzzled.

"Arraigned, Mary," said Shelley. "Going before the judge."

"Oh, was that a bad thing," she hesitantly replied. "Davie going to the court? I mean, no matter what has happened, Moira is still his sister. He did not do anything wrong. If anything, it just goes to show that he's a compassionate man, that even after what she and her husband did to Davie, he still cares for her."

A stunned silence fell between them as the little girl, realising that something was amiss but unable to understand what, stared with trembling lips at her father who reached across and lifting her from the high chair, sat her upon his knee.

Martin stared at Mary, the anger in his face replaced by a strange sadness.

"Mary," he softly said, "If my son doesn't hang onto you, then he's a fool. Of course, you are absolutely correct in what you just said, hen," he nodded and turned towards Davie. "I'm sorry, son, for you did what I did not have the nerve to do. Even after all that has happened, Moira is still my daughter and your sister. Difficult though it might be, we need to support her…and we will. But that does *not* mean that she can be allowed to hurt us again."

He took a deep breath and turning towards Shelley who gave him the subtlest of nods, told them, "I've made the decision and I'm sticking to it. I'm selling the business. There has already been some strong interest from several companies and I intend dividing the profit equally three ways. There will certainly be more than enough for Shelley and me to retire to somewhere warm…"

"Saltcoats," she interjected with a grin.

"Aye, Saltcoats," he nodded with a smile, "though *I* was thinking of somewhere a *little* warmer. I will arrange that Moira's share is deposited with a bank and her legal expenses can be paid from her share. As for you, Davie. Any ideas what you might use your share for?"

His son glanced quickly at Mary and he reached across the table for her hand. "I've always had a hankering to open a small drop-in café or a bistro maybe, somewhere busy like the Byres Road area where there are a lot of shops. Somewhere like that. I'm no good at paperwork or that kind of thing, but Mary has a lot of experience waitressing and knows the ropes and she has also experience in cashing up and did an accountancy course at college…"

"It was only an HNC course," Mary blushingly interrupted.

"Maybe so, but it's more than I did," smiled Davie. "Anyway, I'm thinking that she can help me manage the place."

"You don't want to stay in the business then," Martin said, almost as a matter of fact.

"No, Dad. You have always known that it was not for me. Moira," he bit at his lower lip, "well, she was far more capable for that kind of work than I would ever have been. If she had just waited…" he stopped.

"Well, she didn't wait, Davie. She took advantage of a situation and nearly got you the jail," snapped Mary, who surprised by her own forwardness, placed a hand over her mouth. "I'm sorry…" she began, her eyes widening and appalled, but was interrupted by Shelley who angrily said, "No, Mary, you're absolutely right. It was not just Davie's life she almost ruined. It was Martin's life and wee Elsa's life and mine too. Moira's a grown woman who made her own mind up. Nobody forced her to do what she did, no matter what she might claim."

She turned to Martin and in a softer voice, continued, "But we have survived and we will get over this and let's not forget, Mister Miller, the detective. If he hadn't believed in Davie's innocence…"

"Aye, Shelley. Let's not forget Mister Miller," smiled Martin as he raised his wine glass.

By the time he arrived and was driving along Westbourne Drive, it had got even darker. He slowed as he approached the house and turning the car into the gated entrance, was so intent on negotiating the gravel driveway, he did not see the dark car that slowly passed the entrance and stopped a little further down the road.

He parked in his usual spot next to the overgrown hedgerow, reminding himself again that come the better weather he would get the electric hedge trimmer out and bring the bloody thing down to a manageable size.
His mobile phone rung and squirming in his seat, fetched it from his trouser pocket.
He grinned when he saw the name on the screen and said, "I hope the milkman's gone, because I'm sitting in my car in the driveway."
"I didn't expect you so home soon, so you've just missed him. He snatched his trousers from the bedroom floor and was out the window in a flash," laughed Sadie.
"So, you're in the bedroom?"
"Well, I could be if you hurry up and get your arse in here, Miller."
His brow furrowed. "What about the weans?"
"At my mothers and staying there for a sleepover."
"Oh," was his only response.
"Oh? Is that all you can say? Me wearing my see through nightie, a bottle chilling in the wine bucket on the table for me, a bottle of ginger beer for you, a takeaway ordered for us both and all you can say is, oh?"
He grinned in the darkness of the car before replying, "You've given me a bit of a dilemma, Sadie Miller."
"A dilemma?"
"Aye, have my dinner first or if you're wearing that see through nightie..."
"Well, Miller," she interrupted and pretended anger, "if you *really* need to think about it..."
"Is it the nightie with they wee red tie strap things on the shoulders?" he smiled as he interrupted her.
"It is."
"And nothing on underneath it?"
"Only me."
"Well then, bugger the meal," he was grinning as he reached for the door handle, "I'll be straight in..." he was telling her as pushed open the car door and begun to step out from the Volvo.
He came from the darkness, the silver thin but long bladed boning knife held high in his right hand stabbing in a downward thrust towards Miller's throat, his left forearm pushing the detective back against the car.

Instinctively, Miller raised a hand to fend off the blade, realising though he was a fraction too late, it was just enough to deflect the hand that held the knife, the point of the blade instead piercing his jacket, his shirt, his skin and tearing down through the muscle of his left breast.

He screamed, a high-pitched terror filled scream of agonising pain that echoed throughout the darkened garden and was picked up by the mobile phone that fell from his left hand.

"Charlie!" he could faintly hear Sadie's panicked voice as his phone fell to the gravelled ground.

The mans weight behind his left forearm pushing Miller against the floor jamb was enough to bring them as close as lovers and that's when Miller saw the maddened eyes, smelled the soured whisky breath and when the man grunted, felt the spit of saliva upon his cheek as he recognised the face; Eric Kyle!

Almost immediately, he pulled the knife up and out from Miller's torn flesh and as he drew his arm back for a second thrust, a spurt of blood flew through the air, drenching them both. In a desperate attempt to throw Kyle off, Miller head butted him, but lying against the car as he was he could get no force behind the blow that merely glanced off Kyle's hate filled face.

Miller's eyes travelled towards the knife, now held high and about to be powerfully propelled into his throat. He knew that positioned as he was, his left arm involuntarily jerking when the first stabbing blow had severed tendons and ligaments and now hung uselessly by his side, he could not stop the fatal blow.

Still Kyle had said nothing other than grunt and staring into his bloodshot eyes Miller saw nothing but a frenzied rage and prepared himself to die.

The unexpected flash lit up the driveway for less time than a heartbeat and the loud bang that accompanied it almost deafened Miller, then almost immediately, a second flash and a second bang. Kyle's eyes widened and his mouth opened as though he was about to speak before his body crashed against Miller, his weight causing them both to fall tangled together to the ground.

Suddenly there was a flurry of movement. Kyle was pulled off him and dragged to one side.

"Sir, are you hurt?" a bearded man demanded, as he stood over him and then loudly cried out, "Sir! Are you...*fucking hell*! Willie!" the same voice screamed, "An ambulance! Get an ambulance here now!"

Still in a state of shock, Miller raised his uninjured arm, his fingers attempting to grope for a hold on the car and he tried to sit up, but his left hand felt numb and was sticky with blood. He was gently but firmly pushed back down to lie flat by the same bearded man, his head now lying alongside the wheel of the Volvo.

"Charlie! Let me through! Charlie!" he heard Sadie scream.

He was aware of a number of legs moving about him, the sound of police radios and wondering where the hell everyone had come from.

Sadie, his old gardening oilskin coat that usually hung at the front door coat rack now wrapped about her was beside him, her unrestrained breasts bobbing in front of his face as kneeling she pulled him towards her to cradle his head in her lap. "Charlie Miller," she sobbed, her nightie slowly absorbing the blood he was losing as her lips quivered and her tears fell upon his face, "what the *hell* have you been up to?"

His tongue felt as though it was rattling in his mouth and he tried to speak, but before he could reply, Sadie was unceremoniously pulled to one side and a young man wearing a sports hooded top and smelling strongly of cigarette smoke, knelt beside him.

"Sir, my name's Willie. Listen to me. You're badly stabbed in the left side of your chest, I think it is, and there is a lot of bleeding," the man loudly told him. "I'm going to take off your jacket and try to stem the flow of blood until the ambulance gets here. Do you understand?"

"I've been stabbed, son, but my hearing is still fine," he tried to grin, but his body began to violently shake as the combination of the shock of the attack and blood loss kicked in.

"Oh, aye, right then," the man automatically grinned in response, then roughly manoeuvred Miller out of his jacket and called for a blanket.

"Here, let me do that," Sadie pushed her way back in and took the bandage from the kneeling man and as tenderly as she could, applied the dressing that quickly darkened with arterial blood.

"It was Eric Kyle," he gasped.

"Yes, I know," and he saw her glance over to where Kyle's body had been dragged some ten feet from them.

"Is he…" but he already knew the answer.

"Yes, Charlie, they shot him. He's dead," she sobbed and clutching his hand to her chest, her lips trembled as she stroked with her free hand at his forehead.

He did not feel any pain and staring into Sadie's eyes, heard the distant sound of a siren. The darkened sky appeared to be filled with blue light as now finding it difficult to stay awake, he peacefully closed his eyes.

Almost five hours after Detective Chief Inspector Charles Miller had been admitted for emergency surgery the surgeon finally left the operating theatre.

Pulling off her bloodstained scrubs, she binned them and took a well-earned swig of bottled water, so cold that when the first gulp hit the back of her throat it left her breathless.

Glancing at the wall clock, she sighed then leaving the theatre made her way to the small side room set aside for relatives of the patients. Taking a deep breath, she forced a reassuring smile as she pushed open the door. If she was surprised to see the Chief Constable of Police Scotland in full uniform sprawled across a chair next to the patient's wife, she did not remark upon it. Instead, she nodded courteously to the raven-haired woman who in turn subtly nodded towards the woman sat opposite who wore the dull grey coloured NHS blanket wrapped about her shoulders. The surgeon understood the nod and glancing wearily at Sadie said, "Missus Miller? I am pleased to say that your husband survived the operation and he is now out of surgery and is being transferred to the Intensive Care Unit. However, I must be honest with you and inform you that I still have some considerable concern for his well-being. I am afraid I cannot be more specific than that. Sorry."

Taking the free seat beside Mulgrew the surgeon sat opposite Sadie and leaned forward. "Forgive me, but if I explain this in layman terms it makes it so much easier to understand." She took a deep breath and using her hands to indicate upon her own body, continued, "The point of the knife that was used to stab your husband deeply penetrated his chest cavity in a downward thrust at the left shoulder and travelled through the thorax area, behind the ribcage and entered his aorta; just a small cut, what might be described as a nick, but sufficient to cause massive blood loss from

the heart and consequently, internal bleeding. I'm regret to say the damage was extensive and besides the wound I had to remove minute pieces of material, presumably from his clothing that was carried by the knife blade into the wound. Unfortunately, the knife blade did further damage on its way into your husband's chest and there is also the likelihood of nerve damage to the shoulder where ligament and tendons were severed. To be frank that is not a life-threatening problem as is the issue with his aorta. My colleague and I have worked at repairing the damage to the aorta and we believe we have succeeded in stopping the blood loss. If as we also believe we have repaired the cut to the aorta, there should be no need for further surgery. If not," she shrugged, "the next few hours while your husband is in the ICU will determine if we might have to reopen the wound and try again."
But only if he lives through those few hours, she grimly thought.
"If I may, doctor," interjected Cairney, "what you're suggesting is that it's a waiting game."
"That and if you believe in a deity, prayers," she nodded gravely at the big and rough looking man, but her eyes betrayed her and Cairney saw the despair and hopelessness that she did not admit to.
"You said there's also the chance of nerve damage, doctor," Sadie said, her brow furrowed. "Does that mean he might lose the use of his arm?"
"That would be the worst case scenario, Missus Miller and really," she sighed, "at this time it's a secondary issue. Once I am satisfied that the blood loss from the aorta has been dealt with we can examine the damage to his ligament and tendons in greater detail. I can't with any certainty say the damage is repairable for as I told you we concentrated fully on stopping the bleeding from the aorta…"
"Quite correctly," nodded Cairney.
"…but I'm confident if the damage to the ligament and tendons aren't *too* severe then with physiotherapy and time, we should be able to overcome that problem."
What she did not say was that this would only be an issue if the detective survived her surgery and right now his life hung in the balance or, if you believed in such things, God's hands.
The door opened and a nurse popped her head in, her eyes raised to indicate the surgeon was needed elsewhere and quickly.

Getting tiredly to her feet the surgeon leaned across and placing her hand on Sadie's shoulder, gently squeezed and told her, "Let me find out if he's been admitted to the ICU yet and if he's there, I'll instruct that you be permitted to go and sit with him." Her eyes narrowed as she added, "But you do understand he'll be unconscious for some time…"

"Thank you," Sadie interrupted.

When the surgeon had left the room, Mulgrew quickly followed her into the corridor and called, "Doctor…"

The surgeon turned and staring Mulgrew in the eye, with a shake of her head and a forlorn shrug of her shoulders simply said, "I'm so sorry, there's really nothing more we can do at this time." With that, she turned on her heel and joined the impatiently waiting nurse as they made their way down the long corridor.

Mulgrew bit at her lower lip as she stared after them, then squaring her shoulders returned to the room and said to Cairney, "Sir, with respect there's really no need for you to be here now. Obviously, I will remain with Sadie. I'm certain you'll be anxious to get back to your office to find out the details of what happened."

"Indeed," he picked up his cap and rose to his feet, arching his back as he stretched his arms. "Bloody plastic chairs," he smiled at Sadie, but then his face was more serious as he turned to Mulgrew and added, "I'm at the end of a phone, Cathy. I'll expect to hear about any update, *anything* at all," he stared meaningfully at her. "Okay?"

"Yes, sir, of course," she nodded.

Sadie Miller was an experienced police sergeant with many years service and during that service attended and witnessed multiple situations where individuals had suffered severe trauma. Often she had held the hand of blood-soaked victims and on many occasions attended at homes to break the news of violent or natural cause death. She had comforted distraught spouses and parents, sat in ambulances assisting paramedics dealing with broken and injured bodies, fought with violent drunks and when doing so on occasion suffered her own mercifully minor injuries. However, even with these experiences, entering the ICU and seeing her unconscious husband in bed wearing an oxygen mask with his body attached to monitors almost broke her.

With a sob, her legs gave way and but for Cathy Mulgrew, she would have fallen to the floor.

A nurse hurried forward to assist Mulgrew and together they half carried Sadie to a chair that was set beside Miller's bed.

Mulgrew said nothing, but staring down at her injured friend saw the life ebbing from him. With a reassuring squeeze on Sadie's shoulder, she fought the tears that threatened to spill from her and quietly walked from the ward.

**EPILOGUE**

Prior to 1895, the investigation for all deaths in Scotland, whether by violence or mishap, was the responsibility of the local Procurator Fiscal. However, in that year the Fatal Accident Inquiry (FAI) was introduced into Scots Law to investigate and determine the circumstances following a death or deaths in the workplace or in cases which gave rise to reasonable suspicion, decide if a crime might have been committed. As in common with legislative Law, the Fatal Accident Inquiry was subsequently superseded by the Fatal Accidents and Sudden Deaths Inquiry (Scotland) Act of 1976.

All FAI's are heard in the Sheriff Court where a Sheriff presides without jury and can be held on a compulsory basis for some deaths and on a discretionary basis for others.

It is the duty of the presiding Sheriff to hear the evidence and thereafter produce a determination and in drafting that determination, to consider five relevant details. These details are the time and place of the death, the cause of death and to consider any retrospective precautions that may have avoided the death. The Sheriff must also consider any indication of person or persons who directly or indirectly might be responsible for the death and lastly, to take account of any other relevant evidence.

Acting on behalf of the public interest is the Procurator Fiscal. Other parties that feature in the FAI can if they so wish be represented by counsel or appear in person.

Following the circumstances and huge media interest that resulted in the death of Paula Kyle as well as the stabbing of a senior detective by a fellow detective, the Lord Advocate for Scotland in a written public statement explained his reasoning in calling for an FAI. This statement explained that the Lord Advocate believed the family of

Paula Kyle deserved an account of her death and to know why their loved one had died. It was fortunate for the Crown that the alleged culprit was himself dead and negated any need for a lengthy and expensive criminal trial.

The date was set for the FAI to be called within the Sheriff Court in Glasgow and commenced just less than two months after the stabbing of Detective Chief Inspector Charles Miller.

Court Number Seven within the large three storey, square built building had been set aside for three days to permit all the witnesses in the inquiry to be examined.

At his personal request, the recently retired Sheriff Cooper-Smith was called back to the bench to preside while the Crown Prosecution was represented by the Procurator Fiscal Depute, Missus Susan Duncan. However, as no one from Scotland's legal profession volunteered to represent the interest of the late and unlamented Detective Sergeant Eric Kyle, in a public demonstration of fairness to DS Kyle, Missus Duncan informed the court she was instructed by the Lord Advocate to perform a dual role; when examining all the witnesses to act as both inquisitor and as Kyle's defendant.

The first day of evidence commenced to a court packed with public and media representatives and began with a bewigged, gowned and notably pregnant Missus Duncan providing the Sheriff with a background summary of the murder of the three women in Glasgow city centre. This overview ended with Duncan relating the successful conclusion of the inquiry, resulting in the apprehension of two individuals who following their respective pleas under solemn procedure awaited sentencing.

The media were not slow in noting that Duncan's summary referred only to the murder of three women and with interest awaited details of the fourth murder.

After Duncan concluded her summary, she called the first witnesses, Constables Paul Burton and Siobhan McKay who in turn related their discovery of the body of Paula Kyle.

The witness Doctor Elizabeth Watson was next to be called and provided pathology evidence. Continuing her evidence with the use of explanatory slides upon an overhead projector, Watson detailed to the court her discovery that the weapon used to murder Paula Kyle was similar, but not the same weapon used to murder the three women. This observation she recounted was passed to DCI Miller, the SIO who had managed the multiple murder inquiry.

Further witness testimony was provided by the uniformed officers who had discovered the body of Paula Kyle, believed at first to be the fourth victim of the alleged serial killer.

Constable Iain Bannen was the next witness to be examined and provided information about the morning when Detective Sergeant Eric Kyle approached him and requested he be permitted to lay flowers at the spot where his wife was killed. Missus Duncan spent some time eliciting from the young officer exactly how Kyle had approached him, what had been asked of Bannen and to a hushed court, reminded Bannen he was under solemn oath. Nervously licking at his lips, Bannen quite categorically responded that no, he had not indicated to DS Kyle where Missus Kyle's body had been concealed in the waste bin area nor where to lay the flowers, but had watched the Detective Sergeant walk straight and without deviation from the entrance to the underground car park to the waste bin area where Missus Kyle's body had been discovered.

There followed evidence from Detective Inspector Mark Barclay who related the circumstances that led to Detective Chief Inspector Miller's suspicion of Detective Sergeant Eric Kyle being the killer of his wife.

"You understand, Mister Barclay," said Duncan, "that your evidence about Mister Miller's suspicion of Eric Kyle is in fact hearsay."

"Yes, Ma'am, but might I remind the court that as the Deputy SIO, I was privy to every aspect of the inquiry and I beg the courts indulgence to allow the evidence. It might also be of interest that Detective Superintendent Mulgrew will also be able to corroborate my evidence and was in fact present when DCI Miller decided that based on the evidence I will give, DS Kyle was the primary suspect for his wife's murder."

Duncan turned towards the Sheriff and glanced questioningly up at his bench.

Sheriff Cooper-Smith's eyebrows knitted as he considered the point, then he sagely nodded that Barclay's evidence be allowed and the examination continued.

With no one to dispute the police evidence or argue on Eric Kyle's behalf, the day flowed smoothly and concluded with Barclay's evidence.

The following day commenced with Cathy Mulgrew in the witness box.

Dressed in a crisply starched, white blouse and her bottle green trouser suit, her copper-red hair plaited and hanging down her back, the svelte and very attractive Mulgrew attracted much attention from the media.

Sworn in by the Sheriff, she gave her full name, rank and length of service.

"Thank you, Miss Mulgrew," Duncan smiled at her. "Now, please tell the court of your working relationship with Detective Chief Inspector Miller."

It took her almost twenty minutes to describe Charlie Miller; twenty minutes to relate that Miller was not just a colleague, but also a trusted and valued friend.

"And your working relationship with Detective Sergeant Kyle?" asked Duncan.

While she knew Kyle as a hard working detective, Mulgrew admitted she had no knowledge of the man outside work and her only meeting with Paula Kyle, "…was at a CID dinner about a year previously when Missus Kyle, quite frankly, was completely out of order and made a fool of herself and by association, her husband."

During the examination, Mulgrew paused as if to compose herself and told the court of the weeks of pressure that DCI Miller had been under to solve the multiple murders, pressures from both the media and in particular a police senior manager she did not name, that took their toll on both Miller's professional and family life.

Mulgrew's reference to pressure from a police senior manager caused the Sheriff to sharply glance at her, but in his wisdom he did not purse the issue further.

Prompted by Duncan she explained the reasons why Eric Kyle had become a suspect for his wife's murder, corroborating the evidence already given by Mark Barclay.

Continuing, she told the court of breaking the news of Miller's suspicions and Doctor Watson's findings to the Chief Constable, who fortunately agreed with Miller and whose decision was that Kyle be immediately suspended without pay. She added it was the Chief's firm instruction that under no circumstances was Kyle to benefit in any manner from his crime. It was, she stressed and turned to stare at the Sheriff, the decision of Mister Cairney that if Kyle protested his innocence and intended any legal action against Police Scotland that the Chief Constable would fight it all the way.

"And so we come to the evening when DCI Miller..." Duncan hesitated and staring worriedly at Mulgrew added, "Your friend and colleague...was attacked. But before we speak of the actual incident, Miss Mulgrew, can you tell the court how it came to be that armed officers were on hand that evening?"

She swallowed deeply, as though the memory of the meeting was still fresh in her mind.

"After DCI Miller..." she paused and her eyes flickered as though the memory was distasteful, "and I met with Eric Kyle in Miller's office and where Miller accused him of his wife's murder, Kyle quite naturally denied it. He was very volatile, extremely agitated and threatened Miller. It was no direct threat, nothing specific," she frowned, "just a general threat that he would *get* Miller. To my shame," she exhaled deeply, "I don't think I took the threat too seriously. I know now that I wrongly believed it to be a defensive posture by Kyle, nothing more."

Duncan glanced sharply at her, realising Mulgrew was becoming upset and that she had to move Mulgrew along before the woman became too emotional.

"Miss Mulgrew," she quickly called out, "can you tell me something of DS Kyle's character? I mean, at the time of his suspension you no doubt will have had the opportunity to research his personnel file, yes?"

Mulgrew nodded. "That's correct and I can inform you that on three occasions in his career Eric Kyle had been investigated for allegations of assault; twice against suspects and once against his former wife. I should add there was also an allegation by a friend of Missus Kyle that she had been seen to bear bruises on her body, but in fairness there was no direct evidence that this bruising was the work of her husband."

Duncan glanced at Mulgrew, her eyebrows knitted and a little annoyed wondering why nobody in the bloody police had thought to tell her of that little gem! Taking a deep breath, she continued, "Can I ask why DS Kyle's personnel record and these incidents in particular had not been researched prior to his suspension, particularly as he was now the main suspect for his wife's murder?"

Mulgrew turned pale. "It was an oversight for which I take full responsibility and one that I now bitterly regret," she replied.
"Indeed," Duncan thoughtfully nodded. "So, please tell the court what happened after DS Kyle left DCI Miller's office."
Mulgrew paused as though considering the question, then begun. "While Miller went to the incident room to explain to the inquiry team what had happened, I mean about Kyle's suspension and the accusation he had murdered his wife, I phoned the Chief Constable to inform him of the circumstances. Mister Cairney then instructed that I was to meet with him at Dalmarnock police office."
"And you did meet him there, is that correct?"
"Yes, I met with Mister Cairney and Detective Chief Superintendent Jacqueline Ross who is the officer in charge of the Police Scotland surveillance teams."
"What occurred at that meeting?"
"Mister Cairney was extremely concerned that being accused of his wife's murder, being suspended without salary and being informed that it was unlikely he would receive his commutation," she glanced at the Sheriff, "his final pay-out, my Lord…"
Cooper-Smith nodded as he made a notation on his pad, "…that Kyle might consider taking some form of revenge upon Miller."
"And how was this concern dealt with?" asked the diminutive Duncan as arms folded, she slowly strutted across in front of the witness box.
"Mister Cairney authorised Detective Superintendent Ross to task a MAST team to follow Miller to protect him in the event of any revenge attack upon him by Kyle or anyone Kyle might send against Miller."
"And by MAST team you mean…"
"Sorry, I should explain. MAST is an acronym for a Mobile Armed Surveillance Team. In short, the surveillance unit comprised of a number of authorised firearms officers who would be armed."
"And what firearms would they be armed with, Miss Mulgrew?"
"As I understand it, the standard issue nine millimetre Glock model twenty-six semi-automatic handgun."
Pulling the black gown up onto her shoulders, the diminutive Duncan stared curiously at Mulgrew and asked, "Isn't that rather, if you excuse the term, an *overkill*; arming officers against what was

thought at the time to be merely a *suspicion* that DS Kyle might be considering violence against your colleague?"

"No, Ma'am," replied Mulgrew, slowly shaking her head. "The Chief Constable takes the view that the protection of his officers is paramount where any perceived threat does or might exist. The armed officers were there to combat an extreme threat, but there were also unarmed officers to deal with any form of scaled down threat." She shrugged and added, "As it turned out, regretfully the Chief Constable's worst fear was recognised."

"Yes, indeed it was," Duncan turned away and shook her head. She used her forefinger to push her spectacles back higher upon the bridge of her nose as the other hand unconsciously patted at the pregnant swelling of her abdomen, then said, "Tell me, Miss Mulgrew, was Mister Miller aware of this armed protection?"

"No," Mulgrew shook her head. "Mister Cairney did not wish to alarm Miller and instructed that the surveillance team did not show out."

"By show out, you mean not to alert Miller to the fact he was being followed?"

"Yes."

"In other words, Mister Miller became the subject, the target as it were of the surveillance operation that was for his own protection?"

"Yes, that's correct."

"In your professional opinion, was this a wise decision?"

"In the aftermath of what occurred perhaps not, but we can all be experts on hindsight."

Duncan chewed at her lower lip and stared thoughtfully for a few seconds at Mulgrew before turning towards the Sheriff. "My Lord, I believe that's as far as the Crown need go with Miss Mulgrew today and I request that she be freed from any further examination at this time; however, I do request the right to recall Miss Mulgrew if there should be further need for elucidation of her testimony."

"Granted," replied Cooper-Smith and turning towards Mulgrew, thoughtfully added, "You are free to go, but please remain available Miss Mulgrew in case I should require some further clarification on your evidence."

Mulgrew gave a slight bow towards the Sheriff and left the dock, surprised to find that her legs were shaking.

As he watched her step down from the witness box, Cooper-Smith turned towards the public gallery and said, "Ladies and gentlemen, I think that we will take this opportunity to break for lunch. Thank you."

That afternoon commenced with the testimony of Detective Chief Superintendent Ross who testified as an expert witness on the structure and training of her surveillance unit officers; the authorised firearms officers training and the code of conduct such officers must adhere to when drawing their weapons.
In a loud and confident voice, the tall and austere, thin faced woman explained, "In short there are three basic decisions a firearms officer must take. The first decision is to draw the weapon, the second decision is to point the weapon at an individual and the third decision is to fire the weapon."
"To kill a suspect, you mean?" asked Duncan.
"No, Ma'am, not to kill; to stop a suspect from harming a member of the public, from harming another officer or harming the officer who is pointing their weapon at the suspect. When I use the term harm, I do not mean a punch or a kick. I use the term harm to denote when a suspect intends deadly force to another individual. Officers are not trained to kill, but they are trained to stop someone from committing such harm."
"I see. Now," Duncan waved a general hand towards the public gallery and with a half smile, said, "Like most people I've watched television programmes about the police and I have heard the term double tap that is used in the context of firearms. What may is ask does the term double tap refer to?"
"Double tap is when an officer engages a suspect and that officer will fire twice in rapid succession, always aiming for the large part of the body, the torso. It has been proven that two shots in quick succession, the double tap, will in most situations stop a suspect from continuing to do harm to another individual."
Dismissed after her evidence, Ross was walking from the witness box when Duncan requested of the Sheriff that the witness Doctor Watson be recalled to the stand.
Looking tired and strained, Watson described the post mortem examination of Eric Kyle and with the use of the overhead projector and slides, explained in detail that the two bullets fired by the armed

surveillance officer struck Kyle in the back with such force they almost tore his heart out through his chest. So graphic was the photographs displayed by Watson on the projector that several people left the public gallery for fresh air.

Sheriff Cooper-Smith, conscious that the Scotland Euro qualifier was live on television that evening, decided enough testimony had been heard for that day and concluded the hearing until the following morning.

Testimony on the last and final day opened with the surveillance detective who had fired the fatal shots called to the stand. At the request of the Chief Constable and with the agreement of the Lord Advocate, to protect her anonymity the detective was identified only as Officer A. The slightly built, dark haired police officer, pale faced and dressed in a black skirted suit, her handbag carried upon her shoulder, could be seen by both Cooper-Smith and Susie Duncan, but was hidden from public view behind a screen.

Following routine questioning by Duncan about Officer A's surveillance and firearms experience, she asked, "When you arrived in Westbourne Drive and saw DCI Miller's Volvo car turn into the driveway, what was your brief thereafter?"

"With my colleagues we were to plot up…" she glanced at the Sheriff and explained, "that is, to find suitable locations around the area that would permit us as a team to quickly respond to any threat that might occur to the subject…I mean, DCI Miller."

"And where did you…plot up?" Duncan asked.

"We were travelling behind DCI Miller when I saw his Volvo turn into the entrance of his driveway. My colleague who was driving stopped our vehicle about thirty yards further along on Westbourne Drive and out of sight of the entrance to the driveway of DCI Miller's home."

"This I take it was to avoid what was previously described to the court as showing out?"

"Yes, Ma'am. When DCI Miller's Volvo turned into the entrance, I exited the vehicle and ran towards the entrance to watch that DCI Miller got safely from his car into his home. When I got to the driveway entrance I saw that DCI Miller was still sitting in his car and he appeared to be speaking on a mobile phone. I was on my covert radio telling my team what I was seeing when less than a

minute later, I saw him exit his driving seat and that's when I also saw the figure of a man step out from the darkness of a hedgerow."
"Had you previously noticed this individual?"
"No, Ma'am," she vigorously shook her head. "The first I saw the man was when he stepped from the darkness and quickly approached DCI Miller. Almost at a run," she added in a quieter voice.
"Did you recognise this individual?"
"No, Ma'am," Officer A shook her head. "All I saw was the figure of a large man with a knife in his hand that he had raised above his head as he attacked DCI Miller."
"You're certain it was a knife? Could it not have been perhaps a baton of some sort?"
"Yes, Ma'am, there was no doubt it was a knife. I saw the blade shining in the moonlight when he raised it above his head. A large blade," she shivered slightly at the memory.
Duncan paused before asking, "Let's be clear about this, Officer A. You could clearly see this individual brandishing a knife?"
"Yes, Ma'am," the officer nodded and held her right fist up as though holding a knife to indicate the height of the knife from her body.
"My question might seem to you to be absurd, but it needs to be asked. Did you *honestly* believe this man presented a threat to DCI Miller?"
"Yes, Ma'am. I was in no doubt that he meant to…" she paused and swallowed with difficulty. From his position on the bench, Sheriff Cooper-Smith could see the detective twisting a handkerchief in one hand. "I was in no doubt the man meant to stab Mister Miller," she said at last.
Duncan did not immediately respond to the detectives reply, but allowed her statement to resonate throughout the court. A few seconds passed before Duncan asked, "How did you react to this threat against Mister Miller?"
Officer A again swallowed hard and clasped her hands together so tightly the Sheriff could see her knuckles turn white. He watched as she took a deep breath and replied, "It took me a few seconds to draw my issue Glock from the waist holster. All the time I was watching the man who I then saw bring the knife sharply down and stab DCI Miller…"
"Did the man call out?" Duncan quickly interrupted.

"No, Ma'am, not that I heard," Officer A slowly shook her head. "The first noise was when DCI Miller screamed and I assumed or rather I realised he had been stabbed with the knife. By that time I was holding my Glock in both hands and pointing the gun at the man as I moved forward towards the car. DCI Miller's car, I mean," she turned to glance almost apologetically at the Sheriff.

"Did you call out at all, a warning perhaps?"

"No, Ma'am, I didn't have time," she shook her head again, her face pale as she quietly replied. "To be honest, I had never faced a situation like that before, other than in training I mean. My mouth was so dry I thought I might choke if I called out."

"Were you frightened?"

Officer A blinked several times, apparently taken aback by the question and her brow furrowed. "I'm not sure if frightened was how I felt, Ma'am. It all happened so fast that I don't think I had time to be…frightened. The man had shoved DCI Miller against the car and raised his hand again above his head and I saw that he was still holding the knife and I realised that he was about to stab DCI Miller once more. I reacted like I had been trained and I made the decision to discharge my firearm. I didn't know at the time how far I was from both DCI Miller and the man, but I later learned the distance was assessed to be slightly less than six metres."

She paused and Duncan's eyes narrowed as she saw the young woman's chest heaving as her breathing become more rapid and she reached forward with one hand to grasp at the brass rail that surrounded the wooden dock. "I shot the man in the back, twice."

Not a sound was heard in the public gallery other than the quiet scribbling of journalist's pencils upon their notepads.

Peering at the detective, Cooper-Smith's eyes narrowed at the distressed look on the young woman's face and he said, "Perhaps a drink of water for the officer."

"Yes, of course my Lord," nodded Duncan and fetching a glass from the tray upon the clerk of the courts table, poured water from a jug and stepping behind the screen handed it to Officer A.

Giving the young woman a moment to compose herself, Duncan continued with her questioning and elicited that after discharging her weapon, Officer A saw the man whom she now knew to be DS Eric Kyle fall against DCI Miller and watched as both men then tumbled to the ground. Almost immediately her fellow surveillance officers were there surrounding the fallen men as DCI Miller's wife Sadie Miller run from the front door of the house.

In response to Duncan's probing questions, the young detective explained that having discharged her firearm, she had quickly been removed from the location and conveyed by a colleague to a nearby police office. In strict observance of the Force's guidelines regarding the discharge of a firearm, she was placed within an interview room and other than being provided with a hot drink, remained incommunicado until later that evening when she was interviewed by officers from the Police Scotland's Conduct and Standards Unit.

"Have you since returned to duty, officer?" Cooper-Smith asked.

"Since that evening, my Lord," she turned towards the Sheriff, "I took no further part in the inquiry and I am currently performing desk duties."

"But you will return to operational duties at a later time?"

"Hopefully, my Lord," she turned towards him and eyes narrowing, replied, "but dependent on the outcome of the FAI will determine whether or not I continue as an authorised firearms officer."

"Then," he slowly and kindly smiled at her, "I must ensure that my deliberation on this issue does not take too long, eh?"

Turning sharply towards Duncan, he asked, "Have you any further questions for this officer, Missus Duncan?"

"No, my Lord," she shook her head.

"Then my dear," he smiled again at the young detective, "you are free to go and I thank you for your concise and candid evidence."

Officer A stepped down from the witness box and a few moments later, two court employees lifted the portable screen from around the witness box and removed it from the court.

Susie Duncan glanced quickly at the public gallery and her eye caught that of Sadie Miller who was sat in the second row between Cathy Mulgrew and her mother, whose hand she firmly held.

A tense silence fell across the court as Duncan then leaned across to the clerk and who loudly called out, "Call the witness Detective Chief Inspector Charles Miller."

A tense silence fell among the public gallery as they watched a door open to admit Charlie Miller who wore a charcoal coloured suit, white shirt and dark grey tie, his left arm carried in a black coloured sling.

Mounting the steps to the witness box, he raised his right arm to be sworn in by Sheriff Cooper-Smith, who then asked, "Do you wish to be seated, Mister Miller?"

"No, I'm fine. Thank you, my Lord," he smiled gratefully at the older man.

In the public gallery, reporters scribbled furiously on their pads. Susie Duncan took him through his name, rank, police history and after a brief summary that corroborated why he believed Eric Kyle to be guilty of Paula Kyle's murder, finally commenced her questioning about the events of the evening that concluded with the death of Eric Kyle.

"Prior to arriving home, Mister Miller, did you at all believe yourself to be under any physical threat from DS Kyle?"

"No, Ma'am, no direct threat," he slowly replied. "Of course, since that evening I've given more than a little thought to what occurred in my office when Eric…DS Kyle… uttered his threat, but there is no way that I or *anyone*…" he glanced tellingly across to Cathy Mulgrew as he shook his head, "could have foreseen what DS Kyle intended; no way at all."

"My Lord," Duncan turned to stare at the Sheriff, "I believe it to be unnecessary to go through the attack that was committed upon DCI Miller for there is no doubt he was indeed seriously wounded."

Turning now to Miller, she continued. "There's already been enough testimony to indicate what occurred when you were assaulted, but one question I *must* ask and I ask this question to give his Lordship the opportunity to consider whether or not there was justification for the fatal shooting of DS Kyle."

She paused as though to let Miller consider the gravity of the question she was about to ask. "At the very moment you were attacked, Mister Miller and please, I do realise that the memory of that moment must be painful for you. Can you *truthfully* tell this court that you believed DS Kyle intended to murder you?"

He stared down at her, but in his minds eye he again saw Eric Kyle, his eyes mad with rage, his lips drawn back in a hateful snarl as he raised the bloodied knife a second time. Taking a deep breath, he slowly nodded.

"After he stabbed me, I am in no doubt that but for the actions of the young detective who shot Eric Kyle he would have stabbed me again and murdered me. Thanks to that detective, the prompt action of her

colleagues in getting me quickly to Gartnavel Hospital and the skill of the surgeon," he raised his left arm a few inches as though to indicate his wound, "and her nursing staff to whom I shall be evermore grateful, I would be dead. I owe my life to that young detective and the others and the short answer to your question, Missus Duncan, is yes; Eric Kyle did intend to kill me that evening."
A palpable silence fell across the court, broken when his Lordship asked, "And today, Mister Miller. Are you fully recovered?"
"Not yet, my Lord, but the process is ongoing and I am pleased to inform you that I am receiving full support not only from my wife and family, but also my colleagues as well as the ongoing support from the medical rehabilitation team. Regretfully, I will never have the full use of my arm and can expect a degree of disability in movement, but I'm alive so I won't complain," he smiled at Cooper-Smith.
"Indeed," the Sheriff returned his smile and turning, waved Duncan forward for a quiet consultation.
As Miller and the rest of the court watched, Cooper-Smith and the PF Depute exchanged words for a few minutes and then waving Duncan back from his raised bench, Cooper-Smith loudly asked her, "Does the Crown wish to proceed further, Missus Duncan?"
Shaking her head, she replied, "No, my Lord. I believe the Crown has provided sufficient information to allow you to consider commencing your observations."
"In that case," Cooper-Smith turned to Miller and said, "Thank you for your testimony, Mister Miller and my congratulations on your survival following such a murderous attack upon your person. You are free to stand down."

Two weeks later, in his final act as a member of the Scottish Judiciary, Sheriff Cooper-Smith issued his judgment that as a result of evidence presented at the Fatal Accident Inquiry two counts of homicide and one count of attempted homicide had occurred.
His first judgment was that Detective Sergeant Eric Kyle was indeed guilty of killing his wife, Paula Kyle and thus concluded the then open murder inquiry.
His second judgment was that Detective Chief Inspector Charles Miller had been the subject of an attempted homicide upon his life by Detective Sergeant Eric Kyle.

Sheriff Cooper-Smith's final judgment was that Kyle's death at the hands of an officer of Police Scotland had been justifiable and therefore lawful and was in defence of a fellow officer. The elderly Sheriff further opined the outcome of the shooting of DS Kyle had undoubtedly saved the life of Detective Chief Inspector Miller. In recognition of this act, Sheriff Cooper-Smith praised Officer A's action that evening with the recommendation that his commendation be brought to the attention of her Chief Constable.

In addition to his findings, Sheriff Cooper-Smith commended Detective Chief Inspector Miller for his diligence and tenacity in not only detecting the murderer of three young women, but for uncovering the truth behind the killing of Paula Kyle and recognising but for DCI Miller's doggedness, her murder might not otherwise been solved.

It was a direct consequence of not just Miller's investigative skills, but recognition of his experience and dogmatic approach to detective work that a month after Sheriff Cooper-Smith's judgement, the Chief Constable Martin Cairney decided to promote Miller to the prestigious and non-operational role of Detective Superintendent in charge of Detective Training at the Scottish Police College, Tulliallan.

*******************************

Needless to say, this story is a work of fiction. As readers of my previous books may already know, I am an amateur writer and therefore accept that all grammar and punctuation errors are mine alone. I hope that any such errors do not detract from the story.
If you have enjoyed the story, you may wish to visit my website at:
www.glasgowcrimefiction.co.uk

The author also welcomes feedback and can be contacted at:
george.donald.books@hotmail.co.uk

Printed in Great Britain
by Amazon